Qubyte

Cat Connor

For information regarding permission email the publisher at 9mmpressnz@gmail.com
subject line: Permission.

ePub ISBN : 978-0-4734648-2-0
ISBN Draft2Digital: 978-1-0670072-6-3
ISBN Print: 978-0-4734648-0-6
ISBN: 978-0-4734648-1-3
Editor: Jayne Southern

Messages:

"Cat Connor does it again! *Qubyte* is a fast-paced, tense, funny, and scary thriller. The stakes couldn't be higher, the danger is real, and the premise is frighteningly possible. With plenty of twists and turns, solid wit, and a plot that's as current as today's headlines, *Qubyte* will make you wonder just how safe any of us really is."
- Margot Kinberg, Author of the Joel Williams mysteries (and *Ruler of the Universe*)

"Special Agent Ellie Iverson is a beautifully flawed and relatable character with a brash wit that makes you stick around and see how she deals with the overwhelming chaos which unfolds before her."
- Geoffrey Calhoun, Director of Script Summit, Founder of We Fix Your Script

"Master storyteller Cat Connor and her intrepid Ellie Iverson deliver another relentless nail-biter, packed with clock-ticking action to untangle a bioterrorism plot."
- Lisa Towles, Award-winning crime novelist and author of *Choke*

"Once again the author had me from the get-go with yet another face-paced thriller. If Reacher was a chick, he'd be Ellie Iverson. Lee Child had better watch his back, Connor is closing in."

It all began with a death threat. But first...

Cat Connor has my respect. A prolific and talented writer, Cat understands what it takes to weave a tale with unique and intriguing characters, a pulse-pounding plot, and yet still bring in a great sense of wit and humor. The Byte saga grabs you and keeps you wanting more from *KillerByte* all the way through to *QuByte*. That's ten books of material which is impressive on its own merit and an incredible feat for any author to accomplish. Cat has done it with grace and ease. She's doing what she was born to do, and Cat will tell you herself, she is just getting warmed up.

I am incredibly honored to be asked to write this introduction to Cat's landmark tenth novel to her best-selling Byte series. This saga following Special Agent Ellie Iverson has seen her grow immensely, much like any person would through hardships and trauma. We can see many of the struggles Ellie goes through paralleled in our own lives. This is why she is so easy to relate to and why we root for her so deeply.

It's hard to believe the genesis of this character was born from a death threat. You see Cat, like myself, is dedicated to helping other writers find their voice. Cat ran a large online poetry group based in the US which drew writers from all walks of life and from all over the world, and was incredibly popular in its day. Unfortunately, a few people came in and intimidated the other writers. Bullies to no end. Cat would have none of it. Like Special Agent Ellie Iverson, Cat is a powerful woman with a voice that she makes sure is heard. Needless to say, this ended up with death threats aimed Cat's way. I'm not talking about the off the cuff meaningless slight. I mean a credible and frightening "I know where you live and I'm coming for you" threat. Like a true literary warrior, Cat wouldn't be intimidated or stopped, and eventually, she persevered.

When you listen to Cat tell this story, she laughs. That's who she is. Most people would have taken these death threats to heart and backed off or shut down the writers' group out of fear. Not Cat. No. You see Cat is fearless. This isn't some kind of false bravado. This is who she is. It's in her core. In order to write at Cat's level, you have to be fearless. As writers, we rip open our chests and bleed onto the pages of our creations. That takes a level of fearlessness to do. This trait ends up carrying itself into other aspects of our lives as it has for Cat which is why she is a singularly remarkable novelist. As I said before, Cat Connor has my respect.

Geoffrey D. Calhoun
Top 100 Indie Screenwriter and Founder of WeFixYourScript.com

For Josephine

"Almost all of your life is lived by the seat of your pants, one unexpected event crashing into another, with no pattern or reason, and then you finally reach a point, around my age, where you spend more time than ever looking back. Why did this happen? Look where that led? You see the shape of things." - Ron Perlman

Chapter One
Sell my monkey

From nowhere and without my bidding, stars twinkled on the screen, above a long stretch of country road. A soft glow enveloped the gentle sway of a black horse and rider, the sound of the hooves soft in this comfortable walk. A sharp crack ripped through the air, horse and rider alarmed. Sparks tumbled to the road surface and died as the terrified horse reared and the rider clutched its mane, obviously reassuring and calming the animal, before it fell ...

Jarred and shocked, I squinted at the dimming screen as sunlight chased away the images. Two case files on the screen added to my confusion.

What the hell was that all about?

Kurt stood in the doorway, his hand raised.

"Did I startle you?"

Maybe his knock was the crack I heard.

"You're light on your feet," I said with a bewildered smile.

"Everything all right, Iverson?"

"Of course. Come in," I said, and closed the files I'd been working on before the horse interlude happened.

"Were you watching something?"

"No. There was a glare."

"Everything is all right?"

"Yep."

"Special request," Kurt said and placed a manila folder on my desk and slid it to me.

"That's not a happy face." I waved my index finger in a circular motion at him as he unbuttoned his suit jacket and sat in the chair opposite.

"Take a look."

After scanning the first page, I closed the folder and put it down. With a sigh, I rocked back in my chair. "Since when does Delta A investigate animal rights activists?"

"Since today." Kurt's enthusiasm level matched mine. Zero.

"Who requested this?" It was rhetorical. I flicked open the folder and searched for a name. "Judge Hartwell?"

Kurt leaned forward, his elbows on my desk. "Our beloved judge has wriggled and jiggled this problem to loosely fit our brief regarding serial crime."

"Why?"

"Over the course of several months, six people working in industries known to test on animals have been targeted by animal activists."

"That's an ongoing thing, and they're mostly college kids with bleeding hearts and no concept of reality." Ongoing but not serial.

"Agreed. And normally I'd say not our problem, but it looks like the most recent one was last night ... and it is possible that a monkey infected with a virus was released."

My eyebrows rocketed. "Do we have a potential viral

threat to humans in D.C.?" Because that's a Centers for Disease Control and Prevention problem, not FBI.

Kurt shook his head. "We don't know yet. Judge Hartwell found out about the attack by accident at a dinner party. Her office investigated with some subtlety and discovered the other possibly linked incidents. Mostly threats and red paint attacks against cars and offices."

"Who turned up the missing monkey?"

"Hartwell."

"The company involved didn't report it to the police?"

"Apparently not."

"In what circumstances would a company fail to report the theft of a research animal?" I couldn't imagine a selfless scenario behind that decision.

"Not a moral or ethical one. Maybe they thought they could get the monkey back before anyone found out or perhaps they don't want authorities alerted to their less than stellar security protocols."

Pretty much what I thought. "CDC involvement?"

"She wants us to confirm the threat and confirm the monkey was taken and then notify CDC." I knew that tone. Kurt was unhappy about Hartwell's brief.

"So, we notify CDC right now, and tell them we're investigating alongside them," I said. "As much as I like Hartwell, she doesn't get to dictate how we work."

Kurt grinned, lifted his phone from his pocket, and made a call. While he talked, I emailed Metro and let them know we were looking for a stolen monkey.

Prudent: I didn't want them stumbling into a situation with a disease-ridden monkey without prior knowledge.

"You noticed a rise in the number of sick people lately?" I said when Kurt finished his call.

"Flu season is ramping up, Iverson. It happens."

"Flu jabs, Henderson, we're all offered them."

"You'll always get people who rely on herd immunity to protect them."

An involuntary snort escaped. Stupid is as stupid does. "Judging by the coughing, sneezing, and general unwellness, I don't think it's working for them."

"I didn't think it was that obvious yet."

Yeah, okay, perhaps I'm more sensitive to the presence of germs these days. And now the monkey situation. Germs. Not a fan.

I shrugged. "We should pass out masks and have hand sanitizer by all our office doors ..." Get in front of it and stop the spread.

Kurt's mouth tweaked into a smile. "That's not a silly idea."

"We've got that thing at Quantico." Stolen monkey or not, we had a prior engagement.

"We do. Shall we?"

Chapter Two
More than a feeling.

Lee, Kurt, Dane, Stu, and I waited outside a classroom at Quantico. We waited like bored kids forced to shop with their parents. Lee paced with Argo at his heels. Kurt played with his phone. Dane and Stu messed around playing paper, scissors, rock. I checked Twitter and sent smartassed replies to random people. We were a bunch of bored kids.

The door opened with a *whoosh*. I shoved my phone in my pocket.

"SSA Iverson?" A woman with a warm smile stood in the doorway. "I'm Special Agent Amanda Creed." She stepped forward and shook my hand. "Pleasure to finally meet you."

"Thank you for the invitation. Let me introduce my team."

I ran through quick introductions. Amanda addressed us in a hushed tone. "Are you ready?"

"Sure," I replied. Absolutely not.

"They'll have questions. This class graduates in a few weeks."

Excellent: the ones who were never going to make it to Special Agent should've been weeded out by now. This lot should have eyes on the future, thinking about placements and specialist areas. "Will you introduce us?"

Amanda led us into the room, along the front of the

class. A huge electronic whiteboard behind us listed our names and a bit about the Delta teams. She introduced us and then turned the room over to me.

"Morning! I'm not naïve enough to believe you haven't heard any of the stories that surround me and Delta A. So, let's tackle that first … they're all true." I smiled.

Stunned faces stared back at me. Guess they didn't expect that. I proceeded to talk to the eager class about Delta B and C, and their fields of expertise before moving on to us.

"I'd like to tell you a little bit about Delta A as we're different from the other two Delta teams in the Criminal Investigation Division." I glanced at the board behind me. "I see Agent Creed has also given you some background on the three teams. Now, Delta A … we primarily investigate serial crime, whether murders, trafficking, bank robberies, rape, or other violent crime. If it looks like it's a serial thing, we are notified, and we investigate." And now serial graffiti and a missing critter.

Someone sneezed. A hand went up from the back of the room.

Already? "What'd you want to ask?" I pointed to a blond square-jawed young man about halfway back in the room who'd clambered to his feet.

"Do all the teams have a dog?"

I smiled at the man. "Do you have a name?"

"Sorry. Francis. I'm Francis."

"And no, not all the teams have a dog, Francis. Argo graduated from a program designed to train dogs in victim support. So he's not your typical canine agent."

"Why does Delta A have a victim support dog?"

"We come across a lot of people who need support now, not a few months down the road. If we can provide some comfort right off, then their journey to resolution, whatever that may be, might be smoother. Then the day shit went down might be the day they met an awesome dog."

"Argo could potentially ameliorate their experience?"

"That's what we hope. If we can limit trauma by acting fast enough, it's a better outcome for everyone involved."

Francis smiled. "He's an FBI dog?"

"He is now. He was a police dog but wasn't aggressive enough and came to live with my husband and me." Argo pushed his nose into my hand. "We saw potential in his behavior and asked that he be assessed by our canine division." Argo sat. "If we didn't give him a job, we'd be wasting his intelligence and asking for trouble." The dog leaned on my leg. "No one wants a bored eighty-pound German Shepherd alone in their home."

"You own him and he works with you?"

"Yes. Although he happily works with any of the team. He belongs to my husband and me, and he knows it."

"Who paid for the training?"

"I did. Actually, The Butterfly Foundation did. If you haven't heard of the Foundation, I suggest you look it up and consider donating your time to the cause, all of you." My job as the creator of the Foundation was done for the moment. Argo pushed me. He wanted to play. With a small hand gesture and a whisper he ran through the seated crowd to Francis and sat at his feet. "You can pet him, he's friendly, and he's not working while we are here."

Francis beamed and sat down. Argo made the most of the attention.

"Yes," I said pointing to a redheaded man in his early thirties.

He stood. "SSA Iverson, I am Caeden. How do we get into a Delta team?"

"Delta B and C have an application process. You apply through the division's Human Resources." I paused. "We have a different process. Delta A invites agents to join."

"We can't apply?"

I shook my head. "Not through normal channels. If you were really keen on becoming a Delta A agent, then you'd need to talk to our SAC, be approved by him, and also Director O'Hare. Then, we'd invite you to come in and see how well you fitted."

"Why is it different for you?" Another person this time. A woman.

"You are?"

"Sorry." She stood. "Sarah."

"Because people don't usually leave Delta A." Alive. Don't think about Sam. Just answer the questions. I took a breath. "This team has been together a while now, we're close. We have a different work method from other teams. We have a set of special skills." As I said the words, I heard Liam Neeson. All of a sudden a warm

8

furry body pressed against my leg. My hand touched the top of his head. Argo knew. He knew to come back.

"How did you all end up together?" she asked.

"Our SAC brought Lee Davenport, Sam Jackson, and me together for a serial case a long time ago. We worked well together. He decided we'd remain as Delta A."

"Which one of you is Sam Jackson?" Sarah asked then blanched and sat when a fellow classmate nudged her.

I swallowed. "It's okay, Sarah. Sam was killed in the line of duty almost a year ago."

She nodded and struggled back to her feet. "How did the other three agents get to be part of Delta?"

"By invitation."

Kurt stepped up next to me. "Sarah, isn't it?"

She nodded then coughed into her elbow. "Sorry."

"The other unique thing about this team is me. I am a doctor, and we are the only team with a doctor permanently assigned."

"Why?"

"Because our expertise and skills lead us to find victims of violent crime and they often need immediate medical attention," Kurt said then pointed at another raised hand in the middle of the room.

"Rachel," she said with a hint of southern California and a smirk on her lips. "I heard the reason is that SSA Con – I mean SSA Iverson – suffered more than one traumatic brain injury and needed monitoring." She smirked and whispered to the agent on her left. "And that she's unstable."

Unfortunately for her, we can lipread and my hearing is excellent. I arched an eyebrow in Kurt's direction. He shot me a fast smile before honing in on Rachel.

His whole demeanor changed. "Where'd you hear that?"

"We all know about SSA Iverson's brain injuries during the Son of Shakespeare case and the Hudson Hawk case."

"That's not what I meant. Why would you conclude SSA Iverson was unstable?" He glanced at me and then at Lee before glaring at Rachel. "We saw what you said to your classmate."

"I ... um ... didn't mean anything."

"Then you should've kept your mouth shut," Kurt said.

My eyes roamed over the faces in the audience. They looked back, confused, horrified, concerned – so many expressions to pick from.

"I didn't think anyone would hear me," Rachel said, her voice low and shaky.

"But they did. How did you determine SSA Iverson's state of health? She's never met you. Medical intervention is not in the files you read. Those files contained outlines of incidents, not medical prognosis or recommendations." He took a step back. "Are you a doctor?"

Rachel's slack-jawed slow reaction spoke volumes. A few seconds went by before she answered. "No. I'm not. I heard it from someone in the FBI."

The longer I stared at her, the more she felt like

someone I knew. Someone we all knew. The Wicked Queen. Former Executive Assistant Director Owen. Surely not?

"I'd like to know who in the FBI is so chatty," Kurt said. Quiet authority hardened his manner.

"I'd rather not say." Rachel steadied herself. "I also heard that the only reason Agent Iverson still has a job is that she's best friends with the Director."

Wow. She was all over it with her big mouth and lack of restraint.

Kurt shook his head. Disgust registered on his face. He ignored Rachel and moved to the next person with a question.

I beckoned to their instructor. We met near the door. "Who is she?"

"Rachel Owen."

Jeez. Coincidence? I bet not. Is nowhere safe? "I'm betting she's related to Assistant Director Owen." Who likes me as much as I like her. "I'd also put my money EAD Owen as the source of this gossip."

Amanda nodded. "If that's the case, it might explain how Rachel has teetered back from the brink of failure twice." Amanda checked herself. "I'm not suggesting EAD Owen pulled strings because I doubt that anyone below the Director could have much sway when it comes to recruits. But she should have helped Rachel see the bigger picture and encouraged better behavior."

"How do you mean?"

"Rachel's attitude needs work and so do her

communication skills. From what I witnessed, I'd say she has a long way to go."

"I sense an attitude adjustment in her near future." I left Amanda, joined Kurt in front of the class, and whispered in his ear that Rachel's surname was Owen.

He scanned the room, sweeping his eyes across all the faces then called on Rachel.

"Rachel Owen? Are you a sister, niece, or a cousin to EADC Owen?"

Rachel didn't seem so full of herself all of a sudden. "I didn't mean anything—"

"Stand, please."

She rose slowly, a flush evident on her face. "She's my aunt."

"And she told you SSA Iverson is unstable and the only reason she has a job is that she's besties with the Director?"

The room fell into a palpable appalled silence. Rachel's head nodded.

Unbelievable. Owen, the mega bitch, strikes again. "How did this conversation come about?" My curiosity got the best of me. Argo lay down at my feet and sighed.

"I mentioned at her last visit that Delta A was coming to talk about the Delta teams."

No doubt she couldn't wait to spread her poison.

The instructor stepped in. "Rachel Owen, follow me, please."

The woman gathered her folder and pen and left with her eyes averted.

Kurt smiled at the rest of the worried faces in the room. "Where were we?"

A man in the front row stood. "I'm Charlie. Delta A comprises five agents, how does that work? Does someone work alone?"

"We were four," I said. "Then six, briefly. In the field, we pair up. Lee's been working with our SAC Caine Grafton." An awed rumble crossed the room. I guess they've heard of Caine.

"Thank you, ma'am."

I nodded. He sat down and stocky man with close-cropped dark hair took his place. "I'm Greg. How dangerous is Delta A?"

A laugh escaped before I could check it. "I wouldn't say it's super dangerous."

Lee, Dane, and Stu laughed. All three stepped forward. United we stand. I shot a small smile at Lee.

"We're still standing," Lee said. "We play hard and we play to win. We don't always win and we don't always escape without a scratch or two."

Greg smiled. "Sir, with all due respect, we've heard you do always win and you go above and beyond every single time."

The applause started at the right side of the room and spread until the entire class clapped.

No matter how much I wished, the floor did not open up and swallow me. Dane took a step forward. "On behalf of Delta A, I'd like to thank you. We do our jobs as best we can. Every single time. That's all."

I thrust words in my mind to Dane: Well said. He glanced at me. I picked up: I'm not done yet.

Dane held his hand up to silence the applause. "We are here today to talk about what we do. To encourage you to make the best choices for you. The Delta teams are not for everyone but they're fulfilling as all hell."

I interrupted. "Delta A is a life choice, not a job." Curious expressions met my gaze. "There's a reason it takes a long time for anyone in Delta A to settle down and have a family." I waved a hand across the team lined up beside me. "It's a hard job to leave, even for a few months. It takes a toll on relationships." And life, and all that entails.

Lee eased into the conversation, "If you want a normal family life and a life in the FBI – Delta is not for you." He cracked a cheesy grin. "My former partner in this crazy unit, Sam Jackson, used to say Delta A was a life sentence. The only way out is a body bag."

Gasps fell into dead air.

He ignored them and forged on. "Thing is, he was right. You don't come into this team for a short time. You come in by invitation. You stay because you love it and you're making a difference in people's lives. And you can't imagine any other life."

Family. We are family.

Stu and Dane nodded. Then Stu spoke, "And your place in our unit isn't filled if you're away on leave, it waits patiently for your return." He winked at me. "If you want a life within Delta, any of our Delta teams, then the line forms on our right. Your instructor will have applications for Delta B and C, and contact details for Delta A."

He handed off to me. I checked my watch. "Come talk to us, if you'd like to ask more questions, we have a half hour before we head back to D.C." And find a monkey. Not altogether a glamorous case.

In a heartbeat, fresh faces swamped all five of us, the smell of new blood, idealism, and promise, heavy in the air. I saw Lee, animated and in a conversation with three people. Stu and Dane had a small gathering around them. As the newest to Delta A, I imagined they'd be popular with those considering specializing. Kurt attracted my attention. Amanda had returned and headed our way with two youngish women. I excused myself from the group around me, leaving Kurt to answer the quick-fire questions.

"Agent Iverson, I'd like you to meet Cara and Adele," Amanda said, gesturing to the women with her.

"Pleased to meet you," I said with a smile.

"Can we talk about how you're coping as a female field agent with Delta?" Cara asked.

Straight into it. Refreshing. "What would you like to know?"

"Is it worth it?"

Wow. I studied her for a moment. "I can't answer that for you, I can only answer that for me. For me, yes."

"How do you cope with motherhood?" Adele asked. "Can I ask that?"

I laughed. "You can ask me anything. It's a team effort. Our babies were premature, my husband and I spent their first month beside them in the Neonatal intensive care unit. Once they improved, we took turns."

"How has their birth affected your job?" Cara asked.

"I've reduced my hours. My husband and I have always worked long hours and traveled a lot with work. Neither of us travels as much as we did. Delta sometimes goes without me if the case involves a lot of travel. I'll stay behind and do what needs doing from D.C. Other than that, it was a matter of getting my fitness levels back up."

A smile touched her lips. "We heard hardly anyone knew you were pregnant and you still ran every day."

I didn't realize my life was such a topic of conversation within the walls of the academy.

"I guess that's true."

"Did you consider retiring?"

"Yes, I did." I gave it due consideration. "After a month sitting around watching my babies try to breathe, I felt compelled to go back to work. It's the way I'm wired, I need to stay active and continue making a difference. I don't envisage retiring anytime soon."

"If they're sick?"

"We have family support."

"If you get injured?"

I paused before answering to try to determine what was going on. They were youngish, mid-twenties maybe. I saw life stretching out ahead of them and taking any form they desired. "Injury is a possibility, always. No matter what your job. It's not better or worse knowing I have children at home who need me."

"You've been injured a few times?"

"I have. I'm still here, Adele. The thing with injury is … you recover." Usually. And sometimes with a shitload of medical support and rehabilitation. I smiled. "If that's something you're worried about, I suggest thinking long and hard before becoming a field agent or crossing a road. Sure, seventy-five percent of our job is paperwork but there is a risk."

"How did you know it was worth the risk?"

"I wanted to help people. This is what I've always wanted to do. It's who I am."

Kurt stepped closer to me. "Commitment like Agent Iverson's is what Delta is looking for. If that's there, then finding your way through obstacles isn't that hard. It's planning. It's forward thinking. It's remembering why you do this job."

And sometimes it's tequila straight from the bottle.

Both women nodded.

"Is it true you know the Director on a personal level?" Cara said. "Can I even ask that?"

I laughed. "I do know her. We lived in the same small town once upon a time. I have the utmost respect for Cait O'Hare and the job she does. Agents like her paved the way for us."

Adele spoke, "Thank you both for your candid responses. I have a lot to consider."

Chapter Three
Big Yellow Taxi

The briefing room felt empty. A long wooden table and sixteen functional chairs made no difference to how empty the room felt. I glanced at the whiteboard. Kurt had added a list of potential suspects in the attacks on the companies known to test on animals. Sixteen names, but in reality, we had a hundred possibilities, and then some.

Resting on the end of the table I waited for the team to assemble.

My phone buzzed, amplified by the wood as the noise bounced around the room. Not recognizing the number I slid my finger across the screen. "Agent Iverson speaking."

"Agent Iverson, this is Tahoma Whitehorse. I'm with the CDC and in the foyer of your building with a colleague. Would you have someone met us, please?"

"I'm on my way."

I ended the call, slid my phone into my jacket pocket and walked down to the foyer. Two casually dressed people carrying messenger bags lurked by the reception desk.

"I'm Ellie Iverson." I held out my hand to the woman as I approached.

She smiled and shook my hand. "Doctor Karen Schneider."

Releasing Karen's hand, I turned to the man. "You

must be Doctor Tahoma Whitehorse."

He smiled, his hand was firm and warm in mine. "I am. It is a pleasure to meet you. We have heard stories."

Here we go again.

The desk agent spoke, "They're signed in, Ellie."

"Thanks, Frank." I turned back to our guests. "Follow me. We'll take the south elevator."

The elevator ride zapped by in silence; as tempted as I was to ask what stories they'd heard, I didn't. Sandra called out a greeting from her desk as we neared the Delta A meeting room. Our guests replied in kind.

I opened the door and stood aside. "In here," I said with a smile. "If you'd like to drop your bags, I'll get Sandra to give you a quick tour while I round up my team."

Karen nodded. "That'd be great. Thanks, Agent." She slipped the strap of her bag over the back of a chair. Tahoma followed suit, opting for a chair next to Karen.

"Ellie is fine. Please." I popped my head out of the door and waved at Sandra. "Will you give Karen and Tahoma the guided tour, please?"

"Happy to, O Fearless Leader." I moved out of the doorway as Sandra smiled at the guests and ushered them out of the room.

Sandra's chatter filled the corridor as she explained the Delta team floor layout and background. I went to my office. From my laptop, I messaged the team: Meeting room, five minutes. Everyone, please.

Dane messaged back: Even us?

Me: Do you need a special invitation?

He fired back a smiley face and a coffee emoji.

Me: That's what I thought, text Sandra and get coffee or whatever orders from our guests.

Dane: Consider it done.

I dropped the lid on my laptop and gathered all the information we had so far on the alleged infected monkey and the acts of homegrown stupidity. Even in my mind I resisted labeling the Animal Activist's actions as terrorism. That was a can of worms I didn't want to open, not today, not now. A little yellow duck quacked at me from the floor. I shook my head. "No worms here." He quacked again and disappeared.

Time to get to work.

I set the manila folder and my phone on the table in the meeting room. Kurt and Lee had followed me in.

"Chicky," Lee said with a grin. "Kurt briefed me. So we're genuinely hunting a monkey?"

"Looks that way."

"When did Delta become Animal Control?" He sat at the table, leaving a space between him and the saved seats.

"CDC?" Lee pointed at the chairs and bags.

"Yep." I rocked in my chair. "They mentioned they'd heard stories about me."

Lee grinned and then chuckled. "You're a legend, Chicky."

Kurt sat opposite me, a smile on his face. "Or a warning."

Probably.

"Where are they?" Lee ducked as if searching under the table.

"Not under the table," I said, laughing. "Doing the housekeeping tour with Sandra."

In the event of an emergency, we have two sets of stairs. Here are the bathrooms. This is the kitchen. This is the bullpen. No, Ellie doesn't usually shoot released hostages. Just the once. Three teams work from this floor. Ellie and Kurt Henderson are Delta A SSAs. No, the bullpen has not exploded. There was an IED but it was handled. No, Ellie was never charged with murder. Don't believe everything you hear.

Yeah, I know the drill. All too well.

Dane and Stewart arrived with coffee moments before Sandra returned our guests.

Karen took a deep breath as she walked in. "That coffee smells fantastic."

Dane smiled at her. "Double shot soy cappuccino with cinnamon?"

"Yes, thank you. I'm Karen." She slid into her chosen seat and took the outstretched takeout cup. "And you are?"

"Dane Wesson and this here is Stewart Smith."

Karen's eyes questioned what she'd heard. I shrugged. "Long story. Not for now."

She smiled and nodded. "I'll add it to the list of 'things to ask about over coffee once this is done.'"

Can't wait.

Dane turned his attention to Tahoma. "Black double shot with extra water?"

"Thank you, Dane. I am Tahoma Whitehorse."

I finished the introductions as quickly as I could, without making anyone feel hurried. "Give the door a nudge, please," I said to Kurt, who sat as always on my right.

He reached out and pushed the door shut.

"If you all look at the whiteboard, Kurt has added a list of suspects regarding the growing number of companies targeted by animal rights groups. We will pay a visit to the last place hit by activists as soon as possible, Signal Enterprises. That's the one that may have lost a monkey."

Lee surveyed the list of suspects. "I've come across a few of those names before. But not from this type of activity."

"Which people in particular and where do you know them from?" I asked, pen poised to write in my notebook.

His eyes bounced from the list on the board to me; I saw his mind ticking and hauling in past knowledge. "You know a couple of them too, Chicky. They were at the rec center when we were on the diamond case."

"Stick a big cross next to their names. They're not high priority."

Gangbangers trying to stay out of jail and go straight. They didn't feel right.

Lee stood and added red crosses. He then underlined three other names. "These three I'll check because they ring a bell. But animal rights doesn't feel like their thing either."

"Thanks, that's narrowed our list a bit." I paused and reread one of the names. Then pointed to the name Mendez. A known car thief. "Mendez is someone Sam and I helped out of a situation. How did he get scooped up by our logarithm?"

"Same way the gangbangers did. Parameters are too wide or ..." His words hung for a beat.

"... or, they have a known associate who plays with animal rights folk," Dane said.

"Good call," Lee said. "We'll get to them but first, this lot that we don't know." Lee circled names.

Dane nodded. Stewart agreed. Kurt reached for my pen. I listened to the scratch of the pen nib in his notebook.

My phone rang, I apologized, silenced it, and pressed the send iMessage icon and chose the pre-formed messaged that said: Sorry I'm in a meeting.

Mitch will understand.

Kurt's phone rang. He answered. Then reached over and wrote in my notebook while listening: Someone new to add to the list of victims.

General chit chat ensued while we waited for Kurt to finish. He placed his phone on the table and cleared his throat.

"This morning the front doors and street frontage of the U-Lab building were splashed with red paint. The head of Human Resources over there reported four employees were bombarded by text messages for an hour from five this morning."

"And the content?" I asked.

"'Animal testing scum. You will pay for what you've done.'"

Outstanding. Poetic nut jobs are my favorite.

"Could be something interesting over there," I said. "If it's the monkey thieves then we might get a lead from the fresh crime scene."

"I'm feeling lucky, how about you, Iverson?" Kurt nudged my arm with his.

"Absolutely. The luck is running like salmon up a river." Try as I might I couldn't keep the edge from my voice. Something niggled inside; I kept hearing a malformed word that sounded a lot like *apocalypse*.

My turn: time for quick calls to Fairfax PD, D.C. Metro, Loudoun PD, and Falls Church PD to get them to round up some of the do-gooders. Interesting that so many do-gooders lived in wealthy areas of northern Virginia.

"Lee, can you take Karen and Tahoma? Head over to Signal Enterprises and see if you can verify whether the monkey is infected with something that could pass to humans. Kurt and I will see the latest red paint casualty. Dane and Stewart, you interview suspects as they arrive. Anything that seems off, let us all know."

I glanced around the room; their facial expressions conveyed acceptance of the assignments.

"Safe and alert," I said, standing.

I left the room and called Mitch. "Babe, everything

okay?"

"Yes. Mom is with the babies. I wanted to let you know I'm at work. Maybe we can have lunch?"

I checked my watch. Just after nine. I should be able to make a one o'clock lunch date.

"One?"

"Meet you at PotBelly on 12th?"

"How'd you know I feel like one of their pickles?" I smiled. And a turkey sandwich with that giant pickle.

"Because I know my wife."

"Decent answer. I'll see you at lunch."

Chapter Four
Eve of Destruction

I stood in front of the of U-Lab building and took in the splashes of red paint on the exterior walls and crudely painted graffiti. Expensive to have that cleaned. No doubt the company would like to extract that money from the vandals.

"Messy," Kurt said and pointed to another patch of bright red that had run down the wall. "Looks like something ..." He tipped his head sideways. "An upside-down giraffe."

"Nothing wrong with your imagination." The paint splatters reminded me of blood-soaked fabric. Be wise to keep that to myself.

"We better go talk to the CEO."

We'd stepped four feet inside the paint-smeared door before security pounced. Two guards, hands on the butts of their weapons. The weapons remained holstered which pleased me.

"Sign in over there, please." The bigger of the two pointed to a reception area. "Who are you here to see?"

"Not sure," I replied, opening my jacket to reveal the badge on my belt. His eyes moved from my badge to my holster and finally my eyes. "The CEO, whoever that might be." I spotted his name tag over his breast pocket. "Who would that be, Jacob?"

"Mrs. Amanda Murray," he said. "I'll take you up once

26

you've signed in and have your visitor passes."

Four minutes later Jacob left us outside a grand glass door. Kurt swung the door open. A young woman behind a functional work desk smiled over a computer screen.

"Good morning, how can I help?"

"We are Special Agents Henderson and Iverson, and we would like to see Mrs. Murray."

"Mrs. Murray is on a call and has a do not disturb order in place. Please have a seat." She smiled and gestured to a row of chairs.

We sat. I arched an eyebrow at Kurt. It was all too much like sitting outside the principal's office in high school. "How long do you think she'll be?" I said, raising my voice so the personal assistant knew I was directing my question at her.

"As long as it takes, Agent."

Not the answer I wanted.

Five long minutes later Kurt leaned into me and whispered, "What's wrong with your face?"

"I'm fucking smiling."

"That's not a smile I ever want directed at me," he said. "Dial it back a few notches. You'll scare the PA."

He's probably right.

Thirty minutes later my face ached from smiling and my trigger finger itched. I stood, walked to the desk and said, "Tell your boss we're coming in."

Her eyes widened. Fear? Really?

"Y-you can't. You can't barge in."

"Wrong."

I marched past her, knocked once and flung open the door, a little harder than I expected. A woman in her late fifties scowled at me from across a vast expanse of polished wood. She glared past me without acknowledging my presence. Her shrill voice sliced through the air. "Your job is to stop this sort of interruption!"

I glanced over my shoulder. The PA cowered in the doorway; tears glistened in her eyes.

The woman continued to rip the air with a voice that boarded on a shriek. "Why are you still here?"

"Is there anything you need, ma'am?" Her voice quivered.

"Just get out. I don't need anything from an imbecile!"

The young woman recoiled as the venom-soaked words bashed her.

I turned to face the tearful woman and quietly said, "Get a new job. You don't need to put up with crap like this." She nodded.

Facing Amanda Murray again, I smiled.

Her eyes narrowed. "And you are?"

"FBI," I said and held up my badge before shoving it into a pocket.

"You too?" she said to Kurt.

"Yes."

"Is this about the graffiti and text messages?"

"You'll need to take the text message problems up with your telco," I said. "Graffiti isn't our area of expertise—"

"Then why are you in my office?"

To do my job, you shrewish bitch. "You're not the only company targeted in the last week, but you are the most recent. We were hoping you might have information on those responsible. Perhaps, this has happened before?"

"I suppose it has happened before." With a dismissive wave, she said, "Talk to security, Agent. I can't help you."

Can't or won't. I suspect won't. "How many of your employees received text messages this morning from the perpetrators?"

"I have no idea. HR deal with such things."

Doesn't give a shit about her employees.

A cell phone on her desk beeped. She glanced at the screen without picking it up; before she returned her attention to us we heard four more alerts. "For goodness' sake. This is ridiculous," she said and thrust the phone at me. "Take it!"

I obliged and read the messages on the lock screen then handed the phone back. "You should talk to your telco and get them to trace the origin of the messages," I replied helpfully. "Are these your only messages from the vandals?"

"Yes." Her voice softened. "Can't you do something? This is unsettling."

But a few minutes ago, she didn't care. Guess it's different when she's on the receiving end.

Kurt cleared his throat. "Ma'am, does your company test on animals?"

"I don't see how that's relevant."

"The people who splashed paint all over your entrance

presume you test on animals. We suspect they're the same people who are text messaging your employees and now you."

She harrumphed. "Do you want to use something that has not been thoroughly tested?"

"I don't care either way," Kurt said. "I'm simply asking the question."

And the answer is yes, because if it were no, she would've said no.

"And the graffiti?"

"Police matter."

"Then why are you asking questions?"

"I'm not at liberty to say, it's part of another investigation," Kurt said. "Should we find the people responsible for the graffiti, we will let police know."

"Security may have information."

"Thank you for your time," I said and walked from her office with Kurt close behind.

"Jacob?" he said as he fell into step beside me.

"Yep."

"Stairs?"

"Please."

Kurt tugged the door to the stairs open. I took a breath. I'm a bit of a connoisseur of stairwell air. Fancy building stairwells smell the same as every other stairwell. Running down the stairs to the ground floor cleared my head as much as it stretched my legs. I've always found it hard to resist running on stairs.

Jacob was willing and helpful; I liked him a lot more

than his boss. He handed us two sheets of paper each. Sketch outlines of two people. One male, the other female. Details of clothing included. Attached were printed security tape images of their faces. Groovy.

"Also, here are some soft copies of the images and footage of them doing the painting," he said and handed me a flash drive.

"Thank you. This is great," I said waving everything in one hand. "You made our job that much easier."

"You're welcome," Jacob said with a toothy grin. "Just doing my job."

"Us too," Kurt said, shaking Jacob's hand. "Does this sort of thing happen often?"

"Every year or two."

"Not unusual then?" I said.

"No, ma'am. What's unusual is they didn't hang around and protest when people came into work for the day."

"That's an interesting observation," I said.

"Figured they were first-timers," Jacob said.

"That's a possibility," Kurt said. "You didn't recognize any of them?"

"There were only two and no, I didn't." He nudged his co-worker. "Daniel did you?"

"Nah."

Daniel's a man of few words. "In the past when you've had protestors chuck paint around, did they always stay and harass people coming into the building?"

Thought exercised on Jacob's brow. "This is the only

time I can remember them leaving without annoying people."

The photos in my hand depicted young people. "They look young. Is that usual?"

Jacob nodded. "Most of the protestors we see are college kids or not much older. Full of themselves and trying to turn the world upside down."

I knew the type. We were those kids once. So sure of ourselves and so determined to right the wrongs and things we deemed unjust. I didn't throw paint at buildings or people; I became an FBI agent. Pretty sure Kurt didn't commit a crime to make his point either.

Ah, to be young and idealistic. "Thanks again for this. I guarantee we will use it," I said.

Kurt handed Daniel and Jacob a business card each. "If you think of anything, or they come back, let us know."

"Will do," Jacob said. "Won't we, Daniel?"

"Yep."

Chapter Five
This is my rifle

My closed fist bashed on the plain green painted door four times. No one called out. I bashed again. Neighbors doors opened, heads appeared. I flashed a badge down the hall. Doors closed.

I bashed on the door again.

We waited for a beat.

Kurt shook his head. "Either no one is home or no one is answering."

I sniffed. "Is that smoke?"

Kurt took a deep breath. "Could be."

"Lives could be at risk," I said and took my badge wallet from my jeans pocket and extracted a couple of thin plastic cards, whitish, larger than regular credit cards, and of differing thicknesses. I chose a card and put the other away. "Lives in danger. I'm sure that's smoke."

"What's that in your hand?"

"A slip card," I said and pushed the card into the door jamb beside the lock, gave it a wriggle while encouraging it through the gap. The lock popped. I pushed the door so the lock cleared the door jamb to prevent it from locking again and returned my handy slip card to my badge wallet. New toys are the best. Friends who are locksmiths are even better. Mental note: Tell Pip thanks.

Kurt opened the door. "Hello, FBI. Anyone here?" He called into the living room. He looked over his shoulder at me. "Doesn't look like anyone's home."

A crash vibrated through the floor followed by a shriek. Sounded more animal than human.

"Wrong," I said.

Kurt headed in the direction the noise.

I closed the door. Best not to have a disease-ridden monkey loose in an apartment building.

"Kurt?"

He was nowhere.

"Stay where you are." His voice sounded muffled. "There's a monkey in here."

"Where are you?"

"In a room."

"No kidding." I poked around doing as I was told and not following the sound of his voice. The student apartment came complete with pizza boxes. In the small kitchen area, I found a box of fruit, mostly bananas.

Imagine. "Enough already, where are you?"

The screeching sounds of a pissed animal grated on my eardrums. The noise rose, wavered and grew stronger.

"Call Animal Control," Kurt hollered, his voice clear despite the accompaniment of loud, angry animal noises. "And CDC."

I made the CDC call first. "Whitehorse, we might have the monkey. Actually, we have a monkey, no confirmation that it's the right monkey." I gave Whitehorse the address.

"We're on our way."

"Do you know if this animal is carrying anything

infectious?" I asked.

Kurt's attempt at soothing noises somewhere down the hall failed, to judge by the shrieking distress calls and irritation.

"Waiting on a warrant to access the research data on the missing monkey."

"Their right to demand a warrant I guess." For me, it was another example of how disappointing people can be. More interested in their bottom line than the welfare of the population.

"Try not to get bitten, peed or spat on, and watch out for flying excrement."

"And people want these damn things as pets?" Idiotic. Wild animals are not pets and should not be treated as such.

"Some people wrongly assume they have a right to try to own others, animals included," Whitehorse replied.

"Sometimes I don't like the human race much."

I hung up and moved in the direction of Kurt's voice. "Whitehorse said don't get spat on, peed on, bitten or poop thrown at you."

"Helpful," Kurt said. "Don't come any closer, Iverson. Stay there!" He hovered inside the doorway of the room. Something flew behind him. Kurt's head turned.

"What was that?"

"Shit. The monkey threw shit."

I sucked in a mouthful of air then blew it out to stifle my guffaws. "Are you hurt?"

"Bitten on the forearm."

Fuckadoodledo. "What are we talking?"

"Puncture wounds. Not messy but they look deep."

I flung open a door and hoped for a bathroom. The residual whiff of shampoo tickled my nose. Hallelujah. I scrabbled through a cabinet under the basin for something to clean a bite wound. I found a half-full bottle of peroxide and some disinfectant. Growling, shrieking, and the occasional ear-splitting screech punctuated the air.

I held the bottles up to Kurt, who waited in the doorway of the monkey room. "Which one?"

"Peroxide."

"Where's the critter?"

"I got it into a cage."

"It's safe then," I said.

"No, throw the bottle."

I twisted the lid to make sure it was tight and rolled it down the hall to Kurt. Blood dripped from his hand as he picked up the bottle. I went back into the bathroom and searched for Band-Aids or bandages.

Nothing.

From near the bathroom, I watched Kurt pour peroxide over the wound. Made me wince watching. His lack of expression amazed me. The room behind him went quiet.

"Why'd we leave our bags in the car?" I said more to myself than him.

"Stupid is as stupid does," Kurt responded.

"Now you sound like my dad."

"Do we know yet if the monkey is carrying anything communicable?"

"Nope."

Another dark object flew behind Kurt. He sat down and leaned against the door jam. "That thing has an endless supply of shit," he said. The monkey started screeching, growling, and shrieking all over again.

"If you're okay, I'll run back down to the car and grab our bags."

"Thanks. Go."

Chapter Six

Live and Let Die

Whitehorse followed me back to the apartment and donned gloves and a mask. "You too," he said passing me a mask and a set of nitrile gloves. He greeted Kurt as he walked down the hall to him. "You doing okay?"

"Yeah. Do we know yet if the little guy is contagious?"

"Not yet."

Kurt narrowed his eyes at me. His brow furrowed. "I told you to stay away."

I pointed a gloved hand at my face. "Mask." I dropped his backpack near his feet.

Whitehorse stepped over Kurt's legs and entered the room. The monkey kicked up a racket again and the poo flinging resumed with gusto.

Guess it doesn't like the masked intruder.

I took a dressing pack from Kurt's bag and wrapped his wounded forearm. "You'll need to swing by the ER and have that checked."

Kurt grinned. "Yep. Why do you enjoy it so much when I'm on the receiving end of an injury?"

"That's not true. I don't like seeing you hurt. But I kinda enjoy the whole boot on the other foot thing for a change."

He stood up. I gathered the rubbish from the dressing pack and stuffed it back inside the packet, then shoved it all inside Kurt's bag.

"Where's your colleague?" Kurt asked, loud enough for Whitehorse to hear him over the angry monkey noises.

We semi-squinted at each other. Guess he couldn't drag her name back into memory either. I wanted to say Amanda, but it didn't feel right so I kept my mouth shut.

"Karen is waiting for the warrant," Whitehorse said, then tried the same kind of soothing sounds at the monkey that Kurt had attempted earlier.

I visualized the word Karen, adding sparkles to the letters in the hope that it would stick in my head.

"Watch out, he's crazy," Kurt said.

Whitehorse jumped sideways as the monkey threw something from the cage. It missed. "That was not very friendly," he said using a low soft tone at the animal. "I want to get you back home, but you are making it difficult."

Whitehorse's phone rang. He moved out of reach of any more flying poop before answering it. A few seconds later he pushed his mask down and smiled at Kurt.

"Did you get a flu shot this year?"

"Yes."

"Then you are all right. This little guy carries an A/ Hong Kong/4801/2014-type virus and this year's vaccine contained that virus."

Kurt smiled. I saw relief tweak behind his eyes. I removed my mask and grinned. "So monkey boy has a strain of the flu and he's now contained. So, this is done?"

Whitehorse laughed. "As far as you two are concerned.

We can take it from here and deal with the people responsible with police support."

"Wonderful." Except we don't have the idiots behind the monkey escapade.

I imagined they were in class and might turn up at any point. I made a call and asked the police to provide protection and support at the scene. "As soon as police arrive, I'll take Kurt to the ER and get that wound checked out."

"Good. Get them to do a swab, better to safeguard against surprises later."

"Will do."

Chapter Seven
Walking in Light.

Morning slithered under the bathroom door and spread across the carpet like a flood. Mitch's breathing changed. His arm moved. I knew without looking he'd checked his watch. I also knew my alarm was about to pierce the air, neither of us were ready for that.

The alarm shrilled as my phone rang. The combined noise rose to a crescendo before it crashed over me. I grabbed the phone from the nightstand, interrupting the alarm as I swept my finger across the screen.

"Good morning, Henderson," I said, hoping I sounded more awake than I felt.

"Less good, more morning," Kurt replied, his voice now background noise as Mitch threw off the covers and climbed out of bed. He leaned down and kissed me. I watched him walk across the floor to the bathroom. As he opened the door, light rained down on him. His summer tan almost glowed.

Won't be long before it fades. Winter is coming.

"Iverson, are you hearing me?" Kurt sounded irritated.

"Sorry. Say again."

"I need you in Rockbridge County."

"Henderson, where are you?"

"Stonewall Jackson Hospital, Lexington."

"What?" I really must've missed everything he'd said.

41

"We have a situation. Cait O'Hare is in Stonewall Jackson Hospital. Police are saying she had an accident while riding."

Riding accident. Dammit. His words plucked at every sinew in my body. The video images of a horse and rider on a country road played back. "Clarify that. Riding what?"

"A horse." A modicum of surprise entered his voice. "Explain."

Relief washed over me but didn't last. The horse was better than wrapping her old Harley Davidson around a tree. "She used to ride a Harley."

"Of course she did, I'd expect nothing less."

"And you're in Lexington?" The loud crack didn't happen. If Cait was shot, Kurt would've led with that news. I settled my stomach and removed all traces of the video from my conscious thought.

"Yes. Sean called me in the middle of the night. I drove down."

The relief I felt at knowing it wasn't a motorbike crash evaporated. "How bad is it, Kurt?"

"Bad."

"Where was this accident?"

"Mauryville."

I knew the sheriff down in there. Cait and I both lived there for a time. Small-town life used to hold a lot of appeal. A shiver ran up my spine. Shitty stuff happened in Mauryville and it didn't quite feel like another lifetime ago, yet. Some incredible snippets of life happened there too, no sense getting all bent out of shape over one aspect of the past.

"And you want me down there?"

"She's our Director and a long-time friend to Delta A."

Seriously? There's nothing wrong with my mind. "Henderson, I'm aware who Cait is. What I don't know is why you want me down there if she had an *accident*?" Snippy edged into my tone. "While I'm at it, how about Dane, Stu and Lee?"

"Long night," he said, sounding almost apologetic. "Can't hurt, assemble the gang. I'll expect you in five hours."

"Was it an accident?"

"We'll talk face to face. Get down here."

"We'll be there."

The black screen confirmed Kurt had gone. I lay still and listened to the shower running.

My eyes drifted to the crib. Neither Grace nor Isabella stirred. They spent their first ten weeks in such a noisy environment that even at six months, they'd sleep through anything. Anything except hunger. Grace's small hand opened, her fingers grasped Isabella's sleeve.

Not long till they wake.

Downstairs I heard the sounds of activity. My brain assimilated this and turned it into information. Dad was in the kitchen. He'd let Argo outside. My dad was on baby duty.

* * *

I dropped my bag on the sofa in the corner of the office and planted myself behind the desk. Morning settled on me with a sense of foreboding and a general feeling that something hinky floated in on the wind. Kurt's phone call had started a chain of events in my already acrobatic mind. I'd called my mother-in-law to let her know I was leaving town and that Mitch and Dad might need support. Between her, Mitch, and my dad, the twins would be well cared for in my absence. Didn't make me feel much better about leaving them but this was about Cait, and I had to go.

Voices floated in the air outside my office. I concentrated harder on the screen in front of me. The voices grew louder as they closed in then faded on passing. My eyes didn't leave the screen. Police had emailed a case report for my opinion. The MO matched a cold case. My opinion was we needed to look into it. I typed and sent my reply.

Did we all need to go to Mauryville? Would it be better for Lee, Dane, and Stewart to stay in Washington and work the new case while Kurt and I took care of Mauryville? Or we could postpone the new case until the Director's situation was resolved. Or I could stay behind.

Yeah, not going to happen.

A fresh conversation converged on my closed door and stopped before a knock rang out.

"Enter!"

The door opened. I felt the barometric pressure

change. The door closed. I shut my laptop lid and saw Dane, Stewart, and Lee in front of my desk. Sam Jackson's sudden death left a big hole in Delta A. We plugged the hole as best we could with Dane and Stewart. Fresh blood. It's gotta be beneficial. Argo helped too. In some ways, I felt the team was stronger because of our loss.

"Thank you for joining me. Have you all seen the police request and my assessment?"

They nodded.

"Pull up chairs and let's get into this."

No one moved.

Curious. "Or stand," I said and opened the laptop again to reread the brief police had sent. A waterlogged body found on the sidewalk of 9th Street SW. "It's been sixteen years since the last waterlogged body in D.C. and now the Unsub is killing again, or do we have a copycat out there?"

No reaction. No movement.

Curiouser and curiouser.

"Spill." I made eye contact with Lee, and let my eyes probe his for a second before moving to Dane, then Stewart. "Something on your minds?"

I waited. No one wanted to speak first.

Not a happy sign.

Lee shifted his weight from foot to foot.

"Say it!"

A piece of paper moved in Dane's hand. I hadn't noticed it before. He dropped it on my desk. I raised an eyebrow and skimmed the single page, taking note of the FBI letterhead. From the office of the Executive Assistant Director of the Intelligence Branch, with bold red lettering centered under the letterhead.

Effective Immediately.
Delta teams must cease all working relationships with Russian FSB officers and any dealings with European counterparts must have prior approval from this office.

Signed by Assistant Director Owen.

I clamped my lips together to thwart a barrage of profanity.

Owen strikes again but this time from the Intelligence Division. She hasn't wasted any time throwing her weight around with Cait indisposed. Jump in her grave as quick?

A shudder ran from the base of my spine to my head.

No explanation but if I were honest, it wasn't a surprise given the current political climate. Russia wanted an enemy and we were fast becoming unequivocally that. Pulling back from our relationships with other countries felt short-sighted and knee-jerkish.

"Owen is Executive Assistant Director of Intelligence?" Oxymoron much?

The hinky feeling from earlier gathered momentum.

Dane shuffled his feet. Lee adjusted his expression from disturbed to stony.

"What haven't I heard?"

"The rumor I heard is that Owen is angling for the top job," Stewart said.

I failed to hide my utter horror at that comment.

She's not Director material. She's not even human material. The first fembot director. A bolt of lightning pierced the image, leaving a blackened scar across the silicon face of the fembot.

I knew where this conversation was headed and issued an appropriate warning. In a rough whisper, I said, "Our surmising and complaints do not leave this office. If anyone outside of us ..." I waved my finger around the group, "... gets even a tiny whiff of how we feel, our jobs are history. And that's the least of what will happen to us." I drummed home my point. "This is a safe space, out there, not so much."

The three men nodded.

"Why would anyone consider her?" Lee grumbled, shifting again.

"Think about it, Lee. She's feminine, stupid, Republican, a total suck-up and—" Dane said.

"—all the things he admires in a woman," Stewart finished. "And a freaking puppet."

Puppet or fembot; amounted to the same thing.

"There's more to that. I heard she's a personal friend of POTUS," Dane said. He grinned at me. "I made some inquiries. Casually. Watercooler stuff."

"Crackerjack job."

The word crackerjack glowed in the air. Might take a bit of use for that one to feel natural. Stewart sent an amused question into my mind: New word? I fired a mental shrug back. Crackerjack. Yep, it was going to take work to adopt that doozy.

"O'Hare has held the Director position for ten years?"

"Wow, it must be. That means only one other Director has done the job longer."

Dane nodded. "Rumor has it she'll stay at least another two years before she retires. Even POTUS doesn't want to mess with O'Hare and the job she's doing."

He should hang around the watercooler more often.

"Owen being a friend makes sense," Lee murmured. "Sure as hell isn't job performance."

No argument from me. Always amazes me how she manages to cling to her job. Sure it's by the very tip of her expensively manicured nails.

I leaned back in my chair, pushed the Evil Queen aside and gave thought to the new case. Weighing it against the possibility of foul play in Lexington. Nothing I'd read that morning indicated an escalation in waterlogged bodies. One body turning up sixteen years after the last waterlogged body on a D.C. street was intriguing, but unless we could confirm it was the same Unsub, it wasn't our case anyway.

Dead people don't mind waiting.

On the other front, everything felt stormy and somehow touched by Owen's hand.

I made my decision. "We're going to hold off on this new case. There's a more pressing issue." I surveyed the men in front of me. "Road trip to Rockbridge County."

"Nothing's come through about a case down there ..." Dane said, scanning the tablet in his hand.

"Kurt is there now. He believes there's a case. In light of the current climate here, you can choose to come with, or you can stay and carry on here."

That tweaked their curiosity.

"What are we investigating?"

"Cait O'Hare has had an *accident*."

"Is she all right?" Lee asked.

"I don't imagine she's great. Kurt is there with her. Sean asked him to go down. She's in Stonewall Jackson Hospital."

Half a smile scratched itself into Lee's face. "Lexington feels like full circle, Chicky."

"It's where this version of Delta A started," I said to settle the seething questions I felt mounting in Dane and Stewart.

And maybe where it ends.

Stewart flashed his eyes at me. Was that a warning?

"Iverson, you don't want that to become a self-fulfilling prophecy," he said, in a harsh whisper. His mouth never moved yet I heard him.

Lee spoke, "If you two are done playing mind games. Any clue how we explain the sudden absence of Delta A?"

"Caine," I replied in synchrony with a knock on my office door.

The door swung open and Caine entered.

Lee grinned. "More spooky shit, Chicky."

"Maybe."

49

Caine grumbled, the men stepped aside, letting him through. "Kurt's been in touch. I'm officially sending Delta A to Rockbridge," he said, his voice full of gravel, with a hint of menace.

I gave him a look. "We may have a new case here."

One corner of his mouth twitched. "I suggest you get moving."

"And here?"

"I can handle things here while you're gone."

"I'll give you a hand," Lee said.

"You sure?" Caine turned to Lee.

"We made a fine team so not long ago. I'd like to help, wouldn't hurt to have a Delta A presence around the office."

And throw Owen off the scent. Definitely an ingenious idea. Although now she is attached to the Intelligence Branch she shouldn't be concerned with what happens here in the Criminal Division. But it's the Wicked Queen. Wherever she finds she can meddle, she does.

Caine twitched a lip at me. "That okay with you?"

"I'd like Lee with us down in Rockbridge but we can manage without him. I can see the merit in him remaining here."

Caine's lip twitched again; he shook Lee's hand. "Glad to have you holding the fort with me."

He almost sounded glad. That gave me pause. My mind harked back to hearing him laugh once not so long ago. Scary stuff.

I shook it off and turned my attention to the job at

hand. "Okay, the three of us will head south," I said, "you two stay safe."

I stood and pushed my chair back. Time to go.

A little yellow duck with a noose around its neck waddled across my desk, quacking. I watched as the duck toppled head first over the edge. The rope caught. One sharp snap and the duck flopped lifelessly.

Chapter Eight

Sticky Fingers

Kurt met us in the foyer; I handed him a coffee.

"Thanks," he said, took a sip then passed it back to me. "Hold it for me." Kurt rolled his sleeve up and inspected the bandage on his forearm.

"You all right?"

"Itchy. Hopefully, that means it's healing."

"Maybe get Grant to look at it, later?"

"I'm still taking antibiotics. It's probably nothing." He buttoned his cuff and took the cup back. "Damn monkey."

We followed Kurt through the hospital and down a corridor to a numbered door. Doctor Grant Neal's office.

He swung the door wide. Grant pushed his chair back and bounded around the side of the desk, a greeting spilling from his lips.

"Ellie. Great to see you again. Shame the circumstances aren't better." Grant thrust his hand at me, grabbed mine and pulled me in for a hug and then stepped back and studied me. "Amazing as always." He paused, pushing me to arm's length. "Something is different."

"Really?" I said, with a smile.

His eyes roamed to my left hand then back to my eyes. "Married. It is a *real* marriage this time, right?" He grinned at Kurt. "And it's *not* to Henderson?"

"Not Kurt, and it's real."

"You look well and happy. And I have rounds. I'll catch up for a coffee later?"

"That would be nice."

"And hey, congratulations." Grant let me go. His head tilted slightly to one side like a puppy. If he licks me, he's dead. "There's something else."

Surprised he doesn't know. Maybe Kurt isn't that chatty. "Married with children, what else could there be?"

"Children? Yours?"

I nodded. Certainly didn't find them in a cabbage patch. "Twin girls. They're six months old."

"That is the absolute best news." Grant beamed. "Motherhood agrees with you."

"I reckon it does and thank you."

Grant acknowledged Dane and Stewart as he left.

"Grab seats," Kurt said and leaned his backside on the edge of Grant's desk. Irritation played across his eyes. He was done with small talk.

"What happened to Cait?" I asked, sitting in a chair near him and taking a sip of coffee.

"The official line is horse riding accident," Kurt said. He clenched and unclenched his jaw as he sipped from the takeout coffee in his hand. "She's on life-support."

Life-support. Yep, that's bad.

Questions fired from my mouth. "How did it happen? Prognosis? What do you know that I need to know? Who is with her? Was she alone when the accident happened?"

My brain screeched to a halt then fired back up. "What do you mean 'official line'?"

"Slow down, Iverson. It's been a long night."

"Sorry."

He drank more coffee. "Sean asked me for a second opinion at one this morning."

That explains the jeans, wrinkled shirt, and the need for a shave. "Has she been conscious at all?"

"Not since I arrived."

I knew. I remembered. The process of death wasn't always fast or even straightforward depending on the circumstances. There was a need to determine brain function and activity before the declaration of death.

Don't jump to conclusions, Ellie. Life-support doesn't mean death. "Will she recover?"

Kurt sighed, his eyes met mine. "I don't know."

I heard the words but his eyes told me he did know and I didn't want to hear the answer. "Can I see her?"

He nodded. "Sean figured you'd want to and that Cait would want to see you."

On my feet without realizing it, I started for the door. "How?"

Dane held the door open, Kurt was right behind me, and Stewart behind him. The four of us walked down the quiet corridor. We'd been here before. It didn't feel any better this time.

"The report from paramedics said she was found on the side of the road lying over a black stallion."

A black stallion. A hammer swung in the air.

"Thor. His name is Thor." Nothing felt right.

Nothing.

I stopped walking in the middle of the hallway. Kurt walked a few yards before he noticed.

"What's the matter?" Kurt's eyes probed mine. "You okay?"

"Yes. Where and when did the accident happen?"

"Her last text to her husband was nine-thirty last night. She texted to say she'd head home about ten and that it was a nice night for a ride."

"Where was she?"

"Mauryville."

I nodded, picturing the road in my mind. "It was dark."

"She was out on the road on a black horse in the dark," Kurt said. "No street lights, nothing but stars down that way."

Cait and I shared that road once. Generally, it was quiet. I wouldn't have thought twice about riding or walking home from Cait's at night. What did I know about Cait, Thor, and night riding? She used a dark reflective quarter sheet, a dark reflective safety harness, as well as reflective boots on all four of Thor's legs. The minute headlights hit the horse he shone like a freaking diamond. Shine on, you crazy diamond.

"Iverson?"

"She was visible. Cait used night-riding gear. Always." Safety first.

"The horse could've caused the accident."

Thor's hot-blooded. He pretty much hated everyone except Cait. Guess he could've spooked on the road and fallen. That doesn't feel right. What would spook him? Traffic? An animal? A person jumping out at him?

"The horse?" I needed to look into the situation further to satisfy the niggling in my gut. The gnawing turned into full-blown foreboding. A voice in my head told me to heed my gut.

As if I wouldn't.

"The horse, Kurt?"

Something was definitely up. My hink-dar was off the charts.

"The horse is dead. Sean said they're waiting on an autopsy and the subsequent report."

"So they weren't hit by a vehicle?" Because if the horse died of injuries sustained, an autopsy would be an unnecessary added expense.

"No. The horse may have been spooked by a vehicle though."

I was back on the autopsy: I knew who'd be doing that autopsy and writing that report. Dr. Robinson in Mauryville. "Who gets the report?"

"You," Kurt replied. He watched me closely. "Are you all right?"

My mind still circled the words 'the horse is dead.' Cait loved that animal. She'd had him since he was about five years old. Thor was almost a thousand pounds and seventeen hands of pure crazy Standardbred.

So why don't I believe the horse caused the accident?

Because she trusts him and he trusts her. Could the noise I heard at the end of the inexplicable video have rattled Thor that much?

What did I know about him? He'd been with Cait for eighteen years and had thrown her several times in the early days. Cait told me how long it took to win his trust and how hard she'd worked with him. He was still an asshole to anyone who wasn't Cait or her son, Quinn. Thor lived happily on her property in Mauryville with his friend Freyja. She was an American Quarter Horse and the gentlest creature I'd ever met.

Exact opposites. Poor Cait. Poor Freyja. Thor's passing will leave a giant hole in their worlds. If Cait doesn't recover, her passing will leave a giant hole in her family's world. Our world will change forever.

"Horses don't just drop dead," I murmured as my brain tried to imagine that happening.

"Anything is capable of dropping dead," Kurt said. "Anything with a heart and brain anyway."

Rules Owen out then.

"About the accident ... that's the official line, right? Accident." Stewart's tone suggested he didn't for one second believe it was an accident.

"Yeah," Kurt replied. "Except it's the weirdest accident I've attended."

Silence again.

"Because?" I said.

"Because she came in unconscious but the paramedic notes said she responded to Narcan before and during transportation. Narcan was administered again in the emergency room but with no notable improvement in her consciousness level."

"Fuck."

Stewart and Dane closed the gap between us. Dane whispered, "What's that mean?"

"It means she was under the influence of an opioid."

"And Narcan?"

"Let me," Kurt said. "It's an opioid antidote. It can and often does reverse the effects."

"Why was it administered twice?"

"The effect can wear off quite rapidly. As it appears to have done in this case. Second and third doses are not out of the ordinary."

"O'Hare was a drug user?" Stu said, matching Dane's tone.

"Welcome to the FBI where drug testing is mandatory and random. No, she did not take drugs," Kurt replied. "Plus, I have all her medical records. There has never been any mention of any long-term drug use – prescribed or otherwise."

"Deliberate overdose?" Dane said, looking me straight in the eye.

I gave the merest shake of my head. Why would she? A voice broke into my thoughts but didn't come from Stu or Dane. Why would anyone? We don't know what drives a lot of people to suicide; it's not always obvious, even to close family.

"Did you talk to the paramedics?" I said to Kurt.

"Not yet. I left a message with their dispatch asking that they contact me. Sounds like they had a busy night."

"We need to make sure that whatever happened to Cait is properly investigated and doesn't fall victim to the 'alternative facts' brigade's propaganda machine," I said. It was starting to feel uncomfortable in my country. Maybe the time had come for a change.

Mitch's voice in my mind startled me: We can go back to New Zealand, anytime. Just say the word.

We walked on, all of us thinking, none of us speaking until Kurt stopped outside a single room in a medical ward. I expected to find her in intensive care, not on a regular ward.

"She's in here," Kurt said.

"Kurt, why isn't she in intensive care?"

"No beds."

"Airlift her to a bigger hospital?"

I saw it again in his eyes. The truth. It wouldn't matter where she was: there was no coming back from this.

"Let's go in, Iverson."

I gave an understated wave through the glass door at Sean. He nodded. I entered, with Kurt, Dane, and Stewart close behind. A remarkable amount of shuffling took place as they moved into positions that afforded them all a view of the bed.

"Thank you for coming," Cait's husband, Ethan, said to me, then leaned close to Cait's ear and said, "Ellie is here."

"Any change?" I opted to remain hopeful.

"No." Ethan fished an object out of his pocket. "But the hospital returned her things and there's this." He passed me her phone. Undamaged. "I found a partial text on her phone, never sent, it says 'Not.'"

I opened messages and there it was complete with time stamp. Not what? A suicide attempt or an accident? Did she do this herself and take the horse with her? Of the horses, he was the one who would lose his shit without her.

"So she was conscious enough to try to write a text at the time of the incident." My gaze rested Ethan. "Why a text. Why not call?"

"You lived out here long enough to know the answer, Ellie. There are dark spots on that road, where, for whatever reason cell reception drops."

Nothing much changes down here. Texting used to work better than calling in some places. Guess stronger cell towers aren't a priority in low population areas.

Could've been accidental. Her finger slipping. I don't know how many times I've found random single words in an open text message. It's like pocket dialing.

"Do you know where they found the phone?"

"On the ground near her."

"And she wasn't pinned under Thor?"

"No, well, if she was, I wasn't told. Paramedics said when they arrived she was draped over the horse. I think she was trying to tell us it wasn't an accident, Ellie."

I tried to gauge what Ethan knew but couldn't read him.

Screw it, he has to know about the Narcan result. "You know she initially responded to Narcan and what that means?"

"Yes. That's what I mean, Ellie. It wasn't an accident."

Uh huh.

"So it was a deliberate act."

There was a flash of 'holy fuck' in his eyes as the entire money box dropped.

"Jesus. No. She didn't do this to herself." Ethan clambered to his feet and drew himself to his full height forcing me to tilt back my head to look into his eyes.

Kurt's phone buzzed. He interrupted me before I could speak. "Positive result on heroin, fentanyl and Xanax."

"What the fuck is going on here," Ethan growled, taking a step closer. Sean's hand landed on his arm. He shook it off.

My brain spun around the possibilities while it tried to push away thoughts of suicide.

"Hold up a second." I turned to Kurt. "Cait and Thor fell." I glanced at the unconscious woman in the bed. "Her head?"

"The nature of the incident means it is possible her head made contact with the ground, but paramedics reported she was leaning over the horse, arms around his neck. Her upper body was not in contact with the ground."

"Did her head contact the ground or not?"

"No evidence it did."

She didn't hit her head. The horse went down but she

was still conscious. She was comforting the animal, maybe trying to keep him on his feet.

"So she was leaning over the horse, grabbed him on the way down and stopped her head hitting the ground or as if she was trying to keep him up and calm him when he faltered and started to collapse." I bent down to Cait's ear and whispered, "What do you want us to know, Cait?"

My money was on her wrapping her arms around Thor's neck to comfort him. I swallowed hard as potential scenarios vied for my attention. One stuck out and stayed. Something happened to the horse to cause him to fall, and then something happened to Cait. Somehow heroin, fentanyl, and Xanax ended up in her body.

Horse first then Cait, feels right.

The big question in my mind flashed neon orange and pink. Did Cait cause this?

The respirator hissed.

I straightened up. All eyes were on me.

"Could we be looking for a second person?" Ethan said, sinking back into his chair and picking up Cait's hand. He murmured something I couldn't hear to his unconscious wife.

If Cait didn't do it, someone did. Drugs like fentanyl, Xanax, and heroin don't ever magically appear in someone's bloodstream.

"Yes. We could. Anything to add?"

He shrugged. "Not really. I haven't been out there. Just have a feeling that Cait wanted to tell me it wasn't an accident."

Yeah, but did she want to tell you it was suicide or attempted murder?

"You haven't been out there? Then where were you when the incident happened?"

"On my way back from Roanoke."

Dane stiffened. A word leaped to mind: Croatoan. I shut it down by focusing on Dane and Stewart and thought: Not that Roanoke. Croatoan flashed once then faded. Too many *Supernatural* episodes, boys.

"Had you been gone long?"

Ethan stroked Cait's hand. "Just the day. I was there for business."

Stewart spoke, "What business are you in, Mr. James."

"Security," he said, without taking his eyes off Cait.

"We work together," Sean said. "Ethan advises companies on espionage protection. He runs workshops on espionage prevention, awareness, and investigation. And is our head investigator when it comes to corporate industrial espionage."

Fascinating. I never knew what Ethan's job was, though I did know he was a cop once upon a time. A homicide detective in Los Angeles. How he got from the West Coast to the East Coast, I had no clue, except it had something to do with Cait.

"Who found her?" Dane asked, easily moving the subject back to the incident.

"Someone made a call to the sheriff's office. We don't know who. Kevin said she was alone when he reached her."

I glanced at Dane. "I want to know who made that call, where they live, and why they didn't hang around."

"Who's Kevin?" Dane said, pen poised over his notebook.

"Local sheriff out in Mauryville," I said.

"I'm on it," Dane replied, scribbling in his notebook. "How long do you think we'll be down here?"

"A few days." I turned to Kurt and said, "Let's not stay in the same hotel as last time."

He smiled. A memory fizzed in places it had no right to. A reminder that we'd always have Lexington and we'd nearly had each other.

Ethan spoke, "Stay at our place. There's plenty of room and it's close to the investigation scene."

But not the hospital. That's almost an hour away.

Sean handed me a key. "Stay, El. You know the house, you know the area, it makes sense."

"Thanks. We appreciate it. We'll head out, I need to see Kevin and start slotting some pieces together."

Being back in town might cause a stir. Best head that off before the gossip mill grinds away at my new life.

"Thank you, Ellie," Ethan said. "Thank you for coming, it means a lot to us." He rubbed Cait's arm.

"She'd do the same for me." It's what we do.

Ethan grabbed my hand as I turned to leave. "She didn't do this. She wouldn't. You know her, Ellie."

I hoped she didn't; imagining a scenario that would lead someone like Cait O'Hare to suicide was impossible for me. How well do we ever know someone? I knew her well enough to know there was no way to reconcile Cait and suicide in my mind.

Outside the door, I watched the room for a moment. Our Director. Our friend. My friend. This couldn't be more a Delta A case if someone stamped our names on her forehead.

Stewart arched an eyebrow in my direction. His voice filled my head: There might be something to that, Ellie.

Chapter Nine

Dead Flowers

Kurt motioned to a black Suburban four cars away from mine. I tossed my keys at Stewart and followed Kurt.

Over my shoulder, I said, "Mauryville sheriff's office. See you there."

"Right behind you," Stewart replied.

I waved and climbed into the front passenger seat. It was all so familiar.

"Strange coming back," Kurt said. It wasn't a question. He grew up in Lexington, left, came back a doctor with the FBI, because all hell broke loose. Fun times.

This was different. No one was undercover, I wasn't Kurt's *wife*. Something niggled. Going back even further, I solved an abduction out here once upon a time. The abduction of Cait and Sean's younger sister. And now Cait and Sean needed our help, again. Something Lee said echoed 'full circle.' I settled into the seat and let familiar scenery rush past me. It was as though I'd never left.

Marge looked up from her desk as I swung open the door to the sheriff's office. I smiled. Two beats later she squealed, rushed around the desk and flung her arms around me.

"As I live and breathe, if it isn't Ellie Conway." She stepped back and hollered at a closed door. "Kev, get out here. We got a visitor!"

A door opened. "What's all the commotion, Marge?" came a western drawl from a tall gray-headed man who stepped out of the office. His eyes bounced from Marge to me. "I see the feds have come to town." A smile crinkled an extra few wrinkles in his weathered face.

"Sheriff," I said with a nod.

He held his arms wide. "Get over here kid, and give me a proper hello." Kevin chuckled as he hugged me then let me break free. "How's your dad and that brother of yours. No one's forgiven him for whisking Holly off to the big city. Not the same without her in the bookshop."

I'd imagine not. The local cops liked to hang out in her kitchen and drink her coffee. "Dad's well. Aidan and Holly are married and have a baby girl, more a toddler than a baby now."

Kevin grinned. "And you?" His eyes sparked with life. "You look happy."

"I am." I held up my hand so he could see my wedding rings. "And twin baby girls."

"I never thought I'd see the day ..."

I don't imagine anyone did.

His attention moved to Kurt and then paused as the door behind us opened. Stewart and Dane entered.

"We're all together," Kurt said and extended his hand to grasp Kevin's. "Nice to see you again, sir."

"You too, son." Kevin greeted the other two. "Big turnout. I presume this is related to Ms. O'Hare's incident?"

67

Incident not accident. Interesting. State police must've made the accident assumption, not Kevin. Yay for us. Media will report on a riding accident and not an ongoing investigation. Whoever is behind the drugging and the death of the horse will envisage they got away with it. Might make capturing the person or persons easier.

I'm sure one day the Pollyanna in me will fade and the cynical bitch lurking inside will take over. "Yep, can we get your take on things?" I said.

"Think we better get some coffee and talk."

Marge smiled from her desk. "The diner is open. I wouldn't say no to a slice of chocolate cake."

Kev smiled at her. "With cream or yogurt?"

"Cream, thank you."

Marge was the longest serving of Kevin's five deputies and had worked with him since long before they both turned gray.

We headed over to the diner across the street where the coffee stuck to your ribs and the pie was legendary.

"When did Cait arrive?"

"She stopped by on her way out to Wolfsong three days ago."

"By herself?"

"No, Ethan was with her."

"She was okay?"

"Yeah, they both were. We had a chat about how the young fella is doing at college."

"Any memorable strangers blow through town in the last week?"

Kev shook his head. "Just the usual traffic. It's bear hunting season but not too many new faces stopping, yet. Few folk fishing for trout and so forth. Only seen locals out bear and deer hunting, so far."

I hated the thought of people shooting bears, but the thought of hunters shooting Bambi's mother didn't bother me at all. That's fucked-up. Or maybe it was because I knew about Hunters for the Hungry and that they'd distributed over twenty-five million servings of venison to hungry Virginians.

"No one stood out?" Dane said, breaking the spell I was under and forcing me to focus on Kevin again.

"Not to me." He leaned forward, moved the plate a little before he picked up his cup. "Why?"

The look in his eyes told me he knew why. I matched his posture. "What do you expect happened to Cait?" I said, watching him.

"The horse spooked and took a terrible fall. Bad luck all round."

"It might not have been an accident."

"I gotta tell ya, last night, it sure had the trappings of an accident. I told her when she got that crazy horse that he'd kill someone one day."

He believes it was an accident? "Thor loved Cait." A smile edged across my lips. "It was the rest of us who were in danger."

Kev finished a mouthful of pie. "We can't rule out the horse spooking or even the horse having some kind of a medical event that caused this."

"You reckon it was an accident?"

"I didn't say that, Ellie, but it could've been."

Yeah, right up until the drugs in Cait's system.

"Who called emergency services?" Dane asked.

"We got an anonymous call from a burner phone saying there'd been an accident."

Dane wrote in his notebook.

Burner phone. That's not suspicious at all.

Dane came up from his notebook with another question. "Did you recognize the paramedics who attended?"

"Adam Crutchley was on, with a new partner. Didn't know her. I've seen her a few times but not to talk to."

Kurt made a note. I imagine it was the name. Adam Crutchley. I tried to drag up memories of another time. I was sure I knew his name from somewhere. "Crutchley, he's been with Mauryville Fire and Rescue for a while?"

Kev nodded. "He would've been a high school kid when you lived here."

The memory surfaced, Adam Crutchley lived with his parents on Mulberry Lane. "He still live with his folks on Mulberry?"

Kev smiled. "His mom. Jason Crutchley passed away three years ago."

"He was the Fire Chief, wasn't he?"

"Yes. Cancer got him." Kev shook his head. "I reckon it'll get everyone sooner or later."

Cheery thought.

Forks placed neatly on plates, Kurt and I drained our

cups of aromatic coffee.

I knew we needed to talk to Adam and his partner. "Can you let Adam know we need to talk to him? Tell him we're staying at the O'Hare place."

"Sure thing."

"Who ordered the autopsy?" Kurt wiped his mouth with a napkin then screwed it up and dropped it on his plate.

"I don't know anything about an autopsy," Kevin replied. "You're talking about the horse, I take it?"

"Yes. I'll speak to Doc Robinson, might've been Ethan," I said. Kurt tapped my foot with his. He agreed.

"Let's get out there then while we've still got daylight." Kevin drained his cup and set it down.

Chapter Ten

Dark Horse

"If a vehicle of any description hit the horse there would be carnage, blood, and tire marks," I said. "There isn't even any glass." From the side of the road, I saw a patch of flattened grass on the opposite shoulder.

Kev leaned on his car while the four of us walked up and down the road searching for any sign of vehicular involvement. I found hoof prints in the soft dirt beside the road. It'd rained recently but not since Cait and Thor's unfortunate event.

"He could've spooked and tried to throw her," Kev called out as I walked away from the scene.

"Did he?"

"No. I don't believe so." He bent down and plucked a piece of long grass from the berm. "But he could have."

"Super useful, Kev."

"Here to help."

I glanced back at him. He didn't sound like Kevin. Sandy blond hair and a dimpled grin met my gaze. Chance. Spinning on my heels, I started back to the car. Chance met me halfway. Beyond him, I saw Kevin chewing on the piece of grass he'd plucked from the roadside.

"Hi."

"You here for a reason or is this a social whatever?" I

said.

Chance stepped closer. "What would make a big strong horse like Thor drop at the side of the road?" He placed his hands on my shoulders and focused deep into my eyes.

"Kev could be right, he could've spooked. A snake maybe. A dog could've startled him."

"It's winter, the snakes are asleep. They are as fond of the cold as I am," Chance said.

"A rat or a dog?" Grasping at straws as they slipped through my fingers was a fun game.

"I can't see a big tough horse like him dropping dead of fright because something small and annoying spooked him. Can you?"

Yeah. Nah.

"Not really. What then? He wasn't hit by a vehicle," I said. Irritation fermented.

"Not rocket science El, but it is science."

"A tranquilizer."

"There ya go."

"Did she do this, Chance? Did she kill the horse and overdose?"

"How well do you know Cait?"

How well do we really know anyone? "We've known each other a lot of years. We've been through some shit storms."

"And?"

"I don't believe she would kill the horse or try to take her own life. Her curiosity and passion wouldn't allow that." And I saw it. A video of a horse and a rider on this stretch of road. Dammit.

"What?"

"Two days before the incident." No way to make this sound less insane but then, I'm talking to my imaginary friend. Par for the course. "I saw this, Chance, but didn't know it was this."

"What did you see?"

Not how, but what. Imaginary friends are the best.

"A horse and rider on this road then I heard a loud crack. At the time I thought it was Kurt knocking on the doorframe, but, maybe it was a gunshot."

"Then you know."

"I do."

Chance planted a kiss on my forehead. "Happy to help."

The pressure of Chance's hands on my shoulders eased. He faded into a comic book page that floated to the ground and dissolved.

"Kurt!" I hollered.

He was at the edge of the road, south, away from my position. Kurt spun around when I yelled. We met at a halfway point.

"What if someone fired a tranquilizer dart at the horse?"

"Then we may be looking at an attempt on our Director's life." He stepped closer and spoke in my ear. "Say it, Iverson."

"This was not an accident or a suicide attempt. This is

attempted murder."

As soon as I read my words on the breeze, Kurt called Sean on speaker.

"Can you arrange security for Cait with your company?"

"Yes."

"Do it. Keep it quiet. We're working on the possibility that this was attempted murder. Zero information will be released publicly or to anyone outside Delta A."

Sean blew air before speaking, "Could this have come from within the Bureau?"

Worst case scenario. "It's possible," I said. "Let's nail everything down." While we're at it, let's add some super glue, better safe than sorry.

"I'll arrange for my people to provide security."

"Get a guard stationed outside the door, Sean. Make sure that guard checks the ID of staff going in and out of the room," I said. "No FBI or Law Enforcement visitors without you, Ethan, or one of Delta A present."

"What do you know Ellie? Because it sounds like you know something."

"Something isn't right, but I don't know what. Let's play it safe and close for now."

Her phone flashed in front of my eyes. Her phone. Why did she try to text, why not make a 9-1-1 call? Why not call Ethan? Do we know for sure it was a reception issue?

"Ellie. What?"

"Bag her phone, Sean. I know Ethan and I touched it,

but we should be able to isolate any other prints on it."

"You think someone had her phone? That's why she didn't call for help."

"I do. I think it was given back but it was too late, and all she could do was try to reach Ethan." She was not lucid and incapable of anything more than a partial text on an already open conversation thread. With Sean on the line, I stood where Thor went down. My signal strength dropped to 3G but the call hung in there.

"Do you want me to dust it for prints?"

"No. You're too close. Bag it. We'll do it."

"Roger that."

"How is she?" Kurt said, moving the subject sideways.

"No change."

"That's not a bad thing, Sean." Kurt hung up and pocketed his phone.

"It's not a good thing either," I said and grabbed Kurt by the elbow when he tried to walk away.

He gave me his full attention. "What, Iverson?"

"I need to find out what was given to Thor."

"I doubt it was the same mix that was given to Cait." His voice fell flat, pancaking on the road. "I need to check in with Grant and give him a heads-up about the guard situation." Kurt lifted his phone from his pocket and called Grant Neal at Stonewall Jackson Hospital. While he talked to Grant, I made a call of my own but to a different kind of doctor. The local vet, Doc Robinson.

"It's Special Agent Iverson, has Doc started the autopsy on the O'Hare horse?"

"Not yet. He came in from morning rounds a couple of minutes ago. I'll put you through," his receptionist answered.

The line buzzed. Doc's gentle voice followed. "How can I help?"

"Doc, it's Ellie." I gave him a second.

"You're back. This about Thor?"

"It is. Could he have been tranquilized?"

Kurt nodded his head at Kevin indicating he was going to see him.

"I'll let you know. I haven't had a chance to examine him thoroughly. I did bloods at the site and I'm waiting for results."

"Thanks, Doc."

"Are you coming in?"

"I'll be at your office in about an hour. Don't wait the autopsy for me though, in case I'm delayed. We need to know what caused Thor's death."

"Understood."

Stewart hollered from behind me. I did a one-eighty while pocketing my phone to see what he wanted. He waved then circled his arm in the air. My eyes darted back and forth across the road in the distance. I waved back to let him know I was coming. Where was Dane? As I neared a dark shape moved. Crouched, Dane examined something on the edge of the roadway. For a moment he looked like a squirrel. Guess my nickname for him wasn't too far off.

He stood, adjusted his jacket and grinned at me.

"There was a vehicle," Dane said. He pointed to marks in the dirt at the edge of the road. "Sometime since it last rained."

"Do we know when that was?"

Stu tapped his phone. "We do. It rained two nights ago."

"Heavy enough to wash tire marks away?"

Stu nodded. "Possibly, this area caught the tail end of a storm that dumped about two inches of rain on this side of the mountains."

That accounted for the softer than usual dirt on the edge of the road. Dry and cold was how I remembered this time of year. I smelled the coming snow.

"Okay, so a vehicle. Any guesses as to make, model, color? How about a magical description of the driver and any passengers?"

"You don't want much from a tire impression," Stu said. I spotted a pen in his hand. "We maybe can narrow it down before we get some impressions of the tread." He photographed the tires prints using his pen as a scale. "Pretty sure I'm looking at tracks from a motorbike, Ellie."

I looked back to where the horse and Cait fell: an easy shot for anyone with semi-decent rifle skills, motorbike or not. "Okay boys, this is the thing, pending forensics and the autopsy, this is a Delta A priority case. Attempted homicide of the Director of the FBI. We do not use Sentinel for our case notes. This is need to know only."

Dane and Stu frowned.

"Owen?" Dane said, the lines on his forehead deepening.

"Too wily to do it herself," Kurt replied.

I jumped, not expecting his voice to come from beside me. He laughed.

"Light on your feet, Henderson," Stu said with a chuckle.

"Apparently," he said, with a good-natured nudge. "Sorry."

"Cough or something next time."

Kurt gave a small laugh. "Stu, Dane, we've tangled with Owen before. We know she has lackeys like every evil villain."

And flying monkeys who report back to her and let's not forget her Teflon coating. As much as it pained me to say it, I did. "There is nothing evidential to connect Owen with this." Yet. "Open minds solve crimes."

She's not attached to Criminal anymore; I had to believe that meant something. Maybe she wanted to make a name for herself over at Intelligence. Would make sense; she didn't have the best reputation and could do with a boost. A fresh start.

Wishful thinking.

Frown lines smoothed as Dane repeated my comment. "Open minds solve crimes."

Kurt chuckled. "Poetic, Iverson."

"Painful, Henderson."

The veil parted for a split second allowing ripples of humor to wash over us.

"Where next?" Dane asked.

"Vet." Doc Robinson, a town institution.

Before the drive out to Doc Robinson's I had a quick word with Kevin and this time it was Kevin, not Chance. "Did you come out under sirens to the accident?"

"Nope. Lights, no sirens." He stepped away from his resting place against the car.

"Did you hear any other traffic?"

He thought for a moment. "No."

"Nothing at all?"

"Not a thing, everyone around here was tucked up by their fires." His expert eyes roamed my face looking for clues. "Okay, I give up. What are you thinking?"

"I'm thinking, how many people out here have motorbikes?"

"Depends what you mean by motorbike. You won't find Harleys out this way, but almost every farm has a farm bike. A lot of teenagers ride dirt bikes. Seems by age fourteen a lot of the boys gravitate to dirt bikes and most of the girls stick with horses."

Helpful observation. Cait smashed that mold wide open. "Cait still have that Harley?"

Kevin's mustache quivered into a smile. "Nothing wrong with your memory, kid. No, she sold it a few years back now."

"Thanks, Kevin. How about Cait's son?"

"Young Quinn stuck with horses, but I remember him and his dad playing around with an old dirt bike a few years back." His mustache twitched as a smile grew. "Was maybe six or seven years ago now."

"Why would you remember that?"

"Because young Quinn took a tumble. His ego took a hit but he was fine."

"You were there?"

He nodded. "It was at a barbecue out at the O'Hare place, reckon the whole town was there. First-rate ol' fashioned shenanigans."

"I imagine there were other dirt bikes as well?"

"Can only think one, young Adam. He and Quinn were thick as thieves back in high school."

"Adam?"

"Crutchley."

Chapter Eleven

Reflections of a time long past

My hand slipped off the steel plate on the edge of the door at the vet clinic when I gave a hard shove. It swung inward as I strode to the counter; Kurt grabbed the door before it closed and held it for Stu and Dane.

"Hello there, do you have an appointment?"

"Doc is expecting me. I'm Ellie."

She scanned the computer screen in front of her. Auburn curls, green eyes, wide smile and dimples. Her physical appearance overlaid images in my mind.

The young woman smiled up at me. "Doesn't have anything on his schedule."

"Hannah? Hannah Parker?"

She smiled. "Yes. That's me."

There was no flash of recognition from her. Hardly surprising she was a child when I last saw her. "Tell Doc I'm here, Hannah. Please."

She rose and paused. "How do you know me?"

"I used to live out here, I left about ten years ago. I'm Ellie Iverson, my maiden name was Conway."

Her green eyes lit up. "The Conway property burned down."

Kinda more exploded but hey, pretty close.

"I'll get Doc." Her smile widened. "My grandpa talks about you sometimes. Welcome home, Ellie."

I can imagine the stories she's heard from her grandpa, Mr. Parker, the bee man. Bet she knows all about my hatred of honey. She probably knows about other stuff too. A shudder ran through me.

Doc Robinson followed Hannah into the reception area before my brain ran with details of the other stuff she probably knew. My life is a wondrous place and definitely not for the faint-hearted.

"Ellie!" Doc said, beaming at me as Hannah sat back at her desk.

"Doc, you look well." He didn't look any older. Doc was about my height, his gray hair thinner on top, and his face weathered from the sun. He still looked how I remembered. Fit, healthy. Timeless.

His eyes narrowed as a smile spread across his face. Wrinkles deepened. "So do you. Come on through." His line of sight shifted beyond me. "I take it you're all together?"

"We are."

I made quick introductions and we followed Doc into the surgery area. We passed several clinical-looking rooms. Doc ushered us through the door to his office and took a seat behind an oversized desk covered to over-flowing with sheets of paper and assorted small boxes. File boxes were stacked against two walls, on top of the stacks were more piles of paper; dog toys, animal paraphernalia, samples of medicines and medical equipment spilled across what little floor space was left. Claustrophobia crawled over me as the clutter robbed the room of air and life. Stu pushed words into my mind: Breathe, El. We'll be out of here soon.

I turned my head and nodded at him.

"Sorry it's a bit crowded in here," Doc said. "I need a bigger office." He pushed papers out of his way and picked up a red manila folder. Doc rummaged through the spilling piles of paperwork on his desk until he found what he was looking for. Extracting two sheets of paper from under some books, he added the papers to the folder. The books slid over the edge of his desk and thudded to the ground. He watched them fall, shrugged, and made no attempt to pick them up. "I have the horse prepped."

For a second I wondered how big his operating room was that he could accommodate a horse of Thor's stature. Guess it showed on my face.

"Out back I have a large animal surgery."

"Of course," I said. "What do you know so far?"

"He wasn't hit by a vehicle. There are no signs of trauma apart from grazes from the fall. The horse appeared in tip-top health."

"When did you last see the horses?"

"I was out at the O'Hare property four weeks ago. Annual physicals for both horses and I'd organized a farrier."

"Any thoughts?"

"Not until I open him up and double check that there wasn't a ticking health bomb somewhere."

Fair enough. "You didn't find any marks consistent

with a tranquilizer dart?"

"Thought we could go look together."

"After you."

His large animal surgery was indeed large. Spacious, uncluttered, a clean environment. The surgery came complete with a sling lift, stocks, and an oversized operating table. I quelled uncharitable thoughts about how human hospitals would look in a few years with the ever-ballooning weight of our human population. Probably wouldn't need the stocks.

"Thor's tack is on your left," Doc said waving a hand at a table.

My fingers traced the stitching on a dark reflective quarter sheet, folded on top of a saddle. She did use the quarter sheet. He did glow like a diamond. "A tranq dart would've gone into his neck?" I said.

"Could've gone through the quarter sheet but—" Doc Robinson's stopped as Dane spoke.

"—the shooter wouldn't be able to guarantee the effectiveness," Dane said. "No way of knowing what was under the sheet."

"The young fella is correct."

"Any other way to deliver tranquilizers to a horse?" I said. "Could they be ingested?"

"Yes. Something could've been added to his feed. It's worth checking if we don't find anything here."

I watched as Doc Robinson searched the handsome black beast's cold body for a telltale dart mark.

"Come here," he said, beckoning to me.

"Did you find something?"

He nodded and showed me a small round mark hidden by the hair on the horse's neck but closer to his shoulder.

"Tranq dart?"

"I'd say so. How far away did you guesstimate the vehicle was from the horse?"

I raised an eyebrow at Dane. "How far?"

"At least two hundred yards from where he fell."

"Then whoever shot this probably used a rifle." Doc straightened up and walked over to a big steel cupboard with a combination lock. He dialed in the combination and pulled the doors open. Rifles. I counted six. He took one off the rack and walked back to me.

"Something like this. This is a Model 389 and fires any size RDD device."

"RDD?"

"Remote Drug Delivery."

"How easy are these rifles to buy?"

"Anyone with a Federal Firearms License can buy one or failing that, anyone can have an arms dealer buy it for them. You can buy them online."

Easy then.

"Do you have to know what you're doing with a gun and dart? Can anyone hit an animal anywhere and get the desired result."

"There is a preferable dart placement and it's right where I found the mark."

"So someone familiar with a rifle like that shot the horse?"

"Thor was a moving target, Ellie. They knew what they were doing all right."

"Can you let me know as soon as you get the blood results? Let's find out what drug was used."

"Veterinary drugs require a vet to buy them."

Yeah. I remembered that from another case. The reason I no longer live in Mauryville.

"Thanks, Doc. Keep in touch." I passed him my business card. "As soon as you get results, please let me know."

"Of course."

I touched the big horse on the shoulder. Resting my hand on him for a moment. So unfair that his life was ended like that. Part of me rejoiced that Cait wasn't the one who did this. The air around me fizzed with electricity. I glanced at my feet and saw gravel, dirt, and grass, not the polished concrete floor of the surgery. Thor bellowed. He reared. Panic took hold. His hooves slipped on mud as he fought an invisible assailant. Cait struggled to pull his head up. Something fell from her hand. The horse swayed, his feet danced sideways. She leaned forward and spoke in his ear. He tossed his head, almost dislodging her. Terror radiated from the animal. Foam flew from his mouth. His eyes rolled, he staggered drunkenly then his front legs buckled. Cait clung to his reins and his mane. Urging him to stand. Her efforts to encourage him back to his feet faded as the horse slumped.

A voice broke through the electricity sparking from the

horse.

"Ellie?" I turned my head. Stu was next to me. With a blink, the ground changed. Polished concrete. My fingers moved against the hair on Thor's shoulder. He felt cold. Lifeless. Now peaceful.

"You okay?" Stu said, touching my arm.

"Yeah. He fought hard."

"I know."

Images bounced from Stu's mind. He saw it too. No. He saw what I saw. That's different.

"Something fell from Cait's hand during her struggle with the dying horse."

"What?" Kurt said.

Doc Robinson stepped away from the animal. "There was nothing near the horse when I arrived to remove him."

"Might've been her phone," I said, moving to the door.

Chapter Twelve
Tell me how

Sean slid the glass door open. "Did you come back for the phone?"

I nodded.

He picked up a plastic Biohazard bag from a shelf and passed it to me. "Hope you find something useful."

"Me too."

Sean joined me outside the room. Ethan looked half-asleep in the chair close to Cait; he didn't react to my presence or Sean's. She looked as she did before. Lifeless.

I turned the bag over in my hand. Her phone case bore a few scuff marks and a couple of smallish cracks. Didn't look like it fell from a horse but maybe it hit soft dirt and not the roadway.

"What do you foresee finding, Ellie?"

"Fingerprints, a reason for her phone in her hand before the incident, something that will help us." I smiled. "Hope. I think I'll find hope."

He nodded. "How is it, after all these years you still smile and you still believe there's humanity left in the world?"

"Because if there isn't, we are wasting our time."

He inclined his head to his sister. "She was right about you."

"In what way?"

"You're the updated newer version of Cait O'Hare."

She said that. Unbelievable. "That's pretty funny."

"She calls you Cait point one."

I laughed. "Big compliment. I'm flattered."

"I think you should be scared," Sean said with a smile that reached his gray eyes.

"I'll be in touch." I shook the bag in my hand. "We're heading out to Cait's now."

***

Gravel crunched under the wheels as the cars rolled down the long tree-lined driveway that led to Cait O'Hare's country home. The driveway swooped around the stables and down past the garages to another house set back behind a stand of pines. Sean's house.

We parked outside Cait's huge, beautiful, red-brick home. Stately sprang to mind. Their land stretched out as far as the eye could see in all directions. The O'Hare family estate was impressive.

I climbed out of the car. Hooves pounding shook the ground. My head turned to a considerable fenced pasture to the left of the house. I walked to the five-rung wooden fence and watched Freyja gallop around the field, mane and tail streaming. She passed me, slowed, whirled around and trotted over. We stared at each other for a moment. Steam rose from her flanks. The horse breathed deeply. With a soft whinny, she stepped closer until her nose touched my shoulder. "Hello, Freyja. It's been a

90

while."

She nuzzled my shoulder as I rubbed her neck.

"I'm sorry about Thor and Cait," I whispered, giving her blaze a rub as she moved her head up. Freyja pushed against the fence. "I need to find out who did this. You behave now, ya hear?" I gave her one last rub and walked back to the house to find Dane, Kurt, and Stu waiting on the porch. "We'll go in the back door, follow me."

"And you're a horse whisperer," Dane muttered as I leveled with the porch steps.

"Nah. I know the horse. They don't forget people." I led the way around the house to the back door.

"Didn't realize you were so close to the family," Stu said from the bottom of the steps as he watched me unlock the door.

"Wait a sec, there's an alarm." I went inside and disabled the alarm from the panel in the hallway. Luckily the code was still the same, I'd forgotten to ask Sean. Back in the kitchen, I called out, "Come on into the big house. This is our base while we're in town, so I'll give you all the grand tour."

"And again, didn't realize you were so close to the family," Stu said dropping his messenger bag onto the family-sized pine table in the center of the room.

I took a breath and focused a thought in his direction: Small town.

He smiled. "Was that so hard?"

Kurt glanced from me to Stu. "Did I miss something?"

"Nope," I said, and left my bag on the floor near a

chair. "Not hard at all."

Dane muttered something from the other side of the room.

"Did you want something?" I said turning my attention from Stu to Dane.

"I have a horrible feeling."

Yeah, me too, but whatcha gonna do? I opted to say nothing. They'd pick up on how I felt if I let them. Would I? Time will tell. With that, a steel door slammed shut in my mind and I jumped. That's a no then.

Kurt arched an eyebrow at me. "Give us the tour, Iverson."

"The french doors behind Dane lead to the living room," I said with a wave of my hand. "This door off the right side of the kitchen leads to a hallway that runs the width of the back of the house and leads to a staircase." I pointed. "And this door is a walk-in pantry, and then we have a door to a ... you'll see." I stepped away from the table, crossed the room in two strides and swung the third door open. "Take a look, Kurt."

He ventured into the dark room beyond the kitchen door reappearing several minutes later wearing a quizzical expression.

"Interesting," he said, closing the door firmly. "Very interesting."

"What?" Dane stepped around Kurt, opened the door, and disappeared into the room beyond. I heard his thoughts in a rush. Dane: Awesome. This fills me with hope.

Guess he was taken by surprise. His thoughts were usually harder to hear than Stu's.

Chewing my lip to stop myself smiling, I glanced at Stu. Judging by the look on his face he got the message from Dane too.

"All right, what's in there?" Stu said not waiting for Dane to come back.

"A doctor's surgery," Kurt replied.

"Seriously?"

"Yes. A very well-stocked surgery."

"Why?" Stu tipped his head at me.

"This thing that's happened to Cait. It's not her first rodeo."

Frown lines merged on his forehead as Dane joined us. He closed the door and leaned against it.

"I can't wait for the enthralling explanation for that room," he said.

"Not the Director's first rodeo, apparently," Stu told him, his eyes fixed on mine. "You need to give us more than that."

"Figured." A sigh escaped. "I'll talk while we walk, follow me." I led the way down the back hallway pointing out a bathroom and two offices on the way. "Up these stairs are the bedrooms."

"Rodeo. Go," Dane said from the bottom of the stairs.

"Cait was a deep cover agent with Delta A, back in the day. She built this house then." I paused at an open doorway. "Cait and Ethan's room." I pointed across the hall to a closed door. "Their son's room." Walking on I stopped in front of another door. "Guest one."

"Iverson, spill the tale of Cait's surgery," Kurt said, opening a door across from guestroom one. "Guest two?"

I nodded. "The next two doors are guest three and four. The last room is Cait's private office."

Dane strode down the hallway, he entered guest three. His head popped around the doorway. Calling dibs.

"You wanna hear this?" I called out. He grinned and rejoined us in the hallway. "Cait spent months on end undercover. When she returned from a job, she came here to regroup. Sean was CIA back then. He doesn't say much about that time in his life. He was a specialist." I tipped my head to Kurt. "Like John Miller."

"Specialist equals cleaner, right?" Stu said. I nodded.

Stu nudged Dane. "Told you there was something dark in him."

"And here I was thinking you were overly sensitive."

Stu flipped his brother off.

"Some dreadful stuff went down here. Cait was working inside an organized crime family, they had an informant inside the Secret Service, turned out the informant was on the president's detail. He was a trusted member of the staff. He was also a friend and frequented Cait's home. You know about her sister, Mikki, yeah?"

Blank looks from Stu and Dane suggested they didn't.

"This is a story that requires coffee. Let's go."

Back in the kitchen, I put the coffee on. We all sat at the table.

"Cait and Sean have a sister?" Stu said, leaning on his

elbows.

"Mikki's a bit younger and she's a writer, she was kidnapped a while back and I found her." I expected she'd turn up at some point. She traveled a lot, so it wasn't surprising that she wasn't at Cait's bedside yet.

Their puzzled expressions spoke volumes. Obviously the story of the youngest O'Hare sibling, Michaela Kennedy, never weaseled its way into watercooler gossip.

I let it sit for a moment. It was a story and a half. Cait lay dying in a hospital bed, her life now told by me. There was so much wrong with that scenario I couldn't even begin to explain.

"Anyway, Mikki was out of the country for a few years, studying. She came back during a turbulent time in Cait's life and it's all linked to the Secret Service agent I mentioned before." I tried to assemble everything I knew and turn it into a Readers Digest version for easy assimilation. "Pour the coffee, Kurt, I need to figure out how to best tell this story."

Wishing I could snap my fingers and propel us back in time to see for ourselves what happened out here was fun but not helpful.

A mug of coffee steamed in front of me. I took a sip. "Cait had a way of digging up things no one expected. She put a lot of criminals in jail, took a whopping chunk out of illegal drug supply lines and closed down many avenues of human trafficking. She was a pain in the ass to the criminal community and so effective at taking on other personas that she was hard to spot. What she did was the closest guarded secret in the FBI. She reported to the Director and only one other person was ever aware when she worked anything." I sipped my coffee for a moment. "The other person was her handler, Peter Carlisle. You all know him."

The workings of their minds showed on their faces, no one recognized the name.

"I don't know a Peter Carlisle," Kurt said, lifting his cup to his lips. I waited until he'd set the cup down before speaking.

"How about Caine Grafton, know him?"

"Seriously?" Stu said, moving his chair.

"Yeah."

"Jeez," Kurt said with a shake of his head.

"Then why isn't he here?" Dane asked.

"Because there is nothing he can do here." Because Cait wanted me to investigate this.

"There was no Peter Carlisle on The List," Stu said, referencing the first case we all worked together. Deceased agents turned up freshly dead and it all had to do with a register of aliases.

"You can remember all forty-five names?"

"Actually, yes. And he wasn't on it."

"Probably because Peter Carlisle didn't die, he ceased to exist."

I saw a lightbulb glow in Stu's eyes. "It wasn't a regular FBI operation, was it? They were working a joint task force."

Neither confirm nor deny. "Until I told you, there were

only four people alive who know he operated under an alias and what that alias was. This information goes no further."

Kurt leaned on his elbows. "Cait, Ethan, Sean, and you."

I nodded and waited to see if anyone asked how I knew. No one did. "While she was on a job she discovered the Deputy Director of the FBI Alec Green was tied up with a crime family. Scary stuff. Green had no idea who she was, or at least no one thought he did. Green was buddies with one of the president's men. A guy called Scott, a trusted friend of Cait's. Long story short, a gun battle happened out here in the middle of the night. People died. Green died. Rumor has it a wolf ripped his throat out, but it's an unproven rumor." More aromatic black coffee slipped over my tonsils. "Scott told the crime family. He'd fed them information on the president and Cait for months. They wanted leverage to have a Gun Reform bill quashed among other things. Cait kept getting in the way. She wrecked their operations and she had a tie to the president they thought they could exploit. Green was supposed to dirty her, discredit her somehow. His plan failed."

"Complicated," Dane muttered.

"Gets worse," I said, emptying my mug. "Two senators died and then a couple of congressmen all tied to the organized crime family. Speculation on the subject drew few conclusions that didn't involve said senators and congressmen failing to do their allotted task as assigned by the family. A siege happened out here. Two branches of the crime family attacked the house. Cait's death was reported far and wide. The only people who knew she wasn't dead were Peter Carlisle, Sean, her husband, and Scott. She figured it was someone close to her. With Sean's help, she found a way to set a trap. She caught Scott."

"So the reason Cait has a fully equipped surgery out here is that she couldn't always be treated in a hospital if shit went down?" Stu said.

"Well, when you put it like that ..." I laughed. "That made short work of a long story. Thanks, Stu."

Dane rocked his chair again. "Could her past be the reason why someone made an attempt on her life now?"

"Yes." It's been my experience that people hold grudges for a lot longer than you'd imagine.

"So her past is a potential line of inquiry ... do we slide that in next to the Wicked Queen's interest in Cait's job and see how it stacks up?" Dane said, dropping the chair to the ground with a bump. He stood and paced a bit.

"What's with reprehensible people in positions of power?" Stu said.

"Positions of power attract that type of person," I said. Always have and always will. But not everyone with power is bad.

I clung to that. I had to.

Chapter Thirteen

Help me understand

"Squirrel," I said without thought. Shit. "Dane. Can you dust this phone for latents and run then all of the prints you find through AFIS." I handed the bag to him.

"No problem." His eyes held a question. "What's your best guess on how many people touched the phone before it was bagged?"

"Ethan, me, at least one paramedic, I imagine someone in the emergency room handled it to put it with Cait's clothes. Probably Sean. Potentially whoever shot the horse and drugged Cait to start with."

"Anything else I need to know?"

I shook my head. "Not at the moment." I swiveled to see around the kitchen. "Where's Moose?" Raised eyebrows and a smirk met me when I swung back to Dane.

"Squirrel and Moose have stuck haven't they?"

"Sorry. And yes they have."

Dane chuckled. "Could be worse. Always enjoy *Supernatural* and I'm damn glad I got Squirrel." Dane opened his backpack and took out nitrile gloves and a fingerprint kit. "And I don't know where my brother is."

My phone buzzed on the table. Doc Robinson. "Hey, Doc, you're on speaker."

"Ellie. The horse died from an overdose of Azaperone

with M99 and Xylazine. The amount in his blood suggests it was intentional and also, he would've only been upright for a few minutes before he went down. Death would've been fairly rapid."

That's what I saw. The poor animal confused, staggering, panicking, fighting the drugs.

"What's M99?"

"Etorphine. A very potent opiate used on wild animals."

"Opiates can be reversed ..."

"Yes, even this one, but not when combined with Azaperone. Also, someone has to administer the naloxone and whoever shot the horse wanted him to die."

"And the Xylazine?"

"Another reversible drug but not the way it was used here."

"How would someone get those drugs?"

"On prescription from a vet."

"Thanks, Doc. Anything else?"

"Not at the moment. I'll be in touch if anything else comes back."

I called Kev. "Hey, it's me. The O'Hare case. Definitely foul play."

"What do you know?"

"Someone shot the horse with a dart. Lethal dose."

"Let me know what you need, kid. I'm here to support."

"Thanks, Kev, I'll be in touch."

I leaned back in the chair. The men sitting around the

table were quiet. My last call was to Sean. I let him know it was definitely not an accident and that we had opened an investigation.

Still the men remained silent. I stood up, slipped on my jacket and headed out the door. Freyja waited by the field fence. She watched me walk across the driveway to her, flicking her mane every now and then.

I climbed the rungs and swung my legs over the top bar to sit on the fence. She moved over to stand close to me. "It's awful," I whispered as the horse nibbled my shoulder. I wrapped my arms around her neck. "You wanna do this?"

She pulled her head up. Taking me with her. I swung my right leg over her back, wound my fingers into her mane and turned her to the pasture behind us.

It'd been a long time since I'd been on a horse. This time there was no saddle. Just a winter coat. The warmth of the horse rose through the fleece-lined canvas, the earthy smell, the feel of her mane in my fingers combined to bring a brief pocket of joy. She cantered to the edge of the woods. A gap in the fence led into the dark woods beyond. Freyja and I stared into the woods for a moment. It was her decision to turn back to the house, not mine.

Freyja stopped at the fence where I'd climbed over. I slid off and gave her nose a rub before I climbed out of the paddock.

Boots came into view as I jumped off the last rung of the fence. Following them up a pair of jean-clad legs, I found Dane. Smiling.

"Was that fun?"

"Yeah."

"Should you be riding like that?"

An eyebrow rose. "Don't see why not?"

"I thought maybe that wasn't a safe thing, considering ..." He waved a finger at me.

Don't be mean, El, he means well. "They're six months old, they've been out almost as long as they were in." I smiled. "I'm quite well, Dane."

"I didn't mean to overstep."

Caring. It's how Delta operates. "You didn't."

Dane laughed.

"Why'd you come out here?"

"You left your phone on the table and it's been going non-stop."

I picked my phone up a soon as we arrived in the kitchen.

Dane spun around, a frown creased his brow. "Why now?"

"Cait?"

"Yeah, why now?"

"Why anytime?"

He nodded. "But right now, Iverson, what is so special about right now?"

"I don't know, but we better find out before something else happens."

Five unanswered calls from Sandra and the phone rang in my hand. Make that six calls.

"Sandra, what have you got?" I held my index finger up

to Dane.

"Bad news."

"Bad day."

"I'm about to make it suck more. Iain Campbell was killed in a hit-and-run thirty minutes ago." I circled my index finger.

Dane nodded and disappeared to gather the team.

"Where?"

"Virginia Avenue."

"Where on Virginia?"

"NW."

Maps converged with landmarks in my mind. Watergate complex jumped, jiggled, and settled. Leaving me to wonder why. "Metro Police?"

"Yes, O Leader of the Pack."

"Was Iain anywhere near Watergate?"

"Yeah, almost directly outside Watergate Office Building."

Well, shit. But what does it mean? "Lee and Caine?"

"I've already spoken with them. They'll keep an eye on the investigation."

"Tierney?"

"No word from the CIA. I don't know if Tierney was informed."

"Okay, I'll call him." Later. No rush.

"Is there anyone else I should talk to regarding Iain's death?"

"Not off-hand. Keep me informed, please."

"Will do. How're things down there?"

"Odd. We might be a while." I kept the sigh from my voice. Already I missed the little people in my life and the hairy beast I'd left to help their nana, grandpa, and daddy take care of them.

"Understood."

I hung up, put my phone on the table and frowned at the assembled group in the kitchen.

"What?" Kurt asked. "Something bad happened. I know that look."

I leaned on my elbows and rubbed my temples with my fingertips, blew air out of my mouth, and took a breath. "Iain Campbell is dead." I dropped my hands to my lap.

"Are you going to tell me that's a coincidence?" Dane said.

"Hell, no." My head shook. "I don't deal in coincidence."

Kurt dragged a chair out and sat. "How did Iain die?"

"Hit-and-run is all I know."

"Another accident."

I stared at my phone lying inert on the table for a beat and wondered if it was too early to sound the alarm or circle the wagons.

That was exactly what we needed to do. Circle the wagons.

Chapter Fourteen

Wildfire

A car drove up the long driveway at dusk. I heard it before I saw it through the kitchen window; I didn't recognize the dark blue pickup truck that parked behind our cars. The driver's door swung open. A man got out. I still didn't know who it was.

My phone rang as the man neared the back door.

Kurt stood ready to open it. I answered the call from Kevin.

"We've got a dead body and this might be related to the O'Hare incident."

That was an engaging opener. "Who?"

"The paramedic who worked with Adam Crutchley. The girl."

"Where?"

"In her bed. Looks like an overdose."

"You want us?"

"Yep."

"Okay. Text me the address." Voices at the door drew my attention. I heard the name of the visitor. Adam. "We've got her partner here. He just arrived. Did you tell him to come out?"

"Yes. I saw him in the grocery store this evening and let him know he needed to talk to you."

"Does he know about Alyssa?"

"No."

"We'll talk to him then come meet you. Close the scene, please."

"Will do, Ellie."

Kurt had shown Adam in and seated him at the kitchen table. I introduced myself then slid out a chair and sat down. Dane and Stewart were in the living room doing some research for the case.

"Adam, thanks for coming," I said with a smile.

"Kev said I should." He pushed his hair off his face with one hand. "We have met. It was a long time ago."

Yes. We had. My fingers slipped under my bangs and sought the scar on my forehead. It was a very long time ago. "We have some questions about last night. You attended Cait O'Hare?"

"Yes. Horse accident. He was a beautiful animal, such a shame."

Yeah. It was. "Can you walk me through everything, from the time the call came in until you got Ms. O'Hare to Stonewall."

Kurt stood, poured water into a tall glass and set it in front of Adam. I found the paramedic notes on my phone.

"The call was put through about quarter to ten last night. I didn't speak to the caller. Alyssa took the call, I was re-stocking supplies in the ambulance."

"Alyssa is?"

"My new partner. Alyssa Chadwick. She's been with us for about three months."

"Then?"

"We headed out right away. We ended up following Kevin's patrol car so arrived at the same time."

"Did you see anyone else on the road?"

"No."

"Was the horse breathing when you arrived?"

"No."

"How about Ms. O'Hare, how was she?"

"The patient was unresponsive. We moved her to our stretcher. No outward sign of injury. I inserted a line and immediately started fluids containing glucose." His eyes met mine. "Standard procedure if someone isn't responsive."

"Okay. Then?"

"I administered Narcan."

"Standard procedure?"

"Actually, yes. She responded ... opened her eyes, groggy, and asked about the horse."

I scanned the report on my phone. No mention of Cait talking, I scrolled to the signature, it didn't say Adam. "Was the response due to Narcan or glucose?"

"I thought it was the Narcan but I knew her and couldn't imagine why she'd be taking an opiate, so I went with glucose. Maybe she hadn't eaten in a while before the accident. There was a chance she'd hit her head and we didn't know."

"So, you never assumed drugs?"

"It's not that I did or didn't assume drugs. We did not know why she was unconscious."

Never assume anything. Look at the shit that can

happen. "So you transported?"

"Yes, I drove. Alyssa was in the back with the patient writing up the notes."

"At what point were you aware there was something wrong?"

"Alyssa called out that the patient became unresponsive ten minutes into the drive. I instructed her to administer more Narcan."

That was the second time he'd referred to someone he knew as 'the patient'; it grated on me. "Okay, then what happened?"

"She gave one more dose before we got to the hospital but Ms. O'Hare wasn't responding as well anymore and the last dose did nothing."

Maybe because the last dose was Xanax and fentanyl and not Narcan. "Adam, how well do you know Alyssa?" I stood, poured myself a glass of water and leaned on the countertop.

He swiveled to face me. "We work together. She's only lived here a few months. Doesn't talk much about herself."

"This is Mauryville, Adam. Why did she come here?"

He laughed. "I asked the same thing. She said she'd always wanted to live in a small town."

"They don't come much smaller. Hope she enjoyed it."

"Excuse me?"

"Your partner was found dead tonight."

His face fell. His features melted into a blank canvas. A satisfactory indication that he had no idea. He pushed his hair off his face and stared at me. "Dead?"

"Yes."

"Was it an accident?"

"Looks like an overdose."

His head shook. "No. That can't be. She didn't do drugs."

"Drug testing?"

"Yes. We're responsible for people's lives. Working under the influence is instant dismissal, even doing drugs on your time off, it'd show up in the tests. Then you're gone." His eyes widened. "She did not do drugs."

"Okay." Someone wanted to make it look like she was a druggie. My money was on the tying up of a loose end.

Kurt motioned to Adam's water glass. "Have a drink. Have a think. If there is anything out of the ordinary that might help us find out what happened to Alyssa, then tell us."

Adam drank half the glass of water and set it back carefully inside the ring of condensation it'd left on the surface of the table. We sat in silence. He picked up the glass, finished the contents and again placed it with utmost care in the circle of condensation.

"I can't think of anything. Do you have a card?"

Kurt handed him one of his. "Anytime, Adam. Call, text, email, whatever you want to do, if you recall anything, no matter how small."

Adam pushed the card into his shirt pocket and stood, scraping the chair legs on the wooden floor.

"I'll be going."

Kurt walked him to the door. "Anytime, even if you need to talk, okay?" They shook hands.

Adam nodded at me and waved goodbye.

Chapter Fifteen

Back in Black

Hell fired on all cylinders, flashes of reds and oranges lit my mind. I grabbed my bag and jumped to my feet.

Kurt joined me. "What are we doing?"

My eyes met his. I picked up my phone and called Sean. Amidst utter chaos, I heard him say, "Not now, El."

Shit. I hung up and headed for the door. "Hospital," I said over my shoulder.

Kurt grabbed the door from my hand. "I'm driving."

Stu called out, "You want us?"

"Yes, but not right now. Conduct a thorough search of the property. You're looking for anything that suggests external surveillance. Then head into Lexington and find us. We'll stay in touch." I paused. Then added, "You'll find the security system cameras that Sean installed, so not them, anything else."

"Got it." Stu's words followed us out the door.

Neither of us spoke on the drive to the hospital. Lost in my thoughts, I guessed Kurt was also. We hurried through the hospital to Cait's room. Sean leaned on the glass window outside. Beyond him, Ethan sat by the bed. No nurses. No doctors. No monitors working.

"What happened?" Kurt asked.

"She died."

I watched Kurt. "Did a doctor come in and check on

her earlier?"

He nodded. "About an hour and a half ago."

Not long before she died then, minutes maybe.

"I asked Doctor Neal to check on her," Kurt said.

Sean wiped his hands across his watery eyes. "They'll take her soon. I asked them to wait until Ethan was ready."

"Is it okay if I pay my respects?" I hadn't taken my eyes off Ethan as he sat with his wife's body.

"Go on in, El."

I stepped into the room.

"Sit for a minute, Ellie. She'd want you here," Ethan said without lifting his head. "Move that chair closer."

The chair he referred to was near the corridor window. I moved it closer to the bedside and placed my left hand on Cait's exposed right hand.

Everything in me willed her to open her eyes and be okay. Her eyelids flickered. Her hand moved beneath mine. Ethan didn't react. He still held Cait's hand pressed to his lips. Cait's head turned to me. Her eyes opened.

Words flowed but her mouth never moved. "I didn't do this, El."

It wasn't unusual for me to hold a conversation no one else heard and see things no one else saw, but every single time it made my skin crawl. I took a slow breath and exhaled. "I know. I know. Show me?"

"There isn't much time. The light, it's getting brighter."

The dead fingers wrapped tightly around my fingers. A sharp tug tingled in my hand. Cait clawed her way inside my body. Her incorporeal arms plunged down mine until she wore me like a meat suit. Electricity fired through the synapses in my brain. I was Cait. I could see reins in my hands yet they felt foreign. Astride Thor, comfortable in the saddle, his warmth seeped into my thighs. The gentle motion as he walked on the edge of the road lulled me into a safe cocoon. Darkness swallowed the road ahead. I swiveled to see behind me. A single light on the other side of the road, a long way back. I heard nothing but the horse's hooves. A sharp crack broke the peace wide open.

Thor stumbled. My hands held tighter to the reins. "Shhh," Cait soothed. The horse staggered. My arms went around Thor's neck as he fell, I kicked the stirrups away from my boots. "Come on, boy. Stay with me." Thor fought to remain upright. I felt Cait within me. She was calm. Why was she calm? Her right arm ran down the horse's neck. Cait tugged out a dart and held it in front of my face. "This," she said. "Someone did this." The scene blurred. A brilliant white light sucked Cait from me. I scrambled trying hold onto her, grasping at a light trail as blurriness took over.

With a blink, the hospital bed came into focus. Cait's blue eyes closed.

I wished she'd been able to show me what happened next. I bent my head close to her ear and whispered, "I will find out who did this. They will pay. We will miss you."

Unfurling my fingers from her hand I stood. "Thank you for letting me say goodbye," I said and left the room.

Sean and Kurt were still outside the door.

"Call us, when you're done here," Kurt said. "I'm going to find Dr. Neal."

Kurt tilted his head at me, I nodded. Before leaving, I placed a hand on Sean's arm. "I'm sorry, Sean."

He returned a slight smile. "We've lost our beacon."

"Do you need anything?"

"To turn back time."

Yeah, we all need to do that.

I caught up to Kurt while wiping tears from my eyes.

"Did she tell you anything?"

"Nothing we didn't know."

Grant was in his office with a pile of files in front of him. His paperwork situation rivaled ours. He gave a tight-lipped smile as we made ourselves at home in the chair in front of his desk.

"I'm sorry about your friend," he said, placing his pen on an open file.

"You checked on Caitlin James before she crashed, right?"

He shook his head. "I was caught up in Emergency. By the time I got free she was already crashing, I arrived with the monitors alarming and the crash team."

"Back up. What?"

"I walked in when the alarms were going."

I kicked Kurt's foot to get his attention. "Did Sean say a doctor came in to check on her?"

"Yes, he did." Kurt puffed air. "If it wasn't you, then who checked on her?"

Grant shook his head. "I didn't ask anyone else. We're short staffed as usual." He grimaced. "I was getting there."

Kurt nodded. "I know what it's like when an emergency crops up. But someone else got there. We need to know who."

I left the room and walked down the corridor to reception. There were cameras. I walked to the nearest ward and checked the nurses' station for cameras. They had cameras too. Someone knew Caitlin James was Cait O'Hare. I called Sandra.

"Release a statement to the media, saying the Director of the FBI, Cait O'Hare was treated and discharged from hospital after a horse riding accident."

"Pleased to know our steadfast leader is okay."

"She isn't. I need you to do this."

"How bad?"

"She died a little while ago."

"Oh no." She took a deep breath. "You want me to lie to the media and everyone else?"

"Yes, but technically it's not a lie, it's an omission of the entire truth. It's the framework of the truth. She was treated and discharged, we've simply made it sound a touch more positive than it really is."

"What's going on, O Fearless Foe of the Fourth Estate?"

"This is an ongoing investigation. I want whoever is responsible to think they failed."

"I will release a statement from us."

"If you can get Kirsty to release it from the Office of the Director, I'll owe you free drinks for a month at Murphy's."

"I can do that, do I tell her?"

"No, Delta A only, no one else gets any information other than she was treated and released and is resting comfortably." I'm pretty sure resting in peace is comfortable.

"I'm all over this. Please be careful."

"We will be."

Back in Grant Neal's office, I interrupted the doctor talk.

"The FBI is issuing a press statement saying that the Director was treated and discharged after a riding accident," I said.

"Solid thinking. We don't need a media circus while hunting a killer," Kurt said.

I tapped my head and winked. "Up here for thinking. Grant, there are cameras at reception and at the nurses' station on the closest ward. Are there cameras on every nurses' station?"

I don't remember them from the last time I was here, but then again I don't remember a lot of things from that period of time.

"Every nurses' station and all the external doors, as well as reception, have security cameras now."

Now. So maybe not back then. "I take it they work."

"Yes."

He was already on his feet. Kurt followed suit.

"Where are they monitored and is footage stored?" I crossed my fingers hoping they didn't record in a loop and consequently record over everything all the time.

"Security offices, basement level one. Footage is stored for three months on site then archived with our security company." I stepped out of the door, paused, and directed a question at Grant. "Where's the morgue?"

"Basement, level one."

Of course it is. I love wandering in basements.

Chapter Sixteen

Taste the pain

Stu and Dane met us in the corridor, Dane's usual swagger, minimized.

I pointed to Stu. "You're with me. Dane, you're with Kurt."

Stu turned and fell into step with me as I moved passed them.

"Be careful, Iverson," Kurt said, his words curled around me like a shield.

"Always."

I followed a yellow line at the edge of the linoleum floor, hoping it led to stairs. I didn't feel like taking the elevator.

"Where are we going?" Stu said as we turned yet another corner. The stairwell was directly in front of us.

"Down," I said, swinging the smoke-stop door open. "Basement level one."

Our footsteps echoed in the empty stairwell.

"Because?"

"Because a mystery doctor saw Cait O'Hare and within a half hour she was pronounced dead." I heard him swallow.

"You all right?" Stu said; concern tweaked his words.

"For now."

"Okay."

I slammed the doors in my mind before turning imaginary keys in the locks. That should keep everyone out. The two thoughts I left accessible to Stu and potentially Dane were work orientated. Let's do this thing. There's a job here and it's ours.

Basement level one wasn't too awful a place. Not much different from any other hospital corridor. I knocked on the door with a brass plaque that read 'Security.'

The door opened. A uniformed redheaded woman stepped out. "Excuse me," she said, brushing past us. "Just go on in." Stu shrugged at me and in we went.

The interior room was set out like a break room. An old battered Formica table sat in the middle with magazines and coffee cups strewn across it, some chairs askew and some partially pushed in. Against one wall sat an overstuffed sofa with a full wastepaper bin next to it. Opposite us was a door with a sign that read 'Monitor Station.' Another door near the couch stood ajar and led to a kitchen area. Sounds of washing up spilled from the room.

"Hello!" I called.

A uniformed body appeared. "Can I help?"

I flashed my badge. "SSA Iverson FBI. We'd like to see the monitors. Doctor Neal sent us down."

"Sure." He smiled, dried his hands on the dish towel, and picked up a phone receiver from the wall-mounted phone. "Doctor Neal, please."

The call was fast and ended with the man grinning at us. "Had to check. The monitors are through there." He pointed to the door I'd seen earlier. "I'm David Chu." He thrust his hand at me, giving mine a hearty shake. Then followed suit with Stu.

"Agent Smith. Nice to meet you."

Chu opened the door to reveal a bank of TV monitors, four wide, three high and a husky spectacled man taking up more chair than he should. The air was sharp, an acrid body odor assaulted us. Fighting to keep from covering my nose, I shoved my hands in my pockets – hard enough to keep a neutral expression, let alone breathe that in.

"This is Henry. He'll help you find whatever you need."

"Agents Iverson and Smith." I shook Henry's blubbery clammy hand. "I've got a time frame for you and a ward."

"That'll help, Agent." He moved his head but not far; rings of neck fat wobbled. "Bring those chairs up and settle in."

Stu's eyebrows rose.

My thoughts trickled into his mind: I cannot sit next to Jabba the Hutt.

He nodded and placed his chair next to Henry's. I moved mine up beside Stu. Happy days.

Words landed on me from Stu, yet his mouth never moved: I can't believe you called a member of the public 'Jabba the Hutt.'

My mind laughed and flew a reply: I can't believe the lack of air in here.

"When was it, Agent?" Henry reminded me I needed to pay attention.

"Let's start with one hundred and ten minutes ago on the medical ward. Can you bring up footage of the reception area, please."

"Yes, ma'am."

We watched in silence. Ten minutes ticked by and no one approached the desk. Maybe the sneaky doctor was already on the ward.

"Can you roll it back a bit further?"

"Yes, ma'am."

I had a horrible feeling that the process was going to take forever and I'd suffocate waiting. Stu's voice remained a constant in my head, reminding me I wouldn't suffocate. Every now and then he threw in a comment about deodorant, so I knew it wasn't just me who found it tough near Henry.

Chapter Seventeen

You've got a friend in me

I studied an image on my laptop. It was of the man who potentially killed Cait in the hospital or at least was with her prior to her death. Although we actively sought him, we had no reports of sightings. A face. Nothing more than a face. We should know more by now.

"Did you see the email from Caine?" Dane said. Until he spoke I'd forgotten anyone else was around.

"Remind me?" I get a lot of emails and lately a lot from Caine.

"About the number of cases that Delta A received and solved."

"Yeah. We aced it," I said. "Good times." My focus zoomed back to the photo on my screen. "Who is this guy and why would he be in Cait's hospital room posing as a doctor?"

"A hundred and twenty percent!"

My eyebrows disappeared under my bangs as I witnessed Dane standing by the kitchen table eating a donut and looking very pleased with himself. "What?"

"We aced the case closure. A hundred and twenty percent!"

Holy random conversation, Batman. Without even trying, I gave in to the temptation to wind him up. "Not super sure you know how percentages work."

He frowned. "It's all about context."

"Yes, it is." I waited, but he didn't demonstrate a lightbulb moment. "Our caseload rose fifteen percent from February to March this year."

He nodded. "Uh huh. And we closed off a hundred and twenty percent."

A smile tweaked the corners of my mouth. "No, we didn't."

Confusion blasted from his eyes. "The hell you say."

"Math lesson, listen up. Last year we had forty-five cases over Feb and March. This year there was a fifteen percent increase. We had, let's say fifty-two cases because fifty-one point seven-five cases is ridiculous. With me so far?"

"Yeah. Fifty-two cases is a fifteen percent increase."

"In context, we didn't solve a hundred and twenty percent of the cases any more than you could eat four-thirds of that donut in your hand."

And the lightbulb behind Dane's eyes brightened.

"I might have meant it as a figure of speech."

We laughed.

"Okay, Mr. Figure of Speech, what's one hundred and twenty percent of fifty-two?"

The hamster fell off the wheel and landed on the plug turning the lights out.

"You enjoying this?" He said with a scowl and headed for the back door.

"Yep."

"I'm never talking to you again." He swung the door

open and stepped out.

Laughing, I called after him, "It's sixty-two point four."

"Wiseass."

The door slammed. I jumped. The door reopened. Dane stuck his head around the gap. "Sorry, it got away from me." He shut the door with less force. His footsteps moved away, the gravel crunching in the direction of the paddock.

I glanced from the laptop in front of me to my phone, face down on the table. It rang. Unknown Caller. "SSA Iverson speaking."

A thick Irish brogue replied, "Sorry I couldn't make the wedding. Condolences to Mitch."

"Kennedy. Seamus Kennedy. Been a long time."

"Too long."

"Are you in the US?"

"I am. I need to see you. You're not in your office."

Had a feeling he was though and Sandra didn't warn me. "I'm out of town."

"I heard a rumor. Something about a riding accident."

"What do you want, Kennedy?"

"To see you. Can we meet?"

"Sure. I'll be back in a few days."

"Need to see you sooner than that, Iverson."

Damn. That's not the easiest thing to manage. Shit. My mind spun trying to come up with a location that would work. "There's a roadhouse in Harrisonburg." I checked my watch. "It'll take me an hour to get there. Where are you?"

"Your office."

Knew it! "It'll take you closer to three hours."

"I'll buy you dinner."

"See you at five-thirty. Don't be late." I thought for a beat. "Watch your six."

I stood and walked over to the kitchen window. Dane leaned on the fence railing. Freyja nuzzled his shoulder. Stu ambled over to join him. Where was Kurt?

The stairs creaked. I glanced at the french doors that lead to the living room as the room filled with light from an opening door. Kurt's voice hummed into the phone in his hand.

I drank a glass of water and waited.

By the time I finished the second glass Kurt had come in and put his phone down.

"Anything you need to share?" he said, pouring himself a glass of water from the pitcher I'd left on the table.

"I'm going out later," I said.

"Where?"

"To meet Kennedy."

"Why?"

"I don't know, but he asked for a meeting."

"You want company?"

"Nope. I'm a big girl, I can handle Kennedy."

He finished his glass of water in silence then glanced out the window. "Snow is coming. Make sure you have chains."

"How did the doctor know who Caitlin James was?"

"It's not a secret, Iverson."

I puffed air into my cheeks. "I know that, but she never uses her married name. Everyone knows ..." I readjusted my thinking. "Everyone knew her as Cait O'Hare."

He gave it some thought. "She arrived at the hospital as Cait O'Hare because that's how Kevin knew her."

"Yep, she came into the emergency room as Cait O'Hare. Ethan would've given her married name, Caitlin James, for their insurance, so all the paperwork would be under James."

"I see your point. Someone might have told the doctor she was officially admitted under a different name."

"If he rocked up to reception and asked for Cait O'Hare's room, he'd've got a blank stare."

"Let's keep that in mind."

Chapter Eighteen
With a little help from my friends

I wrestled with my next act all the way to the roadhouse. With my mind made up I called Mitch. "Hey, how's everything on the home front?" My desperation to keep light and easy in my voice shone through.

"What's wrong?"

"I need you to come down to Mauryville, as soon as you can."

"El, is something wrong?"

"We have a potential situation. I can't control it and I don't want you or our kids caught in it." I don't even know what the situation is, but it's something and it's fucked.

"A situation?"

"I'm not a hundred percent sure what is going on yet but Kennedy asked for a meet, and other stuff is going on in D.C. His request cemented the hinky feeling I've had for days."

"Other stuff?"

"Campbell is dead." I listened to his silence for a beat. "O'Hare is dead."

"You want Argo?"

"Bring him too."

"I'll see you soon."

"One more thing. This call stays between us."

"Won't Delta wonder why I've arrived?"

"Come up with something, I'm sure you can." My fingers played with the window button in the door. "Keep away from crowds of people."

"That's an odd thing to say. Are you expecting an attack of some sort?"

"I don't know. Just keep away from people as much as you can."

"We're coming. You take care."

I breathed out and ended the call. Something very fucky was going on in our world and I did not like it at all.

I slid across the center console and flipped the passenger visor down. The mirror reflected what I already knew. I was tired. Not much I could do about that. I ran my fingers through my long hair, reorganized my bangs, and plastered a cheery smile on my face. I exited the car from the passenger door.

My entry into the roadhouse met with curious looks which I put down to the FBI windbreaker I wore. At the back right-hand corner, a hand rose and waved once. Understated, barely enough to let me know he was there.

Seamus Kennedy stood as I reached the booth. We shook hands. I slid into the bench seat opposite him, with my back uncharacteristically to the room. A show of trust on my part. "Have you ordered?"

"For us both."

"Thanks, I hope." A smile crossed my lips. "What's going on?"

"Nothing grand, Ellie. I know the FBI was instructed to

pull back and not collaborate with us Europeans types ..."

The directive extended beyond us and engulfed the entire intelligence community. The IC was gagged. No sharing. There had to be ramifications. "Stupid restrictions. All stemming from POTUS and his wish to distance himself from the Russians and Europe in general. It's not going to help us."

"No, it's not."

"What do you know?"

"There's chatter suggesting a biological attack."

Shit. "Do any of our agencies know?"

"They should, if they're listening." His expression changed from neutral to grim. "I have no idea. Initially, this came from my own intel network and I confirmed with sources within my reach, on the quiet." Seamus took a sip of water.

"How did 5-eyes not pick this up?"

"We don't know they haven't." Seamus finished his glass of water.

Sarcasm crept into my voice without me noticing, "Really? Because I'd expect this to make their weekly newsletter."

A small smile flickered across his face.

"I haven't heard anything." Dammit. I should know this. We should all know this. My mouth opened and recent events spilled. "Cait O'Hare is dead. Iain Campbell was killed in a hit-and-run." Information sources are endangered.

"What? I heard on the way down here that O'Hare was

treated and discharged from hospital after an unfortunate riding accident."

Outstanding; Sandra did well. "That's what we need to people to believe while we find the person or persons responsible."

Seamus inclined his head slightly to let me know someone was coming.

"Two medium rare steaks," a girl said, sliding the plates in front of us.

I smiled and thanked her.

"I'll be right back with some more water." She picked up the empty water jug from the table and disappeared from my view. Seamus watched her for a few seconds.

Steak, fries, and salad awaited my fork. My stomach growled.

"Hungry, Iverson," Seamus commented, slicing a piece of steak and ramming it into his mouth.

I nodded and did the same. I'm always hungry.

Water arrived. I filled our glasses.

We'd eaten half our meals before either of us spoke again. I rested my fork on the edge of the plate. "Tell me about this chatter," I said and leaned on my elbows.

"Finish eating first."

"I'm taking a break," I said with a smile. I knew better than to scoff an entire meal without a mid-meal rest. Something the twins taught me while I was pregnant and one of those things that hung around afterward.

"We've pieced together chatter from multiple sources and it looks like a series of biological attacks is on the agenda," he said, "but I'd sooner talk about O'Hare."

"Let's not talk about that right now." The less said, the less opportunity for someone to overhear.

"All right."

I smiled. "The threat is what? Anthrax?"

"No. Or at least that's unlikely. It never works quite as well as those bozos expect."

"So what then?" Visions of a zombie apocalypse loomed.

"Viral something."

"Okay. How and where will this potential killer flu be released?"

"It's gone quiet."

Shit. "Soon then."

He nodded. "As for where, from what I gleaned ... multiple locations within the US, the UK, Canada, and Australia."

"And those countries all have what in common?" I knew full well what it was. 5-Eyes. They were countries which provided intelligence. Everything I knew about 5-Eyes came to the fore. A country was missing. That's gotta be something, or maybe it was designed to have us chasing our tails. "Why'd they miss New Zealand?"

"My guess would be isolation and small population."

Time to relocate south then. Funny that Mitch suggested it not so long ago. We both held dual citizenship. "How the hell are we going to deal with this? We'll need anti-viral medicine, quarantine stations, shut the borders, vaccines." Disaster. This could be a total disaster. "CDC? Are they at least in the loop?"

"I hope so, but you didn't know, so, it's up in the air."

"Open-sourced intelligence, nothing available regarding this situation?" I picked up my fork and ate more salad.

"I heard General Hayden say, I'm paraphrasing here, Intelligence agencies need to stop being so arrogant and stop believing only stolen intelligence is valuable."

General Hayden former Director of both the NSA and the CIA and someone we should listen to. "Do you think agencies have overlooked open-sourced intelligence in this instance?"

Seamus shrugged. "I'm saying Hayden is right. In my opinion, the arrogance of thinking all intel of value takes subterfuge and hard work to find is damaging, especially now."

"Maybe we need to spend more time on Twitter." I sliced another strip of steak; juices mingled with the remaining salad.

"It's not one virus."

My fork clattered onto my plate. "Jesus." Could it get much worse? "When did you find out?"

"Two days ago. It took me that long to get here."

Cait was drugged then. Before she could be told? There was an emergency intelligence community meeting scheduled, I knew that. Who attended if Cait didn't? I pulled my phone out and called Caine. "Questions. There was an emergency IC meeting called recently, who attended instead of O'Hare?"

"Assistant Deputy Director Owen," he said. "Her new position with Intelligence was announced when Cait had the accident."

Guess having friends in low places was working out for her. "Did Owen share any intelligence gleaned from the meeting?" I pushed food around my plate with my fork.

"Not to my knowledge," his voice rumbled on. "I'm looking for a report but not seeing one."

"We need that report. It's about a potential situation developing."

"Sounds like you need to talk to me."

"Not on the phone. I need you to talk to Tierney. Find out what the CIA know and get hold of someone at Homeland."

Silence filled the airway for a long beat then chattered with keyboard activity.

"You won't believe this. Owen is on leave. Her status popped up as On Leave until further notice."

My mind whirred. Was she running? Shit. "Did she file the report?"

"No."

Shitfuckshit.

I heard a sharp intake of breath from Caine. "ID came back on our waterlogged D.C. body. Deputy Director of NSA. Avalon Kreg."

"That can't be a coincidence."

"Lee and I are going to visit some people. I'll get back to you."

People in prominent places or agencies are dying or

suddenly unavailable. "Houston we have a problem," I whispered.

"Iverson, we have the beginning of a catastrophe," Seamus said.

"Deputy Director of NSA is dead. Director of FBI is dead. The newly appointed Deputy Assistant Director of our Intelligence Branch has mysteriously gone on leave. Iain Campbell, Assistant Secretary of the Bureau of Intelligence and Research, is dead." I hauled in information that tied them together.

The intelligence community: that what ties all of them together.

Seamus leaned across the table. "I have one to add but he's not yours."

I rubbed my temples trying to stem the headache that threatened. "Who?"

"Misha Praskovya."

Shock from Kennedy's words vibrated through my body. Not Misha. My eyes flicked up to Kennedy's. "Not Misha."

Misha stepped straight off a Mills and Boon romance cover and into our team nine years ago. He was our FSB counterpart. We'd worked cases together over the years. Misha was a friend. He taught me Russian and how to drink Vodka. I brushed tears from my eyes before they fell. He was Isabella's godfather.

Just fuck.

"I'm sorry, Iverson. I know you were close."

"How?" My voice cracked and a single word was all I

could cope with.

"He was working a case in Minsk. There was an explosion. Misha died at the scene."

Now I know why Seamus made the journey to see me. "Is it connected?" I swallowed tears and a giant lump in my throat. Now was not the time for emotional outbursts or grief. People depended on me doing my job. With one final swallow, the lump in my throat dislodged and sank.

"My intel didn't mention Russia or Europe beyond the United Kingdom," Seamus said

"Sure, okay, but what do you know about the case he was working?"

"He was tracking a known terrorist. Last I spoke to him, he said he was close and it had something to do with a laboratory explosion in St Petersburg."

"A laboratory?" I felt my internal threat-level monitor zoom up the scale. "How is this not connected?"

"Because nothing I've heard mentioned anyone or anything in Russia connected to this fecking viral disaster."

Hashtag apocalypse. "Open minds."

He nodded. "I am maintaining an open mind, Iverson." Seamus stopped, changed his mind and carried on. "Iain Campbell. He was CIA?"

"He was. He went from there to Homeland and the State Department, then back to Homeland then took the Assistant Secretary to the Bureau of Intelligence and Research with the State Department." Guess he liked paperwork more than me and found it hard to settle after his exciting life with CIA, so he constantly sought out new challenges.

"Fancy title, what does it mean?"

"Means he was part of the IC. He reported directly to the Secretary of State." And received invitations to meetings by the Office of the Director of National Intelligence.

"Bear with me, Iverson, I maybe don't know as much about your intelligence programs as I do ours. How many agencies are represented within the Office of the Director of National Intelligence?"

The struggle to recall that information was real. "A few?" He laughed. I took my phone out. When in doubt Google. "A lot." I handed him my phone.

"Nice that the ODNI has a website."

"I know, right? As you can see ..."

"Everyone."

"Yeah." He passed my phone back.

I scanned the list. Army, Air Force, CIA, Coast Guard, Homeland, Defense, Energy, State, Treasury, DEA, FBI, Marine Corp, Geo-Spatial, National Reconnaissance Office, NSA, and finally, Navy.

"Trying to get a feel for what's happening here. You're telling me some important people are dead and a Deputy Director of Intelligence has disappeared?"

"As I said, Houston, we have a problem."

"How'd Campbell die?"

"Hit-and-run."

"Not at all suspicious."

"Would've looked less so if it was a stand-alone incident."

"You want help?"

"Yes. Let's not mention your offer beyond Delta A."

"Still concerned about your nemesis, Owen?"

"A little bit. Although I doubt Owen will be a problem. I have a feeling she's gone because she knows what the fuck is happening." As soon as I said it, I regretted it. I had no proof other than my willingness to judge her harshly based on our history. Not very professional.

Yet I fully expected to find out the president has decided to leave D.C. for a lockdown at Camp David, safe and sound within the massive bunkers. No visitors. No one coming and going until the threat is over or the world has succumbed.

A tear slid down my face as the thought of never seeing Misha again crept over me. I clung to the images of the last time I saw him in church when we christened the twins. He took his role as Isabella's godfather seriously. The font wavered and shimmered, holy water splashed over the edge dripping into a puddle that spread across the floor. I followed it with my eyes. The puddle became a stream that ran through the church to a coffin in front of the pulpit. The stream acted like a moat and surrounded the coffin with a silvery glow. Misha leaned over and placed a kiss on Sam's forehead. What would I do without Misha?

Warmth touched my hand. Seamus watched me.

"It's never easy, Iverson, letting go, moving on." The

warmth in his lilting voice surprised me. "Are you going back to wherever you came from?"

"Yes. You're welcome to join." I felt work pushing sadness aside and I encouraged the shift. "Where's this virus coming from? Are they importing it? Is it homegrown?"

"Million dollar questions," he said, then revised, "Billion dollar questions. We need to remember that it's viruses, plural."

"Do we know the origins?"

"No. We don't know much but I do know the UK virus is already in the terrorists' hands."

"That have anything to do with you offering to help here?" I smiled.

Seamus's laughter rang like a series of big bells. I imagined that was how humongous leprechauns laughed. "UK has a problem. MI6 and MI5, everyone will be racing around like lunatics and I'm more use here," he said.

Before my eyes, he morphed into Liam Neeson. Seamus had a unique set of skills and we could use him.

"So, Seamus, who else has a virus in their hands? Is it multiple viruses per country or one country one virus?"

"As far as I know, only the UK. That may have already changed. Multiple viruses per country. Before the chatter dampened, I pieced together a jigsaw of code that suggested the first release would be potent and kill a sizeable number of the population ... they're estimating fifteen to thirty percent. Once people start dying, the second virus would hit," he said.

That would cause more panic and more death, especially if they were spread in different ways. Airborne and touch. Hard to avoid multiple viruses. I'd spread Black Death and follow it up with smallpox and maybe chuck in some swine or bird flu for added oomph.

It wasn't the first time I realized I'd be a fairly effective bad guy. One day that might be important.

"Where are these killer viruses coming from?" I asked.

"A research facility or many facilities is the popular opinion."

Time to tell him about the monkey incident. Maybe those idiots aren't animal activists at all. "We had a monkey incident ..." I said, moving a piece of rocket lettuce to one side of my plate.

"Did I hear you right? Did you say monkey?"

"Yep. Crazy animal activists released a monkey from a lab in Washington."

"You think it could be related?"

"Honestly, I didn't think it was related to anything and the monkey wasn't carrying anything disastrous."

"You're sure?"

"Oh yeah. Kurt got bitten. We made sure. CDC ran bloods and came back with a strain of influenza. One that was included in this year's vaccinations."

"Anyone sick? Kurt okay?"

"He's fine. I don't know if anyone else got sick." A look at my watch told me it was late. I called Tahoma Whitehorse anyway. If any of the activists had exhibited signs of illness, he and Karen would know. "Sorry to interrupt your evening. It's Ellie Iverson. Got a question about those bozos with the monkey."

"Hi, Ellie, I'm with one of them now. You're not ruining my evening."

I had a sense it was already in the toilet. "Which one?"

"The girl, Christine Rand, she's ill."

"How ill?"

"Influenza. We're monitoring her as she has asthma, so this could be serious."

"She got sick from the monkey?"

"We expect so. It's the same strain."

"Not vaccinated then?"

"Anti-vaxer. She was raised that way. The male, Jordan Creole, isn't vaccinated either."

"Seriously? Two anti-vaxers stole a sick monkey from a research facility?" Sounds like the beginning of a dreadful joke.

"'Fraid so."

"Darwin Award candidates." A machine alarmed, overshadowing our conversation.

"I'll call you back when I can. This is suboptimal."

Seamus and I stared at each other for a beat.

"That would cause chaos, Seamus. Releasing a disease we vaccinate against into an unvaccinated community." But not as much chaos as releasing something we cannot control into the general population.

He nodded. "You have CDC contacts you can trust?"

"I have new contacts who I would like to think I can trust."

"We're going to need them."

"Wanna guess on the types of viruses the terrorists have?"

"Weaponized smallpox is where'd I'd put my money, along with a genetically modified strain of influenza."

I felt a twinge of disappointment that he didn't say Black Death. What the hell is wrong with me? "Because weaponizing germs is such a great idea." Be nice if they could weaponize a vaccine or a cure and blast the world with that.

My mind drifted to a field of wildflowers. Red Tea. Where did that come from? *The Patriot*? Steven Seagal gave me a nod; it was his movie about a virus and the cure was red tea made from wildflowers. This was one of those times I wanted life to imitate art. I wanted wildflowers dropped from helicopters over everyone, so people could make red tea and be cured. I circled the memory of watching that movie with Cait. Movie nights at her place were relaxed fun affairs as long as the guests liked Seagal movies.

"Hey?"

My eyes focused on the man in front of me. He wasn't Steven Seagal or Liam Neeson. But he was here and he was prepared to help. I couldn't even begin to imagine what we could do against this threat and I'm not short on imagination.

"Yeah?"

"We've been up against it before, Iverson."

"Not like this."

He studied my face. I was about to ask what he hoped to find when he spoke again. "You should go, leave the country, take your family."

A small laugh escaped. "That's never been my thing. It's fucking tempting, but this is me and this is what I do."

"Is there a safe place?"

I knew what he was asking. Bunkers. Was there a safe place for Delta to go if this all turned to brown flying stuff? Yes. Yes, there is.

I nodded and I knew what our next step was. "When we leave Mauryville, we'll make that our base because D.C. is not a smart place to go. But I have a job to do first." I wiped my mouth on the napkin, balled it up and dropped it onto the table before I stood. "Bathroom, then we'll go. Follow me close. We're heading south to finish what I started down there."

As everything Kennedy told me sank in, I knew the call I'd made to Mitch earlier was a sterling idea. Kennedy confirmed that something disastrous was happening, an attack, but not the sort Mitch expected.

Chapter Nineteen
When a hero dies

Habit had me check my mirrors several times as we left Harrisonburg. Making sure Seamus Kennedy was there. Somehow it felt better seeing his car. Gave me hope.

Satisfied, I cranked up the radio and settled into the drive. Not a lot of traffic on the road near midnight. We'd have a clear run to Mauryville. Give me time to mull over what would happen once we arrived. Ethan and Sean would be there. I'd have to persuade them to have a private funeral. Too dangerous now to involve lots of people. Best to keep it small, private, and get it done.

We had no way of knowing if the virus had spread already.

Logic took over. Cait's death was an open investigation. I couldn't release the body for burial until I was certain we had all the evidence we could get from it. I made a mental note to check with the lab and the coroner. That wasn't going to work. I touched a volume control on the steering wheel and turned down the radio. I needed everyone who could help on deck.

"Hey, Siri."

My phone sprang to life. "How can I help, Ellie?"

"Call Noel Gerrard."

I drove listening to the phone dial and then ring. It rang and rang. Eventually, a groggy voice answered.

"El?"

"Yeah. Sorry, I know it's late. There's something going on."

"I planned to call in the morning. Heard some worrisome things." He started to sound more awake. "You know Avalon Kreg?"

"Nope, never met her. I know she's dead though."

"You would've got on, she was a genius, helluva sense of humor, and damn good at what she did. Big loss to the NSA, drowning like that."

Sounded like he knew her quite well. "People don't usually drown on dry land, Noel."

"What?"

Not a hard concept for someone who was ex-NCIS to grasp, surely? "She was the body discovered in D.C. Wasn't in water, Noel. She was waterlogged but left on a street. No water in her lungs. We thought it was tied to a cold case but apparently not."

"Guess not all the details made it to the hallowed gossip channels. Cait's okay, yes? Heard about her accident. Seems there have been a few accidents lately. Mock drowning, hit-and-run, horse riding."

"Explosion."

"What explosion?" Noel was fully awake now. I heard him making coffee.

"Misha Praskovya died in an explosion in Minsk."

"Jesus, El, I'm so sorry. I know he was a close friend."

Tears welled. I fought the rising sobs to continue while wracking my brain for a song or a movie that would tell him Cait was dead without me having to say it and would also clue him into the virus situation and what I wanted him to do. Lifting the tone of my voice, I said, "Hey, remember the last movie night we had?"

"*28 Days Later* is not my idea of a fun movie, El." His words slid down the windscreen and pooled on the top of the console. In the shimmering haze of melted words, new words emerged. I waited, hoping he'd catch up on his own. "Another movie night? This time I'll share my *Mad Max* collection with you. You're in charge of snacks."

Nope, it's not a nuclear threat. Well, not today anyway. "I'd sooner watch *Contagion*."

"Where shall we make this movie night happen?"

"Let's use the Fairfax place." I hoped he got the virus thing and realized I wanted him to go to the bunker.

"Superb idea. We could invite the whole gang and make a weekend of it."

He got it. I breathed a sigh of relief. "This weekend works. You get everything together and we'll see you soon."

"All right. I'll see then you for an underground movie experience."

Final confirmation that he did get it.

His coffee maker gurgled.

"Looking forward to it. No doubt the team will enjoy the rest."

"Anything else I need to know? Access code?"

"You need to talk to Jenny."

"Which Jenny?"

"The Jenny who was born in 1981." Give him a minute. Wait. He can do this.

"Oh, right. Tommy T's Jenny."

"That's the one." Of course, now I'd have Tommy Tutone's 8675309/Jenny stuck in my head. Small price to pay.

"I'll power everything up and get it all ship shape." I heard liquid pouring. He wouldn't be going back to sleep anytime soon. There was a lull as though he was thinking. "Is Cait going to make it to the movies?"

"Nope."

"Not even if I play a Seagal movie like *The Patriot*?"

"I bet she'd be sorry to miss it."

His silence was deafening. Three Mississippi's passed before he spoke again. "No need to torture the rest of us then. *Contagion* it is."

"Thanks, Noel. See you soon." Then I had a thought. "Noel, make sure we have tequila."

His laughter echoed around the car as I touched the screen and ended the call.

"Hey, Siri."

"How can I help, Ellie?"

"Remind me to check with the coroner and lab tomorrow morning."

"What time would you like the reminder?"

"Eight."

"Reminder set."

I always wanted to say thank you when Siri did

anything for me. She was so polite and efficient, it struck me as wrong not to. Instead, I turned up the radio and hoped for some tunes to match my mood. A small laugh escaped; apocalypse rock should be a thing. It might be a thing sooner than the world realizes.

Apocalypse rock to go with an Armageddon virus. I fumbled one-handed in my messenger bag that sat on the passenger seat until my fingers closed around a small bottle. Without taking my eyes off the road, I flipped the lid. A little bit of juggling and I squirted a fat dollop of hand sanitizer into one palm and then rubbed it into my hands.

"Hey, Siri."

"How may I serve, Ellie?"

"Remind me to get more hand sanitizer at ten tomorrow morning."

"A reminder is set."

Misha popped up in my mind. I cleared his image and focused on the road. Glancing at a sudden shadow in the passenger seat I recognized the height, build, and darkness. Misha.

He spoke, words swaddled in a thick Russian accent, *"Podumayte obo mne inogda, moyu prekrasnuyu Elli."* Think of me sometimes, my beautiful Ellie.

"YA budu skuchat' po tebe, moy drug." I will miss you, my friend. *"YA ne dumal, chto my stareyem, no ya dumal, chto u vsekh nas bylo bol'she vremeni."* I did not think we would grow old, but I thought we had more time yet.

"Zhizn' nepredskazuyema. Byt' bezopasnym." Life is unpredictable. Be safe.

I smiled. The edges of the shadow glowed with a soft white light. I couldn't say goodbye, it felt too final and not fluid enough.

"Idite v sleduyushchiy raz." Go well into your next journey.

"Spasibo." Thank you.

A hand touched my arm, I felt a light pressure and he was gone. Oncoming headlights lit the interior of the car for a second. The only thing on the passenger seat was my phone.

Chapter Twenty

Who says you can't go home

I waited for Seamus before going into the house. The kitchen lights were on. The porch lights flicked into action as we neared. Before I could grasp the door handle, the door opened. Dane.

"You waited up. There was no need," I said with a smile.

"You okay?"

"Yep." He looked over my shoulder. I turned a little as I stepped through the doorway. "Seamus Kennedy, Dane Wesson." Introductions over.

The men shook hands. "Pleased to meet you, Dane, is it?"

"It is."

Movement noises from the living room filtered through the partially closed french doors. A door swung open. Kurt appeared. So everyone was still awake. I glanced at my watch. Nearly one-thirty in the morning.

"Thought I heard an Irish brogue," he said with a grin, striding across the room to Seamus. They shook warmly. "What brings you way down here?"

Seamus shook his head slightly. "Nothing grand. We'll talk. Do you think we could have a cuppa first?"

I stifled a yawn. "A cuppa?" I mimicked his accent quite well.

"Cuppa means I'd like a drink of fecking tea," Kennedy said with a crooked grin. "Your accent is shite by the way."

Kurt smiled. "Pretty sure there is tea here somewhere."

Sean appeared from the living room. "Kennedy!"

"Dickhead, how are ya?"

Man hugs ensued.

So they know each other quite well. I don't know anyone else who would ever get away with calling Sean 'Dickhead.'

Ethan and Stu joined us in the kitchen. Turned out Ethan knew Seamus but not as well as Sean. They weren't on insulting nickname terms. Small world, with smaller circles within it. Seamus gave his condolences.

Ethan was doing better than I expected, evidence of exhaustion and a greyish tinge to his skin but it was late and he'd had a few days of hellish stress. Maybe Seamus was the distraction he needed. I knew only too well that his grief would wait for him, and hit him over and over again for the foreseeable future and beyond. He'd carry his loss forever.

The kettle boiled. Kurt even found a teapot and made tea properly, according to Kennedy. We all sat around the big pine table and caught up over tea. So civilized, and not as disgusting as I'd once thought. The conversation turned to why Seamus was in the country and more interestingly, why he was in Mauryville and where I'd disappeared to. We filled everyone in. A big wet blanket dropped over the room. Smiles vanished.

No one spoke. Around the table and I saw concerned, thoughtful expressions. Knowing enough to let the news sink in, I waited. My waiting led to a bathroom break and an unintended meeting in the hallway.

The air shimmered around me. Black lines etched with care along the edges. Color muted, faded, highlighting the black outlines. A door swung open.

I thrust out a hand and connected with the hall wall, steadying myself. A voice resounded from the open door. "Hey, El!" The northern New York, slightly Canadian accent, was followed by a six-foot-tall blond male wearing a soft brown leather jacket and jeans. My focus flipped from the cartoon-like surroundings to a more solid Christopher Chance standing in front of me. Here we go again.

"El, okay?" Chance touched my arm.

"Yeah. Fantastic. And you?" Look at me making small talk with my imagination.

He studied my face for a moment. "Try again."

Guess the small talk was too much? "Important people are dying and there is a biological terror threat which is more an actual thing than a threat. I'm great."

"Sit." Chance grabbed my hand and encouraged me to a chair. It wasn't there earlier. My head swiveled, none of this was here before. No hallway. We were in an office. Chance's office. I sat. And didn't hit the floor. The chair must be real. Welcome to my crazy but rich imagination.

"Why are you here?"

"Seems like you need me."

"No, I need answers. I have questions."

"I gathered there were questions." He shrugged. "Usually they come before the answers."

"Smartass."

"You conjured me up, ask away." His smile almost revealed a dimple. "It's your dime."

"Is this the beginning of the end?"

"Wow, you don't mess around. Straight to the doom and gloom." He leaned on the edge of his desk, crossed his ankles and thrust his hands in his pockets. "It's a possibility."

"Cait's death, is it part of this end-of-the-world crap?"

"Does it look like it?"

I felt my brow crease. "It looked a lot like a single murder but ..."

"But?"

"Iain Campbell is dead, Misha is dead, and the Deputy Director of the NSA is dead." I rubbed my right temple. "And there's more."

"More dead?"

"Probably but *more* more." A sigh escaped. "Biological attacks, chatter in the intel community points to biological attacks here, Canada, Australia, and the UK."

"The UK, not Europe?"

"Yeah, weird isn't it?"

Chance nodded. "Why not Europe?"

"No idea, except the countries mentioned are part of 5-Eyes."

"Is that the intel community where the chatter was

detected?"

"Yeah."

"There's a country missing from your list," Chance said.

"New Zealand."

"Uh huh. Any clue why?"

"Not really. Except they're one of the few western countries that could, in theory, completely shut their borders and contain any virus," I said. "I guess it's not a strategic country for terrorists, not much to gain by decimating the population of a small island nation."

"Who is taking responsibility for this?" Chance moved papers on his desk.

"No attribution thus far."

His eyes met mine. "What's got you so wound up? This shouldn't even be on your radar, should it?"

"Not really. This should be a multi-agency approach including the CDC and military. Our intelligence community should be all over it." But it is on my radar, why?

"I have a question. Why, Ellie, why is this your problem?"

"I don't know." I don't want it. "All I know is there is a breakdown in communication, somewhere, or multiple somewheres. Which shouldn't happen. We've been sharing information freely between agencies and with agencies in other countries since nine-eleven." And then I felt it. A tug in my gut that twitched and squeezed and wanted me to acknowledge something I did not want to consider. The new directives. No sharing. We were shot in the foot. Make America great again? Maybe he wants to make it great by cleaning the slate? Start fresh. I halted all thoughts that screamed treason in my head. It made no sense for this to come from POTUS. The civil war we were charging at full steam would be enough.

A voice interceded, "Would it?"

Chance.

"Would it what?"

"Would civil war be enough? Think, Ellie. Civil war would turn brother against brother, we've been there before. It's long drawn out, expensive, and will destroy infrastructure. A viral threat, now that is almost as suitable as an external war. It'll focus people on a common enemy," Chance said.

Interesting point, POTUS tried war with North Korea but his posturing and foot stamping got him nowhere. Nukes made it an unpopular choice for the majority of the population. A biological attack on his own people and a few other countries would mean he didn't get the blame. That'd land on whichever terrorists were chosen to take the fall. Wouldn't be the first time someone had manipulated a terror group into doing their bidding. Did I really suspect we had a president capable of terrorism? I needed to rein that in and get it under wraps. Dangerous thinking like that could topple us.

"A common enemy is an interesting theory. I doubt that will come about because of the release of a virus. You know what could potentially happen here, right?" I leaned on my elbows and watched Chance. My eyes searched his pale blue eyes. "People won't unite against the perceived terrorists that caused a viral threat, not when people start dying and there is no one to fight."

Chaos, mayhem, anger, violence, and death are the only outcomes of this scenario.

A light went on behind Chance's eyes. "Human nature will kick in. They'll turn on each other as soon as people realize what's happening. Stockpiling arms, food, water, gas and especially medicines."

Humans being what they are, human, once they realize they are all competing for a finite amount of medicine and there is no known cure, the real nastiness of the species will manifest.

"It'll come down to survival of the fittest at the peril of everyone else. Hence we've been on the brink of civil war several times over the last few years."

"This could be a disaster, couldn't it?" Chance sat back in his chair.

Fortunately for him, he doesn't exist. "We're in trouble. And somehow it's my problem."

"What are you going to do?"

"Stop it."

Chance grinned. "Goes without saying."

Something else wriggled across that mental memory board. The new directives came a year after an inquiry into Russian meddling in the presidential election. Prior to the directives, the president seemed to have engineered a situation that distanced the USA from

Russia and other countries. He was downright rude to heads of state; he'd behaved like a petulant child squealing over social media whenever anyone disagreed with him about anything. The world shrank away. He wasn't so much building a brick and mortar wall as a figurative wall and hiding behind it. For the greater good. Maybe he'll chuck rolls of paper towels at all of us from behind his figurative wall. Perhaps boxes of tissues would be more apt.

"El, thinking this is coming from POTUS is dangerous," Chance cautioned.

"Yes, it is. Show me the alternatives."

"Open mind, El."

"What I need is a quantum computer to handle all the simultaneous calculations and help me see what's happening here."

"Isn't that what we are?" Chance wiggled a finger back and forth between us.

My crazy mind played with the notion. Guess if we were qubits then we might be termed an entanglement. Being the inseparable whole that we are. That thought amused me, laughter bubbled up.

"If we could multiply ourselves by four then we'd have a quantum byte and maybe we'd have a real shot at having enough computing power to find the patterns, track the viruses, work out what the deaths of Iain Campbell and Misha Praskovya are all about, and find the motive behind Cait's death and her killer."

"A qubyte sounds adorable," Chance's smile twinkled

in his eyes. "We can do this. You can do this."

"Be easier with a quantum computer ..."

"You've got everything you need." He tapped his head. "And a great team. You got this."

A loud noise jolted me back to the present. Sounded like a car door shutting. Chance's pale blue eyes sparkled then he and his office melted into a watercolor puddle at my feet. Visitors in the wee small hours? A draft hit me as a door opened. I figured it was the backdoor. Fast moving clawed feet skittered on floorboards.

Spinning on my heels, I called out, "Argo!" A barreling blur of tan and black fur slid around the corner and charged at me. He stopped and plonked his butt on the floor, tongue lolling, tail sweeping back and forth across the hall floor. Ears erect. Panting he stretched forward and licked my hand.

"Argo." I sank to my knees and hugged the big German Shepherd. He whined and licked frantically under my chin. "Enough," I said, laughing. He stopped licking but his happy whining continued. "Where's Mitch?"

The dog pulled away, turned his head and looked back down the hall.

"Come on then, let's go." I scrambled to my feet. Argo waited until I moved. He matched me step for step, his shoulder next to my right leg, my hand touching his head. Every two steps he looked up at me. As if to make sure I was still there. Guess he missed me. "That's my boy," I whispered as we walked through the double doors from the living room into the kitchen. A smile spread across my face as my husband stood and crossed the floor to greet me.

"Hey, you," he said, wrapping his arms around me. I sank against his chest and nothing else mattered. A few seconds passed and I felt one arm move. He'd touched Argo's head. "Well done, Argo. You found Ellie. Now, watch the babies."

Argo brushed my leg as he moved. All was well in his world: he had a job to do. I briefly wondered how he'd cope with Freyja. I knew the horse was okay with dogs. Cait used to have a couple of yellow Labradors. Then I registered what Mitch said to the dog. Babies.

"Our girls."

Baby snuggles and those tiny fingers and deep blue eyes. Joy mushroomed. I was glad I'd made the call.

"When you're up in the middle of the night with two babies who refuse to settle, a road trip seems like a great idea."

With magical ease, a plausible excuse for his sudden arrival.

"Babe." I turned around in his arms. Two baby seats sat side by side on the kitchen floor with Argo planted right in front of them. Grace and Isabella slept, giving a fair impression of cherubs. "He's a big help I see."

"Enormous help and he missed you as much as our girls and I did."

The back door opened, a chilly breeze rushed into the warm room. Dane and Stu came in carrying the essentials of baby travel.

"Cold out there tonight," Stu said with a shiver.

"Thank you for unloading the car," Mitch said.

"No problem," Dane said.

"We'll take this up to your room, El. Want a hand with the little people?" Stu said.

"Nah, we got them, thanks though."

"You should be asleep," Mitch said, dipping his head slightly until his breath tickled my ear.

"Yeah. It's been a long night and shitty few days."

"Yeah, figured you could do with a hug and some baby time."

"You're the best."

Kurt caught my eye. "You want to finish this discussion or sleep?"

"Let's get a plan set then sleep," I replied. Mitch and I sat at the table. The babies snoozed blissfully under the watchful eye of Argo.

Thoughts scrambled then tumbled to the ground: pick-up-sticks with words.

"We need to find the person responsible for Cait's ... for Cait." Because I want to know for sure who is behind her death. Maybe then we can start joining the dots. Let's start where we are. Meanwhile, we also need to find the viruses and the release points. Yeah, let's do everyone else's jobs as well.

Big ask.

Amazing team.

We can do this. This is us.

First things first. Cait's killer is priority one. A tiny

yellow head popped out from the sugar bowl, quacked, and shook snow from small wet feathers. With a roar, a snowslide buried the duckling. I blinked the vision away.

I clung to the faith Chance had in me. From deep within I called out to Chance, "Hey, if there's an avalanche, dig me out. Don't fucking stand there holding the shovel."

His voice filled with laughter. "I promise."

Chapter Twenty One

Born this way

Morning rolled around too fast. Argo whined at the bedroom door. I'd decided to break my own rules about dogs in the bedroom and let him sleep with us. Not on the bed, next to it by the portable crib. Something about having Argo close to the babies gave me security. Albeit misplaced. Even he couldn't protect them from a viral threat.

Mitch stretched and threw the covers back. "Coming, buddy." He tugged on jeans and opened the bedroom door.

He and Argo disappeared. I lay in the warmth of the bed and watched the babies sleep in the crib next to me. They'd only woken once during the night. Bonus. I considered my next action. Find Cait's killer. Stockpile hand sanitizer, surgical masks, and nitrile gloves. I moved hand sanitizer to the top of the list.

By the time I hauled myself from the warm bed and got ready for the day I could smell coffee and bacon. Breakfast. Mitch came back up, walking in at the right moment. Grace rolled into Isabella, waking her up. Both babies squawked indignantly. I lifted Isabella from the crib.

"That was rude of your sister," I whispered, cradling her against me. "Let's get you changed, Isabella." I hoisted her bag onto the bed and fished around in it, and one-handed extracting a diaper, wet wipes, fresh singlet and a lilac grow-suit. Glancing over, I saw Mitch cuddling Grace and doing the same thing with her pink bag. We'd gotten quite efficient at one-handed nearly everything. While the babies were still small, it wasn't too hard. Even carrying both babies I could still wrangle a hand free to do a few things. But it was easier with Mitch around.

Carrying a color-coded baby each, we followed the aroma of food.

Dane and Stu ran down the stairs ahead of us following Kennedy who vanished around the corner into the hallway. The call of bacon was strong. I slid Isabella into Mitch's arms and made the babies' morning feeds. I placed two bottles on the table, slipped into the chair next to Mitch and reached for Grace. With her nestled in the crook of my left arm, I wrapped my left hand around and held the bottle; with my free hand, I ate the breakfast that Kurt set it in front of me.

"You two are pretty clever at that," Dane commented from across the table.

"We're learning as we go," Mitch replied with a grin, then shoveled scrambled eggs into his mouth with his left hand. Mirror images, that was us.

Eating resumed around the table; we'd need energy for the coming day. Kurt sat next to me to me with his plate. His fork paused, suspended fully loaded with eggs, midway between his mouth and plate. "We need to take every precaution to keep ourselves safe amidst this potential threat." His hand moved and eggs made it to his mouth.

"You probably don't want to hear this but Bill Gates warned about bioterrorism back in April twenty-seventeen," Mitch said; an element of fanboy leaked out of his voice.

"I vaguely remember something, but not the details," Kurt said, chasing a mushroom around his plate. He blocked it with his knife and stabbed it with the fork. My entertainment ended.

"He said terrorists could kill thirty-million people using genetically engineered versions of viruses like smallpox. He also said the risk was greater than nuclear war," Mitch said.

"Let's give him a call and tell him he was right," Dane mumbled. "I'm sure he wants to know."

Yeah sure, he's probably got a wonderful 'Told you so' spiel ready to share. Even at my most cynical, I didn't believe that. "In my opinion, his warning and this situation shows that people should listen to each other instead of dismissing everything out of hand," I said. "Not just listen but hear what's said. And then act on the knowledge instead of pretending it's not our problem as humans inhabiting the earth with other humans."

That probably was harsh, but dammit, Gates was right and now it was our mess. I didn't want any part of it.

As we ate, I gave thought to how I was going to approach the problems in front of us. Surely the brunt of this is not on us. The intelligence community must know what's happening. How could they not? A little orange glow forced its way into my brain. I stamped it out. Even he can't stop chatter and our community hearing it. Surely. It's not possible for silence to surround this event. There are moving parts everywhere. I imagined a lot of someones knew something before we found out. But now we did know, and action was required.

"What we are about to do is not about you or me or Delta surviving. It's about us all." There were trusting faces in front of me. "It's about Hannah at the vet office and the kid bagging groceries at the store ... we do this because this is what we do. For them." Grace squirmed, pushing the bottle teat from her mouth. I set the bottle on the table and lifted her, leaning her against my shoulder. I rubbed her back, waiting for the burp I knew would follow. And the next generation sitting in our laps, we do it for them.

Stu nodded and raised his hand from the wrist, not the elbow. "Are we going back to D.C.?"

Shit no. Hashtag apocalypse. "No."

Surprise radiated. "Really?"

"Uh huh. When we need to decamp from here, we're going to a secure location. Our base of operation is an underground facility in Fairfax County. The Facility."

"We have a secret base and it's called The Facility?"

Sometimes the good guys have secret bases. It's all very James Bond. I can live with that. We're so James Bond, except there are more of us, and we're not British.

"We do. I asked Noel Gerrard to get it ready for our

arrival, preparedness is reasonable in the circumstances. He's the only person outside of Delta who knows about it."

"Lee and Caine?"

"If this situation gets so out of control that we need to use The Facility then I will make sure Lee, Caine, and Sandra meet us there." We're not leaving half of Delta A behind and we'll need all hands on deck, should this become the dreaded zombie apocalypse.

If the sticky brown stuff fully hits the spinning thing we can get in and out of D.C. from Fairfax County under the radar. Under the river if necessary.

A quote I heard once rambled around my head, something about everything leading to this one moment or place in time. Experience: I could get us in and out of D.C without anyone knowing. I'd done it before. Mac and I did it once. But would that help us avoid contamination? Sure, if we wore Biohazard suits. I imagined us dressed like space cadets trying to negotiate the ladders and manholes that lead to the streets in D.C. A laugh escaped. Ignoring the raised eyebrows, I stayed with the vision.

Ethan refilled his cup. "Cait's killer. That Doctor Sanderson?"

That killed all trace of amusement.

Kurt finished his mouthful of coffee. "What we know about Cait's potential killer won't take long to share." He took another sip of coffee and put his cup down. "Gregory Sanderson is a doctor. He doesn't have a current license to practice in Virginia. He's registered in California but not attached to any hospital that I can find, so far. Looks like he's found a new vocation and isn't practicing medicine. We have a BOLO out, he also made number one on our most wanted list this morning as a person of interest."

"Person of interest ..." Ethan said. His tone suggested he was more than that. Although inclined to agree, we had yet to prove Sanderson's involvement in Cait's death.

"We can't add him as anything else as yet, Ethan. And our press statement says Cait was treated and discharged, we don't want whoever is behind this to know they succeeded."

If they need to verify her death, it might bring them back into the open.

"Who is he working for?" Ethan's stoicism returned.

"We don't know, but we will find out." I sat Grace on my knee facing Mitch.

Dane piped up. "Is this connected to Campbell's death?"

"We have nothing concrete to link the deaths. Best if we remain aware of a possible larger picture but continue to investigate Cait's death as we are."

Fractured focus we do not need. I reached for Isabella's empty bottle and placed it on the table. Mitch sat her up, facing me. She burped and smiled. "Well done, Isabella," I said, kissing her blonde head. Isabella and Grace cooed at each other. Grow-suit encased feet wriggled.

I stood, settling Grace on my hip. Argo rose to his feet and stretched. "Walk with me," I said to Ethan then turned to Kurt. "Could you?" My eyes flicked down to Grace in my arms.

"Happy to." He reached out and took her into his arms with a smile. A gummy smile broke free as she stared at Kurt. "Hello, little person."

Ethan followed Argo and me to the back door. From a coat rack on the left of the door, we took jackets. A fresh breeze pushed cold air at me; I caught the edges of my jacket and zipped it as we walked across the driveway to the pasture fence. Freyja saw us, stopped grazing, and ambled in our direction. I glanced at Argo. He wasn't bothered and plopped himself at my feet, radiating his warmth. My jeans-clad leg appreciated his hairy body.

"Where's Quinn?" I said leaning on the top rail of the fence.

"He'll be here this afternoon. He's still at school."

"Why?"

Freyja pressed her nose into Ethan's shoulder. He rubbed her neck.

"He had exams." Ethan's shoulders drooped. "I haven't told him yet, I told him to come home as soon as his exams are finished. How could I tell him during his exams that his mom died?"

"I don't know. That was your call."

Quinn's absence bothered me.

"I never gave him time to say goodbye."

That was something else for Ethan to wrestle with and

I had no advice worth offering.

"Your plans?"

"Cait always said she wanted to return to the land. Our land. We'll bury Thor next to her in the woods."

Not what I meant but nice to know. "In light of the recent threat situation, do you have plans?"

"We're staying here."

"Keep in touch. Wash your hands a lot, keep away from crowds, public transport. Basic precautions, but sometimes basic works best."

The corner of his mouth turned up. "I told Quinn to drive down not fly."

Really? "When did you last talk to Quinn?"

"Two days ago."

Before Cait died. Before we knew about the threat. Before everything changed. "And I shared intel in the early hours of this morning regarding an imminent bioterrorism attack," I said.

I watched Ethan's profile as he rubbed the horse's neck.

"Gut instinct."

I let that settle for a second. If it were anyone else from outside of Delta, I'd be twitchy as hell right about now. But, this is Ethan. Cait's husband of twenty-five years. Okay. Comforting to know I'm not alone with my tweaky gut calls. Imagine that?

"You talked to Quinn before Cait died and told him to come home right after his exams." I needed to clarify his actions. It told me he thought Cait wasn't going to

168

recover.

"Doesn't matter how much hope you hold onto, Ellie, when your time's up, it's up."

Okay. Maybe he thought she'd hang on longer and the kid would get here in time to say goodbye to his mom. She may well have if Sanderson hadn't interfered.

"If you hear anything, let us know."

"Go catch my wife's killer, Ellie."

"I intend to." I watched Argo and Freyja size each other up. Neither animal showed concern. Something else bothered me. Cait's work phone. "Ethan, do you know where Cait's work phone is?"

His head turned to face me. I could see him thinking. "No, I don't."

"Would she have had it on her person the night of the incident?"

"I wouldn't have thought so. Maybe."

"I didn't see it in the house. Didn't notice it anywhere. Unless it's in your room."

"That's where it would be, I'll have a look."

"Okay." I can talk to Sandra and get her to locate it using the GPS. We have a very special 'Find Friends' app on our iPhones. It's like Find Friends but on steroids. "Do you know if Sean has spoken to Mikki?"

"Yes. She's on her way. Sean said she was in Egypt waiting for a flight to London then home." He paused. "Guess this isn't home for her. She's been living in London for a few years."

"We'll get out of your hair as soon as we can. This is a

family time. The family will draw strength from each other."

"Don't rush away Ellie. The distraction is a useful thing."

Stu yelled out from the front porch, waving something in his hand.

"Think he wants me?" I said to the dog. I swear he nodded. "You coming?" I asked Ethan.

"No."

I left him with the horse. Stu handed me a phone when I reached him. My phone.

"Thanks," I said taking it and looking at the screen. Unknown caller. "Agent Iverson. How can I help?"

"It's Henry."

Henry? Who's Henry? Oh, shit, hefty Henry? Stu's thoughts appeared in my head: Don't say that, El. "Hospital security Henry?"

"Yeah. I saw Sanderson on the lobby camera, two minutes ago."

"Where is he now?"

"In the main hospital building. On a medical ward." I walked to my car, dog and Stu in tow. "Notify police. Tell them you have one of Americas Most Wanted men on site and watch him. I'm on my way."

"Yes, ma'am."

"To clarify, Henry, watch from a distance. Do not approach."

"Got it, ma'am."

I hung up and patted my pockets. No keys. Dane flew

out the back door and chucked keys. Stu caught them. Kurt's head rounded the door.

"What?" He hollered.

"Sanderson. Medical ward. Stonewall," I yelled back.

Stu jumped into the driver's seat; I hurried to the front passenger door. Dane, Argo, and Kurt dove into the back.

I flicked the flashing lights on. We were an hour away. Speed limit? Not today. No need for a siren way out here and I didn't like the idea of that noise all the way into the city.

"Buckle up," Stu said, adjusting the rearview mirror.

I swiveled in my seat. "Clip Argo's harness in, please," I said to Dane.

"Ah, that's what that short belt is for," he replied and attached the belt to Argo's harness.

No one wants an almost-eighty-pound German Shepherd jettisoned through the air in a sudden stop.

Chapter Twenty Two

You can't have everything

I checked my weapon twice as we approached the hospital. Habit. Security. Whatever it was, I felt better for it. I heard Dane and Kurt do the same.

"What's the plan?" Stu asked. "Where do you want to park?"

"First parking space you see near the hospital. This time of day we may not get a park inside the grounds," Kurt said from the back. "And let's not mess around trying."

"Done," Stu replied.

"We liaising with security and police?" Dane asked.

"Yes," I said and checked my phone for any more updates. "Police said he's shut himself in a room on a medical ward."

At least he's contained.

"Why?" Kurt said. "Why would he go back? Why would he shut himself in a room?"

My mind spun. Biohazard symbols rotated through whirling images of Cait, monkeys, and test tubes. The final image pirouetted into view, a caution sign. Why would anyone shut themselves into a hospital room if they weren't sick? Hospitals are a great place to get germs. "I dunno, but we should take basic precautions, glove up and wear masks."

Stu eased into a car park about a hundred yards down the street from the hospital.

"Vest, gloves, masks," Kurt said, undoing his and Argo's seat belts. "You want Argo on the long leash?"

"Yes," I took the long leash from the glove compartment and passed it to Kurt. "If Sanderson is sick ..."

"That's a bridge we can't cross yet."

"But game plan?"

"Contain him until we know what he's sick with, if he's sick. Backtrack his movements as much as we can."

I climbed out of the car, walked to the back and released the trunk. I lifted vests and handed them out. Argo sat on the sidewalk watching and waiting. We put on nitrile gloves. Kurt took masks from his bag and passed them out. We dropped them over our heads, and hung them around our necks, ready for use. I shoved my cap back on my head and threaded my ponytail through the gap at the back. The cold breeze ruffling Argo's fur didn't qualify as wind.

"The masks will help a little but that's all. Do not get coughed, spat, vomited, or sneezed on. Do not touch your faces with the gloves on. Be aware that once this is over everything that came in contact with any kind of body fluid must be thoroughly cleaned." He then handed out small plastic Ziploc bags. "These fit our phones perfectly. Everything will still work even the fingerprint identification."

"Up here for thinking," I said, tapping my head. Much

easier to throw a bag away than mess around later. Be nice if we had something similar for our weapons.

Stu popped into my head: Don't think they make condoms for Glocks, Iverson.

I glanced at him and noted his silly grin.

"We ready to rock'n'roll?" I said.

The three men nodded. Argo waited.

"Alert and safe," I said, running my palm along Kurt's and catching his fingers.

Stu and Dane followed suit and everyone shook Argo's lifted paw. I heard Sam's voice rumble within me, "Chicky Babe." My eyes shot sideways expecting to see him rock up, grinning. Stu's eyebrow rose.

Sam's voice rumbled again, "Alert and safe. Always."

"He's with us today," Dane said.

Kurt smiled. The four of us, and Argo, walked into the hospital grounds. At the main entrance, Kurt whispered, "He never left."

Police stood inside the entrance. I showed my badge as I walked through the door.

A weathered cop took in my badge and then my face. Cogs turned, gears graunched and the machinations of his mind played out on his face.

"You were SA Conway," he stated, his right hand flipped up into a salute.

"At ease, Sergeant." I reeled in memories from Lexington and Rockbridge County. I knew his face. "Alex?"

"You remember." Alex stood a little taller, his

shoulders squared. "The perp is confined to a single room on a medical ward."

"Thank you, Alex, these three are with me." I introduced the team and then Argo. "Any problems?"

He shook his head. "No one has come near him. I have police officers outside the door to the room. There are officers on all hospital entrances and exits."

"Admirable job. Which ward?"

He turned to another officer. "Get Charlie to cover for me on the door, I'll take SSA Iverson and her team to the ward."

The officer nodded and spoke into his radio. Running boots echoed off the walls moments before a redheaded female officer appeared in the foyer. Alex smiled a hello at the woman.

She must be Charlie.

We followed Alex along the corridors, past patients and staff. Mostly, people were preoccupied with their own dilemmas and unconcerned by our presence. One or two noticed Argo and expressed pleasure.

The nurses' station on the medical ward was a hive of activity. Kurt and I stopped to speak with a nurse manager.

"Is there anything we need to know?" I said, leaning on the high counter and reading her name tag. "Cynthia."

"We have moved all the patients from the surrounding rooms down to this end of the ward," she said, stacking charts.

"Have you seen Doctor Sanderson before today?"

She shook her head. "No, he's not a doctor here."

"What happened when he came in?"

She stopped stacking files. "He walked up to the desk, showed me his ID, and asked if there was an empty negative-pressure isolation room on the floor."

"The ID ... what did it look like?"

"It said FBI."

I glanced at Kurt who extracted his ID from his pocket with his gloved hand. He reached across and placed it in front of Cynthia. "Did it look like this?"

She picked it up for a closer look then nodded. "Exactly like that but with his photo and name."

"Thank you," Kurt said, retrieving the card.

"Why did he want an isolation room?" I asked.

"He said he was bringing a patient in and wanted to look at the room to make sure it was suitable."

"Did Doctor Neal give authorization for Sanderson to bring a patient through?" Kurt said.

"I didn't ask, and Doctor Sanderson didn't say. I showed him the room and left him to look around."

"Did he appear at all unwell?" Kurt asked, keeping his voice chatty, unthreatening.

"No, he seemed fine." Cynthia looked from me to Kurt, before her eyes roamed across Dane and Stu and back to me. "He's not bringing a patient in, is he?"

I shook my head. "He might be the patient."

Cynthia nodded. "That explains the gloves and masks. Do you know what he could be sick with and how contagious?"

"No, we don't."

She plunged the top of a hand sanitizer bottle by the keyboard on the desk, squirting a hefty dollop into her palm. Carefully she worked it over every part of her hands.

"He would've come in contact with the top of the counter," she said. "What are we talking about here? How scary could this be?" Her eyes rested again on our gloves and the masks around our necks.

Kurt stepped in. "All we know is that he might be ill and he might be contagious."

Cynthia sucked air in through pursed lips. "I'll alert my staff."

"We'll take it from here," Kurt said and motioned for us to follow him. "Which room?" He said over his shoulder to Cynthia.

"I-25."

"Thanks."

I moved away and spoke to Kurt. "What's different about the room he requested from any other room?"

"You'd put a patient carrying an airborne virus in a negative-pressure room to stop the contaminated air getting out."

For the rest of the corridor, the only noises we made were footfalls and a soft clicking from Argo's nails.

Chapter Twenty Three

You Really Got Me.

The room we stopped in front of was the last patient room at the end of the corridor. Beyond that was a sluice room, a bathroom, and at the very end a lounge area. Two police officers greeted us.

"FBI is here," Alex said to the officers. "You can stand down."

I smiled at the police officers who'd been keeping an eye on Sanderson. "Don't go too far, we might need you yet."

"Yes, ma'am."

They followed Alex back down the corridor and stopped about five rooms away from where there were patients. How the hell police officers would protect patients from a potential virus I had no idea, but, their presence felt reassuring.

An ample window offered a view of the interior of the room Sanderson chose to occupy. The window could be blocked off by a long curtain on a rail inside the room itself. Didn't look much different from any other hospital room. If it weren't for the big red "Isolation" sign and the sign saying "Negative Pressure," I wouldn't have known what it was. A man sat on the edge of the hospital bed. My mind compared his face to the images I'd seen on the CCTV. Sanderson. He didn't look ill. His collar-length sandy hair was thin on top, lines on his face spoke of city miles and long hours more than laughter and sunshine.

Kurt pressed a button on an intercom next to the window and spoke, "Doctor Sanderson?"

The man inside nodded.

"Are you ill?"

The man stood with ease and walked to the window. His voice came from a speaker near the window.

"Potentially."

"Can I see some identification please?" I said.

Sanderson held up an FBI Identity card with an apologetic smile. "I'm not one of you."

Yeah, we knew that. Pleased he chose honesty. "Why the fake identification?" I peered closer. It was impressive. It'd fool us if we didn't know better.

"My employer told me to use it if there was any trouble getting access to the hospital to see the woman in room ten." He shrugged. "I don't have any other ID with me. They told me to carry this one only."

"Do you know who the woman in room ten was?"

"Just that she was FBI. An agent, I assumed."

Never, assume. I gritted my teeth and tried to let it go, but my mind screamed liar. Sure, not everyone in the USA knows the name of the Director of the FBI, but if I were asked to kill someone, I'd want to know more about the target than it's 'the woman in room ten.' The woman in room ten. That jerked about in my head like a fish on a line. I'll come back to that later.

"And you said you are potentially ill?" Kurt said as I

stepped back. "With?"

"An unknown contagion," Sanderson replied.

"And you contracted it how?" Kurt said.

"I understand that I drank from a contaminated water bottle that either contained a virus or bacterium or came in contact with one."

"What would make you say that?" I said, studying the disheveled man before me. I'd seen plenty of killers and he, like the others, was unremarkable.

"The person I met with told me as I was leaving."

"You're irritating me, Sanderson. If you are sick, then we need to know what with. If this is a ruse to prevent us from arresting you, it will fail," I said. "Who did you meet?"

The fact that he thought he'd been exposed to something interested me; given what we knew it didn't seem like a random thing to claim. Nor did his request for a negative-pressure room.

"Juan Garcia."

"Can you describe Juan Garcia?" That had the earmarks of a legit name. Way up there with John Smith.

"Yes."

"Continue ..."

"Approximately five-feet-ten-inches tall. Short dark hair. Brown eyes."

I watched him thinking but nothing else came from his mouth. "Was he white, green, polka-dotted?"

"Mexican."

"He looked Mexican or he was Mexican?"

"Was, is."

"Distinguishing features?"

"A small scar on his chin." His finger traced a small area on the right side of his jaw.

"You're certain he is Mexican?"

Sanderson nodded.

"Where was this meeting?" Kurt leaned on the wall by the window. "How many other people are at risk?"

"A hotel room in Roanoke."

I sensed Dane and Stu stiffen. Their thoughts crashed into mine: Roanoke? Croatoan? Is he kidding? I turned to Stu and whispered, "Myth."

"Roanoke, Virginia?" Kurt sought clarification.

My mind buzzed over Ethan's whereabouts when Cait went riding. That was the first time I'd heard Roanoke mentioned in this hospital since we'd been in Rockbridge County.

Dane shuffled his feet. My eyes flicked to his. "All right?"

"A word?"

I nodded and followed him as he walked a few yards away from the window in the opposite direction to the police. "What's up?"

"Ethan was coming back from Roanoke when Cait was injured. What is it about Roanoke?"

"I don't know." But Ethan is at his house with my children and I need to know. I made a call to Ethan. "Did you go to a hotel in Roanoke?"

"Yes."

"Which hotel?"

"The Hotel Serenity, it's a part of The Serenity chain of hotels. Owned by Dixon. We booked a conference room there for the meeting."

"Is that usual?"

"Yes, we've used that hotel many times."

"Why there?"

"It's a favorite of ours." He paused. "Was a favorite of ours. Cait and I used to have the occasional weekend there."

Dane showed me his phone screen. He'd Googled the hotel. Fancy. Old. I could see why they'd like it. He scrolled for me. Definitely had old world charm and a wow factor.

"Okay."

"Why?"

Dane threw a stop sign into my mind but I carried on regardless. "Because we came across someone else connected to Cait who was in Roanoke recently."

"What does that mean?"

"Dunno yet, but I'll figure it out." I hung up and walked back to Kurt who was still talking to Sanderson. I interrupted. "Sanderson, what hotel?"

"Pardon?"

"Which hotel?"

"The Hotel Serenity."

"Where exactly in the hotel?"

"A room."

He was lucky he was behind glass because the

temptation to grasp the idiot warmly by the throat grew with every half-assed answer.

I clenched my jaw and counted to four. I relaxed my jaw muscles and took a breath. "How about you be more forthcoming with your answers?" I glared at him. "Paint me a picture ... where in the hotel were you?"

Stu moved closer to me.

"A meeting room."

I slammed my palms onto the glass. Sanderson jumped. "Why did you meet Juan Garcia at that particular hotel?" My right hand slammed into the glass again.

He winced. "That's where I was told to meet Garcia."

"Did Garcia stay there? Was he there for any other reason?"

"I don't know. He told me to meet him there. That's all."

"How did he pay you?"

"Cash." He shrugged. "No paper trail."

"And the money is where?"

"In my car."

Money is full of germs and cocaine. It's how it is. That'd be a great way to spread disease. People handle money all the time without washing their hands before cooking or eating or whatever.

"What makes you assume you are infected with something?" Kurt said.

Sanderson paced up and down in front of the window for a few moments before coming to a stop, facing us again. Beads of perspiration clung to his forehead. "He gave me a bottle of water. Looked the same as the complimentary bottled water in the drinks fridge in the meeting room." He stopped talking and rubbed his face. He didn't look ill but he didn't look fantastic.

"Garcia was angry. He said news reports said the agent was discharged from the hospital." He rubbed his face again. "That shouldn't be possible. Unless ..." A slow dawning behind his watery eyes; not the eyes of a well man. "Unless ... you released false information."

That's a win for us; whoever Garcia is he believed our line. Sounded like it sucked out loud for Sanderson. I did not react to his accusation. But my mind spun over something else regarding Cait. The woman in room ten. Her name.

"How did you know how to find her?"

"Sorry?" His head jiggled from side to side. "What?"

Perhaps the question confused him. I tried again, slower with pauses. I felt like William Shatner. "How did. You know. How. To. Find. The. Agent. In room ten?" His head nodded as he listened. That was positive.

"I was told she was in this hospital."

"By whom?"

"Garcia. He sent me."

"I get that. Did he also tell you what room she was in?" If so, we'd know someone within the hospital had passed on information.

"No."

Okay, he found her a different way then. "What was

the name of the agent?"

"Cait O'Hare."

I heard a collective intact of breath from Dane and Stu. Kurt stepped up beside me.

"Cait O'Hare was not in any hospital records. Her name was not on the door of the room. What name was, Sanderson?" Kurt said.

"Caitlin James."

Kurt continued his questioning, "How did you know she was Cait O'Hare?"

"When I couldn't find O'Hare I told Garcia. He got back to me with the other name."

"Where's your phone?" I said, not seeing a phone anywhere in the room. It could be on his person.

"In my car."

"License plate and keys."

"UZX-5555. Keys are locked in the car."

"Thanks. Is it a rental or your car?" I said, writing the registration number in my notebook. "Color and make?"

"It was waiting for me at the airport." He shrugged. "Don't think it's a rental. It's a dark blue Toyota Camry."

Fantastic. I wrote that down.

Kurt took over. "And back to the water ..."

"Right." His eyes darted around the room stopping on the sink before he focused on us again. "I drank half of it before he started laughing and said he'd see me in hell." He wiped his eyes. "I thought it was poisoned, but then he said that wouldn't be any fun."

"Was it only your drink that was tampered with?"

He shook his head. "No, Garcia said he'd found a way of adding his special ingredient to other bottles."

"When did he do that?"

"He said he'd been adding infected bottles to the hotel's supply going back at least four days."

Crapadoodledo. Four days or more. Ethan was there. Four fucking days was bad enough I couldn't think about longer than that. Jesus.

Kurt's mouth moved. Words floated through the air then fell before they reached me. They writhed on the floor like a snake shedding its skin. Vowels and consonants struggled to remain recognizable words. Slowly it all made sense.

"Iverson?"

"Yes." I extracted my phone from my pocket and called Tahoma Whitehorse. He answered on the sixth ring. Counting helped calm my mind. "Have you heard any reports of illness from Roanoke, Virginia?"

As soon as I said it, I thought about the hotel. It's a hotel. Travelers. In the last four days, people with infected water bottles or maybe actually infected people have spread across the country or at the very least the state.

"No. We currently have a small measles outbreak in an anti-vax community in South Carolina and another in a similar community on the West Coast."

"Thanks."

"This still about that monkey and those protestors?"

"No, something new. Not sure yet if it's something or

nothing."

"In such cases, Iverson, it is far better to err on the side of caution."

"Can you meet us in Stonewall Jackson Hospital, in Rockbridge?"

"Of course. I can be there by morning."

"Thanks."

I hung up. "CDC is coming to consult."

"Did he know anything?" Kurt said, keeping his voice low and resting his back against the glass so Sanderson couldn't read his lips. "If we have infected people traveling then we have a problem."

"We don't even know what we're dealing with," Dane said, joining Kurt against the window. "Did Seamus have any idea?"

I shook my head. "Viral is all we know. Whitehorse has heard nothing about any illnesses. That could mean people never got to a hospital or medical care, or no one is sick. Yet." I moved sideways so I could see Sanderson, then banged on the glass to get his attention. "When did you drink the water?"

"I met Garcia yesterday afternoon. Drank the water about three-thirty."

"Then?"

"I drove around. Slept in my car for a few hours last night. This morning I decided to come back here. Figured the FBI would be watching. You would've found me on the security tapes and someone would see me."

"You wanted to get caught?"

His head waggled. "I don't want the responsibility of any more deaths on my hands."

"How long before whatever is it becomes symptomatic?"

"Anytime from about seven hours after contact."

"You feel okay so far? Because you don't look great."

"To be honest, I feel like I'm coming down with something."

A case of death. I heard Kurt's voice on the phone. I walked down the corridor with Argo on my heels. I took him out through the nearest exit for a pee break. I held the door to prevent it from locking us out and told Argo to go toilet. He obliged then had a quick sniff around the grassed area before coming back inside. We rejoined the team.

"I spoke to Ethan and Sean," Kurt said. "Ethan didn't drink the water, but he had a bottle of it in the car and put it in the fridge when he got home. We might be lucky. If it's infected, we might be able to isolate the virus."

"He didn't drink any bottled water while at the hotel?" Double checking.

"No, he had water with him when he arrived and drank coffee during the presentation."

"Why did he bring a water home?"

"Guess he finished his and thought he might need it on the drive," Kurt said. "The important thing is ... Ethan didn't drink it."

"And Sean? Where was he?"

"With a client, not in a hotel."

"Okay." I pressed my fingertips to my temples.

It's begun. And we're already behind the eight ball. Four days behind. There must be sick people somewhere. Airports. Four days. That makes it too late to close the airports within two hundred miles of the hotel.

"Kurt. What's the incubation period for flu?"

"One to five days, most people get sick on day two."

"Could this be a strain of flu?"

"I was leaning more to waterborne disease. Cholera. Typhoid. Norovirus." He tilted his head at Sanderson. "Until he chose a negative-pressure room ... that suggests airborne." Kurt paused to gather his thoughts. "Exploring alternatives to an airborne virus for a minute, cholera and typhoid don't transmit easily, person to person. So you'd get isolated cases of the disease in people who haven't traveled to a country with known outbreaks."

"Norovirus?"

"Fairly easily spread in close groups, like families. And it can be airborne from vomit."

"But would a case of stomach flu kill the number of people the chatter talked about?"

"Norovirus, or stomach flu as you call it, is something that runs through assisted living centers and child care facilities. Death happens but not usually in healthy adults."

Wouldn't be my first choice of viral menace. "Now what?"

"We wait. I want bloods and samples from Sanderson, let's see if we can find out what he was exposed to."

We needed to do something while we waited. I motioned to Dane to follow Argo and me. Stu stuck with Kurt. I walked two paces then walked back, Argo waited. "Sanderson doesn't think it's cholera or typhoid, does he?"

"No, I don't think he does."

I banged on the window to get Sanderson's attention before pressing the talk button on the intercom. "Have you thought about what the pathogen is?"

"Something highly contagious."

"Ebola?" I said. "But that's not airborne, is it?"

"No, it isn't. And I doubt it's Ebola or anything we can avoid by employing normal hygiene methods," Sanderson replied.

"But we can rule out cholera and typhoid?"

"Cholera is treatable, basically you need to replace lost fluids. Typhoid is also treatable with antibiotics and fluid replacement."

"Any ideas?"

"Not yet. I know what it probably isn't, but there's a lot it could be." He waved an arm around. "I have a feeling this is airborne once it hits a human host, because that would make it spread a lot faster than touch."

I went back to where Dane and Argo waited.

"Where are we going?" Dane asked as we walked side by side down the corridor.

"Kurt's going to run tests. Stu can back him up. You and I are going to the nearest Internet café. My laptop is back at the house, and we need to do some research."

Just the thought of visiting an Internet café sent a wave of arctic water through me. Sure I could research on my phone, but I wanted a bigger screen and coffee.

"Do you know where a café is here?"

"Sadly, I do." But I wanted to make a detour to the parking lot first and find Sanderson's car.

Chapter Twenty Four

Get in my car

Argo, Dane, and I stood in the hospital parking lot and surveyed the rows of cars.

If I were Sanderson, I'd park away from the bulk of the cars. Over at the back probably.

"We're looking for a dark blue Toyota Camry. Registration tag: Uniform, Zulu, X-Ray, five, five, five, five."

"We got this. Right or left?" Dane said.

"Right."

Argo and I moved off. I walked down the rows looking for dark blue and occasionally looking up to locate Dane. Keeping tabs. Seven dark blue cars checked out. Two cars circled the parking lot trying to find parking spots. Had a feeling they'd end up on the roadside. This was a full parking lot. I noticed a lot of the cars had parking passes in the windscreens. Staff. Some of the parking rows were painted with blue lines and designated Staff Only.

Dane whistled. Argo stopped and turned. I did the same. He waved, then circled his arm in the air.

A black sedan passed us. Argo moved closer to me. Tinted windows made it difficult to see the driver or if there were passengers. Curiosity got the better of me. I watched as I walked. The car turned down another row and circled back.

"Don't think I like this, Argo," I whispered, switching the dog's leash to my left hand, and holding him a little tighter and closer. Argo watched the car. His ears twitched. Dane whistled again. From the corner of my eye, I saw another black sedan moving in his direction.

Tension built a fire inside me. They were looking for the car too.

I dragged my phone from my pocket and made a call while I walked to Dane. "It's me, send those cops to the parking lot at the back of the hospital."

He issued instructions to the police officers. "Agent Iverson needs assistance." The sound of booted feet moving away filled the phone line for a second then disappeared. The first cop emerged from the hospital exit. I waved.

Kurt talked. "You okay?"

"Yeah, a couple of cars are interested in us. Tinted windows, black sedans. I'd be better if we got some backup out here while we open Sanderson's car."

"Wouldn't hurt."

The call ended when Alex joined me. "What's going on out here?"

I pointed to the two black sedans which had now circled again. "How about a parking lot traffic stop?"

"Done." He waved another four officers over and told them what he wanted.

"I'll be with Agent Wesson. Think he's found the car we want." I donned a set of nitrile gloves that were in my pocket.

"Yell if you need help getting into it," Alex said with a grin. "It won't be like last time, right?"

"Shit, I hope not," I said, matching his grin. "Nah, it'll be fine. Haven't found a bodiless head in years."

My gloved fingers closed around my latest acquisition in my pocket. A tactical pen.

Man, I love that pen. I walked across the parking lot to Dane, without giving the two black sedans another thought. Not my problem now.

Dane was watching the fun. "They stopped both cars and are doing their cop thing," he said.

"Peachy." I peered into the car. The keys were on the driver's seat; walking around to the driver's side, I took the tactical pen from my pocket and with the titanium end, I bashed the window. The result was a satisfying shattering. A zillion pieces of window glass sprayed across the interior. The car alarm pierced the area, dash lights flashed, my brain hated me. I reached in, picked up the keys, shook the glass from them before I extracted my arm and pressed the button to deactivate the alarm.

Easy to unlock a car with the keys.

"That was fun," Dane said, swinging the passenger door open.

I popped the trunk. Empty. My attention reverted to the front of the car. Searching all the pockets and recesses, I found the phone. From my back pocket, I extracted a plastic evidence bag, slid the phone into it and sealed the bag. Felt it should have a Biohazard symbol.

"Got the phone," I said to Dane, climbing out of the car.

"There's a tracker in the car," Dane said, from the backseat. I leaned in the door. "It's attached to the underside of the passenger seat." His flashlight illuminated the underneath of the seat. "See that?"

"Yep. It's a rental ... is that a tracker the company put in?"

"Nope, this one is ..." He shone his flashlight right under the seat. The white light bounced off a sealed metal box securely held with brackets, the rental company logo stuck to the side of the metal.

"Let's bag that extra tracker then, shall we?"

Dane removed the small device from a lightweight mount that held it in place. That it was mounted told us someone went to some trouble to make sure the tracker didn't fall. They didn't want it found.

Footsteps approached then stopped near the car. Alex.

"Hey, what was the story with the black sedans?"

"The cars are rentals. The occupants are from out of town." His stony expression suggested unhappiness. "Both cars contained Inferno Jester club members. They reckon they're looking for parking because they have a buddy in the hospital."

"Maybe they are?"

"Maybe, but it's been my experience that bikers are free and easy with the truth," he countered. "We also found weapons."

It's Virginia, be weird not to find weapons.

The police had the occupants out of the car and handcuffed. Two officers searched one of the cars.

"Can we verify they have a friend in the hospital?"

"I can try."

"Aren't they a motorcycle gang?"

"Yeah, maybe it's too cold for them to ride." Alex chuckled. "Must be hard to be them in the winter."

"I reckon."

"Did you find what you needed?"

"We did. We have the doctor's phone and discovered an extra tracking device. I'm going to take a look at his GPS and see where he's been. I'd like to verify his hotel story and find out what else this car did."

"Let me know when you want us to pull back on the bikers," Alex said, he started to walk back to the cars. "Found with these guys that it's sometimes better to have a chat and let them go on their way."

"I guess not every fight is one you want, huh?" I rolled my gloves off, balled them up, and stuck them in my pocket.

Alex waved over his shoulder.

A female figure darted between cars and headed our way. Long hair in two braids, ripped skinny jeans with neon pink leggings underneath or maybe thermals, a knitted rainbow hooded-jacket fastened up the front with wooden buttons, black Doc Martens, and a less than subtle aroma of pot rising from her clothing. Delightful.

"Lost?" I said with a smile. Not a problem to intercept her.

"Just looking for my car and whatnot."

"Maybe I can help?" My smile was real. She said whatnot.

"It's a blue car and whatnot," she said with a hint of seriousness as she flipped her braids behind her.

"Dark blue or light blue?" I had a hunch she didn't know the make or model. It's blue and whatnot. It took a lot to maintain a professional demeanor in the face of whatnot girl.

"Not like the sky and whatnot, more like the sea."

Holy shit balls. I didn't need to look to know Dane struggled not to laugh. "Like the sea, so a green-blue?" I'm helpful.

"More like a deep ocean blue and whatnot."

I bit my tongue hard. Whatnot girl peered around me and spotted Dane. She pointed at him.

"He's cute," she said to me then called out to Dane, "Hey, what's your name and whatnot."

I took a slow breath in and a released it in increments to prevent laughter. It had been a stressful day and now it felt as if we'd been dropped into an episode of *Disjointed* complete with Olivia as Whatnot Girl. I thanked the gods we didn't have Dabby in front of us. No way I would cope with that insanity.

"Dane," Dane said, leaving out the agent part; he swallowed his laughter but I heard it all the same.

"That's the car!" She squealed and launched herself at Dane. "You found the car and whatnot."

He grabbed her by an arm and swung her back around.

"You sure it's your car?"

Her head nodded like one of those bobble-headed toys someone had flicked too hard. "It's absolutely the car and whatnot." Her face crumpled as she saw the broken window. "Someone is going to be mad and whatnot."

Shoot me now.

"Think you've got the wrong car. What's your name?" Dane said, steering her to me.

"Really, that's it," she squealed trying to duck under his arm. "That's the blue car and whatnot."

A light bulb moment exploded. "Oh hey, do you know Jerry too?" I said, friendly, and opting for a name that sounded almost like Gregory.

The girl grinned, her head bounced forward, then flew back. How does she not get whiplash nodding like a bobble-head?

"He's not feeling well. I thought I'd get him his phone and whatnot."

"I have it," I said. "I'll take it to him." I am so helpful.

Her face froze. I could see a dim light in her eyes grow brighter then fade. "Jerry asked me to get it, I should get it and whatnot."

"We could do it together," I said. My smile wouldn't quit. "If you wait for me for a second, I'll call Jerry and ask him what we should do."

Dane struggled to keep it together. I called Kurt knowing he'd play along with whatever and whatnot.

"Hey Jerry, did you send someone to get your phone? I bet those nice police officers would help fetch it."

"Iverson, I take it you want the cops to your position. Call me Jerry again, twice for yes."

"Jerry, Jerry," I said.

"Done."

I hung up and pushed my phone into my pocket.

"Jerry said we can both take it to him," I said. "What's your name? I'm Ellie."

"My name is Yvonne. Are you a special friend of Jerry's and whatnot?"

Fuck a duck.

Dane's eyes met mine. He grinned so hard he looked demented. "Incoming," he said and inclined his head in the direction of our approaching visitor.

Alex called out from a few yards away, "Iverson, you need me?"

I spun around. "I do, indeed."

He smiled. "I'm all yours."

Turning back to Yvonne I said, "Stay with Dane for a minute. I need to talk to my friend."

Alex and I walked back a few yards until we were out of earshot. "Yvonne here might have something to do with your biker dudes. She wanted the doctor's phone, says she's a friend, but she didn't know his name is Gregory, not Jerry."

"Ain't that just a biscuit looking for gravy."

I blinked. That was a new one. "We should chat to a few of those bikers and see if they know Yvonne. Also, she reeks of pot, so, we can probably hold her on suspicion of drug use."

"Always a fun time when you're in town, Iverson."

"I know, right?"

"We'll go have a talk with the boys over yonder and see if they remember Yvonne." We watched her for a moment, hitting on Dane. She wasn't the most subtle person ever.

"We're going to take Yvonne in to see Sanderson. Because that'll be fun." I'm in dire need of some fun.

"Hell yes, it will."

Alex left. Yvonne wriggled around but Dane had her arm in a firm grip. She pointed with the other hand to the bikers' cars. "That big guy."

I followed her finger and saw four big guys. "Which one?"

"Next to the bald one and whatnot." Her finger still pointed at the group. "That's Emmett."

"And Emmett is?" A little voice in my head said, "Emmett is a biker, soon he'll be a lifer." I had no idea where the voice came from.

"I told you and whatnot. Him!"

Silly me.

Dane moved her forward. She took a few steps. Then waved like a crazy person at Emmett. He did not wave back. His hands were cuffed behind his back. Mental note made to speak to Emmett later.

Together we walked Yvonne into the hospital and through the corridors to the isolation room. We stopped before the window, so neither party could see each other. Kurt and Stu joined us.

"This is Yvonne, she's a friend of Jerry's." I handed Sanderson's phone to Kurt.

"Hey, why'd you give it to him? Why is it in a bag and whatnot? My brother is going to be cross and whatever."

Whoa. She deviated from her speech pattern. "Jerry's your brother?" I said, knowing it was highly unlikely.

"No, Emmett is. This is going to make him mad and whatever."

Her brother is an Inferno Jester. That's great.

"What happens when Emmett is mad and whatever?" Stu said and leaned against the wall, looking down at Yvonne.

Yvonne wriggled in Dane's grip. "I'll let go as long as you stay here," he said with a smile. "You seem like a nice girl."

She nodded, braids bouncing. Freed, she dragged up the sleeve on her right arm. Scars. Burn scars. Looked like a cigarette had been ground into her arm. I did a quick count. Fifteen times. Judging by the degree of fading on some of the scars and the pinkness of others, it'd been happening over time. Torture. Her brother is an asshole.

"When Emmett gets mad he tells someone to hurt me and whatnot."

"Yvonne, no one is going to hurt you. Okay?" Dane said, pulling her sleeve down. "No one is allowed to hurt you."

Those braids bounced all over the place under the forceful nod. Stu stood up straighter to avoid the flying hair.

"Come with me," I said, beckoning her to follow me to the window. "There is someone in this room and I want you to tell me if you know who he is."

She hesitated.

"You're not in trouble, come over here and tell me who you see."

She took two paces and stopped. We waited for a moment. She gathered herself and walked to the window. Sanderson was sitting on the bed. He didn't lift his head, his eyes flicked up then back to the floor.

"Have you seen this man before?"

She shook her head, braids flew, almost hitting me. The movement caught Sanderson's attention. He brought his head up.

"Yes! Yes! I have seen him and whatnot." She bounced on the balls of her feet and pointed. "It's him. It's the doctor from the hotel and whatnot."

"What hotel?"

She shrugged, her brow furrowed. "Um, not here. Um. I don't know."

"Do you know his name?"

She shook her head; I leaned away to avoid a braid in the face. "Emmett does."

"You were at the hotel with Emmett? Anyone else?"

"There was another man in the room, I saw him before they shut the door. I wasn't in there and whatnot."

"Where were you?"

She smiled. "I was sitting in the bar working on my

movie script and whatnot."

Sorry – what? "Film script?"

"Uh huh, I'm a scriptwriter."

"That's great," Stu said. "Been writing long?"

"About a month and whatnot."

"Excellent." Dane grinned at Stu before turning his attention to Yvonne again. "I'd love to read it."

This crazy crap needs to stop. "Okay, and the doctor," I said, pulling the conversation back to work. "Did you meet him?"

"No. I wasn't allowed in the room and whatnot. Emmett brought me along to keep an eye on me." She sighed. "He treats me like a kid. I'm twenty. I'm not a kid and whatnot."

"What happened after the meeting?"

"Emmett and me ... No, Emmet and *I* went home."

Stu tapped her on the shoulder and waited for her to look up at him. "Did anyone give you a bottle of water?"

"Yeah, fancy bottled water with a picture of the hotel on it. I wanted to keep it, but Emmett wouldn't let me and whatnot."

"Did you drink any of it?"

"Nope, he took it off me when I tried to open it. I thought he was going to open it for me, but he got mad and threw it in the trash."

He probably saved her life. But I bet it was because he was scared he'd get infected, not to protect his sister. "Why were you getting the phone?" I said to Yvonne, my voice light and chatty.

"Emmett told me to. He dropped me off in the other parking lot, you know, out the front part of the hospital and whatnot."

"Yes, I know where that is," I said.

"He told me to go through the hospital and out the other side ..."

"Uh huh."

"He said I should look like I'm going to my car and whatnot."

"How were you going to get into the car?" I dangled keys in front of her. "Without these."

She frowned, then plunged her hand into her jacket pocket and held out a matching fob and key. "Emmett gave me this one and whatnot."

How handy. "Then what?" Because it felt like the plan went screwy somewhere along the way.

"Then I give him the phone."

"But you didn't get the phone so what happened?"

She sighed. "I used the bathroom inside and got all turned around when I came out, then I accidentally went out the same door I came in and whatnot."

"Whoops."

"I went back in and tried again, and a little girl talked to me. She liked my jacket and whatnot."

Give me strength.

"By the time I got out, you'd found the car and I saw Emmett and his friends were already waiting for me. And Emmett didn't look happy and whatever."

Right back to the whatever. Emmett is an idiot, and he

sent a stoner to do a job. What was he thinking? I imagine he thought she'd raise less suspicion than a big-assed biker snooping around a parking lot.

Might've worked too. "Dane, would you take Yvonne to the female cop we saw by the front door? Charlie, I think her name is."

"Sure, protective custody?"

"Please. Let's keep Yvonne safe so she can write that script."

Yvonne's smile radiated. She willingly walked away with Dane. Waving goodbye to the three of us as she went.

Kurt nodded, plunged his hands in his pockets and said, "Nicely handled, Iverson."

"Poor kid has a rough deal from life," Stu said. "Hope she does write a film script and someone other than Dane reads it."

Agreed.

I bashed my hand on the glass to get Sanderson's attention. "You never mentioned anyone else at that meeting in Roanoke."

"The meeting was with Garcia, not his thug."

Shitballs and whatnot. "What else haven't you told us?" I placed both hands flat on the glass and glared at him.

"Nothing. I told you everything."

"How about you tell me why you injected whatever it was you injected into the Director of the FBI's IV line?" Because you haven't told us that.

205

Sanderson shrank down and almost folded into himself.

Kurt walked me away from the window. "Sanderson contacted a burner phone, he texted saying there was no O'Hare admitted to the hospital."

"And?"

"And the reply came within a minute telling him to wait. About twenty minutes later another text said to look for Caitlin James."

"Twenty minutes. So if Garcia was on the burner phone, he needed to check with someone."

"We're on the same wavelength. Who did he ask is the question here," Kurt said.

"Alyssa?"

"Cait didn't use her married name. How would Alyssa know her name?"

He had a point. Unless her whole purpose in moving to Mauryville was to cause harm to Cait, but why? Cait's married name isn't a secret, she prefers not to use it in a work setting. I put a pin in that and moved on.

"The shooter. I still think someone had control of her phone so she couldn't make a call." Then again, reception on that stretch of road has always been problematic.

"Unless it fell to the ground while she struggled to keep the horse upright and calm," Kurt said.

That makes sense. "Potentially, but she had the phone in her hand because there was a partial text."

"Someone picked up the phone and handed it to her?" A degree of incredulity crept into his voice. "What would the point of that be?"

"To throw us off? I have no clue. It feels like the shooter may have had control of Cait's phone after shooting the horse and delivering drugs to her. Or it fell to the ground." Straws fell from the sky, slipping through my outstretched fingers.

"Are you hearing yourself?" Kurt said.

I smiled. "Yes, I am. And it was her personal phone, not her work phone. The phone had her contact details in it as Caitlin James." I still thought that the phone had something to do with Garcia finding out who she really was.

"If the shooter didn't tell Garcia Cait's surname, then who did?" Stu said. "Because I'm FBI, and it never even occurred to me she had another name."

"See?" I said to Kurt. "It's not common knowledge even within the Bureau."

"Someone from Mauryville ..." Kurt said. "That's what you're thinking isn't it?"

"Yeah. I am." Someone who had possession of her phone, or someone who knew her well.

Twirling thoughts sent colored light through the air. Little rainbows spread from the center of one revolving thought in the middle of the twirling mess. That thought glowed with pure white light. Someone who knew her well enough to know she liked horse riding at night and that her husband would have her admitted under her married name.

"We got a tracking device off his car too," I said,

inclining my head to Sanderson. "I doubt he knew about that."

"So that's how Garcia's thugs knew how to find him," Kurt said. "Makes sense."

"Alex the cop has the bikers cuffed outside. Dane and I should go talk to Emmett, Yvonne's asshole brother, before Alex lets them loose."

I heard Dane's footsteps coming back up the corridor.

"I'll stay here with the phone and him," Kurt said.

"I'll keep you company," Stu said.

"Once we're done with Emmett we'll go find a café." Despite my reservations regarding cafés in Lexington, I wanted coffee. Memories eased in and took effort to evict.

Kurt studied me. "We met outside a café in Lexington."

I smiled. "We did. And you said you never wanted to have dinner at my place."

He chuckled. "You told me there were groceries in the trunk of your car ... and I was tending to a woman who passed out because she saw the contents of your trunk."

Visions of dismembered limbs danced before my eyes. Fun times.

"You two look happy," Dane commented as he joined us.

"Kurt was reminiscing about the day we met," I said with a smile. "I make a great first impression."

Dane's eyebrows rose and Stu laughed. "You practically accused us of being imposters."

Actually, I did accuse them. Live and learn.

"Awesome first impression," Dane said. "Awesome."

"Shall we?" I said, to Dane. "Wanna come chat with Emmett?"

He nodded. His jaw set in a firm line. "I do."

Chapter Twenty Five
Born to be Wild.

Alex had the bikers separated and more officers on the scene than before. Two officers were still searching one of the cars.

"We'd like to talk to Emmett," I said to Alex.

"Do you know which one he is?"

I surveyed the line of bikers; apart from the two bald ones, and one with a long beard, the others pretty much looked the same. Big. Long-haired, scruffy. They all wore black jeans, boots, long sleeves, and cut-off jackets. I picked one that kinda reminded me of Yvonne. Same hair color, nose, face shape. Dane and I conferred and agreed.

"Emmett?" I said standing in front of the big man. I figured he was six-four. Not the biggest guy I'd come across. Lee was taller. Sean was six-seven. Height I could handle.

"Who wants to know?"

"I'm SSA Iverson and this is SA Wesson, We'd like to talk to you about Juan Garcia."

"I don't talk to feds." He spat on the ground. "Especially DEA."

"We're not DEA. We're FBI." Could be Garcia is in drugs which might be why he hangs out with bikers.

"I have nothing to say."

"You know nothing about the virus? About the water

bottles at the hotel? Wasn't you who took a water bottle off your sister and threw it in the trash?"

"I don't know what you're talking about."

"Okay." That's fine. "Your sister is sweet. She seems to have a plan for her life."

His eyes hardened. All light left them. "Keep away from her," he said, his voice low and menacing.

"Nah. That won't work for me. I like her. We're already besties."

Dane smiled and said, "She's hot, that sister of yours. And she *likes* me."

I stepped back, turned, and walked away. Hot? Of all the adjectives in the world, he chose that one?

Dane and Alex followed me.

"Riled him up good," Alex said when I came to a halt at the edge of the parking lot.

"He's involved in a developing situation. We need him held, can you do that?"

"Of course. Found drugs in the car he drove."

"Something worthy of holding him?"

"Methamphetamine."

Schedule II drug. He'd get bail more than likely, unless it was for distribution. "How much? Are we talking supply or own use?" He didn't look like a tweaker. Too big and healthy looking for that.

Alex motioned to another cop to join us. He showed an evidence bag containing six very small Ziplock bags.

"Looks to be about ten grams in each of those baggies," the cop said. "We'll weigh it back at the station."

"Looks like a distribution charge right there. Five years minimum," Alex said.

I smiled. "We'll try and get him on a raft of charges. We'll get the District Attorney to contact you, a-sap."

"Thanks for that, Brian," Alex said to the other cop. We watched Brian walk away. "What's going on, Agent Iverson?"

"We have a potential viral threat." I thrust my hands in my pockets. "Emmett was at a meeting with the sick doctor, and someone called Juan Garcia in a hotel in Roanoke."

"Jeez. Before or after the doctor got sick?"

"Before the doctor got sick. I think Emmett is probably okay."

Alex frowned. "I hope so, Agent, he's been spitting and carrying on."

"I saw. He's a real charmer." And they were welcome to him and his unwashed pals. "I suggest that you wash your hands often and thoroughly and get your officers to do the same."

"There's been nothing on the news and nothing come down the line."

"There will be, soon, take precautions. Don't wait."

"Sure thing. You look after yourself, y'hear."

"Planning on it."

Emmett's voice rang after us. "That fucking doctor better hope he dies."

I spun around and hollered back, "He's probably thinking the same about you."

Dane and I hurried away. Leaving Emmett to wonder if he was infected after all.

Chapter Twenty Six
Little Lies

I parked the car under a familiar tree. Nothing much had changed at the café, not outwardly anyway. Twigs crunched under my boots as I climbed out of the car. A sudden movement caught my eye, a squirrel raced up the tree trunk. Maybe Lee's comment about full circle was closer to the mark than I realized. I stared at the red-brick building. The smell of roasted beans and brewed coffee wafted from the café.

Coffee. We need coffee. Nothing bad is going to happen here.

Dane had switched Argo from his working leash to the shorter leash. They waited beside me. I sensed their hesitation and confusion. They both picked up on my lack of enthusiasm for the red-brick building in front of us. I shrugged it off. All in the past. No one is actively killing my friends today.

Everything in me froze as images of mom played and I heard her say, "Are you sure? Because seems like someone is indeed actively killing your friends and everyone else."

I took a deep breath. My decision to ignore the specter of my mother in my head gave me room to take another breath. As I exhaled, I smiled. Fake it until you become it. "Come on. The coffee here is fantastic."

Dane grinned. "Do they have pie?"

We walked through the door together. I pushed my sunglasses up on top of my head and gave my eyes a second to adjust to the dim interior. The aroma of buttery piecrust cooling from the ovens mingled with coffee.

"Yep. Get the cherry, it's freaking phenomenal," I said. "Also, get me a slice. I'll order the coffee." Dane and Argo walk away before I'd finished. "Ice-cream and whipped cream."

"Of course," he said with a bright smile. "What flavor?"

"Vanilla."

"Okay, Argo, you're in charge of remembering that." The dog looked up at him and appeared to accept his role.

How anyone could eat pie without cream and ice-cream, I wondered to myself as I leaned on the counter waiting for the barista to take our order. A red scrolling banner along the bottom of a big flat screen television on the wall behind the counter caught my attention.

"Ma'am, may I take your order?"

"A quad-shot espresso in a mug with extra hot water and an Americano." I pointed to the television. "Can you turn that up?"

He glanced over his shoulder and nodded. Picking up a remote near the coffee machine he pointed it at the TV. The volume rose to an audible level.

"Is that okay?"

"Yep, thanks."

Dane joined me holding a number. "What's up?"

"Watch."

An announcer read the words that scrolled along the bottom of the pictures of destruction. His voice droned but the words were clear, "Just before midday an explosion ripped through a laboratory in Atlanta, killing twenty-one people and destroying the complex."

"What laboratory?" Dane said.

"I don't know. We should know, so let's find out." I called Tahoma Whitehorse. My call went to voicemail. I tried Karen's cell. She answered, flustered.

"Karen, it's Ellie Iverson. What laboratory exploded?"

"A big one," she replied. "A company called U-Lab, they make flu vaccines among other things."

"Didn't we deal with U-Lab over the monkey incident? They were the ones who were hit last by the monkey thieves and gave us descriptions that led to the arrests." And Kurt's bite.

"Yes. That's the company. This is their southern laboratory with a manufacturing lab attached."

"Did they keep viruses there? Like ones that would be dangerous to humans?"

"You mean weaponized viruses or dangerous in general?"

"Can I pick C, all of the above?"

She laughed lightly. "They had a government research contract but they were not designated BSL-4, so they didn't have anything considered fatal to the general population. They definitely had various strains of the flu and other viruses they were creating vaccines for."

"Could anything have escaped?"

"Unlikely, the best way to kill pathogens is under extreme heat, and an explosion that became a flaming fireball would do that."

"Thanks." At least we had no other nasty pathogens to worry about.

"We're headed your way soon."

"Tomorrow?"

"Sooner than that, we've managed to get the CDC whirlybird."

"See you when you get here."

The barista pushed our coffees across the counter to us. I paid. We moved off to find computers and wait for pie. May as well enjoy pie while eating pie in a café is still a thing we can enjoy.

I choose a computer. Dane sat next to me instead of opposite and did the same. Argo lay beside my chair and a server brought a bowl of water for Argo as soon as we were settled

"Thank you, that's very considerate," I said, taking the bowl from the girl and placing it near the dog.

"You're welcome. I thought he could do with a drink."

"I'm sure he could. You can pet him if you'd like, he's fond of attention. His name is Argo."

She crouched next to him and let him sniff her hand before rubbing behind his ears. She tipped her head back and said, "I'm January. He's an agent like you two?"

It wasn't a guess. He was wearing his FBI vest, and we were kinda obvious too. "Yes. He is."

"He's beautiful." She stood, smiled, and carried on

with her job.

I turned my attention to the computer and logged into a search engine using an incognito proxy server. I didn't want my search easily found by the next person to use the computer.

"What are we looking for?" Dane said, picking up his cup.

"As much information as we can find on viruses and disease that can be spread by water or survive in water."

"Okay."

Someone coughed on the other side of the café. Dane and I caught each other's eye for a split second. A shudder ran through me. It occurred to me that maybe a café wasn't the best choice of venue given the circumstances. We needed to know what we were dealing with and how damaging this was going to get. I settled into search mode.

Tahoma and Karen should be able to shed some light on the situation, once we brought them up to speed. I focused on the facts. No reports of illness from Roanoke.

"Sanderson said he didn't know who Cait was …" Dane typed without looking up. "But administered something to finish her off."

"He said he didn't know and yes, he did something to end her life quicker than it would've ended given the circumstances."

"Is it possible that he didn't know he was murdering the Director?"

"I don't know."

"And the paramedic who potentially administered a drug cocktail in the back of the ambulance is dead."

I knew what he was thinking: Sanderson was probably going to get very ill, if not dead.

"Loose lips sink ships."

"It's not World War Two that we're fighting," Dane said with a chuckle. "Tying up loose ends?"

"Yeah, but more than that. They've played their part. The paramedic was killed, not infected, or we don't think she was infected. If she was, she died before the virus made itself at home and changed the decor. Why?"

"Why not infect both her and the doctor. She'd carry on working, infecting people unknowingly. That would make sense. If you're spreading a virus, wouldn't you use your loose ends?"

I nodded. "Yes, I would. I'd use them until they died and hopefully they'd spread the disease a helluva long way before that happened. Why kill her quick and leave him to suffer?"

"Because she knew more?"

"Sanderson has given us a description ..."

"Maybe she knew something else, more, not appearance related. I mean really, Juan Garcia?"

Maybe.

I abandoned my virus research and opened Facebook. "She's bound to have a Facebook account, won't hurt to see who's on her friends list." It'd be super unlucky for us if she didn't have a Facebook account.

"I'll keep looking for potential viruses." Dane typed

then stopped. "You can freeze them?"

Permafrost isn't going to provide a virus stasis medium in this case. "Yeah, I'm sure I read that somewhere. But they won't stay frozen in the water bottles and he wouldn't be able to get an ice-cube of the frozen virus into the bottles." I suppose he could, if he used customized ice-trays, but that would require a hands-on approach. If I had a virus that killed I wouldn't want to be handsy with it. Of course, it could all be done in a lab with all the protective gear, but still, it would take time and you'd need lab access and the ability to work undiscovered.

"This could be a new virus that's been mutated to survive in water."

"Yes. It could."

I felt Dane looking at the screen in front of me. "Anything?"

"Can't see her friends. Yet."

I picked my phone up from the table and called Sandra.

"How may I serve, O Leader of the Ragtag and Lost?"

A smile spread across my face. Always with the astonishing titles. "I need to get into a Facebook account."

"Just give me the deets and let me at it," Sandra said with accompanying knuckle cracks. Do we need a warrant?"

"We should get one ... can you organize that while you're doing what you do?"

"Judge Hartwell owes us a warrant I believe. I'll get the paperwork out of the way and you'll be in that account in a jiffy."

"Super, quicker the better. We have time constraints."

"On it. I'll hit you back as soon as I gain access."

"Email coming at you."

I signed into my work email and sent the Facebook link to Sandra.

"Got it. Make sure you clean the browser history when you're done. That didn't come from your laptop."

"I will." I hung up and waited.

Pie arrived. I sat quietly working my way through an enormous slice of pie with their freshly made vanilla ice-cream and a big dollop of whipped cream. The decision to enjoy this moment in life felt like the best one.

We don't know what's going to happen, could be the last time we'll be out in public having anything as civilized as pie and coffee. If this apocalyptic scenario plays out then before long, there'd be avoidance of people, mayhem, looting, and panic.

Dane paused before shoveling another forkful of pie into his mouth. He wiped cherry juice from his chin. "This is awesome."

"I know, right?"

An email alert sounded. Sandra.

I opened it on the computer and clicked the provided link then followed the instructions from Sandra. We'd danced this dance before.

I forked pie into my mouth with my left hand while

scrolling through Alyssa Chadwick's Facebook page. She was an active social media user. Very active. Scrolling, scrolling, with no clue what I was looking for just hoping it'd jump out and wave a flag so I knew when to stop.

She moved to Mauryville almost four months ago. Started the job as a paramedic a few weeks later. So what happened before she arrived in Mauryville? What caused the desire to live in a small town? Something triggered that move. "Dane, can you get into her boyfriend's account?"

"Yeah, with Sandra's help."

"Cool, gimme a minute."

I found him in the relationship part of her Facebook page. Journey Wahlberg.

That didn't sound right. I called Kevin. "Hey, it's me. Alyssa Chadwick's boyfriend?"

"A guy called Allen Buchanan, that's Allen with two l's and an e."

"Not Journey Wahlberg then?"

"Ah, no. What the hell is wrong with parents these days ... how is Journey a name?" There was a pause. "Didn't mean to offend, Ellie. But tell me you didn't name your babies after fruit or vegetables or anything stupid."

"Kiwi and Kumquat."

A rush of air followed the deafening silence.

"What the four-lettered-expletive is a kumquat?"

Not my kid, that's for sure. "A little tiny orange thing ... never mind." Flippant is my middle name. "Grace and Isabella. Our girls are Grace and Isabella."

This time a moment's silence was followed by a sigh of relief. "You had me going, kid. Your kids will thank you when they're older for their real names."

Unless I change them to Kiwi and Kumquat. Kinda liked the way they sounded. Mitch's voice broke into my thoughts, and he was not amused. No to changing their names then. Back to work thoughts. "Allen Buchanan?"

"Yes."

"Thank you." I hung up.

Dane's eyes were full of questions. I headed them off before they popped out of his mouth. "Facebook says she is in a relationship with Journey Wahlberg and Kev says Allen Buchanan."

I searched her friends for Journey then Allen. No photos of either man, although they both had profiles. Their friends' lists were hidden. "Okay, Dane, sending you both links." I emailed them to him. His phone buzzed seconds later.

"Got them, I'm using my phone for this."

"Okay." I heard him typing and figured it was to Sandra. Reading the Facebook posts left by Alyssa, I determined fairly quickly that she liked to bake and YouTube cat videos were her thing. Looking for anything that suggested she was keen on an end-of-world scenario or had a reason to want to hurt Cait O'Hare started to seem like a long shot.

I changed my line of thought. What was missing from her profile? I scrolled. I searched for other people with the same surname. I searched for anyone she'd tagged as family. Nothing. No family on Facebook. Sure that happens, but it's unusual in a young person.

Phone time. Dane stared at his phone.

"You still talking to Sandra?" I said.

"Nope. I'm in Journey's account and there are no photos of him. At all."

"Photos of his girlfriend?"

"No photos of a girlfriend or any friends."

If he avoided photos, then that'd be why no selfies of them together popped up on Alyssa's timeline, but it still struck me as odd, especially for youngish people. Millennials loved selfies.

"Journey doesn't say a lot. But his profile does say he's in a relationship with Alyssa and has been for five years," Dane said.

"Yeah, same on hers. Any posts of interest?"

"Only posts about the weather and food."

"She posts about food and cats."

"I'm moving to the Mauryville boyfriend now."

"Send me the link to Journey's Facebook page, please. It's an open link? Or do I need his password?"

"It's open. I'll send the password in case it's required," Dane said.

I wanted to see their posts on a big screen, side by side. I wanted to see them on my laptop. Using public computers was far from ideal. Just as I opened the Facebook page in a separate browser, a shadow dropped across the screen and table. Creeping cold slinked through me. Slowly my head turned to the window to see what'd caused the shadow. I almost didn't want to look, fully expecting to see the IP address I was using written in condensation on the window. The shadow vanished. I saw nothing but weak winter sunshine.

Light streamed in, unobstructed. Blowing air out of my mouth to calm myself did not go unnoticed.

"You okay?"

"Yeah. Memories linger and some I'd sooner not revisit."

"Sure?"

"I'm fantastic." Movement caught my eye. The door swung closed, but I didn't see the person who'd entered or left. Wind? My gaze shifted to the window nearby. Wind would explain the shadow, probably a tree branch. Nothing moved or swayed outside.

Swiveling my head back to Dane, I turned fast enough to see someone rounding the edge of the counter. "Lee!" Relief swamped me. I waved. He waved back and strode over.

"This takes me back," he said, with a smile. He dragged a chair from the end of the table over to us. Said hi to Dane then moved to the other side of me.

He put a laptop case on the table. "Need this?"

"Yes. Thank you. How?"

"I left Caine in D.C and turned up at O'Hare's. Mitch handed me the laptop and said you'd come into the city. I went to the hospital and Kurt said you were looking for an Internet café. Figured this is the only one."

Unfortunately.

Lee and I switched places; he dealt with wiping all trace of me from the café computer while I fired up my laptop and opened the links.

With both Facebook pages open I compared the images they'd posted. I checked the dates of posts over the last three months. Drugging Cait felt as though it'd been planned for some time. The plan needed enough fluidity that it could happen any day at any time. The important issue was the initial administering of the first dose of drugs. Alyssa didn't do that. She administered more drugs in the ambulance. If she was involved – and it appeared she was – it had to happen on her shift. So planning was imperative. Someone had to know where Cait was and when she'd be on that road.

Cait didn't broadcast her whereabouts. We didn't even know where she was when she wasn't in Washington. She could've been anywhere. Who would know?

Kirsty or Ethan.

Her PA or her husband.

Kirsty is the only person in the FBI who always knew how to get hold of Cait. The first suspect in a murder is almost always the closest to the victim. The spouse, suspect number one. My whole body cringed. Open mind. Just keep an open mind. Everyone is capable of murder when the stars align and the circumstances are right.

"What's happening in your head?" Lee's voice startled me.

"Dark shit."

"Spill," Lee said.

"Who knows how to get hold of Cait at any time?"

"No, El, no." His head shook, disbelief crammed into the lines on his face. "No."

"You never went there when you heard?"

I saw it in his eyes, he did, and he couldn't deny it. A heavy sigh dropped to the keyboard in front of Lee. "That's our first port. Of course I went there, briefly."

"And dismissed it, why?" I said, hoping Lee had something I could use to take Ethan out of the equation altogether.

"He wasn't home."

That isn't enough.

"What?" Dane stopped scrolling on his phone. "You talking about Ethan?"

"Yes," I said. "Only two people always know where Cait is. Her husband and her personal assistant."

"He was not involved." The confidence in his words gave me pause.

"And you know that for sure, no doubt in your mind?"

"So do you," he said with a small smile. "In the interest of the investigation, I remain open-minded. He could be hiding something."

Yeah, it might not be all roses and champagne at Casa O'Hare. "Do you know Kirsty? Cait's PA." Perhaps an appropriate time to shift away from thoughts of Ethan, and give the next person our attention.

"Only as a gatekeeper. Can't get to O'Hare's office without going through her." In the air above him, I saw a penny rattle around a slot then drop and disappear into his skull. "What motive could she have?" Dane didn't look impressed with the idea of agent involvement.

"Not saying she did anything. I'm saying that the only person that's not Ethan who ever knows Cait's whereabouts in advance, is Kirsty."

"Duly noted. Let's file that away for now, shall we?" Lee shifted his attention to my screen and the waiting Facebook pages. "Tell me what you can see?"

"I'm seeing dates of posts that correspond. He posts on his wall. Then she posts on her wall. They're mostly within minutes of each other. A few of them have long gaps between. Could be because she was working and unable to post. But look ..." I scrolled through the last two weeks of posts. "He always posts first."

"They don't even like each other's posts, do they?"

"No. Never. He posts a picture. Then she posts a picture."

"A conversation with photographs?" Dane said, moving closer.

"That's the theory," I said lining two pictures up. "What do you suppose mac and cheese and a cupcake mean?"

Lee reached over and scrolled one of the timelines then sat back with a harrumph.

"You're the resident code cracker, Ellie, what do you see?"

"I see food and it's making me hungry." I scooped the remnants of pie and melted ice-cream from my plate before focusing on the pictures in front of me. "I imagine this code, if it is a code, was devised well ahead of time and in person."

I double-clicked a photo of a piece of pie Alyssa had posted because something on the table smacked of familiarity. It wasn't as sharp as the pie, but the colors drew me. I double-clicked again and zoomed in on the round object near the edge of the plate.

"What does that look like?" I mumbled. "Is that a drink coaster?"

"Can you get it any sharper?"

"If I zoom any closer it'll blur more."

Lee pointed at the semi-circle of color. "Blues and greens."

Dane stood and walked away. He returned fast holding a blue and green circular object in his hand. A drink coaster.

"You're fucking kidding me," I said and took it from him to compare it with the blurred image on my screen. "She was here."

Dane left again.

Lee scanned the walls and ceiling. Video cameras would be handy. They used not to have them but times have changed in the nine years since we'd been in the café. Lee pointed at three cameras.

"When was she here?" Lee said.

"Well, let's try to work it out," I said, looking at the pictures. "Check this out. There are five different meals he posts, that she posts against. She uses one of fourteen different baked goods in reply." I scanned images. "I doubt it has anything to do with the actual day and time the picture is posted."

"Weeks and days?"

I scrolled through more pictures before I agreed with Lee's assessment. "Weeks and days, but also a time of day. Morning or afternoon. How do they decide which week is which?"

"Does she talk about moving at all?"

After a while, I found a post, dated six months earlier, where she mentioned wanting a new job. "Here. He's got a corresponding post of more food."

Dane attracted my attention with a loud whistle from across the café. He circled his arm in the air.

"Keep looking here, Lee. I'll go see what has Dane all riled up." I joined him at the counter and was introduced to the manager.

"Alyssa came in a few times a month, the days varied, she was often in uniform," the manager said.

"Did she meet anyone?"

He nodded. "Yes, a man. She'd come in, order, then look around for him."

"When did you see them last?"

"Monday morning."

And it's Friday or Saturday now. What day is it? A word shimmied into my consciousness. Saturday. Cait was attacked on Tuesday night.

"You're certain it was Monday morning?"

"Absolutely."

Finally some progress. "Tell me you have operational

security cameras."

"I do."

"Would you show Agent Wesson please, and see if we can get a picture of Alyssa and whoever she meets?"

"Yes. Whatever we can do to help, Agent."

Yay, and without screaming about a warrant. "Thank you."

I left Dane to the manager and hurried back to Lee. "She was here Monday morning. Let's find the posts that arranged that meeting, then we have a place to unravel their code."

"You're thinking something ..."

I am. "What if we used the code against Journey? Post a picture of our own once we've worked it out and see if he shows. If he thinks he killed her but didn't stick around to find out then he'll want to finish her off. If he didn't kill her, then he'll see the post and presume she needs to see him."

"If he killed her and stuck around to check he's going to know something screwy is going on."

"True, but I'm picking he'll need to verify it's not her. He's not the end of this chain, he's a link, so someone above him will need verification."

"El, meatballs and pie on Friday."

"Okay, so that could mean next week. It could mean Monday morning?"

"Yeah, they might not even use weeks as such but this week, next week, week after next, last week of the month."

"She picks the place. Go through her photos, let's find all the meeting places. I'm betting every photo would have a place, either subtle like metadata or open like the actual name showing or like this blurred coaster."

Dane appeared next to me. Before he could speak, I did. "Hey, did you ever find out who called emergency services to alert them to the accident?"

He flipped his notebook open and read me some notes. "Call came from a burner phone, it bounced off a cell tower in Mauryville. No identity. Nine-One-One said the caller may have been male, was calm, and hung up as soon as he'd given an approximate address."

"Not super helpful."

"Nope. The video surveillance might crack your picture code completely as far as meeting places and times go, but it's not going to help us locate the mystery boyfriend."

"He knew about the cameras from the first day?"

"Oh yes. We can see him, the back of his head, a cap he's wearing. We can probably build an accurate height/ weight profile, we don't have a face, at all, anywhere."

"Staff?"

He handed me his notebook. Three descriptions, all different.

"And they were here working on the days he met Alyssa?"

"Yep."

"Wow."

He's a thirty-something, forty-year-old with green, hazel, and blue eyes. His hair is both brown and blond.

He wears a collar-length ponytail, that's short and tidy, with a buzz cut. Mullet maybe? Business in the front, party in the back? He's somewhere between five-feet-eight and six feet in height. His build was described as both wiry and big. Dane had tried to get clarity on the body type. It didn't help: he was either short and thin or tall and overweight. I stopped reading for a moment.

"What are they smoking in this café?" I knew only too well how varied descriptions and statements can be after a crime, but this was recall, there was no trauma involved. "It must be some remarkable shit."

I read on. Distinguishing features were enthralling; a limp but no consensus on which leg, and a long scar on his right hand. A sketch of the scarred hand showed it extended from between his index finger and middle finger to his wrist on the back of his hand. I glanced at my hand then at Lee and Dane's hands. That's a big scar.

I handed the notebook back to Dane. "No one knows what Alyssa's boyfriend looks like. That's splendid." But he has a limp and a scar, so that's better than nothing.

"I'll plug what we have regarding that scar and his limp into our NGI system."

"Make it so Number One."

Dane and Lee chuckled. "Do you have to say that every time anyone mentions Next Generation Identification?" Dane said directing an eyebrow lift in my direction.

"Yes." I grinned. "Don't forget the surprising discovery that he has three eyes and they're all different colors."

He turned to Lee. "Has she always been like this or is

this the result of one too many blows to the head?"

"More like to six or seven too many blows in the head department, and yes, always a wiseass."

"Don't mind me, I'm delighted to sit here and listen to you talk about me."

Chapter Twenty Seven
She lied to the FBI

Kurt walked into the café. I saw him standing inside the door and waved my arm high in the air. He nodded and came over.

"Tahoma and Karen are at the hospital. It's best if I let them do their thing."

I peered past him. No Moose. "Where'd you hide Stu?"

"He wanted to walk over."

"I'm glad you're here. This thing with Alyssa, the paramedic, is captivating."

Kurt sat opposite me.

"You want something to eat and coffee?" Lee stood and leaned over the table to shake his hand.

"Yeah, I'll come," Kurt said. He motioned to Dane and me. "Get you anything?"

"No thanks," I replied.

Dane shook his head.

"Iverson, I offered to bring you food and coffee. You feeling all right?"

"Very funny."

I went back to the Journey's Facebook page. He'd posted regularly for about six months, before that there was a break. Just over two years of no posts. Where was he for those two years? Did he take a Facebook break? Was that scar on his hand and his alleged limp the reason for the break?

I compared the pages. Alyssa had posted during that time. And traveled. A few weekends away. Every few months she went away, or at least changed the type of pictures she posted. Pictures of parks and beaches. She never mentioned him. He never mentioned her.

"Dane, we ran his name?"

"Yeah, nothing."

"Nothing at all? No Social Security Number attached?"

"Nothing. Looks like he uses a fake name on Facebook. It's not hard to change your name on social media and smart to do so if you don't want people knowing who you are, I guess."

I wriggled in my seat, stretched my arms over my head then relaxed. And tried to get my focus back. The antsy feeling grew. My calf muscles twitched and feet refused to keep still. Ridiculous. Argo whined and stood. He leaned his head on my knee. "I need to stretch my legs and so does he."

"You do that, I'll do this."

I pocketed my phone and walked to the counter where Lee and Kurt were choosing items from the extensive blackboard menu. "We're going for a walk. I need to get air."

"Want company?" Kurt dragged his eyes from the menu board long enough to know I was with Argo.

"Nah. You guys eat. I'll be back soon." I hauled open the door and then threw words over my shoulder. "Pie, grab me any pie."

Outside, the cool fresh air hit me. Argo and I stood a few feet from the café on the edge of the parking lot. Breathing in, I let all the smells tell me a story about the area. Someone wearing lilac as a scent walked through the parking lot. My eyes automatically scanned the vicinity; a woman a hundred yards away walked down the sidewalk. Probably her. A dog peed on the oak tree near our car. In the other direction, I saw a man walking a small ball of fluff. "Hardly qualifies as a dog," I muttered. Argo nudged me. I took that as agreement.

A whiff of chlorine triggered a dark thought that could spiral this case straight to hell: what if Kirsty was somehow tied up in this mess? It took real effort to shift that thought sideways. I glanced at Argo. "Come on, let's go for that walk."

A voice rang out from behind me. "El, wait up!"

I turned and saw Moose striding up the street. His jacket flapped as he moved to reveal his gun with every second step.

"Seems we have company after all," I whispered to Argo knowing that the words formed in my head and that Moose could see them.

He caught up. "I can go get coffee if you don't want me around."

"I don't mind, but I need to free my mind up."

"Okay. I can walk quietly."

Ten minutes later, the need to know how Alyssa and Journey and the Unsub knew where Cait would be, mushroomed into something I could not push aside or ignore. No matter how much I didn't want this situation to emanate within the FBI, that avenue needed exploration.

But why?

Why was Cait targeted, and why like that? And was it something to do with the viruses or was that an aside? I couldn't bring myself even to think coincidence. My gut told me we had more than one scenario unfolding.

Argo concentrated on reading the latest dog blog on a tree and leaving a suitable comment as high as he possibly could while I mulled over the events that led us here. They led us here. Led us.

Was that the intent? The words circled the tree then fell into the gutter. I watched as they splashed in the dregs of rainwater before slipping down the drain. A hand reached out of the stormwater drain and beckoned me.

Nope not going there. A red balloon squeezed from the drain and floated skyward. Fuck that.

"El?"

I jumped. My insides bounced unhappily against my ribcage then dropped. I glanced at Moose but it wasn't him who spoke. His brow creased. Guess he saw me jump.

Laughter followed. Only one person I knew laughed like that. Spinning around I came face to face with Christopher Chance. This will be eye-opening. Life faded to black and white. Muted colors crept across my line of vision.

"Chance."

"Sit."

"Where?" We were in the middle of the sidewalk.

He motioned to a park bench on a patch of grass. "This is for us," he said, dimples showing as his smile widened. "Come on, Argo."

The dog gave me a side-glance then followed Chance. Seriously? Now my dog can see my imaginary friend. Ain't that peachy. Not. I'm spreading my particular brand of crazy to my dog. I thought he was smarter than that. Disappointing. My eyes darted around. No Moose. Where'd he go? Trees sprouted from what was once the road. I expected to see Moose walk out of what was now a wooded area. He didn't.

I sat next to Chance with Argo at my feet. The seat felt cold and unforgiving against my back.

"What's happening El, you look worried."

"Because I am, what'd you do with Moose?"

Chance laughed. "He's still right where you left him."

"Okay." What else could I say?

"This concerned expression is about O'Hare?"

"No, it's about the weather. Will winter will ever start properly?"

"You always gotta be a wiseass?"

"You have to ask?"

"Okay, tell me. I know you, and this is not a happy Ellie Iverson."

"We're battling viruses, people are dying in supposed accidents, Cait died of an apparent drug overdose. The person who was supposed to administer an antidote gave her more of the drug. Her boyfriend found her dead in their home."

Chance interrupted me. "Let's cut to the part I can help with—"

"Can you though? I dunno."

"What is it you need, El?"

"I need to know why the dead paramedic overdosed Cait. I need to know why she's communicating in code with her former boyfriend who may still be her boyfriend. And he's not the boyfriend she lived with in Mauryville. I need to know how anyone knew where Cait was. How did this happen, Chance? How the fuck did someone take out that horse with a tranq dart and then drug Cait? Why did a doctor finish her off?" I sucked in air. "And why is Misha dead. Why the fuck is he dead?"

"Wow, come here." He threw an arm around my shoulders and wrapped me in a tight hug. "Shh. You got this, El. You do. This is no harder than any other investigation."

"There's a fucking virus, Chance. It's been released in Virginia. We don't even know what it is."

"That's not ideal."

"No, it's not. And ..."

"There's more?"

My head rubbed against his shoulder as I nodded.

"No one knows where Cait is when she's not at work. It's a thing. No one knows if she's in Washington or at the shore or out of state or down here. So how was someone waiting for her?"

"Someone knew, El, they had to."

"Yeah, but that someone might be her husband, or her personal assistant, Kirsty."

"Discounting her husband as the killer because I don't believe you really believe he did this. Her assistant is FBI?"

"Yeah."

"Shit."

"Yeah."

"Breathe, El, you're not alone working this. You've got Delta and you've got this big hairy beast." Argo leaned against my leg as Chance scratched behind his ears. "And me. I'm here."

"True." Imaginary friends for the win.

"One step at a time. What's next?"

"Finding the supposed boyfriend and working out why he disappeared for a few years to reappear six months ago."

"Why him?"

"Because he's connected to Alyssa, the paramedic, and she overdosed Cait in the ambulance. He's all we've got when it comes to a lead that might get us up a rung on the ladder."

"What about the doctor?"

"He might be sick. Doesn't know what with but he told us his contact infected bottles of water at a hotel in Roanoke. The doctor is in hospital. CDC is involved. The virus is their problem for now. Our problem is finding

Cait's killers."

"Okay, so let's ignore the virus and concentrate on Cait."

"I'm trying to, but it's a murky windy trail and I don't know where it's going or why."

"Working backward then, you know how but don't have a who or a why."

Story of my life.

Chance twisted on the bench until he faced me. "What do you know?"

"Same as you. That the reason the Journey boy wasn't Facebooking for a couple of years might have something to do with that scar and limp. But more, because if he had Internet access, he'd probably still be on Facebook."

"Prison."

"Or?"

"Somewhere like that, somewhere that doesn't allow access to the outside world." Hospital. No, patients aren't prisoners. Unless they are prisoners. "An asylum for the criminally insane." I was half-kidding because it smacked of a Batman episode. "Arkham Asylum."

The muted colors surrounding us deepened until they were shades of greens, grays, and black. Lightning flashed across the trees. A shiver ran through me. Argo whined and hid his face under his paws. Chance grabbed my hand. In his eyes, I saw the asylum and a parade of inmates. The Joker, Two-Face, Poison Ivy, The Riddler and Harley Quinn. Poison Ivy and Two-Face revolved around each other while the other faded into the stone façade.

"You made the world a dark place all of a sudden," Chance said, as street lamps came on.

"What's Two-Face's real name?"

"Harvey Dent," Chance said.

"Oh, yeah." That didn't feel right. "Poison Ivy is Alyssa, in this weird little Batman scenario we've got going on here."

"Okay. The boyfriend is Two-Face?"

"I think so."

"Two-Face was in an asylum so was Poison Ivy. Could they have met there? One working, the other an inmate?"

"Perhaps."

"What are you thinking?"

"That he has a link to Two-Face somehow." A sigh escaped; using my phone, I searched Batman on IMDB. Harvey Dent was played by Aaron Eckhart, Tommy Lee Jones, Billy-Dee Williams, Nicholas D'Argosto, Richard Moll and Tim Nugent. The character was created by Bill Finger and Bob Kane. Something about seeing the name Finger made me think I was on the right track.

"What's the boyfriend's name again?"

"Journey Wahlberg."

"Like Mark Wahlberg?"

"Yeah, but not as cool." A small laugh escaped. "Wahlberg has the same number of letters as Williams."

"Could be his real surname."

"Yeah, but what's his first name, I know it isn't Journey. He's no Hollywood brat."

"If we think about it as a J name—"

"Way ahead of you." I had my notebook and a pen busy working on all the anagrams of Journey. "One Jury, Joey Run, Joey Urn, Eon Jury."

"Going with Joey."

"I'm going with the song, 'Run Joey Run.'"

Chance frowned. "I don't know it."

"Let me play it for you."

By the time the song was finished we were grinning like idiots at each other.

"The dad didn't shoot Alyssa. The dad shot Joey," I said. "Except I doubt he was shot, more likely it was a blade." A long one, like a sword or a machete.

"Brutal," Chance said with a grimace.

"Were they going to get married?"

Chance nodded. "Maybe elope."

"Okay, Joey was badly hurt and went to the hospital then probably rehab but where does the asylum come in? They didn't meet there but maybe they saw each other again there ..."

"Rekindled the romance."

"Except now he's bitter and twisted and suddenly decides to kill Cait?"

"I think we've missed a few steps."

"Alyssa felt guilty for what happened to her boyfriend. He used that guilt to manipulate her into helping him." I had a hard job believing someone sworn to help people turned into a killer overnight. The thought shoved me back into the bench. A doctor killed Cait. A doctor finished her off when she was already dying. Shouldn't be that hard for me to believe a pretty little paramedic administered a dose of heroin and Xanax instead of life-saving Narcan. Why did I think she didn't? Because I can't function in a world where 'trust no one' is the catch cry anymore. "Why did he want Cait dead?"

"Joey Williams is the key to that question, El. Run his name through everything. You'll find the answer."

"Will I find him?"

"Have a little faith in yourself."

"Easy for you to say. I'm staring at a dark hole and it's sucking humanity into it."

"Don't let it, El. You can do this. You can find Williams and find his motivation."

"Could this be linked to the virus situation?"

Chance shook his head. "I don't think so. That seems like a giant leap."

Fair enough. So two separate situations and the other deaths are not mixed up in this either. Then Owen disappeared because she thought she was a target not because she had a hand in Cait's death.

Part of me saw that as a possibility but another part didn't want to end up with the job of protecting the Evil Queen. A third scenario popped up; she might have gone on vacation. Then a fourth scenario jumped at me: or taken personal time for whatever reason. "I gotta go, Chance. Thank you."

"Happy to help, I did help, right?"

I smiled. "Yeah, you helped."

"Take it easy, El. Those babies need their mom."

The light flickered then died. Green, gray, and black swirled into a tornado and flew away.

"Argo." The dog sat up and leaned on me. Moose stood in front of me. "Stu, we need to go back. We've got work to do."

"Yeah, I know. What the hell did I see?"

Shit. He saw. "Chance. He pops up sometimes and helps me work stuff out."

"You were sitting on a park bench in a comic book."

"Uh huh."

Best to leave Moose to process what he'd seen. Best to leave him to it. We walked in silence.

Chapter Twenty Eight
Run Joey Run

Back in the café, I said, "Get something to eat, Moose."

His right eyebrow rose. "We doing the nickname thing again, are we?"

"Looks that way." I hurried over to the table where Dane, Kurt, and Lee were deep in conversation. Pie waited for me. I sat down, forked a piece of the golden-crusted delight into my mouth. Apple. The tartness of the apple balanced the sugary crust to perfection. Argo drank in great gulps from the bowl on the ground.

"Champion choice." I glanced at Kurt. He pointed to Dane. "Thanks, Dane."

"Thought cherry twice might be overkill."

I finished another mouthful of pie before speaking again. "I got something, perhaps I have something. Journey Wahlberg might be Joey or Joseph Williams." I paused before stabbing another piece of pie. "How'd you get on with the soft biometrics?"

"Turns out about two hundred and fifty people in the database have scars like Journey's and almost three thousand have a limp of some description."

Super helpful.

Dane tapped on his phone screen. "Approximate age?"

"I reckon the same as Alyssa or close to it."

"Have we got her details?"

Shit. Have we? I scrambled through information and tried to remember.

"We do," Kurt said.

Kurt to the rescue. I concentrated on eating and left him to give Dane the details. In truth, I expected someone to ask how I came up with the name.

"El, there are about forty Joseph Williams around Alyssa's age. Can't narrow it anymore, can you?"

I smiled. Because I can. The names of the actors who'd played Two-Face scrolled past my eyes. "Look for a Joseph Billy hyphen Dee Williams."

Dane's line of vision went from the screen in his hand to me. "How do you do that?"

Moose sat next to Dane and peered at the phone screen, a smile spread across his face.

"He's there, isn't he?"

They both nodded. "Joseph Billy-Dee Williams, and he's a year older than Alyssa. Last known address Greensboro, North Carolina," Dane said, shaking his head in wonder.

"Is that a current address?"

"He updated his address with the Department of Motor Vehicles five months ago."

"DMV, so we have a photograph?"

Dane nodded and handed me his phone. After a few seconds, I gave it back.

The DMV had perfected five looks when it came to male drivers and their license photographs. Biker, car salesman, stoner, contractor, and lunatic-slash-tweaker.

Joseph's picture fitted the lunatic-slash-tweaker category.

A blind dog could take a better photo. Somewhat disappointing to find he didn't have three eyes.

"He's not as astounding as his description, is he?" Dane said with a grin.

"So how come I get the feeling he's not living in Greensboro now?" Moose said, moving his arms so a server could put a roast vegetable salad in front of him.

Lee spoke, "Because he's not. He's living in Rockbridge County somewhere, I feel it in my bones."

With a laugh, I said, "I thought that was a change in the weather you felt in your bones."

Lee grinned at me. "That, too. Snow's coming."

"What do we know about Joseph Williams?"

Dane and Lee typed. Kurt and I rocked back on our chairs. Moose ate his salad.

"It was Chance, wasn't it?" Kurt smiled at me from across the table.

"Yeah. Nah. Kinda. He was my sounding board but I'm going to credit myself with the name." I bumped the chair legs to the floor. "I started talking to Chance about the big gap in Joseph's timeline and speculating on the reason."

"How was that for you?" Kurt said, addressing Moose.

"Interesting. Fucked-up, but interesting."

I shrugged. "Seems Moose saw some of what I see." Back to business. The song returned and threw darts at my memory. The father.

"Look up Alyssa's father. Is he alive?"

Much typing ensued while I finished the last crumbs of

pie.

Lee and Dane spoke at once, "Dead. Two and a half years ago."

"Details?"

"Getting them ..." Lee said. "Searching for his death certificate."

Dane jumped to his feet. "Got it!"

Didn't know it was a race, but whatever. "And?"

"There's a court entry tagged in this death certificate. He died as a result of a gunshot wound received while attacking Joseph Billy-Dee Williams."

"Williams had a self-defense plea?"

"Uh huh and it was upheld."

Kurt cleared his throat. "Running on pure adrenaline and the need to survive, he could've inflicted life-ending injuries on Alyssa's father, even with his hand cut to pieces and whatever happened to his leg."

"Hold it, I have that information," Lee said. "His leg was broken in two places and almost severed by a long-bladed weapon. His right hand was pretty much split in half, that scar is all the way through. The weapon was a machete."

"I'm sure someone else was there and dealt with the father before he could finish Joseph off," Kurt said, reading a more detailed report on Williams's wounds. "If he had a gun why didn't he use it sooner? He sure as hell didn't fire right-handed with his hand messed up like that."

"Why weren't these questions asked during the

inquest?" I said, pushing my plate away.

"They were. Williams was adamant that he fired the shot that killed the father, he said he fired left-handed."

All our heads shook.

"Alyssa was there?"

Kurt nodded. "She testified that Williams killed her father in self-defense."

"Alyssa did it," I said. "Not Williams. That's why he could manipulate her. That's the hold."

Kurt clicked a link and read more documents pertaining to Williams. "He was locked up for about seven months. He was in the hospital for a long time after the attack, then rehab for several months. He was released, didn't do well back in the world. Developed a drug habit, a dependency on prescription pain medication, during the healing process. Oxycodone. He was an Oxycodone addict then he started mixing his drugs. A couple of psychotic episodes led to him being locked away in—"

"An asylum," I finished.

"Pretty much."

"There we have it folks, the Batman connection." Jeez. My innards shriveled as I realized I'd said it aloud.

"Arkham Asylum," Moose said with a grin. "That's what I saw."

Maybe if I kept talking, no one would pick up on the Batman thing or Moose's comment.

"Williams effectively did time for Alyssa. Right?" I said and leaned back in my chair.

"Yes, I suppose he did in that he was horribly injured, needed rehab, addicted to pain meds, and finally psychotic which did get him locked away. She was able to carry on her life, he clearly was not," Kurt said. "The Batman thing is not going away, Iverson. We'll talk." He turned to Moose. "I'll be talking to you as well."

Okay, woohoo. Moving on. "Let's find Williams, shall we?" Then we can talk to him and start to understand why he wanted Cait dead. "Did Sanderson have anything interesting to say about Cait and why he was asked to make sure she died?"

"No. Juan Garcia apparently did not elaborate," Kurt said.

"Do we have two people working independently, wanting to kill Cait?" Fuck. It was very much looking like that.

"Really?" Kurt said.

"Or three?"

"Who the hell shot the horse and delivered the first drug load to Cait?" Dane leaned over and moved the mouse pointer on my laptop until it touched the email icon at the bottom of my screen. "Go there."

"Email," I said, clicking the icon and opening my email. I saw an email from Dane.

"Well yeah, but this email in particular." He clicked on the email from himself and moved the pointer back and forth over an image of Williams. "Easier to find a picture if you know who you're looking for. I found him. Now look behind him."

Shit. I know that place "That's Cait's Mauryville property. That's the horse. That's Thor in the pasture."

"It looks like he knew Cait," Kurt said.

"Why was he at her house?" Lee said. "Why would he be out there?"

"Can someone tell me what Williams did for a living?" I scanned their faces.

Heads shook.

Surely he did something that got him out there. When was that? "Where'd you find the picture?"

"Searched the inter-webs for his name and it popped up, along with another hundred images that aren't him."

"Any context?"

"Yeah, a blog post about horses. But no mention of why Joseph Williams was in the photo or why the photo was taken at Cait O'Hare's."

"Who owns the blog?"

"Someone called VetGirl."

"That's something, Dane. A big something."

Time to talk to Doc Robinson. I made the call and discovered he was out on a call. Hannah answered the phone. I played a hunch. "Hey, it's Ellie Iverson. Hannah, are you VetGirl, who writes the blog about horses?" Dane found the blog and showed me the latest entry. Images of her grandfather's horses.

"You know about that? Wow, I've actually got a reader."

"I saw it today. Love the photos of your grandfather's horses." I enlarged the photos to see the captions. Names.

Handy. "Especially love the gray he called Shady."

"Thank you, Agent Iverson." She sounded pleased.

"Who's the guy in the photo with Thor?"

"Oh, Joe. Shame I didn't get a photo of Ms. O'Hare with Thor before the accident."

"Yeah, it is. Was she there that day?"

"Yep, she was in the stable with Doc and Freyja."

"How long ago was that?"

"Late summer."

I heard the bell chime over the vet clinic door and chattering voices. "Do you often go with Doc on calls?"

"Not really, but it was a nice day and I asked if I could go along to take some photos."

"Ever met Joe before?"

"No. He was nice. The horses loved him."

"Thanks, Hannah. Nice work on the blog."

I called Sean, stood, and walked away from the table while I waited for him to answer.

"It's me. Do you know Joseph Williams or Joey Williams?"

"Don't think so."

"You sure?"

"Yeah."

"Is Ethan around?"

"Yeah, hang on." Footsteps filled the airway. Then voices. A baby cried. Grace.

"El?" Ethan's voice rang out cutting Grace's cry in half.

"Do you know a Joey or Joseph Williams?"

"Nope."

"Do you know anyone who goes by the name Joey or Joseph or Joe and is approximately thirty-two years old?"

"I know a Joe Wahlberg."

You're kidding me. "How do you know him?"

"Joe used to come out and spend time with the horses, muck out the stables and do whatever needed doing when we were in Washington. He worked here most of the summer."

"He do anything else?"

"Bit of gardening. General yard work."

"When did you last see him?"

"I haven't seen him in over a month. Cait mentioned him a few weeks ago." A door closed. "She was talking about letting him go."

"Any particular reason?"

"She said he wasn't working out."

"He'd been there all summer and now he's not working out?"

"Never really had the opportunity to discuss it properly. But now you mention it, it seems a bit out of the ordinary."

"I need you to give it some thought. Hit me back if you come up with anything."

"Why are you asking about Joe?"

"He's a person of interest in the death of one of the paramedics that treated Cait at the scene."

Silence. Another door closed. "El, what aren't you telling me?"

"Nothing. Just give it some thought and hit me back if

you remember anything." I paused, a gust of wind swirled a silver candy bar wrapper in the air. It slapped into the window and stuck there. 3 Musketeers. "Hope the babies aren't too distracting."

"They're not, El. It's nice having life in the house." He laughed lightly. "You know what I mean."

"Yeah."

"Any messages for Mitch?"

"Tell him I'll be there when I can."

I hung up and walked back to the table. "Ethan said Joe Wahlberg worked at their place most of the summer while they were in Washington. Also that Cait was going to fire him. He wasn't working out apparently. He didn't know the whole story."

Lee stood up. "We should head out to Mauryville. I don't like that Williams had some kind of beef with Cait. We don't know where he is. Quinn is on his way home. Mitch and the babies are there. All excellent reasons to make sure nothing else happens."

"Kennedy and Sean are out there," I said, didn't make me feel any better even though they were seasoned and well-trained. Between them, they had an impressive resume. There was no scenario in which I envisaged a cripple getting the drop on them. Yet I felt apprehensive.

Concern bubbled spitting droplets of boiling water into the air as the media release crept into mind: Cait O'Hare was treated in hospital and discharged following a horse riding accident.

Kurt and Moose pushed their chairs back as they

stood. Dane followed. Everyone packed up. We were out of there.

"What about Tahoma and Karen?" I said as Kurt ushered me to the car.

"They're fine. They've got police backup, and unknown pathogens are their thing. They'll be in touch if they need us."

"The pathogen thing is not making me happy," I muttered. "We don't deal with shit like this all the time."

"It's not quotidian if that's what you mean," Lee said with a small smile.

My eyes rolled before the words formed. "Crosswords again, Lee?"

"Word of the day," he said, his eyes drawn to Dane who had stopped walking and typed frantically. Both thumbs moved at speed.

"Quotidian means an everyday occurrence." Dane stopped and made eye contact with me. "Or something to do with malaria."

"In some places that is still an everyday disease," I said then stopped.

"An everyday disease ..." Dane echoed.

"A flu," Lee said.

"Vaccinations," I replied.

"Not if it's new to humans," Dane said.

"We can't vaccinate against something we don't know about."

"True."

Haunted by the line of thought and direction of the

conversation, I saw the outcome: death for tens of thousands of vulnerable people. Pandemic. No vaccine. Could be hundreds of thousands or even millions.

The Last Ship. We were heading for a last ship scenario.

"If it is new to humans and a premeditated release then wherever it was created or mutated, there could be a vaccine?" Dane offered.

Unless the creators were okay being collateral damage. Different from a suicide bomber but not by much.

Kurt gazed at us, one by one, and with his usual calmness said, "CDC is on it. It's their job. Whatever this virus is, they will find out and deal with it."

"What if it's not a virus or anything contagious?"

Kurt's eyebrows met as frown lines knotted on his forehead. "Where is this going?"

"What if we're looking at a nerve agent?"

"You're thinking poisoning?" I nodded. "I'm listening … lay it on me, Iverson."

"Soman is a candidate. Even if the contaminated water drips or splashes on your skin, you will get sick and potentially die. It can be delivered via aerosol, food, water. Symptoms appear within seconds from the vapor but minutes or hours from ingestion."

"You've given this thought and research time?"

"More hauling things I've read in the past into focus, because until we know for sure what we're dealing with, the possibilities are frightening and extensive."

"But Soman?"

"It's a short-lived threat. It'd cause utter chaos, then be over."

"I'm still listening. What else is going on in that head of yours?"

"That's not scary enough?"

"It's plenty scary but I know you and this is the tip of the iceberg."

My turn to smile. He knew me well. "VX is another potential suspect. That shit can last months in the environment, so, I'd sooner it wasn't that."

Kurt gave a small laugh. "Yeah, me too."

"And ... A-234, it's already been used in the United Kingdom. Recently."

His eyes met mine. All trace of humor vanished. "Novichok. Salisbury poisoning of Sergei and Yulia Skripal. Do you really want to continue this thought?"

"We're told to stop collaborating with our FSB counterparts and now there is a potential contagion threat? Makes me consider alternatives, such as maybe this is not a contagion. Maybe we have a situation whereby someone is introducing a nerve agent."

Or maybe we have an unknown contagion from Russia. Either way. We could be looking at Russia. The bromance is over. Or China wanting payback for trade sanctions. Or North Korea because ... do countries even need a reason?

Kurt was reading something on his phone. "Here we go, March 12th, 2018, Sergei and Yulia Skripal were found unconscious on a park bench in Salisbury. Police later released a statement saying a nerve agent was to blame. The Russian-made Novichok. Sergei was an ex-spy. Three people were hospitalized that day and all were subsequently discharged."

"Three?"

"The police officer who found them was exposed as he had no idea it was a nerve agent at the time."

"How long does Novichok last in the environment?"

"I don't know if anyone knows the definitive answer to that question. Media speculated at least four months when the second couple was exposed in Salisbury."

I remembered the reports and the panic waves that washed across the world. Details popped into view from further reports after the woman died. She'd found what she thought was a perfume bottle and sprayed a bit on her wrist. So technically it wasn't in the environment it was contained in a bottle. The woman died, her boyfriend survived. I had my doubts as to whether or not that perfume bottle was dumped after the park bench poisoning. If someone got that shit on their skin, I'd expect death to follow. No one from the initial poisoning died. So what was the point? To cause terror? To send a message? It wasn't to kill. That nerve agent is certainly capable of killing if delivered to the skin or ingested or breathed in. "If the Russian's are looking to cause havoc and disrupt, using Novichok would do it."

His head nodded. "It would disrupt and cause widespread panic. People would be afraid to leave their homes."

He was right because it's something they know about. My mind spun over the potential of something as innocuous as a small perfume vial containing Novichok on an airplane. A couple of squirts somewhere in the toilets on board and you have a planeload of the walking dead. Coordinated attacks on multiple planes would ground air traffic as well as kill or cause serious illness in a heap of people. An effective way to halt air traffic. If they also attacked cruise ships, then we'd have boats floating at sea full of the dead and dying. But would that situation be worse than a contagion?

I glanced at Kurt. "More so than if we have a contagion situation?"

"Potentially. Tell people there is a new strain of flu and they'll wash their hands more, keep away from crowds, take precautions where possible, but mostly carry on. Tell people there is a nerve agent loose in their community and it'll get ugly fast," Kurt said.

"And if someone told them it could be in their water or food ...?" Or on their door handles or sprayed onto random packaging of innocuous goods in supermarkets.

"There's no way we could manage the situation and create a satisfactory outcome."

"Whatever this is, it will take some skill to manage," Stu said. "Are we going?"

"Yeah. Let's go."

Mitch's voice filled my head. I heard the tone, not the words. He wanted help.

Chapter Twenty Nine

Taking it Back

Caine called me before we were five minutes into our drive from Lexington.

"How's it going up there?" I said, touching the speaker icon. "You're on speaker."

"Five media outlets ran with a story about the monkey theft. Did you know the girl died?"

"No. I knew she was ill."

"She's dead and the boy is critical."

"They were anti-vaxers," I said, my words so dry they crunched like autumn leaves. "The monkey posed no threat to anyone who received this year's flu vaccine."

"The Fourth Estate floated a different story."

Of course they did. They'll print anything that vaguely looks as though they can get a bit of mileage out of it or a dig at the Establishment. Hence we kept our media release regarding Cait brief and more of an outline of the truth.

"There's nothing to see here," I said.

I heard a newspaper rustle. Old school. Caine didn't read his news online like the rest of us.

"Ellie, they're saying the monkey was stolen from a secure laboratory in Washington and that the death of the girl was caused by a virus the monkey carried."

"Partially true. But The Facility can't have been that

secure if those two bozos could break in and *Free Willy*."

"That won't stop the media stirring up shit and carrying on about the monkey and its viral payload," Kurt said. "Are they saying anything else? Anything we should be worried about?"

"They've linked the research facility that burned down in Atlanta to the monkey."

"I thought they were different companies," I said. "The research facility was manufacturing vaccines and owned by U-Lab. The monkey came from Signal Enterprises."

"It appears that the monkey came from U-Lab in Atlanta and was re-homed in Washington at Signal Enterprises."

"Was it already infected when it traveled north? How did they ship it?"

"Working on it, Ellie." Caine's gravelly growl deepened. "One other thing. Iain Campbell was killed crossing the road after coming out of the Watergate Office complex."

"Yeah, I know."

"Do you know what's underneath that building?"

"No."

"A black hole."

"A what now?"

"A high-security underground research facility housing some of the most dangerous viruses and bacteria known." The grumble in his voice vibrated the speaker. "The thing with that facility is it's not Government funded and therefore doesn't have to adhere to our rules regarding physical security."

"You're kidding me."

Kurt shook his head. "He's not, Iverson. BSL-3 and BSL-4 labs receiving government funding have a set of rules they must follow to keep microbes from escaping and to prevent staff from becoming ill. Private facilities need a lock on the door. The government is more concerned with their paperwork than viral containment protocols."

BS what now? "Explain the BSL thing please."

"Biosafety level three is for microbes we can cure or vaccinate against. BSL-4 is for things that will kill us and keep on killing us."

"Things that will kill us. What about things designed to kill us, weaponized anthrax and so forth?"

"They're included."

"Nice. And the Watergate facility, Caine?"

"BSL-4. Before funding was cut four months ago, they were working on weaponizing human pathogens."

"So it's been shut down?" I said.

"No. Government funding was stopped. They're now funded privately. It's still a BSL-4 lab but there are no rules ... as long as that door is locked it's all rainbows and lollipops."

Right in Washington. Damn. "Surely they wouldn't have removed all security procedures that were already in place?"

"We don't know."

"What do we know?"

"That Iain Campbell left the building and was killed. We picked him up on a foyer elevator camera. He exited from the private elevator that goes down to the lab facility."

"What was Iain doing over there?"

"Trying to find out. He didn't say anything to you?"

"Haven't heard from him for a month or more."

"I'll keep on it, Ellie. You all right down there?"

"Yes. I'd like you here as soon as possible. Eventually, we need to make an announcement regarding Director O'Hare's death and it should come from you."

"I saw the announcement regarding the treatment and discharge. You have an acceptable reason for that?"

"Yeah, I don't want whoever is behind this to know they succeeded, yet."

"All right. Be careful."

"Always."

"I'll spend another few hours working on the Campbell Watergate situation then drive down to meet you all," he said with a deeper than normal growl. "Where?"

"We're on the O'Hare estate. Ethan wants us there and won't hear of us moving our base to a hotel in Lexington. I'll suggest we use Sean's home to give Ethan and Quinn some time to adjust to their new normal." Sean's house was as big as Cait and Ethan's, it made sense to transfer over there.

"I'll come to the O'Hare property. We can look at any arrangements that need making when I'm there."

"Be safe, Caine. Make sure you wash your hands. A

lot."

Chapter Thirty

Reunion

Chickens. All over the driveway. Pecking away. Kurt slowed the car to a crawl. One chicken took notice. Its beady black eyes stared at the car then it resumed its pecking. Kurt braked.

"I didn't know the O'Hares kept chickens," Kurt said.

Argo whined from the backseat. He moved from side to side and stared out of each window at the chickens.

"Me neither."

Made me wonder if they were planning on moving back here permanently, and soon. Maybe that had something to do with Cait letting Joey go? Perhaps she planned on spending more time here and didn't need him. Could the answer be that simple?

I opened my door and climbed out. Flapping my arms and walking to shoo the chickens to the house. "Come on, girls, let's go. Driveways are not for ladies like you."

A rattling noise caught their attention. The flock stopped, heads cocked at the noise which moved in our direction and sounded as though it originated around the side of the house near the back door. As the noise came closer the chickens ran to greet the rattler. Ethan, rattling a box of something they obviously wanted to eat.

He called out, "One of these chickens is smart. They got the back gate open."

"Clearly, those chickens are organized," I said and laughed as he pied-pipered them round the back of the house leaving the driveway clear. "I'll walk," I said to Kurt leaning into the car before I shut my door. Argo whined and watched me as Kurt drove on with him still in the car.

As I walked along the driveway, I heard more noises, this time not chickens. The double doors to the living room opened, Mitch stepped out carrying a baby in each arm. I picked up my pace and he walked down to meet me. The girls babbled as they saw me. I scooped Grace from Mitch's arm and kissed Isabella on the head. Mitch stooped a little to kiss me.

"Glad you're back. I'm getting multiple reports from D.C. of a flu outbreak."

"Could be seasonal and nothing to worry about," I said with a half a smile. I shifted Grace in my arms. She hooked her tiny fingers into my hair and held tight. "Who's talking flu in D.C.?"

"My brother said we've got fourteen staff out sick as of this afternoon."

Shit, that's a lot. "You offer vaccines, yes?"

He nodded. "That's why this is concerning. Has it started, El?"

"Sounding like it." I shifted Grace again and unwound her fingers from my ponytail. "Meanwhile, there is a real possibility that one of the people responsible for Cait's death worked here on the property until she fired him recently." I shivered and cuddled Grace tighter as we walked to the house. "Let's go inside."

Mitch scanned the driveway. "That person could be out here?"

"Yeah. I'd say it was a possibility. We released a press statement saying Cait was treated and discharged. Which means the killer thinks she's still alive."

A sharp crack rang out. Before my brain caught up, I thrust Grace into Mitch's arms and drew my weapon. I spun on my heels and scanned the area as he hurried through the door with the babies.

Seamus Kennedy appeared in Mitch's place. Gun in hand. "What is it?" he said, we both crouched below the front steps.

Freyja tore up the pasture, galloping hard to the woods. I watched for a moment. Dark splatters flew off her as she ran. "She's bleeding," I muttered. "This is unfortunate."

"Someone shot at the horse?"

"I dunno, but she's bleeding and I'm pretty sure that was a gunshot." It was definitely a gunshot.

Another crack rang out. Dust puffed on the driveway about five yards in front of us.

"Definitely gunfire." Kennedy grabbed my hand. "Inside, now."

We ran. A bullet hit the steps with a small thud as the door shut behind us.

"Mitch!"

He moved into view. He was in the hallway behind the living room with the babies, Argo, and Kurt. "We're here, we're okay."

"There's a tunnel entrance in the downstairs office. Grab what we need for the babies in case we have to leave."

Kurt spoke, "Stay here, I'll go up and get everything. It's not rocket science ... I can figure it out."

Mitch thanked him. Dane took Kurt's place. Argo paced the hallway. A yell came from the backyard. Ethan.

"Stay here, Kennedy. No one comes in the front door." I hurried to the kitchen. Moose covered the back door. "Sean?"

"He went to his place," Stu replied. "Ethan is out back."

"Armed?"

"With chicken feed."

No, then. Maybe he'd have a shot if they were geese out back not chickens. Scary mother fucker guard geese. "Kennedy is in the living room. Dane, Mitch, the babies, and Argo are in the hallway downstairs. Kurt's gone upstairs."

"Quinn. Ethan's kid. He was in here a few minutes ago."

I spun around. "Quinn! Quinn!"

No sign of Quinn as I checked the surgery, pantry, bathroom, and living room. I walked back into the kitchen, shut the door, and a bullet shattered the window over the sink. Glass shards flew everywhere, missing me by about a foot.

Stu shook glass from his hair and removed pieces from

his clothes.

"Are you hurt?"

"Nah." He flapped his arm sending sparkly pieces of glass raining to the floor.

The curtain blew in the cold breeze from the gaping hole, then snagged on jagged glass. Another shot hit the wooden window frame.

Stu and I dropped to the ground, keeping well below the kitchen windows. Glass crunched as we duckwalked to meet each other near the table. We stood up, moved chairs, and sat at the table.

"One shooter?" I said, flinching as another round hit the wall outside.

"It could be our guy."

"Yeah. What the fuck is he playing at?"

"Let's go stop him and find out?"

"Commendable proposition," I said with a hasty smile.

A voice from the hallway said, "It's an abysmal idea. Stay put." Sounded like Dane but I wasn't certain.

"Dane?"

"Coming in." He joined us at the table. "Well ventilated in here." His eyes rested on the torn flapping curtain and the glinting glass on the floor.

"We can get out, right?" Stu said, with a raised eyebrow in my direction.

"There's a tunnel. So, yeah. We can get out in two directions. To Sean's or to the woods." Because everyone needs a tunnel system under their house for emergencies or sieges. James Bond wishes he had houses like these.

"We leave Kennedy and Lee to hold the house and go get this prick," Stu said.

"No, we don't," Lee said, walking into the room. He stopped and chose his path with care to avoid sharp pieces of window remnants. "People should stop shooting at us."

"Where were you?" I said.

"Bathroom."

I smiled. "I knew you were somewhere."

A bullet smashed another window but this time not in the kitchen.

"Enough of this. We don't need a siege situation with some fucktarded gunman," Lee said with a grumble.

Crying in the hallway reached me. I closed my eyes for a split second. Isabella. She wanted feeding. If she were hungry then Grace would be as well. I heard Mitch talking but not the words. I stood, ducked my head a bit and hurried to the fridge. I swung the door open picked up two bottles from a shelf with one hand and counted how many were left. Four.

Something hit the door and vibrated it in my hand.

"Ellie, get away from there," Dane said.

I shoved the door closed and noticed a hole. Oops. Ideally, I would warm the bottles but I knew that wasn't going to happen. I scurried to the back of the room. Tucking the bottles under one arm, I extracted my phone from my pocket and made a call.

Kevin answered on the fifth ring.

"We're out at the O'Hare property and have a spot of

trouble."

Silence followed. Then a sigh. "Last time you said something similar to me—"

"I know. We have a shooter out here. Whoever it is, has pinned us inside the house. Ethan and Quinn are unaccounted for."

"I'll round up the troops. Staties?"

"Couldn't hurt."

"You know the drill. Keep your head down. I'll let you know when we arrive."

"Come in quietly, Kev."

"Will do."

I hung up and shoved my phone back in my pocket then slipped out into the hallway.

"Hey," I whispered, taking Isabella from Mitch and leaving a bottle in her place. "Shh." I cradled Isabella and made a decision. "We should take them down to the tunnel."

Kurt rocked Grace as he walked up and down the hallway. "That's a fine idea."

"I gave Kevin a heads-up. He's bringing state police with him."

"Okay. Now let's get these babies to safety," Kurt said.

Mitch pushed the bottle he held into Isabella's bag. I handed him the other bottle and watched him stow it in the same bag. Teamwork.

"Make it happen," I said to Kurt. "It'll be safer underground."

Kurt shook his head at me. "You go with Mitch. I'll

follow."

For a split second, the old Ellie reared her head and readied for a fight. Isabella sucked noisily on her fist. Old Ellie shrank back into the shadows. Life won. On the floor by the stairs was Isabella's bag, I bent down and picked it up. Mitch hooked up Grace's bag then took Grace from Kurt. Kurt picked the babies' cuddle rugs from the banister and tucked one around Isabella, then one around Grace. Good thinking.

"Let's go," I said. Isabella grizzled but gave the impression she was content enough for the moment. Thank goodness. I held Isabella tighter and opened the hidden door in the office. It was somewhat familiar. We had a similar setup at home except our hidden door went to a panic room. "Argo! Go!"

The dog ran past me and down the stairs. I followed him and paused at the top of the steep stairs to run my hand along the wall. My fingers connected with the light switch and the stairs flooded with a yellow glow. Mitch followed me down. At the bottom, I moved a few yards into the tunnel and waited. An arrow on the wall facing the stairs pointed to an S, another arrow pointed in the opposite direction to the word 'woods.'

If we went to the woods I knew we would come to a small room that contained survival equipment. Maybe something I should tell Mitch. "Babe, if something happens, something I can't control. If you go that way," I pointed, "there's a room near the end with survival gear. If anything turns to shit, take Argo and go. Promise me."

"Cavalry is coming, right?"

"Sort of."

If Beau Bennett and Walt Longmire's love child and his deputies the Keystone Cops could be referred to as a cavalry.

As much as I loved watching *The Ranch* and *Longmire*, I didn't need Kevin turning into some weird compilation of Beau and Walt. Especially when Kevin was no spring chicken. The weirdness scale slid along another few notches.

Mitch smiled. Calmness washed over me. "It'll be okay, El."

Yeah. It will. I hope. "Promise me if this gets out of hand that you'll go."

He gazed deep into my eyes. "I'll keep our girls safe. I'll take Argo. We'll go to the woods."

"Thank you." I turned in the direction of the S. "This way, babe."

S stood for Sean. We could get into the house, as long as the code was still the same. The house would be the best option for the babies.

I said to Mitch. "We're going to Sean's."

"Is he there?" Mitch asked, falling into step next to me.

Argo brushed my leg to remind me he was there and waiting for instructions. "Argo, point."

The dog moved ahead of us at a trot until he was far enough ahead to warn of danger.

"I don't know. You would've seen Sean last, Mitch."

"Haven't seen him since you went into Lexington. I

don't think any cars left but yours."

"He's probably at home then." I adjusted my hold on Isabella, tucking the rug closer around her. She squawked and grabbed at my hair again. "Shhh, it'll be okay little one. Mommy will feed you soon."

Soundproofed underground, I had no idea what was happening up top. By the time we got to the stairs that led to the entrance to Sean's place, I was antsy and desperate to find out what was happening. Argo ran up the stairs and back down. Guess he was antsy too.

Sudden running feet behind us chilled me to the core. I pushed Mitch gently to the stairs. "Go. The code is seven-seven-four-two." He took Isabella and her bag from me and juggling babies and baby bags, he moved quickly up the stairs.

I slid my Glock from my holster and leaned back against the wall beside the stairs. Argo stood alert next to me. It's Kurt. It's gotta be Kurt. While I forced calm into my body, my index finger moved on and off the trigger. Breathe. Deep breath in. Hold. Long slow breath out.

The footfalls slowed. Argo leaned on my leg. His ears pricked, head cocked.

"Iverson!"

Kurt. Argo gave me his patented side-glance. I flicked my hand into the depths of the tunnel. He ran.

"Over here," I said, letting my voice carry into the dimly lit tunnel. The words followed Argo, bouncing on the tip of his tail.

Kurt's feet pounded as he ran again. I waited until I

saw him and Argo before holstering my weapon. A small cry trickled down the stairs. I turned to face the sound. My foot hit the second stair before Kurt joined me. Argo squeezed his hairy self in next to me.

"What's happening up top?" I asked, walking one stair above Kurt.

"Lee thinks there are two shooters."

"Two? Joey has a friend?"

"Maybe."

I heard something in his voice. He didn't believe it was Joey. The door loomed in front of us. Closed. No sign of Mitch. At least he was in the house. I knocked twice, pressed in the code and opened the door. Warmth, light, distant gunfire. Two of those things were great. "Hello!"

An answer came from deep within the house. "In the living room, El," Sean said.

Kurt closed the door and followed Argo and me through the house. Mitch was on the sofa with both babies in his lap. Argo nudged him and then the babies; he did a quick patrol of the area then flopped onto the floor. Sean leaned near a picture window that overlooked his front garden and driveway, watching outside. His reflection showed the stress on his face that his posture tried to hide.

"You okay, El?" Sean said without turning around.

I squinted into the reflection of his face. "Yeah, I'm fine. Is Ethan here?"

He shook his head.

Fuck.

"Thought he was with you."

"I saw him leading the chickens back to the yard but haven't seen him since. Gunshots happened within minutes of Ethan taking the chickens off the driveway."

"Was Quinn next door?"

"Didn't see him. I hope he's with his dad."

Sean nodded.

"Are we getting backup?"

"Yep. State police and Mauryville's finest are on the way out."

"I'll go find Ethan and my nephew," Sean said. "Make yourselves at home."

"You want help?" Kurt said.

"No. Stay here with El, Mitch, and the babies. They need your gun more than I do." Kurt squared his shoulders. Sean must've sensed the argument building. "I'm quicker on my own. This is our home. I know where I'm going and can get around without drawing any attention."

Kurt nodded. "Sure. Call me if you need help." He made a phone sign with his fingers, Sean nodded and left the room.

Until that moment I'd never thought of the O'Hare's property as anything but their home, but it was way more than that. It's a sprawling compound without the security at the gate. Memories wriggled and squirmed. There was security. It was low key in as far as there was no gatehouse or guard to pass but the property had cameras. Everywhere.

"Kurt, somewhere there is a control room. There are cameras everywhere outside. I don't know if Sean's system will let us see video feed from Cait's place, but ..."

"Worth a shot. I'll find the control room. Yell if you need me."

Isabella screwed her face up and cried. Her patience had run out. Bottles. Where were the bottles?

"Mitch?"

"In the bag. I dropped them both in Grace's bag."

I unzipped the bag and fished out both bottles. I set one on the sofa next to him and took Isabella.

"Come on little one." Dropping the bag I had onto the floor, I sank into the sofa near Mitch and uncapped the bottle. They were still cold although not fridge cold. Not that Isabella cared. She sucked hungrily.

Before long, the room was filled with thirsty sucking noises in stereo. I tried to relax and enjoy the cuddles and feeding time but my mind had other ideas. I silenced the noise and focused on Stu. Trying to get an idea of what was going on. The pictures I saw in my mind were scrambled. Jumbled pieces of chaos. Unacceptable.

Gunshots. Broken glass. A dead chicken. What the actual fuck? I didn't need another dead chicken in Mauryville. At least this one wasn't nailed to a door. The chicken lay on the driveway near the back door. Return fire. Freyja galloped around the paddock. Panicked. She kept trying for the woods but turning back. What would turn her back from her escape route? Another shooter?

I tucked Isabella's bottle under my chin and wriggled

my phone from my jacket pocket.

"Hey, Siri, call Kennedy."

"Calling Kennedy."

Nothing happened for a few seconds then the phone rang and Kennedy answered.

"The horse keeps trying for the woods and turning back. There could be another shooter there."

"Thanks. We have two pinned down." A small laugh followed his words. "One is using the stable and one is in the cover of the trees at the edge of the driveway."

"What the hell is happening, Kennedy?"

"No idea, Iverson, but whatever this is, it is not the best."

"Keep your head down, look after Dane and Stu. Sean is trying to find Ethan and Quinn. Where's Lee?"

"He's on the end of a rifle at the other side of the house."

"Stay alert and stay safe."

"I'll keep an eye on the team."

I pressed the end call button and went back to holding the bottle with my hand.

Chapter Thirty One
We don't run

Mitch lifted Grace to his shoulder. Within a few minutes, she let loose a gigantic burp and smiled groggily in my direction.

Battle noises broke the calm of Sean's living room. Hooves thundered. Shots rang out. My brain skittered sideways into a civil war reenactment then bounced back with force as reality hit me. The fight was close. There was a little over a mile separating the houses, but it sounded like twenty yards. Hooves pounded on the cold hard ground. She was panicked and looking for shelter. I took a breath. Isabella pulled away from the bottle. Finished. I put it on the floor and lifted her. Patting her back I stood. She burped. Mitch held his free hand out to me. Cradling Isabella in my arms, I bent and kissed Mitch.

"I have to go out there," I whispered.

"I know. Give her here."

"Will you be all right?"

"Of course. We'll be fine." He smiled. "We're safe here, El. You go do your thing."

Kurt's voice rang out from somewhere to my left. I smiled at Mitch and followed the sound of Kurt's voice. Argo walked next to me until I got to the hall doorway.

"Stay with Mitch," I said, patting his head. "Guard."

Argo spun around, his tail wrapped around my leg as he moved. I watched for a second. He paced the edges of the room then sat on the floor next to Mitch. I breathed. Argo would do his best to keep them safe.

Kurt called out again.

"I'm coming," I replied.

He was in a spacious office. Kurt saw me as I entered. "There could be more than three shooters."

"Crap on a cracker." I moved a chair out and sat down next to him. On the wall above the desk were three big screens, labeled at the top. Cait, stables, Sean. Each screen showed video footage from various cameras. Four feeds per screen.

"Look at the screen in the middle. There's a camera that faces the woods from the stable on the bottom right."

I watched. "Where's the horse?"

"Running free somewhere. She jumped the fence a little while ago."

"Is that a person?" I pointed to a shadowy area at the edge of the woods. Wasn't the best image. The shape was almost out of camera range.

"Yeah. I saw the person move before ... think there are two of them over there."

Kurt had his phone on the desk. Lee's face lit the screen. I reached over and slid the green icon right then touched the speaker icon. "Lee, okay?"

"We all need rifles and this needs to end," Lee said with practiced calm.

"Cavalry is coming," I said. "We need to hold them off

for a little while longer."

"How many shooters do you estimate we have?" Lee's voice trailed off. Then it was back with a vengeance. "I've had eyes on two in the last half hour."

"Maybe four," Kurt replied.

I watched the screens. Movement at the top caught my eye. For a second I thought it was a police car then I realized it wasn't. "Fuckadoodledo."

Kurt looked up. I did a silent count while watching the footage from the driveway camera.

"Five armed men climbed out of an SUV up by the driveway entrance," Kurt said.

"Get word to the others. Hold your positions as long as you can," I said.

I blew air out of my mouth and tugged my phone from my pocket. We were going to need more than the Keystone Cops and state police.

I scrolled quickly through recent calls and tapped Andrews' name. He answered fast.

"How can I help, Iverson?"

"Be airborne in twenty and break the sound barrier getting to Mauryville?"

"That doesn't sound ideal." Over the phone, I heard movement. "What's going on?" He gave instructions while walking.

"We're on the wrong side of a siege down at Cait O'Hare's property. Local and state police are on the way. FBI SWAT would be helpful."

"Let me translate that for my boys." His attempt to

muffle his voice failed. "Wheels up in fifteen. Iverson needs a hand."

A voice I recognized shot back, "Nah, she needs a rifle. Bringing it!"

My smile returned. "Make it ten and tell Dixon that would be useful, thanks."

We needed some vantage points. My mind scoured possibilities. Barn roof. Stable roof. Can I get up on Sean's roof?

"See you soon. I'm dispatching THU as well. Their flying time is shorter. Stay safe."

Lee's voice echoed from Kurt's phone. "Andrews and THU. I almost feel sorry for these gun-toting lunatics."

I watched the screens as armed men dispersed. One glance at my watch told me Kev and his team would drive right into a trap. I called him. "Hey, a carload of armed men arrived, they've set up along the driveway in the trees."

His phone crackled. Man, I love the countryside and dodgy reception.

"Ellie, we'll drive in across the fields on the northeast side of the property."

The woods are northeast. There's no driving in from there. I chewed my bottom lip and let his words take shape.

South West, walk in across the field. That made more sense. I needed to tell Kev I'd contacted D.C. and that the cavalry was coming. Time for a little game I like to call, 'How well do you know Ellie?'

"You know what'd work right now? Music. Oh yeah. I'd like to hear some Rick Springfield."

"What song tickles your fancy, kid?"

"I'm partial to 'My Last Heartbeat,' put it on for me. " Come on, Kev, you can do this.

"Marge showed me how this fandangled phone plays music." Music flowed. He did it. Right after Springfield mentioned the cavalry coming, Kev stopped the song. "Thanks for the song recommendation. I appreciate your thoughtfulness."

"You're welcome."

For a second I wondered how well Kev knew the property but I didn't want to mention tunnels over the phone. Kev talking in circles meant he wasn't happy with saying much over the phone either.

I hung up, put my phone on the desk, and watched the screens. There was a lot of activity.

"There!" I pointed at a screen that showed the driveway immediately in front of Cait's home. A man walked across the driveway to the stable. "What's he wearing? What is on his back?"

The man paused for a second and stared over his shoulder. Kurt snapped a photo of him then enlarged it on his phone.

Another car drove into the driveway. Another five men exited the vehicle, taking long guns with them. Shotguns or rifles or both.

"And?" I said. Waiting for information on the man on the driveway.

"It's a patch. He's a gang member."

"What the fuck is going on here?" I leaned back in the chair. What were the odds of coming across a gang after our gang experience in Lexington, I wondered. "Which gang?"

He passed me his phone so I could see the logo on the patch. A snarling wolf's head with red dripping from its fangs. A snarling blue wolf's head with red fangs. The words 'The Alpha Brotherhood' arched over the top of the wolf. Underneath was Richmond. I had never seen the patch before. Nor had I heard of The Alpha Brotherhood. But coming across another gang so soon after meeting Emmett from The Inferno Jesters didn't feel like a coincidence.

"Are these idiots bikers or a street gang?" I mumbled passing the phone back. "And what the actual fuck?"

Kurt swiveled to look at me. "We need someone who deals with gangs." Without another word, he called work and asked for Claude Finklestein, then tapped the speaker icon. "What do you know about a gang calling themselves The Alpha Brotherhood, they seem to have claimed Richmond?"

"Kurt. We heard there's trouble down yonder. You all right?"

"For now. Tell me about this gang?"

The sound of fingers on a keyboard filled the room before Claude said, "They haven't been around long, five years tops. They're bikers. Affiliated with some of the bigger gangs. They come under the protection of The

Inferno Jesters."

Well, hello connection.

Four more patched men crossed a camera. This was serious. "No motorbikes that we've seen or heard, Claude," I said. "We could have fifteen men out here."

"They'll have stashed their motorcycles somewhere. The last skirmish they got into, they stashed their bikes in a warehouse they owned and traveled in rented cars."

"We came across some of The Inferno Jesters in Lexington earlier today. They were driving black SUVs."

"I saw mention of the Jesters in Lexington in a report on Law Enforcement Online, they're being held on a raft of charges with more pending, mostly drug related and one member had family violence charges pending."

Yes! That should keep Emmett off the street for a while.

"Can you find out if they own or have access to somewhere they could stash bikes down in Rockbridge?"

"They hail from Richmond, anything to suggest they didn't drive the whole way in the cars?"

"No."

More keys tapped. "Bikers were seen traveling west from Richmond last night. There's a police report. Apparently, twenty members of The Alpha Brotherhood and fourteen Inferno Jesters cruised into Rockbridge County two-thirty in the a.m. Six bikers were arrested at Stonewall Jackson Hospital. Two of the bikers arrested were Inferno Jesters, the others were Alpha Brotherhood." He paused. Fingers tapped keys. "The rest have not been seen since they arrived in town in the early hours."

"That's a lot of trouble to vanish into the ether," Kurt said. We watched the screens as more gunshots resounded. "There is no way those guys out there know how many of us are inside or who is inside."

"I'm going through files to see if I can find out what they're doing out there. I'll call you back as soon as I get something."

"While you're at it, see if you can find their motorbikes. Solid opportunity to get some trackers on them."

"Yes, it is. I'll see what we can do."

"Thanks, Claude."

Kurt touched the red icon with his index finger and ended the call.

We needed a meeting. We needed a strategy and we needed to tally up the weapons available. Looking up I saw the injured horse gallop across a screen, foam flying from her back. As soon as practical, I'd find a way to stable her and get Doc Robinson out.

Mass text time. I opened an app we use when we're not sure how secure our communications are and linked everyone to the message: The shooters are members of The Alpha Brotherhood and The Inferno Jesters motorcycle clubs. Thirty-four bikers crossed into Rockbridge during the night. Six were arrested today in Lexington.

Another two cars arrived. More men, more weapons. A

small cry from the living room sent a shiver up my spine. Bikers, weapons, and babies do not go together. A knot formed in my gut and tightened. Did I need to get back into Cait's house and get those last two baby bottles from the fridge before the babies needed feeding again? Bits and pieces of the night and morning slid into place in my mind. I'd made the bottles. Where did I put the formula? Back in Grace's bag. A sigh of relief washed over me. Those bottles can stay in the drafty kitchen at Cait's. We'll be fine.

I sent another group text: That means there are twenty-four bikers unaccounted for by local LEOs. There's a chance they're here. We need a strategy meeting. Stay alert. I'll be in touch.

Twenty-four armed bikers. Eight armed people in the house. The odds were in their favor, three to one. It was worse than that. Not all eight could be warriors today. We needed to protect civilians. We might be outgunned but we're not outsmarted.

We got this.

Chapter Thirty Two

Surrender

Twenty-four bikers. "Kurt, he said thirty-four?"

"Yes."

"We can account for maybe twenty-four here, and six in holding cells. Where are the other four?"

"More are here or more are coming?"

I nodded. "Both."

Sean's voice rang down the hallway, followed by exclamations of irritation, the noise exploded into the room. "Henderson!"

Kurt jumped to his feet and took off out of the door running to the commotion. I followed. Catching up, it was easy to see the cause of the distress and urgency in Sean's voice. Ethan, supported by young Quinn and Sean, blood spreading across the right side of his shirt.

Dammit, this was not ideal.

Kurt relieved Quinn. "Quinn, go find my bag. In the living room."

Quinn ran.

"My room," Sean said, steering Ethan to the expansive hallway. "It's the closest."

I ducked under Sean's arm and grabbed Ethan. "Go," I said. "We've got him."

Ethan grunted but said nothing. Sean paused; for the first time since I'd met him, he faltered, unsure of his next step.

I let Ethan go at the edge of the bed, Kurt helped him sit, then tossed the pillows across the bed onto the floor on the far side. Supporting his shoulders, Kurt encouraged Ethan to lie back. He struggled to get his legs onto the bed.

Quinn spoke from the doorway. "Your bag."

Kurt walked over and took it from the young man. "You want to stay?"

Quinn wavered. Indecision flowed over this face. Ethan rolled his head to see his son. "Quinn Jameson James, Go, Get out of here."

Indecision became frustration and annoyance.

"Don't tell me what to do, not now," he said, his voice hardened. "I'm not a child." The young man planted his feet and squared his shoulders.

"You're pre-med, right?" Kurt said, opening up his bag and not looking at him.

"No. I've completed my third year in medical school."

Kurt continued unpacking his bag. "You've done the OSCE?"

"Yes."

"Explain please," I said watching Kurt place items in sterile packages in a line on a blue plastic sheet.

"OSCE is Objective Structured Clinical Examination, it's given at the end of the third year of med school and is used to assess clinical skills and competencies," Quinn said.

"Thank you."

"What was your elective surgery?" Kurt glanced at me with an eyebrow raised.

I knew that look. The kid might be useful after all.

Ethan moved.

"Stay still, Dad," Quinn said, he crossed the room to his bedside in three strides and placed a hand on Ethan's shoulder. "I'm staying. I'll assist." Quinn directed himself to Kurt. "Elective surgery was ENT. I could probably take out his tonsils." The kid grinned at his father.

"Leave the dad jokes to me, Quinn," Ethan said with a feeble attempt at a laugh.

Quinn smiled. "And did a two-week elective in geriatrics."

Ethan groaned. "I'm not that old."

"Other than Geriatrics and ENT, I did six weeks of general surgery."

"That's more like it," Ethan mumbled.

"You're assisting me," Kurt said to Quinn. "We'll go slow and steady. Anything you're not sure about, ask."

"Got it."

"If you two don't need me, I'll go back to check the cameras," I said.

"We'll let you know if we need you back. Don't go too far," Kurt said. "I'd prefer to do this in the other house in the surgery. See if that's possible, Iverson."

"I will." My head shook. Kurt knew it wasn't going to happen.

I left Ethan in capable hands; with or without a surgery, Kurt would do all he could.

Chapter Thirty Three

Dream Police

My phone rang in my hand. I glanced at the screen as I walked. Lee. Touching the green icon, I spoke before he could. "Ethan was wounded."

"I know. This is getting out of hand."

Battle sounds permeated the house sneaking in through closed windows, rattling the panes. It was also closer to us. I stuck my head around the living room door to see Mitch pacing the middle of the room. The babies were asleep in a comfortable armchair close to the interior wall. He'd pushed two of Sean's big leather red armchairs together to create a makeshift crib. Problem-solving since forever.

I leaned on the hall side of the wall and talked to Lee. "How are you doing?"

"Hanging in there. Kennedy and I are keeping a lid on the area surrounding the house."

A shot rang out. Glass smashed. Sure sounded like they were keeping a lid on it. "Any glass left?"

Lee laughed. "Not a lot."

That was comforting. Glass is replaceable people are not. "Listen out for the helicopters. I haven't heard back from Andrews, but I doubt I'll hear until they're close."

"Everything okay over there?"

"So far so we're doing fine. Mitch is antsy."

"Not surprising, Chicky."

I closed my eyes for a second, conjuring Sam in my mind. If ever there was a time that Delta needed SSA Sam Jackson, it was now. His deep voice rumbled in my head. "You got this, Chicky Babe. Have a little faith."

For a split second, Sam's smile lit the dark within. I got this. "Where's the horse?"

"Lost sight of her about half an hour ago."

"Squirrel and Moose? They've been real quiet."

"Dane was worried about the horse, that occupied him a bit. The four of us have a corner of the house each. They're okay, Ellie."

"Let's keep it that way." It'd be bad form to lose the two newest members of Delta so soon. I heard a clink then the sound of a magazine pushed home, which led to my next question. "Ammo?"

"We got plenty. Found O'Hare's stash in the office."

"Keep in touch. Stay safe."

I hung up, swung around the doorway and came face to face with Mitch. He wasn't smiling but he was okay, that much I knew. I saw a firearm in a holster on his belt. I knew he could and would use it, which was even better.

"Any news?" He took a step closer. Blue eyes searched mine.

"Not yet. Ethan is wounded. Kurt and Quinn are tending to his injuries as best they can here. Delta and Kennedy are holding their own. Bikers are firing indiscriminately at the house."

His right eyebrow rose. "Indiscriminately?"

I nodded. "If they had a plan they haven't executed it. There are enough of them that they could take both houses. They haven't. Sure, maybe they don't know how many of us there are. But they're firing from cover, mostly, and shooting up the house." I had a feeling Ethan's wounding was more wrong-place-wrong-time than someone trying to take him out. Considering what was happening around us, that was a pretty weird thought. I stuck by it.

"Maybe that is the plan?"

"Pretty stupid if it is. They have to know reinforcements are on the way." Oh, shit. Kevin. Did I tell him more bikers arrived?

I glanced at my phone in my hand and watched as it rang. Kevin's name sat on the screen surrounded by the noise of the default iPhone ringtone.

Mitch grinned. "Love when you do that."

Yeah, me too. Not. "Kev."

"Hey, kid. Thought seeing you like honey so much, I'd get you some of old man Parker's special reserve to take back home with you. What do you say? About eight jars do you?"

Nothing I'd hate more. Which gave me pause. Kev was telling me something. I needed to pay attention.

"Eight jars sounds perfect. What's so special about that honey?"

"He tells me it comes from a rare flower that grows in his southwest pasture. Healthy for animals too, I hear."

"Would that flower work for a dog that's scared of

storms?" Silence. Come on, Kev, you got this.

"Sure would. That ol' dog of yours would love the healing properties of this honey. Mr. P swears by it."

"Watch out for her, will you? She was chasing a rabbit and hasn't come back."

"I'll put the word out. Maybe she's gone visiting. Friendly soul, that pooch."

"Had a bit of thunder out this way, probably frightened her."

"No doubt. I'm sure she's fine. But I'll keep an eye out in town in case she comes mooching around after the contents of my cookie jar."

I let all the conversation filter through my mind. Eight jars of honey became eight horses. If Freyja had run southwest, she'd see them and probably join them. If she ran south, she'd still hear the horses. I hoped if she did, she'd find them. She'd need comfort and all the horses roundabout knew each other. There was a full-on Western about to unfold. The cavalry was actually coming. Holy gun smoke. "Let me know if you see her."

"Of course. I'll send a picture of her happily munching cookies."

"Thanks." I hung up. Send a picture. If we could get some images of the area then I could send pictures to Kev and his posse, as well as SWAT and THU., Make it better for everyone. Zero surprises. Could I do that? I could if Mitch had a drone in the car. There was a fair chance. He more often than not had a prototype he was testing in the trunk when he arrived home from work. He didn't expect me to ask him to come here so maybe he hadn't taken all his stuff out of the trunk before heading down.

Yes. Yes. I could do this. An idea hatched. It was dangerous but damn if it worked it'd be worth it. I stuffed my phone in my back pocket and looked up at Mitch. His eyes widened.

"No." His head shook. "No. El. No."

So he does have a drone in the car then. "We need it."

"You cannot get to the car."

Pretty sure I can. "Let's say I could. What else would I need besides the drone case?"

"Spare batteries."

"Trunk?"

"Glove compartment."

My mind darted over the scenario. I needed to get into the trunk and the glove compartment. Okay, I can do that. "How big is the drone case?"

"Thirteen by ten inches and I'd say four inches deep."

If I could reach it from the backseat, I could probably pull it out the pass-through.

The rear seat of our car is designed with a built-in armrest and cup holder. It folds back into the seat when not in use. If it is in use, the center seat cannot be used. Usually we don't use the armrest because that's where Argo sits. I listened to the voice in my head explain how to use the pass-through and tried to put a face to the voice, with that the voice became an instructional video complete with a mechanic who resembled Christopher Chance.

"To use the armrest, simply fold it down out of the seat back. To use the pass-through:

1.   Slide the knob on the cover downward.

2.   Pull up on the cover.

This will open the pass-through allowing access to the trunk from the back seat."

Chance straightened up and stared into the camera. "PS: Your death wish is showing. Just stay safe and wait for the cavalry."

His laughter bounced around my skull as the video ended.

Okay. I got this.

Mitch grabbed my hand. "You can't."

Actually, I can. What I can't do is ask any of the men to wriggle their bulky selves into the back of our car and reach into the trunk. None of them are under six foot and none of them are thin enough. Muscle is bulky. I doubted Lee or Kennedy would be able to get their arms into the pass-through and bring their hand out with the drone case. Visions of Winnie the Pooh with his hand stuck in a honeypot sprang to mind. It'd be exactly like that. I controlled the urge to smile.

Logic then. "I'm the smallest person here, no one else can conceal themselves in the footwell in the back of the car or bring the case back out the pass-through." My eyes searched his for a moment. "You know it's true."

"Getting to the car, it's suicide."

"I sure hope not. I'm taking Argo. He'll watch for me."

"This is insane."

"We need that drone. It gives us an advantage. We have cops on horseback coming in, we have helicopters coming in. I have a feeling they'll hear the choppers and open fire. If we have a bird's eye view—"

"I know, I know. But I don't want you out there."

"You're reading A.A. Milne to the babies, yes?"

He nodded and I knew he saw where I was going. "You can't stay in your corner of the forest waiting for others to come to you …" Mitch's voice trailed off leaving an empty sadness behind.

"I'll be okay. I've got Argo watching my six." Time to adopt the tone that reminds him this is my job and it's time for me to go do it. "Trust me. We'll go out of Sean's back door. We have a better likelihood of getting to the car from here than going through the tunnel."

His arms circled me and held me close. "Promise me you'll be careful."

"You know I will."

My hair ruffled as he spoke, "That's not a promise. Say the words."

"I promise." My fingers weren't even crossed. Our lips met. Heat bloomed. Oh, I was coming back, simply for more of that. I stepped back and ducked under Mitch's right arm. Both babies slept. Their faces all innocence and calmness. As it should be. I kissed their heads, lightly, so as not to disturb them.

Mitch held my hand until I moved out of the doorway. "Three things," he whispered, as our fingers separated.

"Three things." I eyed the dog next to me. "Come,

Argo."

Chapter Thirty Four
I got friends in low places

At the back door, I switched my phone to silent and checked my weapon. One in the chamber and a full magazine. Two spares magazines on my belt. Argo watched me. Friction bristled in the air. We'd trained for situations like this, and all his training was about to come into play. No vocal instructions. This time I'd use hand signals and facial expressions. His eyes glued to my face, waiting, the excitement coming from the dog palpable. He loved to work.

I took a deep breath and opened the door. The dog crossed the threshold first and waited outside the door while I closed it quietly. I circled a finger at him. He slunk away to check the vicinity. His posture on return told me there was no threat close by. I led the way around the house. Opting for a more cautious approach, I stopped. We had over a mile of ground to cross and needed to keep to cover as much as possible.

Gunfire echoed.

Hugging the wall, I edged along to see if anything was there. Inching ever forward, listening to gunfire. For the most part, it was occasional single shots. Once in position, I held my breath and peered around the corner. Did a quick scan, and then pulled back before exhaling.

Argo used the wall as cover as he slunk around the

garage to the driveway. He came halfway back and waited at the midpoint for me to join him. More shots rang out. Sounded as if they came from near Cait's driveway and the front of the house. Suited me.

Where did I last see Mitch's car? In the vicinity of the back door. He'd parked quite close to the house to allow Ethan and Quinn access to the three-car garage at the back of the house and to keep the shared driveway clear to allow Sean access to his home.

I figured I could get close to the house via the rose garden on the far side of Cait and Ethan's garage. Depending. Time to call Lee and pinpoint an accurate location for him and Kennedy. And I couldn't call. Not if the bikers were intercepting communications. Well, okay, we had no proof they were, but hell, I would. I touched an icon on my screen which opened an app. All calls made through the app were scrambled. Thank you, NSA. All our phone numbers popped up on the screen. I touched Lee's. Seconds later he answered.

"Hey," I whispered. "I'm outside, need to get to Mitch's car. Where are the shooters?"

"All over. Like freaking mushrooms. Every time we form an idea of where they are, another one pops up somewhere else firing like a fuckwit."

Fuckadoodledo. "I have to get to Mitch's car."

"You better have a fantastic reason for flaunting your death wish."

What is it with everyone and the death wish bullshit? I ignored his comment. "There's a drone in the trunk. We need the drone."

"Hell, yeah, we do. And you need a distraction."

"Please."

"Give me a few minutes. You okay wherever you are to wait for a few minutes?"

"Yep. I'll hold here with Argo." I glanced at my watch and noted the time.

"Stay safe, Chicky."

Leaves rustled. Argo's ears twitched and turned. I pocketed my phone and plucked the Glock from my holster as I listened to the noises around us, a weird mix of gunfire and chickens clucking. The chickens were at the back of Cait's house on the far side of the rose garden. Why would they be making noise? It's been my experience that chickens don't much like gunfire and disruption, they'd be more likely to hide than anything. Argo's head turned at the chicken noise. His ears swiveled back and forth.

Why aren't those chickens hiding?

Somewhere inside the farmyard noises, I detected something else. Movement. A person maybe? I watched Argo. He stared at the chicken run obscured by a fence and the back gate. His hackles rose. A low growl rumbled in his throat. I touched his head silencing him. Through the gaps in the fence palings, I saw a moving shadow. Argo took a few steps closer to the gate.

I checked my watch. Two minutes was up. Right on cue, a yell pierced the air from the other side of the house.

The gate moved. My finger slipped onto the trigger. Waiting. Watching. Hinges creaked as the gate widened. Legs came into view. I followed them to a face. Squirrel grinned at me. Over his shoulder, I saw a dark shape. Shit.

Training my weapon at the darkness, Squirrel frowned. Argo growled. Squirrel dove to the right, I fired. The ground vibrated under my feet as the shadow dropped.

"You all right?" I said, not taking my eyes off the shadow.

"Yeah." Dane joined me, brushing his clothes off. We both checked the body. I kicked the weapon the biker had out of the way and nudged the burly man with my foot. No reaction. Not that I expected one. The tidy hole in the middle of his forehead and the brains blown out the back of this head kinda implied sudden death. I leaned down and poked a couple of fingers under his chin seeking a pulse. Nothing. Peachy.

"Headshot or no shot," I muttered, holstering my weapon and searching him for identification. "Help me roll him."

Squirrel and I grabbed the man by the clothes and dragged him to us until he toppled face down on the path with a deadened thud. From his jeans back pocket, I extracted a wallet and tossed it at Squirrel. Argo growled. I scanned the area expecting more trouble. My Glock found its way back to my hand.

"There's a driver's license. Looks like our man. His

name is Gregory Richmond."

All of a sudden Gregory is a popular name. "Wait what?" Greg's a fed.

"Gregory Richmond."

"The hell it is," I said, holding my hand out for the license. Squirrel placed it in my hand. It said Gregory Richmond. And the photo was very similar to our dead man. Guess more than one Gregory Richmond could live in Dinwiddie, Virginia. I scanned around, we were still relatively safe, so I used my phone and accessed headquarters to pull up Gregory Richmond's personnel file. Same date of birth, same address, same height, same eye color, different face.

What the actual fuck?

"Problem?" Squirrel said, looking over my shoulder before looking at me.

"A fake? What else is in that wallet?"

He removed credit cards and bank cards. The credit cards said Gregory Richmond. The bank cards had no names.

"Why fake?"

"Because Greg is a fed and I have a hard job thinking there are two Gregory Richmonds living in the same house in Dinwiddie, especially two with identical everything except their faces."

"I take it Greg doesn't look like that guy?" Squirrel thumbed at the corpse.

"Not at all. Greg's more banker than biker."

Argo jumped the body to get to the gate. Hackles

raised. Teeth bared. Scuffling, running, and a ground-shaking thump.

I glanced at Squirrel. He'd moved back and to the side of the fence. More running feet joined the first set. Squirrel, Argo, and I walked fast but with care toward the objective. Time to leave.

Gunshots ahead of us came from the house. Lee and Kennedy no doubt, laying down cover fire to distract the rest of the gang. Sounded more like engaging than distracting, but as long as the bulk of the bikers stayed focused on the far corner and side of the house, our movements would attract less attention.

Two cars were parked in front of the garage. Mitch's car was harder over by the house than I thought but far enough away from the back door to make the area slightly safer. I needed to cross about fifteen feet of ground to get to the car.

I touched Argo's head, pointed and raised my hand slightly. He turned, his tail swished. Argo walked back a yard or so and stood watching for signs of trouble.

Squirrel nudged me, mentally. My thoughts zeroed in on him. Images filled my mind. The car. The backseat. The pass-through. Once sure he knew my intentions and was on sentry duty, I holstered my Glock and crept across the top of the driveway to the back passenger door of the car. The door opened easily. I controlled the hiss of relief and climbed into the car, closing the door as I went. Without the babies' seats in the car, I had ample room for me to maneuver. I semi-knelt in the footwell and reached to the back of the seat, pulling the middle armrest down with a sharp tug. Squirrel's voice found its way into my brain. "Don't be long."

The interior of the car muffled the gunfire and sounds of breaking glass. Concentrate.

A metallic ping resounded. I turned my head and saw a stream of light flow across the front seat from a new hole. I slid down the panel behind the armrest and peered into the darkness. I could see nothing. Climbing through to the front I broke the beam of light and opened the glove compartment. A bubble pack of batteries. I shoved them into my pocket. Underneath a few maps and receipts, I found the flashlight.

From the backseat, I shone the light into the trunk. The metallic case shone like a puddle of quicksilver in the dark trunk. Satisfied that I knew where it was, I dropped the flashlight and reached in, fingertips barely grazing the edge of the case. Another metallic ping. A beam of light shot across the trunk illuminating my hand.

Squirrel's voice edged with fear within my skull. "Hurry up." Return fire came from his position.

Stretched to full capacity, I reached the case with my fingertips, dragging it closer until my fingers gripped around the edge.

More gunshots peppered the car. With a last big effort, I grasped the case and dragged it to the gap. More twisting and I extracted the box. Beams of light streaked across the interior. The shooter or shooters were close to the garage. I popped my head up for a quick look. The cars in front of the garage displayed definite battle signs. Windshields broken, bullet holes, gashes in the panels.

Lee and Kennedy were doing a great job keeping the bikers away from me. I squashed a sigh. There were a lot of them. They had no hope of keeping all of them occupied. Time to go.

On a deep breath, I flung the door open and scrambled out, running for cover as soon as my feet hit the dirt. Squirrel grabbed my arm and pulled me behind him near the side wall of the garage.

"You leaking anywhere?"

"Nah, no leaks," I said, moving the case to my left hand and drawing my weapon with my right. "Let's get out of here." I glanced back the way I'd come. Yeah, not that way.

We'd have to use the smashed up cars as cover until we could get to the other side of the huge garage building and then run like hell.

Chapter Thirty Five
Wanted dead or alive

Gunfire filled the air. Rounds hit the dirt, puffs of dust danced above the ground. The garage hadn't fared too well. Argo took off in front of us. His job was to find us a safe way out. He came back fast and touched my leg, his 'follow me' signal.

Squirrel and I followed Argo, keeping low, and moving as fast as possible. The dog adjusted his pace to account for the clumsier and less-agile humans. A fierce gunfight erupted behind us. I listened as we moved. Our guys had found automatic weapons and were exchanging fire with the bikers. Bonus. That'd help keep their attention off us.

"How far is Sean's place?" Squirrel said, keeping step with me.

"Mile, or maybe a mile and a half from Cait's."

"Shit, this property is huge."

If you had the land, it made sense to spread out. Tremendous having family close and all but no need to live in each other's pockets. It was the size of the property that made using a drone even smarter.

The ground shuddered under my feet. Subtle at first, then with increasing strength. Horses. Or maybe one galloping horse. Argo changed direction then stopped. The vibrations underfoot increased. I stilled, trying to judge where they came from.

"What is it?" Squirrel said, touching my arm.

Really? "You can't feel it?"

Squirrel shook his head. Maybe it was farther away than I imagined.

"Hooves."

"Freyja?"

"Think we're about to find out." I motioned to Squirrel to follow and ran to where Argo waited under a substantial oak tree. Smart dog. Not easy to get squashed by a rampaging horse under there.

The rumble underfoot increased until the wild-eyed wounded mare broke cover and galloped at the oak tree. I whistled. She swung her head my way, eyes wide, mouth foaming. For a second she gave the impression she'd slowed, but she veered away and galloped past. Gunshots echoed. With a panicked whinny, she whirled around and galloped back where she'd come from. Maybe this time she'd find Kev and the posse.

She bore a long wound that suggested a bullet had grazed her right shoulder, rather than lodged in it. Blood had dried and sweat flew from her.

Could've sworn the horse wore a winter rug last time I saw her. I wanted Kev to catch Freyja and get her to safety before worrying about us. We were okay. We could hold on longer than her. The panic filling that poor horse could potentially drop her.

We waited until the sound of her hooves was nothing more than a distant vibration, just in case she turned back and caught us without cover. Being in the path of a panicked horse was not my idea of a fun time. Argo scouted ahead. We didn't budge until he came back to give the all-clear. Following close behind I let him lead us to safety. Winding through trees, around structures, Argo delivered us to Sean's backdoor.

The door swung open. "Saw you on the camera," Sean said. "You all right?"

"Yep. Dane found me."

"I saw that. Hey, Dane. Welcome."

Sean shut the door and bolted it behind us. I carried the case into the dining room and placed it on the table. Mitch appeared, smiling. He wrapped his arms around me in a warm, welcoming embrace.

"Babies still sleeping?"

"They are."

Lucky. "I got the drone. Can you get it airborne as fast as possible, please?"

He let me go, stepped sideways, and unclipped the case latches. I went into the kitchen and drank a glass of water. Sean and Squirrel talked in the surveillance room as Sean showed Squirrel the camera set up. Soft conversational noises stopped and started from way down the hall. I surmised it was Quinn and Kurt talking as they patched up Ethan. Distant gunfire punctuated the calm of the house, reminding me we were at war with bikers. Why were we at war with bikers? Because no one knew Cait was dead except us? Why would they want Cait dead?

I imagine the discovery of their dead buddy wouldn't

please them. My phone vibrated in my pocket. I switched the sound back on as I answered the call.

"Ellie, it's Karen. The doctor is dead."

Holy shit balls. "Shit."

"Yeah. We're waiting on lab results before we know more."

"Any more reported cases of sudden illness or death?"

"Two guests at a Roanoke hotel died about half an hour ago."

A shudder hit me so fast I felt vomit swish the back of my throat. We weren't wrong. It's definitely happening. "What hotel?"

"The Garden Inn."

Not the hotel where Sanderson met Garcia. "That's a different hotel. Sanderson told us Garcia doctored bottled water at The Hotel Serenity."

"We have samples and they are at the lab for analysis. These things take time. Some of the bottles were still in circulation within the hotel. We're expecting more deaths."

"I take it the hotel was happy to comply without a fuss?"

"Yeah, the thought of patrons dying swayed them." There was a smile in Karen's voice. "We've contacted all the Roanoke hotels with the help of local police and requested they send us guest lists and also remove any bottled water."

A bullet smashed through the window in the kitchen. I slid to the floor and sat with my back against the cabinets under the sink staring at a bullet hole in the wall in front of me. I chose to ignore it. "I've heard reports of a widespread flu outbreak in D.C. What do you know?"

"Yes, we're aware. We're having a busy flu season."

"Is it this?"

"At this stage, we don't know. I'm inclined to say it's the flu that can be deadly enough for some people."

Another round flew through a window pane in the kitchen and lodged in the wall.

There was something else, I felt it. "What else is happening?"

"We were notified of three cases of meningitis at the FBI Academy in Quantico."

What the actual fuck? "Is that a thing that can randomly happen?"

"College campuses have their fair share of meningitis, thing is, we vaccinate against it."

"And this?"

"Looks like these three contracted Neisseria meningitidis."

We were there. "We were there, all of Delta A, we were on campus talking to the graduating class."

"It'd be unlikely for you to catch anything ... when was this?"

"Last week, this week, I dunno." The days ran into each other like the gunshots through the kitchen window. I'd lost count.

"Is Kurt Henderson with you?"

"Yes."

"Tell him to prescribe antibiotics for the team as a precaution."

That felt like something a doctor would say to stop someone worrying. To be fair, it'd probably work. Another shot smashed through the remaining glass and into the wall. "Will do. Keep me posted."

"Are you all right?"

Yep, it's not the first time I've sat on the floor in a kitchen in Mauryville while someone shot at me. History is doomed to repeat. Huh, history. I needed fifteen minutes to take a closer look at Cait's history. "There's a bit of a situation out here. You and Tahoma should stay away from O'Hare's place until we give the all-clear."

"Jesus, Ellie."

"We'll be okay," I replied as Grace wailed from the living room.

"A baby?"

"Two. Mine." Not the best situation to find ourselves in with infants. "Keep me in the loop regarding the virus, it is a virus, right?"

"As far as we know. Waiting for the test results to start coming in and will do." She stopped but I knew she wasn't done. "Definitely get Kurt onto an antibiotic script for you all."

Sure will as soon as we can actually fill a prescription. Bit tricky in the current climate.

I hung up, dropped my phone into my top pocket, and considered my next action. Another bullet hit close to the last.

This was getting old. Grace's crying kicked up a notch and Isabella joined in. Decision made. I crawled into the living room, avoiding the broken glass. We needed to un-fuck this and fast.

I found Mitch with his feet sticking out on the other side of the makeshift armchair crib. I crawled over and sat next to him on the floor. He had both babies with his back against the wall. He passed me Isabella without speaking.

"It'll be okay," I whispered rocking her. "Mommy and daddy are here."

Her bag was close enough for me to reach. Hooking the bag with my fingertips, I dragged it closer and rummaged in it until I found her pacifier. Her crying ceased the instant it entered her mouth. Silence enveloped us once more. I glanced at Mitch and Grace. She too had her pacifier.

"Were they gunshots, before?"

I wanted to say no but couldn't. "Yes. A couple of bullets flew into the kitchen."

"And you were in there?"

"Yes."

Mitch adjusted his hold on Grace and reached for my hand. Our fingers entwined.

Squirrel ran into the room. "I couldn't find you!" Relief rang through his words as his eyes landed on me then Mitch. Squirrel lowered his voice, "Sorry. You all right?"

"I'm fine."

He crouched in front of me. "What happened?"

"Someone shot at the kitchen." Or me. But probably the kitchen. "There's some glass on the floor in there, watch where you step."

His eyes studied me. His head shook side to side. "Not that. That I heard, clearly."

"The doctor died. Two more deaths were reported at a hotel in Roanoke."

"Same hotel that Ethan was at?"

"No."

A frown slipped over Squirrel's face. A small tornado formed in his eyes. "It's really started."

I nodded. "There's something else. A meningitis outbreak at Quantico."

"Is that part of the big picture?"

"I don't know. Karen told me. She said meningitis is a thing that can happen on campuses, so maybe it's a random event."

His eyes sparked. "I'm sorry, what? Are you saying it's a coincidence?"

Ridiculous. We all know how I feel about such nonsense. "We don't know if it's related, is what I'm saying." I steered the conversation to something closer to home and more concerning. "Ethan?"

"He's okay. Kurt and young Quinn are finished. They're cleaning up."

My attention shifted to Mitch. "We need that drone up and flying," I said, motioning to the drone sitting on the coffee table in the middle of the room. "Can we fly it out of a window?"

"It's ready when you are and yes," Mitch said. "I need my hands though."

I leaned over and took Grace. She grizzled a complaint then settled into the crook of my arm, her leg kicking her sister's, which didn't bother Isabella. Mitch clambered to his feet and retrieved the drone. It was small but not tiny, about eight inches in diameter.

"How big a window?" Squirrel stood next to Mitch inspecting the small machine.

"Be easier if it wasn't a fanlight but an actual window. My piloting skills aren't lousy but they're not perfect."

I struggled to imagine Mitch at anything less than spectacular with any of his skills set.

Squirrel grimaced and whispered, "No one wants to know about his special skills, Ellie."

"Get out of my head," I muttered. The walls within my mind surrounded my personal space and clanged shut. The smart and safe way to go.

My stomach growled. When did we last eat? I couldn't recall eating since the pie at the diner. It was less about me and more about the babies and my team. Everyone was low on reserves and in need of sustenance.

This was turning into the cluster fuck of the century. But on the plus side, I doubted the bikers had eaten or had access to food.

The babies felt heavier in my arms prompting me to stop watching Mitch ready the drone and get the app functioning on his phone, and pay attention to the dual bundle of arms and legs in my arms. Isabella's dark blue eyes met mine. She smiled and cooed. "Mommy has to work. How about you sleep like your sister?"

Isabella's gummy smile widened, her fingers grabbed my hair and tugged. That's a no then.

I struggled to my feet striving to not wake Grace or drop either child. Upright and stable, I slid the sleeping baby into the makeshift crib, unwound the small fist from my hair and slipped Isabella into the other end, making sure she couldn't kick out and disturb Grace. From her backpack, I took her teddy and handed it to her. She cooed and babbled at the bear. Argo nudged my leg.

"Guard," I told him. He planted his furry backside in front of the armchairs without hesitation.

Time to recce the contents of Sean's fridge and pantry. From the hall door, the damage to the kitchen was minimal ... if you ignored the broken glass all over the counter and floor and didn't look at the holes where rounds lodged in the wall. I crouched below the window level and duckwalked to the fridge. Someone outside would see the fridge door open. I tugged the door from the bottom. A bullet smashed through a corner of the remaining window pane, puncturing the door and killing a jar of pickles. Brine ran all over the floor. Crouching in pickle juice, I surveyed the contents of the shelves. Bread. Butter. Cheese. Eggs. Pickles everywhere. Salad fixings in a clear plastic container. A white bag caught my eye. I unwrapped it, sliced ham. Another bullet hit the door. A carton of milk sprayed all over me. Swell.

Jumping to my feet, I scooped everything edible into

my arms, slammed the fridge door shut and ran back to the living room, leaving the kitchen awash in milk and pickle juice, and trudging milky pickle footprints into the carpet. It would stink to high heaven if left. Me too.

Squirrel took some of the food from me and placed it on a smaller coffee table at the end of the sofa. "Didn't feel hungry until I saw food," he said.

I added the rest of the haul to the table. We needed a knife. With a sigh, I went back. The utensil drawer was easier to get to than the refrigerator. I managed without drawing fire. Back in the living room, I rummaged in Grace's bag for a spare long-sleeved tee shirt. I kept one in each bag and whipped off my shirt to pull on a clean one.

"El, I'm ready," Mitch said. He held the drone in his right hand and his phone in his left. "Safest window?"

I pointed to two grand sliding windows that ran a quarter of the way down the living room.

"Someone is shooting at the back of the house, but this is more elevated, with no vantage point for a shooter outside."

Squirrel opened one of the windows. The light breeze caught the drapes for a moment then died down. Mitch fired up the little drone. There was a slight hum and nothing more. Squirrel held out his hand. Mitch placed the drone on his upturned palm and used his phone to control it.

"I've sent the camera feed to your phone so you can see what's going on below the drone. I've got the operating system," Mitch said, sending the drone out of the window.

I stuffed a piece of cheese into my mouth before clicking on the link to the drone's live feed. I had a drone's eye view of the ground below.

Chapter Thirty Six

My eyes have seen you

"Take it right, Mitch," I said, watching my phone screen. "What am I looking at?"

Squirrel leaned closer to me. "Can you enhance the image?"

"Can you move your head?" I said, nudging him out of the way.

Squirrel moved back. The image on the screen sharpened. The biker held something on his shoulder. "Is that a rocket launcher? Fuck!"

Squirrel spoke and I realized he was on his phone. "Rocket launcher. Get out of there."

"SRAW pointed at the top floor of Cait's house." I watched in horror as the rocket impacted with Quinn's bedroom, and filled the sky and surrounds with debris. I reached out and took Squirrel's phone.

"You okay?" I said into the phone. Nothing. I stared at the screen for a second. All I saw was Stuart and Lee's names.

"Stu?" Nothing.

"Lee?" Nothing.

Two icons popped up on the screen. Call ended. Call back? Shit balls.

"Ellie?" Mitch said.

"Uh huh." I watched my phone screen and shoved

Squirrel's phone back into his hand. Another person and another SRAW. This time they took out an end bedroom. "Sean!" I hollered, not even thinking about the babies. "Sean!"

His fell shadow over me as he entered the room. "Problem?"

"They're using Predators. We lost contact with Stu and Lee."

Grace wailed. I handed Sean my phone so he could see the drone feed then fished Grace's pacifier from where it had fallen and popped it back in her mouth. "Shush, sorry, little one." My fingers brushed over her soft hair before my attention returned to the clear and present danger. Argo stood and peered over the arm of the chair. Grace went from stifled cries to gurgling joy.

There was nothing to stop the bikers from turning the rocket launchers on this place. We were farther away but all they had to do was walk a hundred yards or so up the driveway with one of the SRAW's and pow, we were toast.

Then I heard it. A dull faraway *thwok thwok thwok*. Helicopters. Rocket launchers and helicopters were an unsatisfactory mix. I knew that from experience.

"Helicopters inbound. We need to warn them and get those launchers disabled."

Squirrel made the call to Andrews' cell phone. I heard his voice plainly as he said, "Do not approach target. I repeat. Do not approach. Until all-clear given." I couldn't hear Andrews's reply but I could imagine his annoyance.

Sean beckoned me to follow him. He led the way down

the hall into an office. He opened an enormous gun safe and passed me a rifle, then took one himself. Squirrel ran into the room.

"Helicopters are waiting for the all-clear." His eyes hit the weapon in my arms. "Nope. That's a no." Squirrel tried to take it from me.

Sean leaned close. "If you're more accurate than Ellie under pressure, then you and I go. If not, back off, buddy."

Squirrel's hand dropped. "This is not wonderful."

"It is what it is," I said with a small smile as I successfully quashed Chance's voice in my head telling me my death wish was showing. "Can you get me my jacket? It's on the arm of a chair in the living room."

Squirrel grumbled but did as I asked. He thrust the jacket at me and held the rifle while I put it on.

"If Mitch can guide us, we get to the big oak tree this side of Cait's garage. Think that's the best place for a sniper nest," Sean said.

Yeah, it was almost perfect. The big branches and the murky brown autumnal foliage still clinging in clumps made it a viable tree for us. Beside it grew colossal fir trees which provided more cover and camouflage but were crap to climb.

Sean flicked through a pile of fabric on a shelf in a cupboard and removed two brown digital camouflage shemaghs. He wrapped one around his neck and head, then did the same for me with the other. My leather jacket was close enough to dead-leaf brown, and my indigo jeans were dark enough to blend into branch shadows as were my brown boots. I'd wear my black leather gloves. Sean put on his gloves. I scanned the screen in my hand. "There's another guy with ..." I paused trying to see what he had. "Looks like another Predator SRAW moving onto the driveway."

"No time to piss around," Sean said.

With the rifle cradled, I hurried Squirrel back to the living room. Mitch glanced at me, anxiety danced in his eyes at the sight of the shemagh. I took my engagement ring off but kept my wedding band on. Mitch held out a hand and I dropped my engagement ring into it. "Keep that safe for me."

He smiled and pushed it into the coin pocket in his jeans. "Of course."

Removing my gloves from my pocket I plunged my fingers deep into them and then made a fist a few times to make sure I could move freely. Easier without my engagement ring to twist and catch inside my gloves.

I gave my phone to Squirrel. "The big tree we were under earlier, Sean and I are going up it. We gotta get rid of the threat before they take out helicopters."

"Can't the helicopters take them out?" Mitch said.

I tipped my head up to look at him. "Really?"

He shook his head. "I know, I know, the sons of bitches guys have too much cover. Pine and fir trees are a pain in the ass."

They sure are and the driveways are lined in them, not to mention the stands of pine dotted about the land.

The tree we headed for was slow at losing its brown leaves. Sitting among the silvery spruce, blue cedars and deep green of the pines, the oak looked dead as it hibernated for winter. We were lucky there hadn't been much wind and the branches of the oak were still thick with foliage, albeit brown and crispy.

"Can you get the drone in among the trees without compromising it?"

"Done it before. It's tricky but doable."

That's what I want to hear.

Sean tapped my shoulder and gave me an earpiece. I moved the scarf and stuck it in my ear. Sean handed one to Squirrel as well then he disappeared but his voice whispered in my ear. "Saddle up."

"Coming," I said in a whisper.

"Roger that." Sean's voice came back loud in my ear.

Microphone test complete. Without looking at the babies, I joined Sean in the hallway and let him lead the way to a door. He opened it revealing a staircase leading down. He and Cait sure loved staircases. "Garage is down here, we can get out that way."

A much better option than the back door with a shooter taking pot shots at the kitchen. A low soft bark startled me. Turning I saw Argo, head cocked, waited to see what I'd do. I nodded at him. "Come on then, Argo. You're on our six."

Squirrel's voice filled my ear. "SRAW is lining up to hit another top floor room, over."

"Roger," I said. "Try to locate Kennedy and our boys.

Iverson out." We walked down the carpeted stairs followed by Argo in stealth mode.

Sean unlocked the bottom door and pushed it open. The darkness in the garage felt safe. As the door closed, a cool, inky security blanket fell over us. I knew that beyond the comparative safety of the garage walls a battle raged but right then there was nothing but the soothing quiet of the garage. My eyes adjusted to the dimness and capable of picking out shapes and shadows, we moved again. Sean led. I clamped a hand on his shoulder so I could stick close. We passed two cars and he stopped.

"Door."

It was tempting to hold my breath when he unlocked and opened the door. Sunlight swamped us. Outside, he closed the door quietly. With my hand on Sean's shoulder, I gave a squeeze. He moved. From cover to cover we made our way to our objective and rapidly covered the three-quarters of a mile to the giant oak tree near Cait's garage.

Timely warnings from Squirrel regarding bikers' movements enabled us to avoid engagement. It was a different story as we closed in on the tree.

"Biker at your eleven," Squirrel said then paused and changed his mind. "Shit. Correction. Your ten, eleven, and three." We held our position. Argo scouted ahead looking for the best way through.

"Is the drone having trouble with the trees?" I said in a whisper.

Squirrel replied, "Yeah, Mitch doesn't want it too low

or it'll be compromised."

That made sense. We needed its camera. Having it shot from the sky would be highly annoying. And knowing drones, blow my budget; I didn't want to explain that to whoever our new Director would be.

Argo returned and signaled me to follow him. The dog was worth his weight in gold. He guarded the bottom of the tree while we made our ascent. Climbing with rifles had a definite challenging aspect to it. In an adrenaline-rush kinda way. From within the branches, Argo was out of sight. Squirrel gave us a rough idea of where the unfriendlies were from our hidden position, which he couldn't see from the drone camera. His only references became the trees and the garage close by.

I straddled a huge branch with my back against the trunk. Sean was somewhere close by on another massive limb. We were as high as we could get and still remain mostly covered by the dead leaves. An explosion rocked the area. Another Predator. The house was falling apart. Smoke filled the air. It stank. I drew the shemagh up from my neck and over my mouth and nose. Wrapping my legs around the branch, I stretched out with the rifle until I lay prone on the branch, praying it didn't break. Shifting leaves with the muzzle until I had a clear view through my scope I lined up the area the bikers' favored and waited for the next one to emerge.

Sean's voice in my ear told me he was ready too. His job was to protect me with cover fire if necessary. He was far enough away from me to draw the fire from me, we hoped, so I could line up a second shot if needed.

Squirrel spoke. "Multiple targets moving. Out."

Great. I waited. Finger on the trigger. Breathing slowly. A biker with an SRAW came from the trees alongside the driveway, he moved into an open area. I sighted through the scope, lined up his head. He was side on to me. Gently I squeezed the trigger. Red billowed out the far side of the biker's head as he dropped to the ground.

I reloaded and watched the confusion below from my nest. They had no idea where the shot came from. Squirrel confirmed their confusion as two bikers attempted to drag the body away. Another picked up the SRAW. Three shots fired in quick succession from within the tree, but from above me and to my left. Sean. Bikers dropped, blood sprayed. The SRAW hit the ground. I waited.

Squirrel warned me another SRAW was moving.

This time the biker broke cover, pointed the SRAW at the garage, and swung it to the trees hiding us. I breathed. Lined him up. Squeezed the trigger. The back of his head sprayed all over the driveway. I reloaded and waited. I could do this all day. Part of me even enjoyed lying along a big branch among crispy leaves and smaller branches. But not the part poked by twiggy bits of the tree.

Squirrel warned another biker was on the move. The drone followed a group of four as they tried to flank our position.

Sean whispered in my ear. "Got a bead on them."

A smile flittered over my lips, another biker crept out into the clearing. No SRAW. He had a grenade launcher. Nice. I fired. He dropped like a sack of shit. I heard Sean firing.

"Hope someone is keeping count," Sean said as a blanket of silence dropped over the area.

"No movement. Over," Squirrel reported.

"Keep watch. They're taking stock. Over," I said.

"Rough guess ... how many more SRAWs do they have? Over."

"Call in the helicopters. Over and out," I replied. Letting my answer speak to his question.

Sean and I stayed where we were, watching. Waiting. A low growl from Argo warned us someone neared the base of our tree.

I tapped the microphone button on my jacket lapel. "Squirrel, can you see anything near us? Over."

"Looking. Wait one. Over."

Argo's growling increased; even filtered through dead leaves, it was a frightening sound. He meant business.

"Squirrel? Over."

"Unfriendly approaching from the east of the tree. Over."

I wanted to climb down, but everything I'd ever been taught told me to hold my position. The dog had a job to do. This was helluva test for a dog that wasn't fierce enough for police work. My heart lurched as growling became a snarl that led to a vicious bark and more snarling. Running booted feet, then a blood-curdling scream mingled with snarling.

"Dog got him. Over." Good boy, Argo. Good boy.

Silence dropped again, this time broken by the *thwok* of incoming helicopters.

Gunfire from the trees lining the driveway popped at random intervals underneath the sound of the helicopters. We hadn't heard firing from the house since we set up the nest, which didn't fill me with warm fuzzies. Using my scope, I watched six men fast rope from the first helicopter hovering over the pasture in front of the house. The second helicopter flew over us and circled the property before landing.

Once the area was secure, Sean and I climbed down.

Argo waited. Bloody-faced. A few yards from the tree lay a biker. I walked over and toed him with my boot, cradling my rifle, ready for trouble.

He groaned. Not dead then. Blood trickled from a wound in his neck and bite marks on his arms. Guess he tried to protect himself from Argo's teeth. Fool.

"I'd stay still if I were you," I said. Argo growled from near my thigh.

"Keep him away from me," the biker said, shuffling back along the ground.

Not so tough now.

Argo stepped up and growled again.

"Stay still," I told the biker. "Or he'll bite again."

Chapter Thirty Seven

Friends will be friends.

For a few minutes, the chaotic noises of battle resumed. It was short-lived. All around us men in green rounded up gang members. My name rang out across the driveway. I turned to see Andrews striding across the gravel, rifle in a sling in front of him, another rifle held in his left hand. He grinned.

"Guess you don't need this," he said, lifting his left hand.

"Got one," I said with a smile and moved the rifle in my arms up a little. "But thank you."

"Thank you for clearing the way. Where is everyone?" Andrews' eyes flicked from me to Sean and back to me. "We haven't met. I'm Andrews."

Sean smiled. "Sean O'Hare."

Andrews nodded upon recognizing Sean's surname. "Related to our Director?"

"Yes."

I interrupted. "You got men near the house over there?" I replied, pointing to Cait's place.

"Yeah."

"I'm going in with them," I said and took off running for the house. I tapped my mic and said, "Sean. Go back to your place. Over."

Andrews matched me stride for stride. I heard him

speak to his men, but not his words. In my ear I heard Squirrel. "Where are you going? Over."

I tapped the mic, "To get Lee, Stu, and Kennedy. Keep the drone airborne. Out."

Squirrel and Sean voiced protests. I ignored them both. From the front veranda of Cait's place, I saw the damage. There wasn't a lot left of the top floor. The main living areas fared slightly better although there wasn't an intact windowpane anywhere.

Andrews gave orders. I walked up the steps. Part of the broken veranda roof hung over the french doors. I ducked around it and pushed the middle of the doors. With a creak they gave way. The door I thrust ground to a halt, jammed on something. I pushed again. It wouldn't budge so I shoved the other door and slipped in through the small gap I'd created and checked the room was clear of people and then dragged debris out of the way for the team.

"Clear," I said leaving them to make their entrance. I moved to the kitchen. Not much left without damage. Smashed windows, bullet holes, broken glass strewn all over. I saw brass casings on the floor. One of my team had used the kitchen. No sign of life. I set my rifle down in a corner of the room and extracted my Glock from my holster. Easier inside with a smaller weapon.

I called out, "Lee! Stu! Kennedy!"

The only noises were from Andrews' team walking around in the living room. Methodical footsteps moved up the hallway.

Andrews stepped into the kitchen. "Bet this was a really nice house."

"Yeah, it sure was." I motioned to him to follow and headed for the surgery. Andrews stood on the hinge side of the door; he'd follow me in and go left. No sound filtered through the door. The room could actually be empty. It was a safe room. No windows. No other access. The Pollyanna in me hoped at least one of my team was holed up inside.

I twisted the handle. It didn't yield. With a closed fist I bashed on the door and hollered, "Iverson, entering!"

Andrews and I listened, my ear to the door. I shook my head. Nothing. If locked, then someone locked it.

"Andrews, got anything useful to breach this door with?"

He'd already slung his pack to the ground. Seconds later he produced a shotgun. "This do?"

"Breaching rounds?"

"Hell, yes."

"Then yeah. Beyond this door are a scrub room, another door, and a surgery."

Breaching rounds limited the danger to anyone inside the room; made especially for breaching and designed to destroy the target then disperse into a powder. Sam loved them. Sam used to love them.

Andrews pressed the muzzle of his shotgun between the door handle and the doorframe. I stepped back behind him.

"Firing!" He turned his head away and squeezed the

trigger. The round shot through the locking bar. Andrews poked the door with the muzzle of the shotgun and it swung open. I walked past Andrews into the scrub room. No one inside. The second door was closed, but I knew that had an automatic closer on it and no lock. No door handle, a push plate, designed so the door could be opened by walking a shoulder into it, rather than touching a handle with sterile hands. I pushed the door and saw light when the door moved. I swung the door hard, shoved my foot in front of it so it didn't come back on me and scanned the room down the sight of my Glock. Andrews squeezed my shoulder and placed his foot behind mine. I stepped inside and to the right. He followed to the left.

The door closed. Lights stayed on. On the far side of the room, beyond the operating table, and against the cabinets I saw a shape. Familiar light-brown hair.

"Lee!" I plunged my Glock into my holster and strode across the room to him. Andrews slid to a stop on the other side of Lee's slumped body and searched for a pulse. Bloody wrappers from dressing packs strewn near Lee, combined with his blood-stained his hands, told a tale.

I saw no one else. Where were they?

I tapped Lee's collarbone. "Hey, eyes open!"

Nothing.

Andrews nodded at me. A pulse.

"Cowboy the fuck up, Davenport." I opened his torn shirt to reveal a saturated wound dressing on his abdomen. I lifted the edge and saw more blood. Nasty. I reached into the nearest drawer looking for dressing packs, figuring they were close enough for him to reach without moving far. I ripped one open and jammed a thick wad of gauze on top of the soaked mess in his stomach, pressing it firmly against him. "Oh man, I don't wanna find myself wrist deep in your guts again, Davenport."

"Again?" Andrews said.

We watched Lee's face. His eyelids flickered but didn't open.

"Again," Lee croaked. "What can I say ... she ... is enchanted by my entrails."

"Glad, you're not dead," I said, smiling. "Andrews, can I use your phone?" Mine was trapped in my back pocket.

Andrews pushed his phone into my free hand. I glanced at it. iPhone. Excellent. "Siri, call Kurt Henderson."

"Calling Kurt Henderson for you Mr. Stark," Siri said, in a British male voice.

I filed that away for later. Lee smiled. Andrews laughed. "Secret's out."

Kurt answered.

"Need you at Cait's place. Lee has an abdominal wound."

"Gunshot or something else?"

Apt question; hard to tell because of the bloody dressing

"Lee, gunshot?"

"Knife."

Andrews reacted swiftly. For us, it meant there could be an unfriendly inside the house. I knew Kurt was on the move so I carried on talking.

"Anyone else hurt?"

"Don't know. Haven't found Stu or Kennedy yet."

"I'm coming through the tunnel with Sean."

"Okay, I'll let Andrews' boys know."

I passed the phone back to Andrews. "There's a tunnel entrance in an office down the hallway before the stairs. Kurt will come in that way."

"I'll take two men and go meet him, we don't want any unwelcome surprises getting to him first."

"Thanks."

I sat cross-legged on the floor next to Lee. "Guess I'm with you."

Andrews returned with my rifle. He placed on the floor near me. "Just in case."

"Thanks."

Lee moved his legs. Grimace lines on his face made it clear he regretted that decision. "How about you stay still until Kurt gets here?"

He gave me a half-smile.

I let my breathing even out to pull my heart rate down. Adrenaline, useful in a fight, was less so now. My free hand trembled and it took concerted effort to bring everything back under control and turn my attention to Stu. He'd dropped off my radar. That was odd. Usually I could sense him and Squirrel. And the occasional thought popped into my head despite my ability to put up mental walls. I focused my energy on Stu. No walls. Come on, Stu, where are you?

Squirrel's voice broke through my thoughts. It wasn't internal. It was from the earpiece.

"Have you found them yet? Over."

I tapped the mic button. "Only Lee. Where are you? Over."

"Coming in the front door. I have to find him, El. Over."

"I know. I'm in the surgery with Lee. Let Andrews' guys know you're inside. Be careful."

Radio silence resumed. Cold seeped through the linoleum into my bones and torso. If I was cold Lee must be freezing. Blankets. I grabbed Lee's hand and pressed it against the gauze. "Just for a second. You need blankets before hypothermia sets in."

He didn't react.

I hauled myself to my feet. Where would blankets be I wondered? Opening cabinets and low cupboard doors. I found them near the exit door. Four blankets would be enough. I carried them back to Lee. He tried to lean forward for me to get a blanket around his shoulders, unsuccessfully. Instead, I draped blankets over him.

"We're going to get snow," I said, settling back down next to him. I pressed on the wound again. His hand had already fallen by his side. "My phone said it was twenty-three degrees before I climbed the tree."

"You climbed a tree?" Lee said, his voice quiet, his

337

usual drawl missing.

"Yeah, and Sean. Took a couple of rifles and climbed a tree."

Lee opened one eye. "Fun?"

"Yeah."

I heard the skittering of paws in the distance. Argo. A dog on a mission.

"Here boy," I said, following up with a whistle. I counted. The door moved. On the second Mississippi, Argo slid to a stop in front of us, still a bit dirty from his tussle earlier but otherwise okay. "Atta boy."

"He come by himself?"

"Probably followed Squirrel in. We can't find Kennedy or Stu." I took advantage of Lee's coherence. "Where'd you last see them?"

"Upstairs. I was holding the kitchen until ..." He faded again.

Upstairs didn't exist anymore. I didn't want to say that aloud. It's enough I thought it without the benefit of partitioning. Argo lay down beside Lee, so his body touched as much of Lee as possible. Part of what made Argo outstanding at his job was his ability to sense what was needed. Hurt people needed comfort and warmth.

Lee's eyes closed completely. I let him rest. Argo would keep him warm. I'd sit there for as long as it took, keeping pressure on the wound. My mind wandered, looking for Stu and Kennedy, then trying to understand what happened and why. I was missing large chunks of information and without them, the biker gang siege made no sense at all. I considered that it had something to do with the biker that Cait fired. But why the siege, that was above and beyond. Was that the bikers' plan all along? Was their intention to cross several counties to lay waste to someone's home and they stopped by the hospital on the way because Sanderson interfered with the initial plan? It didn't surprise me too much that they had Predators. Bikers were pretty adept at getting hold of weapons. Guess it was one of their superpowers. Mine was exploding heads from a tree. Horses. Where was the cavalry?

So many things needed answers. Numbness set in as I listened to Lee and Argo breathing. As long as Lee's breathing remained steady, I wasn't too worried.

Ten minutes later Kurt announced his presence from the scrub room doorway. "Coming in!"

"About time," I called back as he strode across the room.

He went on one knee next to Lee. "Fine work, Argo," Kurt said, patting the dog on the head while his other hand checked Lee's pulse. "He's nice and warm."

Kurt turned his head to me. "The dog needs his face washed. Looks like he's chowed down on a zombie."

I smiled. He did. "Lee's been quiet for about seven minutes."

Lee opened an eye and peered at us. "Sleeping here," he said, in a whisper.

I lifted my hand so Kurt could get clear access to the wound.

"Not very pretty," he said. "Think we'd better take care of that."

Kurt looked at me. "Have they cleared the area?"

"Mostly, I can check, now I'm able to move." I wiped my bloody hands on my jeans, withdrew my phone from my back pocket and called Andrews. "Are we clear downstairs?"

"Yes."

"Fantastic. Kurt would like young Quinn over here from the other house."

Kurt smiled and nodded.

"I'll have him escorted, can I ask why?"

"He's at med school. Kurt needs a hand with Lee."

"He'll be with you very soon." Andrews hung up.

As soon as Quinn arrived, I picked up the rifle and left. Dixon waited in the well-ventilated kitchen for me.

"Long time no see, Iverson," he said, as our fists met in mid-air.

"It's been great," I said with a grin.

"You don't mean that. I know you've missed this shit," Dixon said, sweeping his arm around the destroyed room. "They're still searching upstairs."

Couldn't deny it. We'd always had fun working together. Wow, maybe I do have a warped idea of what fun is? "I figured it'd be a mess. See Dane?"

"He's up with them. I'm here for you, so where ever you want to go, I'm your shadow."

Yay me.

A slow drawl telling someone he was the sheriff alerted

me to Kevin's presence outside the kitchen. Silver hair came into view through a smashed section of wall as the voice came closer.

"Kev! In here!" I hollered.

Dixon covered his ears. "Jesus, warn a man first."

I shrugged and threw a grin at him. Kevin found his way to the front steps. We met him in the living room.

"I got the horse, two of my deputies are escorting her across the fields to Parker's place, Doc Robinson is meeting them there."

"Will she be all right?"

"Hopefully. She's scared but not too badly hurt."

"Thanks, Kevin," I said smiling. "I'm sure Ethan and Quinn appreciate it too."

"Where are they?"

"Ethan is wounded and at Sean's. Quinn is in there." I tipped my thumb to the surgery. "Helping Kurt patch up one of my team."

Kevin spun around on the spot. "What is it with you turning houses to rubble in Mauryville?"

"Wasn't about me this time," I said. "And that's kinda unfair."

It's not me and houses in Mauryville. It's me and houses period. Two of my homes have exploded in my life. I'm willing to accept that that's not normal.

Kevin laughed. "Guess this one didn't explode."

Well, it actually kinda did. Decided to leave out the rocket launcher part for now.

"Lucky there."

"Saw a dead chicken. I assume she was a friend of Abigail's." Kevin said without a single twitch of his mustache. Impressive. I'm never going to live down my pet chicken and her untimely death.

Dixon stood at ease listening to our conversation. "You two go back aways, huh?"

Kevin's mustache twitched. His eyes sparkled. "She's the reason I've got gray hair."

My eyebrows rose. Oh really? I cleared my throat and put an end to Kevin's stroll down memory lane. "Everyone rounded up out there?"

"They're still sweeping the property to make sure, but it's looking good. Lot of bikers in cuffs face down on the driveway. Few bodies out there too."

Yeah. I stopped the smile that wanted to shine and reminded myself that they were someone's children long before they became gang members. A life is a life. I took a few today, and it should not be an easy thing to wipe away.

Chapter Thirty Eight

(Don't fear) The Reaper.

A feeling of impending doom crawled over the rug and touched my hand with its icy fingers. A shudder ran through me. Caine stood in the doorway. No clue how long he'd been there. "Can I help you?"

"I have some news."

"And?"

"One of the new agents from Quantico died. Owen's sudden leave was a family emergency. She went to her niece's bedside."

Crap. What did Karen tell me about Quantico? Meningitis hit three of the students. Wake up, Ellie, that's why we're all taking antibiotics. Lucky for us all, Cait's surgery contained a decent supply of antibiotics that Kurt happily doled out three times a day. Just in case.

"Meningitis."

"Yes."

"The agent who died, was it Rachel Owen?"

"Yes."

"Guess I shouldn't have had such uncharitable thoughts about Owen's sudden absence from work."

"Probably not."

The corner of his lip twitched. "Where is everyone?" His grumbly voice reminded me of an old teddy bear. It went well with the deep lines and a weary expression.

"No idea," I replied. "Are you coming in, or pretending you're a door?"

The other side of his lip twitched. Decision made. He walked in and sat in one of the armchairs near the sofa, with his leather briefcase on the floor next to him.

"Are you expecting your team back from No Idea soon?"

My eyes met his. "Did you make a joke?"

His lip twitched. "Are you?"

"Yes. Are we waiting?"

"That would be an excellent idea."

"Do you mind if I finish this report then?"

"Carry on. I've got some reading to do," he said and tugged an iPad from his briefcase.

"Excuse me but since when do you use an iPad?"

"Since you all disappeared south and left me and Sandra high and dry."

Oh, Sandra taught him. "You came down with her, right?"

He nodded. "She's talking to Lee and Ethan."

I went back to the report and finished telling headquarters what happened at Cait O'Hare's property as best I could. All the bikers left alive were under arrest and now held in Kevin's jail. It was crowded. He had state police helping him interrogate the prisoners and four FBI agents out of Richmond who were experts in The Alpha Brotherhood and The Inferno Jesters biker gangs. Delta A was not involved. Potentially we were targets along with the O'Hare family. Until anyone knew otherwise, we weren't allowed anywhere near the bikers.

I felt I could breathe again but I knew that would be short-lived. Tahoma and Karen from the CDC were coming out to update us on the virus situation. Lee was recovering and chose not to go to the hospital. His decision was helped by the virus situation. Ethan was recovering. He also opted to stay out of the hospital. The only two who had zero choices were Stu and Kennedy. They were airlifted to the Naval Medical Center in Portsmouth. I had no idea if either of them would make it. Dane insisted he was fine and refused time off to accompany his brother and Kennedy. He said we needed him more. He was right, but it didn't stop me from fretting that he should be with his brother. If Stu died, he'd have a hefty amount of guilt to live with. Meanwhile, I sent my team out riding. Mr. Parker let us borrow some of his horses, and I encouraged everyone who was well enough outside in the snow.

The virus threat was out of hand. Reports had hit the media of an outbreak of flu. News reports suggested a pandemic, a potentially new strain of flu attacking the northern hemisphere's already severe flu season. Then I saw media reports of another illness. The Black Death. Bubonic Plague. I knew that there were usually a few cases of Black Death a year in the USA; it wasn't eradicated as most people thought. People were advised against gathering in public places due to the flu outbreak and instructed on the benefits of thorough hand washing.

A general air of hysteria shrouded North America.

That would get worse once people grasped there was a new illness in play.

I'd wait for Tahoma and Karen, they'd be able to tell us more. Grace squawked from the armchair crib. Isabella cried. Nothing like waking babies to pull me back to the insular world around me. That was the end of my report writing or the meandering around in my mind searching for answers. I glanced at the screen. I'd written two words since Caine arrived. Not helpful.

Caine grumbled his ancient teddy bear growl. He stood looking into the armchairs. Cries turned to babble and happy noises.

"They like you," I said, putting the laptop on the coffee table and standing.

"Foolish babies," he said, doing his best to remain gruff and imposing. They saw straight through him and giggled.

"You can't fool them," I said. "They're smarter than all of us. And probably hungry. If you entertain them for a minute, I'll make some formula."

"Do they eat actual food yet?"

"They more spit it and choke on it than eat it. We've called a halt to weaning at this stage," I said from the kitchen.

While I made the bottles, I heard Caine explain to the babies how much joy they would one day get from a decent steak. No doubt they would. One day. I shook the first bottle to disperse the powder, watching out the window as I did. Sean had replaced the glass already, which was a blessing. In the distance, I saw horses. I almost wished I was out there with them. Almost. Isabella made happy gurgling noises. Her voice had changed recently; it was huskier than Grace's. Our identical daughters; maybe they'd be slightly different after all.

"Which one wears purple?" Caine said.

"It's lilac and that would be Isabella."

"Judging by the aroma she needs a fresh diaper."

Yay. Because it amused me, I said, "Diapers are in the lilac bag along with baby wipes."

I mixed up the second bottle and carried them into the living room. My eyes met with a sight I didn't expect.

Isabella lay on a rug on the floor and Caine knelt in front of her, dirty diaper in hand. Clean diaper on the baby. No words. I had no words.

Instead, I set Isabella's bottle on the ground near the sofa and scooped up Grace. I didn't even watch Caine stand and leave the room. I heard water running and when he returned, he settled on the sofa next to me with Isabella to feed her. The entire feed of the babies went by in silence. Probably as stunned as I was.

Conversational noise filtered in the back door. Sounded like the guys were back from their ride.

Relief swamped me. I could now pretend I hadn't witnessed a domestic scene involving our SAC. The comfort zone violation was over.

The babies lay on their tummies on a blanket, facing each other and babbling happy noises.

"What's the next plan?" Lee asked, moving gingerly across the room.

"Healing," I replied.

"I'm almost there already."

Bullshit. "Right then. We need to know what the biker gangs had to do with O'Hare and why that creep she let go led them here."

"I'm going out on a limb and saying they arrived here because we told the world Cait was treated and discharged, so whoever commissioned the job thought it wasn't finished," Kurt said.

"Interesting that you said commissioned," I replied.

"And who killed the paramedic? And why did that paramedic drug Cait in the ambulance?" Kurt added, folding himself into a chair.

"And where Juan Garcia is and why he hired Sanderson to kill Cait," Lee said.

"And who shot Thor and administered the overdose one to Cait at the side of the road," I finished. Seven ducklings waddled across the floor. One tried herding the others but they scurried in all directions, quacking with annoyance. The plump noisy duckling chased its nest mates in circles until it exploded in a cloud of yellow fluff.

Dane stretched. "We know the virus distributor, Garcia, hired someone to kill Cait, so he was responsible for at least shortening her death phase once she was in the hospital." He paced, then stopped and turned. "We know Garcia worked with Emmett from The Inferno Jesters Motorcycle club. We found Emmett with methamphetamine but it doesn't mean they're not distributing other drugs."

"We have a link between the gangs, Garcia, and Cait," Lee said. "But we are still short on a motive for Garcia wanting Cait dead."

"Why not find a way to infect her and have her death attributed to some random illness? Why go about it the way they did?" Dane said. "So messy."

That exact question had been screwing with my thoughts since we found out about Sanderson and Garcia. It felt like two scenarios. Viruses. Cait's death.

But Garcia and the biker had a hand in that death. Was it dumb luck that the biker supplied the paramedic with a similar cocktail to the original found in Cait's blood?

Fuck.

I held up my hand.

"The drugs we found in Cait's system and the paramedic's and her home, are close enough to the same that the same person could be responsible. Was that dumb luck or did the biker supply the original shooter?"

"Kinda stupid if he did," Lee said.

"Exactly."

"Something fucky going on in biker land?" Dane said. "Or maybe the drugs also came from Garcia."

"Finding Juan Garcia should be priority one," I said.

"Garcia?" Caine grumbled, passing a toy to Grace.

"Moving too fast for you?" I muttered with a smile. "Garcia hired Sanderson to finish off Cait in the hospital. High probability he hired the person who shot the drug load into Thor too."

"Sounds like Mr. Garcia did not like our Director," Caine said. "Think we need to find out why he wanted her dead and why he didn't infect her the same way he did the doctor."

Yeah. The biker siege thing wriggled and jiggled inside me.

"Swinging back to our loser biker who got fired. A grudge might be enough for him to lead the gang out here, I guess." Chance emerged at the living room doorway and gave me a cheesy grin and a thumbs up. Something right then. "I got the sense that he wasn't the most popular biker in the club, bit of a loose cannon which probably irritated the older guys." Another thumbs up from my goofy imaginary pal in the doorway. "Bet his standing would improve if he went back to the clubhouse after he was dismissed from his job and told his buddies that he knew where Director O'Hare lived and that she was at her country estate and unprotected and recovering from a riding accident."

"Okay, that's a theory. Loser biker leads gang out to the estate not knowing Cait is already dead. But it's possible he'd already killed the paramedic … we thought the biker killed Alyssa because she failed to kill Cait," Kurt said.

"What if that was Garcia who killed Alyssa, not our biker?" I threw that into the mix and waited to see what would happen. I got another thumbs up from the goofball in the doorway. He was playing the cheesy nerd card for all it was worth.

"Whoa, what?" Dane said, cross-legged on the floor near the babies. "You're saying the biker didn't kill the paramedic? But we found their coded images and thought they were meeting. We have proof they were meeting."

"Yes, we do. But we have zero proof he killed her or blackmailed her. That was an idea we played with because we knew they were in communication and he did time. Could be another reason for them meeting." I glanced up and saw Chance's thumb flick up again. It was getting harder and harder not to laugh. "They might be friends."

Jeez.

"Okay," Kurt said. "Let's say for shits and giggles that Garcia supplied drugs to the bikers for distribution. Garcia coerced the paramedic, not the biker."

"How would he know about the relationship between the medic and biker?" Lee said, wincing as he stretched out a leg.

"Be careful moving, I don't wanna re-do those stitches," Kurt cautioned. "Let's chuck this out and see if it floats." Kurt crossed his legs. "If I wanted to do business with a gang like The Inferno Jesters and their sidekicks, The Alpha Brotherhood, I'd do my homework. I would have bios and background info on every person in those gangs. I'd be looking for anything I could exploit if things went sour."

That made sense.

"And in doing his homework, Garcia found a weakness. A patsy if you will," Caine said.

It was easy to imagine a biker as someone who would blackmail a former girlfriend especially if he'd done hard time for her. You're a worthy adversary, Garcia. You had us looking in the wrong direction. Another voice broke into my thoughts and warned me not to get too cocky. We still might be barking up the wrong tree.

"We need to talk to our idiot biker ... what was his name again and did he survive the battle?" I said.

Kurt flipped through his notebook and found the name.

"Joey Williams."

"That's right, no clue how I forgot that."

Kurt then checked his name against the list of bikers involved in the siege given to him by Kevin.

"Joey Williams was killed."

Shit. A flash of holy fuck hit me. A niggly thought grew. Might not have been us that fired the bullet that ended his miserable life.

"Who killed him?"

"Waiting on autopsy results and ballistics."

"Can we get ballistics to put a rush on all rounds taken from corpses?"

Kurt shook his head but made the call to Kevin to find out what laboratory he needed to squeeze for results.

Dane stood up and walked to the windows. He leaned on the wall and peered out of a window. "We should talk to the paramedic's partner and boyfriend."

"Yes," I said. "You want to do that with me?"

He turned around and looked at me. "Yeah."

"Did anyone ever speak to the boyfriend?" Lee said.

Did we? "Kurt and I didn't," I said. Should've, but shit happened and he never got interviewed. Unless Dane and Stu did. "Dane? Did you and Stu talk to him?"

"He was on the list, next up in fact, and then Sanderson happened, so nope."

"Right, let's make him first this time around. Let's go see what he has to say about his girlfriend and his lack of selfies on Facebook."

"Now?"

Caine stood. "I need to talk to you all before you take off in different directions." All eyes were on Caine. "Iain Campbell was a colleague and a friend to this team which is why I'm very interested in a song he emailed me before he died."

A smile spread across my lips. "He sent you a song? Can I see the file?"

"Of course." Caine nodded at Sandra who carried her laptop over and planted herself next to me.

"The song in question is a little ditty called 'The Man Comes Around' by Johnny Cash," Sandra said.

We grinned at each other. Before we met Iain Campbell, he'd sent me a song and inside that song was a file. So it was reasonable to believe he'd done it again, and he'd done it because he knew he wasn't going to get out of whatever situation he was in, alive.

Sandra compared the music file to the size of the same

file she downloaded from iTunes.

"Ours is bigger," she said a hint of triumph nestled in her words. "Do you think he put the passwords into the information about the file?"

I nodded. "Of course."

And there it was. The title of the song written a little differently from how you'd expect but not enough for anyone who didn't know there was a hidden file to figure out something was up.

"OpenPuff," I said.

"Oh yes."

Within a minute Sandra had extracted the hidden file from the song and opened it to reveal a cipher. It sat there on her screen. A collection of As and Bs.

Bacon cipher. I did not feel up to cracking that by hand despite having done it before. I reached over and lifted the laptop onto my knees.

"Do you mind?" I said not waiting for an answer. "We're using a secure connection?"

"Yes."

The top of the screen told me she'd opened an FBI browser. I entered search terms for a Bacon Cipher encoder/decoder. Found a suitable app and downloaded it. I dropped the text into the empty decode field. Just like magic, I got Iain's message.

The Watergate office complex BSL4 laboratory was breached. They were working on a weaponized bacterium called Q fever and mutated it. It's now behaving like a virus. It is deadly. This viral bacterium or whatever it is, is in the hands of bioterrorists here. They are planning to release it in bottled water.

I stared at the words in front of me in silence. Fuckadoodledo and whatnot.

Sandra read it; her usually pale skin paled more. I read the words aloud.

Everyone stared at me. We knew there was a threat, but now we *knew* there was a threat.

Life rocketed back into me. "We need to know everything we can find out about Q fever and this mutation." I reread the words. "When did he send this?"

"I re-watched the video footage of him exiting the elevator from the laboratory. He stopped inside the main doors to the building and had his phone in his hand at that point." Caine passed a toy back to Grace. "There you go, little lady."

"He didn't leave right away. He was in the lobby for a few minutes," Sandra said. "The time stamp on the email matches the time Iain was in the lobby."

"Can we get someone into that lab and find out what the hell is going on?" I said. If Iain figured stuff was happening there, then he must've got that information from somewhere. "Iain didn't randomly walk into a BSL-4 lab in D.C. and decide to go nosing around. Let's find out who he'd been talking to before his death."

"Anyone spoken to Tierney?" Kurt said. "CIA always knows more than they tell us. Wouldn't be a bad place to start."

"All right," I said as my next course of action spun out

in front of me. "Kurt, you're on the Tierney/Campbell angle. See if Tierney knows anything about Watergate."

Kurt nodded. "I'll check with Karen and Tahoma regarding this Q Fever/virus/bacterium and see how far they've gotten with identifying the thing that killed Sanderson."

Sandra carefully took her laptop back. "I'm here for whatever y'all need," she said.

"Dane and I will talk to Alyssa's boyfriend. Lee and Caine, go over everything we have on Garcia, find me a link to Cait that makes sense."

A murmur of compliance filled the air. I stood, gathered the empty baby bottles and took them into the kitchen. I found Ethan and Mitch at the kitchen table.

"I'm heading into town with Dane to do some interviews," I said, rinsing the bottles and standing them upside down on the counter. I opened a cabinet under the counter and found a substantial stock pot with a lid. Dropped the bottles and teats in, filled it with water and set the pot on the stove top. "Keep an eye on the bottles, don't let the water boil dry. Ten minutes should be long enough to sterilize them."

"I won't boil it dry." Mitch smiled. "Be careful," he said. "Are you taking Argo?" I knew his tone meant I should take Argo. It was a suggestion wrapped in a question that wasn't even a recommendation. He was worried.

"Of course."

"Ethan, how you doing?"

"Getting there."

"Take it easy. I'll see you when we get back."

I leaned down and kissed Mitch. He tasted like jalapeños. Sandwich remnants sat on a plate in front of him. "Did you let Sean make you a sandwich?"

"I did. He sure likes jalapeños and spicy salami."

I laughed and left the room. Never thought to warn Mitch about Sean's sandwiches. Whoops.

Chapter Thirty Nine

Lie a little better

It took us a while to leave the O'Hare estate. Car issues. Most of the cars were riddled with bullet holes and missing windows. At Sean's suggestion, we took one of his vehicles from his garage. Funny but I had no recollection of what was in his garage when I passed through it during the battle. It was dark in there and I was focused on the task ahead.

I buckled Argo into a regular seatbelt in the middle of the back seat of Sean's immaculate twenty-seventeen Ford Expedition XLT. He didn't seem to care and Sean was okay with dog claws on his cream-colored seats.

Dane stared at the twenty-eighteen yellow Shelby GT 350 also parked in Sean's garage. Yeah, no way in hell were we getting near that beauty.

After a comfortable drive into Mauryville, we stopped by the sheriff's office and found Kevin.

"Kid, you all right?" he said as I opened his office door after Marge sent me through. Argo followed me in and made straight for Kevin. Dogs always know who'll pet them and make a fuss. Kevin ruffled the fur on the dog's neck.

"Yes. We need to talk to a few people in town today and see if we can get to the bottom of this madness," I said, sitting in the hard wooden chair in front of his desk.

Dane talked to Marge in the outer office.

"I've some bikers sitting around doing nothing, interested?"

I nodded. "Very much so. I take it you're holding them on the attempted murder of federal employees?"

His mustache moved and his eyes smiled. "I am."

"Add anything and everything you can think of to the list of charges, so far it sounds like we can put together a pretty long list. I'll have the DA throw everything he can at them."

"I singled out the head honcho. Just waiting now to see if he tries to lawyer up."

I fully expected him to. But that he hadn't so far was almost encouraging. Maybe he's looking at his third strike for acts of violence and would rather not spend life in prison. Maybe we can dangle the death penalty? Words drifted on a sea in my mind. Waves washed them to the shore where they assembled in the sand. *The Code of Virginia*. Title 18.2-31. Capital murder defined. The punishment for conviction of a Class One felony is death. The tide dragged words along the beach back to the sea. All that was left baking in the sand were the seaweed-covered images of Cait O'Hare and Doctor Sanderson. Both Class One Felonies.

"I need some leverage before I talk to the motorcycle club members." Also, I shouldn't talk to them at all but I didn't think Delta A were targets. I doubt they had the first clue we were there. Must've been a delightful surprise.

His eyes sparked with life. "I know that look," he said, as his right eyebrow rose. "What are you thinking?"

"I'm thinking none of this makes sense and I need to follow the threads until it does."

"I'll babysit these boys until you're ready. Take it easy, Ellie. There's something in the wind."

Yeah, there is. "I'd like to speak to that paramedic and the boyfriend of the dead medic first." I knew their names but they wouldn't weasel their way off my tongue. I tried again as Kev patiently waited, petting Argo while I hauled names from the edge of the abyss in my mind. "Alyssa's boyfriend, Allen Buchanan. What do you know about him?"

"He arrived in town with her. He didn't give the impression of a troublemaker. Got a job real quick. Works with Johnny Adams in the workshop."

Johnny Adams. I didn't recall any Johnny Adams from when I lived here.

"What does Johnny Adams do?"

Kev leaned back in his chair causing the wood to creak. "Suppose he's new in town as far as you're concerned, Ellie. He's got the old mechanic workshop on Chambers Run. You'd know it as the Donaldson place."

"Fred Donaldson, the tractor man?"

"Yeah, although he probably prefers diesel mechanic," Kev said with a half-smile.

So, he's not dead then. "How long ago did Johnny Adams take over the business?"

"Fred moved to Florida nearly eight years ago now."

He paused, the lines on his forehead deepened. "Must be all of that. He got tired of the cold winters. Said it was killing him."

"He wasn't old was he?"

"Nope. In his early fifties but riddled with arthritis."

That didn't sound fun for someone so young. "And this Adams guy? Any trouble there?"

"Nope. Quiet as a church mouse."

"And Allen Buchanan is a mechanic?"

"That's what he was hired as, so that's where my money is."

"You don't happen to know if our helpful paramedic is on duty today?"

"We can find out." He lifted his desk phone from its cradle and dialed. "That you, Janine?"

I couldn't hear the response and had to settle for listening to Kevin rumble on about the weather and how horrible it was that Cait O'Hare came off her horse and the tragedy of the horse's death. He then became diplomatic over the presence of two gangs out at the property and his borrowing of horses to ride to the rescue. "Now, now, Janine, no harm done. It all turned out in the end."

Looked like she disagreed, from the expression on his face. He finally found an opening to speak and asked about Adam Crutchley. "Adam in the ambulance today?"

Words filtered through the receiver to become unintelligible by the time they reached me. "Oh, I won't disturb him, then." He hung up and smiled. His heavy mustache twitched. "He was on overnight. Janine says he'll be home and tucked up in bed. He's on nights all week."

"At least we know where to find him. Thanks, Kev."

"Not a problem. You two take it easy. Holler if you need a hand."

I nodded, stood, and joined Argo at the door. Kevin swung the door open. Marge scurried out of the way. Eavesdropping? Dane smiled at me and confirmed Marge was eavesdropping with a single clear thought about nosy neighbors.

Did I miss small-town life? No, I didn't. I gave Dane a rundown on our next stop.

We parked in front of the workshop. Big blue lettering on the front of a huge garage-type building proclaimed it Johnny Adams' Repair Shop. One of the two massive roller doors was open. A man inside the building worked on a tractor.

Fat snowflakes drifted from the sky and flattened themselves on the windshield. Glad of my leather gloves but wishing I had a beanie not a cap, I stepped out of the vehicle at the same time as Dane. Then let Argo out from the back. I gave him a quiet command and he headed for the nearest patch of grass to relieve himself. We caught up with Dane in the open doorway of the workshop.

Dane called out, "Hello in there."

A head popped up and a deep voice asked, "Can I help?"

"I hope so. Looking for Allen Buchanan, that you?"

The man wiped his greasy hands on a rag hanging from his pocket. "No. That'll be the young fella." He turned as if he expected to find him right there.

I scanned the workshop but couldn't see anyone else.

"Know where we can find him?" Dane kept his tone friendly like he was dropping by to say hey.

"Here," the man said. "He was right here a few minutes ago."

"Bathroom break, maybe," I said.

An engine rumbled to life somewhere out the back of the building. No. Don't run. Fuck.

I jerked my thumb at Dane. He nodded and ran for Sean's car. I took off through the building with Argo, found a back door open, and ran through. A young man sat in an old car. Didn't sound as though it liked the cold much.

I waved my hand at him and signaled him to wind down the window. I figured there were two ways out: the driveway that curved around the barn-sized workshop or through the workshop. Dane would have the driveway blocked and I stood in front of the only other exit. Not sure that he wanted to squash me, but he didn't look like he wanted to get out of the car either. Perhaps some encouragement.

I opened my jacket and showed him my badge and weapon at the same time. His eyes flicked from the gold to the black then up to my face. Again, I knocked on the window and signaled him to wind it down. No way was I going to raise my voice to be heard over the sound of the rumbling V8 as it warmed up.

He finally complied. "Who are you?"

"Agent Iverson. I'm investigating your girlfriend's death." Not a total lie. That was definitely part of our investigation scope. "This is Argo." I motioned to the dog next to me. Argo watched with interest.

"You investigate overdoses?"

"Turn the engine off, come inside, and we'll have a chat." I did my best at non-threatening and even managed pleasant. It wouldn't last long so he'd best make up his mind to cooperate.

He turned the key. The noise stopped. Allen swung the door open and climbed out. "How I can tell you anything you don't already know, Agent?" He tugged his beanie down over his ears and shivered.

"You never know what you might remember that could help. We'd like to hear your take on the situation. Everyone has a slightly different point of view." I walked beside him to the workshop where the other man was waiting. "You must be Johnny," I said, offering him my gloved hand.

"I am, and you?"

"Agent Iverson. We're investigating Alyssa's death." I pointed to Dane who hurried across the workshop to meet us.

Dane addressed Allen, "Allen Buchanan? I'm Agent Wesson." He shook his hand. "We're together."

"Cool."

Johnny ran his hands down his overall legs. "Allen,

why don't you use the break room." He glanced from me to Allen. "He shouldn't even be at work. But he won't stay home."

"I don't want to stay home, better if I'm busy," Allen said.

"I understand that," Johnny said, "You look shattered. You need to grieve and there are things to organize for Alyssa."

With a determined firmness, Allen said, "It's better if I have something to do. I'll make the arrangements when her body is released." He beckoned to me. "It's this way."

Dane and I followed him. Johnny returned to work.

The room was clean and tidy. A pale wooden table with six chairs took up the center of the room. Along one wall was a counter and sink; at the end of the counter on the floor stood a fairly tall refrigerator. Allen opened the fridge and took out a bottle of water from a six-pack of water bottles. He offered us water. We both declined. He broke the seal and downed a third of the bottle before setting it on the table and pulling out a chair.

Dane turned the bottle so we could see the label. Shit. A picture of a hotel.

"Something wrong?" Allen said.

"Do you usually have that brand of water here?" I took a photo of the bottle and sent it to Kurt and Karen.

"I dunno. It's water. I drink whatever is in the fridge."

"Seen that brand here before?"

"We finished one of those six-packs yesterday, so yeah." Allen picked at the edge of the label on the bottle.

"What has water got to do with Alyssa?"

Hopefully nothing but who knows? "Where were you when Alyssa died?"

His eyes lifted. "Here. Working. It's what people with bills do."

"Do you know her friends?"

"She didn't have the kinda job where she could socialize a lot."

"Friends?" Dane pushed.

He shrugged. "Not really. She used to go into the city sometimes and have coffee with an old school friend."

We both perked up. "That sounds nice." I kept my voice chatty. "Do you know the old school friend?"

"No. We didn't meet until after we'd finished with school. Alyssa was already a paramedic and I was finishing my apprenticeship."

"So you never met her friend?"

He shook his head. "Just didn't work out that way."

"Male or female?"

He shrugged. "Girl, I suppose."

My phone rang. A FaceTime call from Karen. "I'll be right back," I said, standing and walking out the open door looking at the woman on my screen. "The water?"

"Same brand. That brand is bottled exclusively for The Serenity group which is a chain of hotels owned by Dixon."

I knew where that was going. "Crap. The tampering was done in the bottling plant, wasn't it?"

"Yes, it was. Check the batch number on the bottle. We

have evidence pointing to the contamination beginning at batch number zero-zero-four-three-two-nine-zero-eight and ending at one-zero."

"So you stopped it?"

"We did but I'd be surprised if this was their only avenue. The CDC shut down the plant for decontamination late yesterday." A brief smile linked her words. "Batches up to zero-seven are probably safe. Not a definite."

"They finished a six-pack yesterday. If they're going to get sick how long have they got?"

"They're probably already contagious, do not get any body fluid on you. Wash your hands. Don't touch your face, eat, or drink anything, without scrubbing your hands."

"I have sanitizer in the car." Dread took hold. I did not want to take anything back to the O'Hare place.

"You need to use it. A lot." Karen sighed. "See if you can find out where they got the water."

"How many hotels are we talking about with potentially contaminated water?"

"That chain is all over the USA, Mexico, Caribbean, South America, Europe, with one hotel in Australia."

"They wouldn't all drink water from the one bottling plant though?"

"No. We don't know if other bottling plants are compromised. Even if it's only East Coast hotels, we're still in trouble."

She was right. "It's not a budget hotel either, so, we're

talking about people who travel widely using them?"

"Yes, we are."

"And the other hotel with deaths in Roanoke?"

"The virus was injected into pats of butter."

"Shit."

"Also not a budget hotel."

I scanned the workshop. My position allowed me ample view of the expanse. Guess it took a lot of space to accommodate some of the larger farm vehicles and trucks. Johnny was back working on the tractor.

"I'll go talk to the owner about water. Hey, Karen ... if they're infected how long before symptoms appear?"

"They've been drinking the water for at least a day. If they're not sick yet, they're lucky. Six to twenty-four hours for symptoms to appear."

"Do we know what it is yet?"

"Our lab is working on it."

"Okay. Did Kurt contact you?"

"He did. We are trying to verify the existence of Coxiella burnetii at the Watergate laboratory."

"And that is?"

"It's the bacterium that causes Q Fever and has the potential for bioterrorism. It's highly infectious ... fifty percent of people exposed will get sick. It's resistant to heat, drying, and many common disinfectants."

"Oh, crap."

"Generally infection is spread by inhaling contaminated dust. It spreads from cattle, sheep, and goats, to humans. Q Fever has been previously weaponized for biological warfare but to our knowledge, it was not held in D.C."

"Could Q Fever be mutated into a faster-acting, stronger, nastier bug, is that what they did when they weaponized it?"

"Scientists are capable of almost anything. It's highly likely that if they've based this illness on Q Fever, that they're created an antibiotic-resistant form. Or they may have taken qualities of Q and recreated them in a virus, like a Chimera Virus."

"And that's what?"

"A virus that looks like one thing but is something else. A virus in disguise really. We could take action to treat a flu but it's a delightful cross between Ebola and smallpox. It's also possible to create a virus that triggers two diseases at once."

"What is wrong with people that they can justify playing God and contribute to the wanton destruction of lives?" I didn't require an answer. Karen understood. "Is it a bacterium or a virus?"

"At this point, I can tell you that Sanderson's system was fighting an infection, and it took hold fast. Whether that is from exposure to an agent or because he was already ill, I can't tell at this stage." She took a breath. "The way scientists are developing new and improved ways of killing, it could be a Frankenstein of a creation. The worst parts of several things cobbled together into one."

"Any advice?"

"Be careful."

Karen hung up. I pocketed my phone and walked across the expansive concrete floor to Johnny. All of a sudden it felt like mankind was doomed. Pollyanna has left the building.

"Sorry to interrupt but where'd you get the bottles of water?" There was no other way to ask than run the risk of him getting defensive.

"A buddy of mine dropped some in the other day."

"And he got it from?"

"Oh, right, he delivers bottled water to hotels and restaurants. Why?"

"Wondering ... because that water was supposed to go to a Dixon hotel."

He straightened up and wiped his hands. "Thought they were a bit fancy for us. Must've dropped the wrong ones here. Bet he got chewed out when the hotel was short a case."

A case. They had more then.

"Bet so. Where's the rest?"

He took a step back. "You're a fed, right?" I nodded. "Am I in trouble for this?"

No, probably dead though. I smiled. "Nah, I'm curious that's all."

He smiled in return. "In the break room, under the sink."

I nodded and walked back to the break room. All was quiet in the room. Dane and Allen sat facing at one another. It wasn't an awkward silence. They watched when I walked in, crossed behind the table and opened the cabinet under the sink. Sure enough, there was a cardboard box with the same logo as the water on the table. I dragged it out. It originally contained twenty-four bottles of water. Twelve were left, in cardboard six-packs.

I pushed it back into the space and closed the door. With a sharp pull the fridge door opened, I took a water bottle from the open six-pack. Spinning it in my hand, I found the batch number. It ended in zero-nine.

Dane's eyes drilled into the back of my head as his thoughts probed mine. I let him. Better than saying aloud that the water might be contaminated with a virus or bacterium that potentially will kill them.

I put the bottle back, rubbed my gloved hands down my thighs, as if that would remove any germs from the leather and sat back at the table.

"Everything all right?" Allen said, sipping more of his water.

"Yeah, I asked your boss about the water. Looks like it was delivered by mistake. We recognized the logo. That's all." I smiled. Settled and resumed my chat with Allen. "You never met the friend. You were at work when Alyssa supposedly took the drugs. Did she often use?"

He shook his head. "Never. Random drug testing. She'd lose her job."

"Which begs the question, why would anyone suspect suicide or accidental death?"

"She was taking antidepressants."

"That's the first time we've heard that," Dane said,

leaning on the table with his elbows. "Since when?"

"Maybe six weeks. She was down for a few months, struggling, with I dunno what. She wouldn't talk. Her doctor put her on some antidepressant."

"Anyone else know?"

"Not as far as I know." He sighed. "She didn't have friends here. I tried getting her to come out with me on her nights off, you know, go places where people were, but she never wanted to."

A depressed woman overdosed. But no one knew she was depressed, except her boyfriend. We had no way of knowing if our dead biker knew or not. If he knew, then staging a suicide wouldn't be suspicious, except to everyone else.

"Was she ever suicidal?"

Allen nodded. "She had suicidal thoughts once. I took her to the doctor. He gave her Ketamine." He paused. "I'd heard of it." Allen shrugged. "I wasn't happy about it either. But it worked. Fast."

"Ketamine?" Dane said, he shot me a look of disbelief.

A horse anesthetic. A fun party drug if it's done right. Or a fucked-up trip down a k-hole if it goes wrong. This was a question for Kurt. I made the call. "Is Ketamine now an accepted drug to treat suicidal thoughts?"

"Hello to you too. Hold a minute, I heard something about Ketamine trials." I heard his fingers tapping, household noise, the babies gurgling and babbling. Hearing them made my heart soar. The thought of Q Fever plunged my heart into my roiling stomach acid.

Kurt's voice drowned out the babies. "Short answer, yes. Some doctors are using a low dose, reportedly it acts fast and removes suicidal thoughts. It's used as an intervention."

"Thank you."

"You're welcome."

I ended the call and placed my phone face down on the table. "Ketamine to treat suicidal thoughts in an emergency is a thing now." Color me amazed.

"Allen, no one knew about Alyssa's mental illness?" Dane was clarifying.

"As far as I know."

"What about her partner?" Dane said. "He'd know, right?"

"Dunno why she'd tell him. She didn't like him much."

Oh, really? We were led to believe they were close. "What was it about him she didn't like?" I said, watching Allen flick the edge of the lifted label. I wanted to grab the bottle and rip off the label. Took a lot of restraint to let him carry on flicking at the curled corner.

"He made her uncomfortable."

"In what way?"

"He came onto her. Kept trying to find excuses to touch her."

Whoa. What now? "Touch her how?" I said.

"Get too close and brush her boobs or grab her ass, then say it was an accident."

He might find he has an accident if that's how he carries on. "How did Alyssa handle him?"

"She threatened to go to the sheriff. She should have, he's a prick and he was doing shit, sneaky like, making it hard to prove it was on purpose." Anger bubbled in his words, spilling over his teeth and onto the table. "Why would someone do that?"

"I don't know," Dane said. "No excuses for intimidation or sexual harassment, Allen. None."

"Could that behavior be behind her depression?"

Allen nodded. "That's what I thought. She reckoned it wasn't that simple, that depression isn't caused by one thing."

Yeah, maybe, but living with constant harassment isn't one thing. It's bullying. It's undermining. It is disbelief wrapped in pain.

This provided a much clearer picture of Alyssa, and it was nothing like the initial images we had. I stood and walked to the window over the sink. Looking out at falling snow I let everything come together. Snowflakes touched the window and slid down to pile up on the sill. Everything I knew about Alyssa piled up with them. Her only haven was Allen. At work, she was harassed. She was more than likely also intimidated and manipulated by Joey the biker. What if killing herself was her only way out of the hell she was living.

But why would she administer drugs to Cait?

Why?

Can't have been Joey's idea. It looked very much like he didn't know Cait was dead. What if Joey wasn't a super asshole? What if he went to Cait with his concerns regarding Alyssa? What if Cait said go to the police and next minute Alyssa is dead?

No.

Another snowflake slipped down the windowpane.

Joey wanted Cait to pay for something, more than likely for firing him from a job he enjoyed because of his gang ties.

No. Not that. Okay, stop. Think.

Alyssa's link to Joey. Guilt. The prospect that he did time for her. High odds he got stabbed by her father protecting her. She had a history of men bullying or abusing her.

I spun around. "Hey, Allen."

He turned in his chair. "Yes, ma'am."

"What do you know about Alyssa's father?"

A cloud crossed his face. Anger? Sadness? Hatred? Everything jumbled into one.

"He was an asshole, beginning to end," Allen said, his voice low and seething with anger. "An asshole. Who beat his wife and his daughter."

"Did you ever meet her family?"

"No." He fished a piece of paper from his pocket and handed it to me. "Alyssa wrote this. She used to carry it with her in her wallet."

I unfolded the paper with care. Blue ink on white paper. I read the words to myself then aloud. "'When everyone's dead, and everyone's gone. There's no one left to carry on. Safe at last. Home free. Burying the pain under an old oak tree. Creaky boards on wooden floors.

Pictures stuck to painted doors. Gray shadows flicker on a white wall. Clouds floating up the empty hall. Before I become someone's prey. Find a place to hide away.'"

"What?" Dane cast his eyes to me. "What does it mean?"

She was talking about her life. "Not sure."

"It's not the happiest poem I've ever heard," he said to Allen. "When did she write it? Alyssa did write it?"

Allen sat quietly but surprise registered on his features as if he hadn't heard it before. "Yes. That was a poem that Alyssa wrote."

"Then why do you look surprised?"

"She used to recite it all the time. All. The. Time." His eyes met mine. He did not look well. "But, it always ended with the oak tree."

"You never read it for yourself? The whole thing?"

"No. I knew what the piece of paper was when I saw it folded in her wallet. I took it and put it in my wallet. I didn't look at it."

Guess he would've eventually. "Do you know what it means?"

"No, not really. I thought it was about her family but I don't know about the stuff after the tree."

Beads of sweat glistened on Allen's forehead. It was snowing. Yes, it was warm in the break room, but not hot, and fresh, cool air filtered through from the open workshop main doors.

"Are you feeling okay?"

"Bit of a headache," he replied, swigging more water.

"Did Adam Crutchley know Alyssa told you about his behavior?"

He nodded. "He sure did. I had a word with him over two weeks ago. Told him we were going to the police and that was that."

"How did he react?"

"The prick laughed. He said she couldn't prove anything, it's his word against hers and he grew up in this town." Anger spilled over his words. "Who did I think the sheriff would believe?"

"And then?"

"I punched him."

Well done. I resisted a smile.

"He swing back?" Dane said.

"Nope, he lay there crying like a baby."

Oh shit, he knocked him down. Time to talk to Adam 'the baby' Crutchley.

"If you recollect anything else, call me, right away, okay?" I said and pressed my card into his hand. "You should rest up."

He rubbed his right temple with his fingertips. "Think I will. Thanks for trying to help find out what happened to Alyssa," Allen smiled, I sensed him pushing anger down deep.

"It's what we do."

"How did you know to investigate her death?" He half-smiled. "Can I ask that?"

"Of course. Something didn't feel right," I said. And apparently Alyssa agreed, judging by the poem now stuck in my head.

He looked increasingly unwell. "Feels like I'm coming down with something."

"Flu season," I said. There was a couch against the wall by the door. "Maybe you should lie down."

Dane and I went into the main workshop and found Johnny working on the same tractor.

"We've suggested Allen lie down. He doesn't look well. How are you feeling?" I said, smiling, no big deal, it is flu season. Chimera flu season. Everything nasty you could think of crammed into a run of the mill flu.

"Not great, but not too bad." He wiped sweat off his brow with the sleeve of his overalls.

"There is a lousy strain of flu going around. We'll send some people to assess you both."

"Is that necessary?" Panic flashed in his eyes.

"For your wellbeing." I smiled as reassuringly as I could. I hoped I didn't look creepy. "Close up. Rest."

"If it's that bad we'll go home."

"Be best if you stayed put."

"What aren't you telling me, Agent?"

"You might have been exposed to a new strain. We don't know anything more than that, except what we were told. Anyone who looks ill should stay where they are and rest. We will send medical help."

"You'll be in danger now?"

I hoped not. "We'll take precautions. Just shut the doors and rest." Maybe a red X on the door so everyone knows it's contaminated. Because that wouldn't cause panic.

"My wife?"

"Give us your address, we'll send someone to her as well. Do you have kids?"

"Not yet. Our first is due in four months."

Oh shit. "Congratulations. What's your address?"

He gave it to me, and I typed it into notes.

We left the workshop and drove a hundred yards down the road before Dane pulled over. I took off my gloves, opened a Ziploc evidence bag, dropped my gloves in it and squirted hand sanitizer in my hand then tossed him the bottle. He did the same.

"Fuck," I muttered, putting the bottle of hand sanitizer in the console between us.

I called Karen. "Send a team or whatever you do. The young man at the address we just left is sick. This about the bottles." I fired off a text with the exact address.

"On it. How many people involved on site?"

"Two. One is definitely sick with something and the other doesn't look great. The boss has a pregnant wife at home." I copied the home address and texted it to Karen.

"Thanks, Ellie. We'll deal with it."

"Could be a regular flu though, right?"

"Of course," she said, her words coated in a lie that felt better than the truth. "Latest data showed that only thirty-seven percent of the adult population received influenza vaccines last year, a decrease of six point two percent from the previous season. Dropping vaccination numbers would show as an increase of reported cases of influenza."

Statistics helped.

Chapter Forty
Lilac Wine

"Dane, swing by Alyssa and Allen's house."

At the intersection, he turned right. "Why?"

"Because we might find something." And right now, might is enough. The poem repeated in my head until it made me dizzy.

"An old oak tree?" Dane said then broke into an awful rendition of 'Tie a Yellow Ribbon.'

"You're killing me," I muttered, covering my ears with my hands.

Dane laughed and stopped. "What do you expect to find?"

"A reason."

"For?"

"Her death, what Adam Crutchley was doing, for Cait's drugging, for some clarity of purpose."

"The drugs came back as identical to the ones we found on the bikers, El. Garcia is linked to that mess."

"We think. We need proof."

"And a note from a dead girl will do that?"

"If she's the person I feel she was, then I have a feeling she kept a diary, so yes." If not, we're chasing rainbows on a snowy day. It wouldn't hurt us to look.

Dane flicked the indicator and turned down another road. Two more turns and half a mile of straight country road and we drove into the driveway of Alyssa and Allen's rented home. At the end of the driveway, the big limbs of a tree extended over the garage. Brown leaves, frosted with snow clung to the branches. Oak. I pointed. Dane agreed. We left the warmth of the car. I shoved my hands in my pockets as we walked to the backyard. Under the big tree was a seat. The sort with built-in storage underneath it.

"What is the point?" Dane said when faced with the charming wooden seat.

"I have one in my backyard. Crackerjack place to keep smaller tools and whatnot."

He broke into a grin. "I can't believe you said whatnot with a straight face."

I couldn't believe I'd said it at all, especially with crackerjack. Who even am I?

Dane's cogs were turning. "You garden?"

"No. My dad gardens." I lifted the lid. Inside I found tools. Trowels, forks, a couple of claw things I couldn't recall the name of. I moved the hand tools out of the way. Underneath them, I found plastic pots, string, a pair of pruning shears, and under that a metal box. I moved everything out of the way so I could lift out the box.

"A metal box under an oak tree," Dane said, watching me with interest. "How lucky do you feel?"

I lifted the lid. With a grin on my face, I said, "Pretty lucky."

The lid fell back revealing nothing. Shit.

"Okay, now what?" Dane said, tucking his hands into

his pockets. I pointed to the house.

"Really?"

"Yep."

I put everything back the way I'd found it. Snow fell harder, obliterating our footprints as we crunched across the partially frozen ground to the back porch.

Dane peered in a window. I ran my fingers across the top of the door frame. No hidden key. I checked under plant pots. Dane swung the meter box open.

"Looking for this?" He said, handing me a small magnet box.

I slid the cover off it and tipped a key into my hand.

"Looks like a door key, shall we try?" I held it up.

Dane grinned. "Sure."

I plunged the key into the keyhole where it flopped around like a dying fish. I pulled it out again. "Front door?"

We walked around the house to the front and tried the key again. It wriggled around inside the keyhole and did nothing.

"Or not," Dane said.

As I walked around the outside again and placed the key back in its hiding place, my new plan involved breaking and entering. Probably not the best idea but Allen was unlikely to mind too much.

Out with the slip card and into the house via the back door then.

Dane waited. I released the lock and swung the door wide. No sounds of life. Skittering of paws or otherwise.

"Wipe your feet," I said, stepping off the doormat and into the kitchen. "Room by room."

The house was warm, dry, and clean. Dane stood in the middle of the kitchen.

"If I were a diary, where would I be?" He turned around faced the hallway. "Bedroom?"

"Yeah. Do a walk-through first then we'll search their bedroom."

We walked through the small, tidy house.

"Wooden floors all through," Dane said, more to himself than me.

Wooden floors and area rugs, a long, well-worn rug in the hallway. A cozy kitchen. Two bedrooms. One living room. One bath. Not a lot of room to hide in or get lost.

"That poem mentioned wooden floors," I said from the main bedroom doorway. "Haven't noticed any creaking floorboards, have you?"

"No." Dane's voice came from over my shoulder. "We going in or hanging here in this very ordinary doorway?"

I stepped into the room where Alyssa died and held my breath. Being unsure of what to expect struck me as odd. It was a bedroom. No body waiting to talk to me. No residual feelings of sadness or loss. Why would I expect anything? Then it dawned on me. The room felt peaceful. Peace. Alyssa was at peace.

"You okay?

"Sure."

"Do you think Allen has been sleeping in here?" Dane asked, opening drawers in the tallboy.

"Don't know."

"Think I'd take the sofa rather than sleep in the bed my girlfriend died in," he said, moving piles of tee shirts then replacing them.

I checked the nightstands. An old-fashioned wind-up bell alarm clock sat on one, its red enamel battered and chipped from years of service. The absence of ticking caused me to glance at my watch to confirm the alarm clock wasn't working.

"If he is sleeping in here he hasn't wound the clock," I said, opening the bottom drawer of the two drawers in the nightstand. I found notebooks. Sitting on the bed, I took a closer look. Three notebooks. Flipping through them I discovered someone was a list keeper. One contained grocery lists. One contained household chore lists. The last notebook contained lists relating to errands. The next drawer up contained a small jewelry box and some perfumes. "This must be Alyssa's side of the bed."

Dane opened the closet and moved clothes hangers.

"Anything interesting?"

"She kept notebooks with lists. She was pretty organized."

"This closet is tidy, nothing hidden. The shoe boxes on the shelf contain shoes."

Who does that? I'm pretty organized, but shoe boxes in my closet contain photos and letters and treasures. Shoes live in the shoe rack.

The other nightstand contained nail clippers, a book, a

flashlight, and a parts catalog for John Deere Model D tractors. Allen's side of the bed.

Still nothing like a diary or a notebook. Dane moved to the second set of drawers and I turned my attention to the bed. I lifted the mattress all the way around, shoving my arm in as far as it would go. Nothing.

Dammit.

I shifted my feet and a floorboard creaked. Frozen on the spot, I looked at Dane.

"That sounds promising," he said.

I rocked my foot. The board creaked again. "Give me a hand."

We pushed the bed over about a foot, I pushed down on the creaky board and it lifted about half an inch at the opposite end. Dane grabbed it and lifted. Inside the hole was a book inside a Ziploc plastic bag.

I took the book from the hole and tipped it out of the bag onto the bed. As soon as I opened it I knew this was Alyssa's diary. My fingers traced an embossed silver tree on the dark green cloth-bound cover; above the tree were five tiny silver dragonflies. It was a beautiful journal.

"Jackpot," I said with a smile. "Let's put everything back and go see what we have here."

Ten minutes later, shivering, I slid into the passenger seat of our car and closed the door.

"Coffee?" Dane said as he shut his door. "Diner?"

I nodded and left the book safely inside my jacket, intent on exploring its contents with pie and coffee at the diner. Who knew how many more chances we'd have to eat pie like that? A small laugh escaped. I thought the same thing last time we ate pie.

One of these times it will be the last.

"Something funny?" Dane chose a car park outside the diner.

"Just thinking how last time we ate pie I thought that was our last pie for a while."

"Right, the apocalypse an' all."

"Yeah."

"The dead won't reanimate and turn into zombies, though, right?"

I shrugged. "Fuck knows. If they've created this thing, then it could do anything."

"Headshot or no shot."

"Damn straight."

I wished I had gloves to put on the minute I opened the car door. The temperature must've dropped another five degrees, the snowfall heavier. Dane opened the diner door for me. A rush of heat hit us as we entered. I unzipped my jacket and caught the notebook before it fell. I ordered two coffees and two slices of cherry pie warmed with vanilla ice-cream.

I slid across the shiny blue seats in a booth near the back. Dane sat opposite me. Tiredness drew lines on his face.

"You checked in on Stu?"

I knew he hadn't since we'd partnered up. Dane's eyes met mine. "He's fine."

"You called?"

"No. I'd know if he wasn't."

I believed that was true. Had a feeling I would too and everything in the Stu part of my brain felt okay. Quiet but okay. Kennedy was a survivor. I expected him to be fine.

My phone rang. I tugged it from my pocket, and set it on the table while I removed my jacket. Debbie Barnes. The FBI's specialist in the creation of false identities and new lives. I answered, tapped the speaker icon and folded up my jacket.

"I have something that will interest you," Debbie said.

"Okay, what is it?"

"A list of names came through from Mauryville and as it was a list of bikers' names, we ran it through our database."

I didn't even ask why. I'm pretty sure every gang had an undercover cop or fed in it at some point. "You find something?"

"Shane Radford. He's been missing for two years."

"Missing person."

"Missing DEA agent."

"Oh, shit. What name has he been using?"

"Dave Holloway, also known as Freddy."

"I'll see if he'll talk to me. Will you notify DEA that he's in custody and see how they want to proceed?" Lost agents aren't always lost. Sometimes they're deeper than anyone expected.

"I will." There was a pause. "On an unrelated note, I was going to drop by and visit Mitch and those adorable babies tomorrow."

"Mitch and those adorable babies are down here with me," I said with a smile. "I'll let you know when we're back."

"I'll look forward to it."

"Thanks, Debbie. Catch up soon."

After I hung up, the server carrying a tray with pie and coffee headed our way. Neither of us said anything until the server left.

Dane pulled a plate of pie across the table. "One of the bikers is an agent." He shoveled a forkful of pie into his mouth. The expression on his face as he chewed said it all. It was excellent pie.

"Yes, to the agent," I said, taking a smaller amount of pie than Dane. Half my pie disappeared before I turned to the first page in the notebook.

The diary began in the middle of summer. Alyssa wrote every day to start with. She loved Mauryville. Small-town life, she wrote, was comfortable for the most part. I skipped days and flipped pages until I came across the initials AC. She worked with AC and he'd asked her out. She turned him down and commented he knew she had a boyfriend so what was his problem. And from then on he became an asshole.

"Listen to this," I said to Dane. " 'AC made another excuse to brush past me today. This time he pretended to trip and grabbed my boob.' "

"Prick."

"She mentions going to have coffee with an old friend, uses the name Journey."

So we were right about the food photographs. They were a code of sorts. Now to find out if it was sinister or friends mucking around.

"How did that go?"

"Doesn't say. But she did say she told Journey about AC and how horrible he makes her feel."

"Did she talk about Allen?"

"Yeah. She said Allen wanted to smack AC around but she doesn't want him getting into trouble." I read some more then paraphrased. "The doctor adjusted her medication because she was complaining of increased anxiety."

"Anything to suggest she knew who was behind Cait's attack and the biker visit?"

"Not yet."

I forked pie into my mouth and a wayward cherry escaped and bounced on the table landing with a plop on the notebook. I scooped it up and dropped it back in the plate. A fat round red stain remained. Setting the fork on the edge of my plate I carried on reading.

Better to read now and eat later.

Dane's sense of humor was about to get the better of him. I held one finger in the air. I felt a smile grow from within, let it come, and carried on with the task at hand.

Flipping pages, scanning for anything that felt relevant took time. Twice I closed the book and took mouthfuls of pie and drank coffee.

The third time, about to close it, I inadvertently turned an extra page. I shut my eyes. Opened them. Stared. The page was filled with little symbols, crazy stick figures. Doodles but not doodles. I flipped back through other pages. She hadn't drawn anything like them before, not even as little drawings in the margins. I thumbed through a few more pages. Some contained writing, some the weird, doodle-type stick figures and no writing.

Code. But not one I'd seen before. Was she worried that her boyfriend would read her diary? Or was she worried someone else would? Who had access to her house? Why would anyone have access to her house?

"What's up?" Dane said. He leaned in, waiting.

"It's getting interesting. I found code."

"She wasn't a teenager so why write in code in a diary?" He lifted his cup to his lips but put it down before taking a sip. "Can you crack it?"

My right eyebrow arched. "Pretty sure I can. Gimme a minute."

I reached for a napkin from the dispenser at the end of the table, Dane handed me a pen. He stood up and joined me on my side of the booth.

"This is cozy."

"Uh huh."

Dane peered at the open pages. He tapped the first page. "It's not a code as such, it's a language."

"Code is a language."

He sighed. "Yes, but this is a mixture of two languages. Or maybe one language and one alphabet."

My finger traced over the grouped doodles. They weren't hieroglyphs. Moving my finger along the page, I stopped at a different group of doodles. He was right. There were at least two forms of language used. "What does that look like to you?"

"Armenian? Yiddish? Hebrew?"

"No idea then?" I moved on two lines and came to yet another style. This time the sticks had little circles attached at the joins or the ends.

"I've seen that before." Dane used his phone and took a picture. "We had a weird case once with symbols like that drawn on objects. I think it's Angelic."

Because angels just rock on over and draw in people's notebooks. "Angels. Well, then, let's locate one and start pulling feathers until it decodes this for us."

He ignored me and sent a text message.

I decided to go back to my usual way of working out codes. With the pen in hand, I searched for shared features in the groupings. Vowels were always the best place to start. Samuel Morse thought 'e' was the most used letter, followed by 't' then 'a' 'i' 'n' 'o' and 's.' Looking at the jumble in front of me, I took a breath and looked for the most used symbol.

I drew a circle with a vertical line through the center. That was the most common symbol on the page and gave me a starting point. And accepting that 'the' is the most commonly used word in the English language gave me more to work with. I scoured the page for three-letter words ending in a circle with a vertical line through it. From that, I determined 't' was an upward arrow and 'h' was a vertical line through the middle of an X.

Before long I had enough letters decoded to guess at the longer words. By the time Dane's phone buzzed on the table I had partial sentences.

"That was Stu," Dane said, reading the screen. "He said it is Angelic, and sent us an Angelic alphabet."

"Because everyone has one on their phone?"

Dane laughed. "Remember when we met and I said we worked strange cases as well as the Wayward Son Protocol?"

I did indeed recall that. "Angels though?"

"Takes all sorts to make this crazy world we live in."

I used the image on his phone to decode the few words written in Angelic. We had a page we could read, if not all the words, then ninety percent.

"Okay. She's talking about things moving in the house. She woke up for her night shift and the coffee mug she thought she left on the table in the kitchen was on the counter in the bathroom." I read more. "She thinks she's losing her mind because she doesn't remember taking the cup to the bathroom."

"Any mention of why the code?"

"Just read that. She thinks if Allen reads this by accident he'll take her back to the doctor, and it's not the first thing she's found somewhere she didn't leave it."

"Paranoid?"

"Could be."

Alyssa went on to describe how AC made her feel horrible that night on shift. He leered at her. Suggested she unzip her flight suit a bit to make herself look more feminine. When she told him to stop behaving a dick, he sulked for the rest of the shift. She said she was worried he'd follow her home. He'd done it before and sat at the end of the driveway watching her. She'd told Journey about those incidents, and also Allen.

Dane's phone buzzed again, pulling me away from Alyssa's private hell. I glanced at Dane. He showed me the text.

Stu: The other code is based on a runic alphabet. See image.

He'd attached a photo of a complete runic alphabet and another text followed quickly.

Stu: The person who is writing in runic has mixed two known alphabets, here's the second. You should be able to decode everything now.

I nodded at Dane. Deep inside my head, I cleared a space and thanked Stu. His reply came back quickly. I knew that meant he was recovering.

Back to reading. I quite enjoyed that Alyssa wrote 'Joey' and 'Allen' in Angelic script but 'AC' and 'asshole' appeared in runic-like for the bulk of her journaling in the latter pages. I found no reference to Joey or Journey that wasn't positive and friendly, likewise to Allen. Those two were not an issue in her life; they were support. What was strange was that neither displayed much awareness of the other. Joey knew about Allen, Allen did not know who Joey was and they'd never met.

From all the things I learned from reading her private thoughts, the one thing that stood above everything was how awful AC made her feel.

A server filled our cups and moved away. She popped back minutes later and cleared the plates.

Dane placed a hand over the notebook, blocking the text. "At what point are we going to talk about our exposure to the mystery illness?"

I hadn't planned on talking about it. I knew we couldn't go back to Sean's; that would put everyone at risk. Every. One. Until he voiced the words, I had pushed all ramifications of the meeting with Allen so deep even Mitch and Stu couldn't find my thoughts.

A can of worms fell from the sky, exploding on impact. Little bits of worm wriggled all over the table. Some stuck to the notebook. I picked pieces off and flicked them to the floor. A fluffy little yellow duckling quacked and waddled across the table. It stopped. Surveyed the banquet of worm guts on offer. Quacked again and left. The mess writhed and wriggled.

I took a deep breath. A cacophony of voices filled my head. On another deep breath, I closed the open portal in my mind and silenced the outcries.

"We'll be fine," I said and pushed his hand off the page. "Let's get on with this."

"Sure we will." He sipped his coffee. "I'm sure we will."

It sounded a lot like 'the fuck we will.' With an internal shrug, I got back to the task at hand.

Chapter Forty One

Can't keep a good man down.

Coughing and spluttering – potential illness – funneled down the diner and reached our booth. "We should probably leave." I tucked the notebook and napkin I'd written on into my waistband and shook out my jacket, shoved my arms in the sleeves, zipped it over the book, and rose to my feet. Dane scooted around the table and retrieved his jacket, his wallet out and already at the till paying. I walked past an unwell-looking man near the door and paused long enough to say, "You should be home in bed, sir."

He stared at me, blinked, and mumbled, "Heading there now."

I stepped out into the cold but fresh air. Dane caught the door before it closed and hurried after me. The car lights flashed, I opened the passenger door and jumped in, slamming the door shut behind me.

Safe in our little bubble away from the germy public we stared at each other. My mind rampaged and a few of Dane's thoughts reached me. I sent them back. They weren't helpful. I grabbed the hand sanitizer and squirted a large dollop into my palm before passing the bottle to Dane. This was our life now.

Instead of allowing despair to take hold, I summoned a smile. Attitude is everything. If ever there was a time for an injection of Pollyanna it was now.

"We need an operations base," I said. "Somewhere away from people."

"We also need masks and nitrile gloves."

"I might have a solution." I wrestled my phone from my jeans pocket and made a call to Grant Neal. He answered faster than I expected. "Ellie?"

"My partner and I are in need of a few things and somewhere away from people to use as a base."

"Okay." I waited while he thought. "There's an empty building on the hospital grounds."

"Can we get to it without going through the actual hospital?"

"Yes, drive through the carpark and down the lane that leads to Emergency then keep going out the back. There's a larger car park and beyond that a grass area, the building sits back on that, down a long driveway. In the old days, it was the nurses' home."

"Sounds perfect."

Actually, it sounded droughty and cold but far enough away from people to keep them safe from us, in case of infection and us safe from them in case we weren't infected.

"What do you need? I'll take it over there now. I'll leave the door unlocked and the key in the kitchen."

Kitchen. Peachy. That'd be helpful.

"Is there power?"

"Yes, it was never cut off. It's an historic building now and we let people use it as a hostel and for retreats and so forth."

"Even better. Thanks, Grant."

"Is there something I should know?"

"Yeah. Dane and I have been in contact with someone who was exposed to the illness that killed Doctor Sanderson."

"And two of my nurses. Even though he tried to be careful."

Shit. "I'm sorry."

"Not your fault, Ellie. You didn't go round letting a lethal virus loose." He stopped, a small laugh escaped. "Did you?"

"No. I did not."

"I'll stock the place with whatever medical supplies you'll need. Can you get food?"

"Yeah."

"I nearly said see you soon. I won't see you unless you get ill. Hope I don't see you."

"Thanks, Grant."

I hung up and stared at the phone for a moment. The gravity of the situation settled on my shoulders.

"Okay?" Dane said, his hand on the ignition key. "Where to?"

"Yeah. Let's finish what we need to do here and then we'll go to Stonewall Jackson Hospital and our new accommodation. For now, let's go park up on the road out of town. Pick a spot."

Kevin walked out onto the porch of the sheriff's office and waved at us. I waved back and made a sign with my hands indicating I'd call him later. He smiled and nodded.

I wanted to talk to the bikers. That wasn't possible until we knew we weren't carrying a lethal virus.

But we don't know whether they are carrying.

Dane picked a spot on the shoulder of the main road. The snow had all but stopped dropping from the low gray sky.

"I'm going to read more of this." I tapped the book and willed it to contain something usable. I flicked through to the last page I'd read and started the painstaking task of converting the squiggles and stick-figure type symbols into words that I could read without causing a migraine.

Dane called Kurt and let him know what we were doing and what our plans were. I heard Kurt's voice even though he wasn't on speaker. Unhappiness resounded in every word he said and distracted me from my task. Concentrate.

I blocked out everything around me. Winter no longer existed. The car no longer existed. Alone at an imaginary desk with the notebook open in front of me, I learned to read the code without needing to translate each letter.

When I finally extracted myself from the pages, I knew Adam Crutchley was a liar.

My phone rang. "Yep," I said, not even aware enough of the call to use my name.

"Ellie, is that you? It's Doc Robinson speaking."

"It is, sorry." I focused. "What's up, Doc?"

He chuckled. "Never gets old, Ellie. I have something

for you." I heard the gear change in his voice. "The horse was in fantastic health, no question that he died of a massive overdose of drugs."

"Thank you for that, Doc."

"There's something else. My wife has a bee in her bonnet over a credit card receipt she found while doing the books. You remember Cookie, she does my accounts."

"I remember Cookie." Hard woman to forget. She was genuine southern lady until riled and then, from memory, she could chew nails and spit out a barbed-wire fence. "Tell me about the credit card."

I heard an annoyed female voice in the background. Just sitting in his cramped untidy office would be enough to make my voice shrill and temper rise, never mind trying to work in that environment.

"She found an emailed receipt from a company that I have in the past purchased my tranquilizer rifles from. The receipt was for a rifle. She thinks I have a big enough gun cache as it is and is displeased at the thought of a new rifle."

A blind person could see where this was headed. "Was that the only purchase that you didn't make?"

"No. About an hour later she found another receipt this time from a new drug company, one I haven't used before."

Uh huh, I do understand what new means. "Any name on those receipts?"

"Only mine. Ellie, I did not make those purchases, and the credit card used is not mine."

"Doc, have you been away at all over the last month? Did you leave anyone helping Hannah hold down the fort?"

"Not really," he said.

"That's a yes, not a no," I said. "Who did you ask to keep an eye on things or maybe back up young Hannah in an emergency?"

"I didn't really. But I spoke to Adam Crutchley and said I'd be away and if Hannah got into trouble, could she call on him to help out."

Well, what do ya know about that? "Can you read me that credit card number, please?"

Doc did and I wrote it down so I could check it out. Couldn't help but wonder what the odds were of the card belonging to Adam. Guess it depends how clever he thinks he is.

"Tell Cookie not to worry, it wasn't you. I will get to the bottom of it."

"Thank you, Ellie."

"No problem."

As soon as the call ended, I opened an app we liked to use to run credit card numbers. The card number came back fast as a pre-loaded Visa gift card. No name. The great thing about gift cards is someone had to purchase it. I needed to dig deeper, so I sent the information to Sandra. And waited.

I turned my head to find Dane's seat empty. Swiveling in my chair, I peered into the back. He was sleeping. My phone buzzed. A text from Sandra. The gift card was purchased using a credit card belonging to Adam Crutchley.

We got the little fucker.

Nothing I like more than beating a criminal with their stupidity. "Dane?"

He was semi-reclined on the back seat. With Argo stretched out next to him.

"Dane!"

He grumbled and rubbed his eyes. "Yep." Dane sat up slowly and climbed back into the front.

"I got something. We need to go wake Adam Crutchley and have a wee talk."

"We are potentially infected with something evil," Dane said.

"Yeah, but we've got a few hours before we're contagious, right? Fifty-fifty we won't get sick at all."

He shrugged. "Suppose so."

"We'll be fine."

He rubbed his face. I got out of the car and stretched, then let Argo out for a bathroom break. Dane joined us on the side of the road. "I'm going over there and check out that tree," Dane said, flashing me a smile.

"Must be nice being a man," I said, letting Argo back into the warm car. I buckled him in, back in the driver's seat by the time Dane returned. He jumped into the passenger seat, shivering, took hand sanitizer from the glove compartment and rubbed it into his cold hands.

"Let's go see Crutchley," I said, tapping the indicator lever.

"What'd you find out?"

"Alyssa was driving the ambulance that night and Doc Robinson's wife is pissed because of a new credit card that was used to purchase a tranquilizer rifle."

"You ran the credit card?"

"I sure did. It was a gift card purchased by Adam Crutchley."

"That ramps things up."

Chapter Forty Two

Don't laugh at me

I knocked hard on the wooden edge of the glass-paneled front door of the Crutchley house. Dane, Argo, and I waited.

The door opened. Mrs. Crutchley smiled out at us. "How can I help you?"

I opened my jacket to reveal my badge. "I'm Agent Iverson, Mrs. Crutchley. We need to talk to Adam."

"Oh, I am sorry he's asleep," she said. "Bless his heart, he was out saving people all night."

Of course he was. "I'm afraid we have to wake him," I said.

"But he has work again tonight."

"I understand that, ma'am." My patience vaporized. "We can talk to him now, here, or we can arrest him and take him to the nearest field office. Your choice?"

She stepped aside. Thought so. "His is the second door on the right down the hall."

Dane and I walked down to the room. The door was shut. I knocked then flung the door open hard enough that it smacked into the doorstop.

Fuck him, he's a bully and an asshole. He can wake up my way. I flicked on the light.

Jerked awake Adam sat up and peered at us bleary-eyed. "Agent Iverson?"

"Yes."

"What's going on?"

"We have some questions."

"Can they wait until my shift tonight, I can come to you and we can talk then?"

"No. Now. Get up."

"I can come to you tonight. I know where you're staying."

"Get up."

Reluctantly he swung his legs over the side of the bed. I was relieved to find he wore sweatpants to bed. He stuffed his feet into Ugs. I fought a rising Beau Bennett/ The Ranch moment and didn't ask 'What the fuck is on your feet?' In case it slipped out, I clenched my teeth.

Adam stood, put on a robe from the closet, and tied it around himself. "The kitchen is always warmer," he said. "Follow me."

I let him settle at the table. His mom fussed around until I asked her to leave us alone.

"What's this about, Agent?"

"Who drove the ambulance the night Cait O'Hare had her accident?" Dane said, moving around the table until he and Argo were next to Adam.

"I did. I told you already."

"You don't want to reconsider your answer?" I said.

His eyes met mine. I saw a reaction that came across as arrogance. That would be a mistake.

"No, I do not."

"Okay." I flipped my notebook open to a page filled

with information from Alyssa's journal. Trusting a dead girl. "Alyssa drove the night you attended Cait O'Hare's accident."

A modicum of smugness faded. He shrugged and rebounded with renewed vigor. "You were there, were you?"

"You took turns. She was the driver that night." I left no room for confusion. "Two weeks ago, her boyfriend knocked you to the ground."

"He's a crazy person. I should've pressed charges."

"Huh, because that's what he was saying about Alyssa. She should've pressed charges against you for sexual harassment."

"That's ridiculous. I didn't do anything she didn't enjoy or want me to do."

"So Alyssa gave verbal consent to be touched, fondled, and leered at by you?" Let's clarify that.

"She didn't not give it."

Dane bent down close to Adam's ear and said, "That's not consent."

"She was a druggie anyway."

I shook my head.

Dane unclipped Argo's leash. "Seek," he said, and the dog started searching.

"You can't do that. You need a warrant."

"No, ya see, your mom invited us in and the dog will find what the dog finds, we can't control what he does, his leash is off."

"But he gave him a command."

"Agent Wesson, did you say something to my dog?"

"Nope," he said. "Just took his leash off."

"I heard him." Adam's voice squeaked.

I gave a half a shrug. "Our word against yours I guess." I scratched my head. "Wonder who will be believed? Two federal agents, or you, a proven liar."

"You can't do that. It's against the law."

"And you can't go around breaking into people's houses and moving their stuff and watching them sleep," I said producing a photo I'd found in the journal.

"I didn't do that," he said.

"Funny that, because you were the only person pressuring her to go out, making excuses to touch her, and behaving like a bully because she kept turning you down and telling you to leave her alone."

"How would I get into her house?"

"Ya see, Adam. I know who owns the house that Alyssa and Allen are renting."

All of a sudden he didn't look so pleased with himself.

"Would you like to tell Agent Wesson how you stuck that photo of Alyssa sleeping on the bathroom mirror for her to find when she woke up?"

He shook his head.

"Okay then," I stood up and walked to the kitchen doorway. "Mrs. Crutchley, would you come in for a minute, please?" I said, in the sweetest voice you could imagine. Then I turned back to Adam. "It wasn't the only photo. Alyssa left me another four."

She was scared but also scared of what Allen would do

if he found out; she didn't want him in trouble. She told Journey about one of the photos. I wished she'd gone to the police. Kevin would've acted and could've saved her life.

His mom entered the room. "What did you need, dear?"

"Are you renting a house out to that lovely young couple, Allen and Alyssa?"

Her face fell. "I am. That poor young man ... she was so lovely."

"Do you have spare keys for the property?"

Adam glared at his mother. "You don't have to tell them anything," he snapped.

She frowned at him. "I don't have the keys," she said. "We used to always keep one in a key keeper in the meter box, but Alyssa and Allen had the locks changed."

"So you no longer have a key?"

"I did, of course," she said. "Alyssa gave me one of the new keys for emergencies." She paused at a groan from her son. "But Adam borrowed them to pick up something from the garage over there once. And I'd forgotten until you mentioned it."

Dane tapped my foot with his. Argo was back and I knew by the look on his face that he'd found something.

"Adam, you need to start telling the truth," I said.

His mother's mouth opened in horror. "What on earth is going on?"

"It has something to do with Alyssa and with Mrs. James."

Neither of them blinked when I said Mrs. James.

"That was a dreadful accident. I was so pleased to hear she was discharged from the hospital. Cait and Ethan were so sweet to us when Adam's father became ill."

"Do you mind if I have a look around your home?" I said, wanting to see what Argo found.

"Not if it helps you, dear," Mrs. Crutchley said. "You've had your fair share of loss, haven't you, Ellie?"

I paused for a beat. "I didn't realize you remembered me."

"Not right away but I got there."

I smiled. Argo walked ahead of me, taking me straight to Adam's room. He sat next to the bed. I crouched down and felt underneath it. When I hit a big object, I gave it a closer examination. A medical bag. The backpack type that Kurt carried. Gimme the prize.

I dragged it out and carried it to the kitchen.

"What's in this?" I asked Adam putting the bag on the table.

His mother answered before he did. "I thought you lost that bag, that's why you got the other one."

"Found it again," he said. "It's a paramedic's bag, it has medical stuff in it."

"Okay to open it then?"

"Personal property. I don't give my consent."

I spoke his mother. "Do you own this house?"

She nodded.

"Did you give me permission to look around?"

"I did."

I unzipped the bag. At first, I only saw the usual stuff that I'd seen in Kurt's bag. Dressing packs. Syringes. Stethoscope. Saline irrigation vials. Normal stuff. At the bottom, I found a box. When I opened it I found money. Cash, folded, with rubber bands around it. Under the cash, small Ziploc baggies, containing a white powder with a sticker that read Alprazolam. I texted Kurt and asked him what it was. He replied within seconds: Xanax.

In a bigger Ziploc bag, I found more small bags of white powder. Not labeled. Then tucked in the corner, I discovered ten mil ampoules of fentanyl citrate. In a hidden pocket, I found a burner phone. I spread it all out on the table.

"Do you have anything you'd like to say?"

He shook his head.

His mother had a few words to say. "Adam, are these illegal drugs?"

He nodded.

"What on earth are you doing with drugs?"

He looked his mother square in the eye and said, "Making small-town life bearable."

"You don't use," I said, looking at him, he was way too healthy looking for a user and I got the impression he enjoyed the apparent status of life as a paramedic. "You sell." Dane photographed everything we'd found. "Distribution, and the same drugs that were found in Cait O'Hare's blood and in Alyssa's."

Mrs. Crutchley walked around the table and smacked her son upside the head. "I should've done that a long time ago," she said, with disgust. "Did you sell the drugs to Alyssa? I struggle to believe she was a drug addict."

My turn. "He didn't sell it to her, he injected it into her. She was probably asleep at the time. Your son is a murderer." I couldn't grab her fast enough, she ducked around me and smacked him again. Bet he saw stars that time. Dane whisked Mrs. Crutchley away to another room. I picked up the phone. There was a sticker on the back with a phone number written on it.

"You can't disrespect me like that, in my home, in front of my mama."

"And yet I did. You're lyin' like a rug." I shifted in the chair and dropped my voice. "And you're a shit ton of stupid. But go right ahead and be offended. I'm pretty fucking offended by what you did. So that seems fair."

I flipped pages in my notebook until I found the number that made the call to emergency services and informed them about the horse and rider accident. It was the same as the number on the back of the phone. Just to check I called the number. The phone on the table vibrated.

Dane picked up the phone and answered the call. He grinned at me. "We have the drugs and we have the phone."

"So what?" Adam said.

"Oh yeah, I nearly forgot." I smiled and arched an eyebrow at Dane.

"Yeah, the other thing."

Adam didn't look happy, but he wasn't quite scared or

sorry enough for my liking.

"The person doing Doc Robinson's accounts found two receipts for a credit card that isn't his, one for a rifle and the other for drugs, the same drugs that were used to kill Caitlin James's horse, while she was riding."

A modicum of bravado returned. "It wasn't me."

My mood dipped into 'fuck you and the horse you rode in on.' It felt okay because horse shit is good for roses. And I like roses. So pass me a goddamn vase.

"You need to stop being such a liar," I said, opened messages on my phone and brought up a screenshot from Sandra that unquestionably showed Adam Crutchley as the purchaser of the gift card, with both the gift card and his credit card number displayed. I handed him the phone. "Anything you want to add?"

He shook his head. I removed my phone from his grip.

"Do you own a motorbike?" I said to Adam.

"Yes."

I didn't imagine it was a Harley. I bet it was some kind of off-road type machine like a KTM. Not exactly big tough-biker territory.

"You may as well talk. We're arresting you for the attempted murder of a federal agent and the murder of a paramedic, for possession of Schedule I and Schedule II drugs for supply and distribution."

He covered his face with his hands for a moment. Dane came back into the room and sat down next to me.

"I've sent his mother to the neighbors."

"Smart thinking."

Adam dropped his hands into his lap. "I met with Garcia a month ago. I owed him money for product. Didn't have the money to pay him. Before I knew it, I'd told him I knew where the Director of the FBI lived and I'd know when she was in town. She wouldn't be hard to get at because she was relaxed here."

Fuck. Not Joey at all.

Before he knew it, my ass. He knew what he was doing when he gave up O'Hare. There was more to it. "Why did you give up Cait O'Hare?"

"She came into the station, pulled me aside, and she told me if I didn't stop annoying Alyssa she'd get involved and make my life hell. I didn't need the FBI involved."

How did Cait know about Adam's dick behavior to Alyssa? Maybe Joey told her, could he have gone to her for help, and then Alyssa died of a suspected overdose. I'm sure if Joey thought Alyssa died because Cait didn't help, he'd be plenty mad. Angry enough to go along with whatever the gang was planning.

"And killing her was the answer ... you couldn't stop being a dick?" Perhaps that was too easy.

"I was in debt. She threatened me and she was going to talk to mom."

"Like you threatened a woman you worked with, like that?"

The District Attorney should be pleased we had a table between us because I wanted to whack him like his mother did. No, I didn't. I wanted to pistol whip him. Teach him a lesson he would never forget.

"Why'd you ask about a motorbike?"

"Because that's the only way you could've gone from shooting that horse and shooting up Cait, to the station in time to jump in the ambulance and ride out like a hero."

"If it was me."

I shook my head. "Don't even try that bullshit, pal." I read my notes from Alyssa's journal once more. "The night of the so-called accident, you were late to work. Alyssa had to wait five minutes for you, knowing there was a call."

That meant he made the call on his way to work. Not from the actual scene of the incident.

"So you came up with a plan to shoot the horse. Where's the tranq gun and the rest of the drugs?"

Adam started to laugh. It was quiet at first then gathered momentum until he howled with laughter and tears poured down his face.

We waited. While we waited for him to control himself, I made a call to Caine. "We have the person responsible for the death of Thor and the attempted murder of our Director."

"Nice work, Ellie. A biker?"

"No. A paramedic. Have a BOLO put out on Juan Garcia, he sent the bikers out there thinking Cait was still alive but the paramedic told him where Cait lived. He also offered to kill Cait to wipe a drug debt, which is what started this whole ugly mess."

Our duplicitous press release flushed them all out, but the human cost was high on both sides.

"Why did Garcia want Cait dead so badly?"

"I doubt he's the biggest fish in this pond. Could've been trying to curry favor with his boss. Taking out the Director of the FBI would be an impressive feather in his cap, I suppose."

"We'll find him." Caine's gravel-filled growl softened. "You doing okay out there?"

"We might've been exposed to this new virus. We're fine for now and are going to Stonewall Jackson. I've cleared it with the hospital."

"Keep me posted," Caine said and hung up.

Adam gasped. "You're infected and you're here. My mom was here!"

"First, we don't know if we're infected. Second, we're not contagious yet if we are infected. We have jobs to do because you can't accept that no means no." I leaned close to him. "So if your mom gets sick, pal, it's on you."

He tried to glare at me and failed, because I got there first.

That's right asshole, this is on you.

His lip trembled. A long time ago I perfected a look that can make grown men cry.

Not so tough now.

"You have no idea what it was like watching Quinn James get everything in life, two parents, med school. His mom and dad were here a lot while my dad was sick. I gave up college because of the medical bills and Quinn Jameson O'Hare James sailed on through like he walked on air. Like he's charmed. His fucking parents dripping approval and money all over him."

Wow.

I leaned over the table bringing my face close to Adam's. "You make your own breaks in this world, Adam, and you make the best of what you have, it's no one's fault your dad got sick. It sure as hell wasn't the fault of the James family."

I made a call to Kevin. "Got any more room in that jail of yours?"

"Not really, you got someone else for me?"

"Adam Crutchley, but it's okay, I'll get a couple of FBI agents out here to pick him up."

"I'll take him until they get here."

"Thank you. He's at home. Waiting." I paused, rallied my thoughts and carried on. "Hey, Kev, don't be long."

"I'm halfway out the door, kid. Be there soon."

I hung up. Argo pushed his nose into my leg. I looked down at his brown eyes looking up at me. "You're a good boy," I said rubbing his ears.

Dane forced Adam to stand up, dragged his hands behind his back and handcuffed him, then pushed him back down into the chair.

Chapter Forty Three
I'm Already There

We stopped and got groceries at the first supermarket we came to in Lexington. We wore nitrile gloves, used the self-service checkout and avoided contact with everyone. Then Dane stopped at the very next bottle store. He came out with a bottle of Patron tequila.

Crackerjack choice. If there's a chance, we're going to die we may as well make a party of it.

Our sanctuary at the back of the hospital, set in what in spring and summer were probably lush lawns, was a snowy white expanse.

We unloaded our groceries and took our go-bags, and everything we had or might need into the building. It was nice inside. Warm. I noticed the warmth as soon as I opened the door and figured Grant had turned the heat on for us. The groceries stowed, I fed Argo in the kitchen, we left him to his bowl of kibble and explored the house. An odd patch of cold grew then shrank in my head.

Upstairs were sixteen bedrooms and two communal bathrooms containing six showers and toilets in each. Downstairs included two offices, a staggering living area, a catering kitchen, and a dining room with a massive table that seated at least twenty.

Caine called. "Hope you two aren't getting too comfortable, it's not a holiday camp," he growled.

I hit the speaker icon. "You're on speaker. Did you call to say hello or was there something else?"

"Garcia was stopped driving north." That didn't feel like the whole story. I waited. Dane waited. "He was apprehended with another viral payload. This time the delivery system was aerosol cans disguised as air-freshener."

"How north are we talking?"

"He was almost in Loudoun County."

"Dulles International Airport is in Loudoun."

I had a feeling Garcia was nothing but a link in a very long chain.

"Is he going to give us the person above him?"

"He doesn't have a lot to lose, it all depends on how charitable he feels."

"Criminally, are we talking charges and punishment?"

"Death penalty is on the table, so are consecutive life sentences. But I'm talking about something a little faster-acting than the judicial system."

Crap on a cracker. "He's sick."

"You didn't even need to buy a vowel," Caine said with a grumble that suggested he was not *Wheel of Fortune* game show host material. "There's an interrogation team talking with him now. He's in an isolation room at The Facility."

Apart from a safe place in times of threat and our bunker, The Facility was somewhere we could hold, treat, and interrogate suspects who have illnesses we wouldn't want out in the world. Well, on one floor, the other floors

418

housed laboratories and living quarters. The whole place could be sealed completely. Had its own power supply, water, air purifying system; it was the whole nine. And I'd sent Noel Gerrard there to make it feel like home. Now I knew he had company.

"Excellent, three floors underground and in isolation is the best place for him."

"I'll let you know if we get anything, but I'm not expecting much."

"We'll be hanging out here waiting ... about the pathogen, do we at least have a name for it yet?"

"Whitehorse and Schneider are calling it Qu Pathogen," Caine said.

"So they still don't know if it's a virus or bacterium?"

"They say it's manufactured and it's both."

Wonderful. "At least we have a name for it. I like to know what it is that can potentially kill me."

"It's not going to kill either of you." Caine's gruff voice grated along the airways. "Whitehorse said the quarantine has to last at least seventy-two hours."

I glanced at the tequila bottle on the table. We needed another bottle for a seventy-two-hour lockdown.

"If someone is coming into town can they drop a bottle of tequila on our doorstep? And make it a top-shelf bottle. This is no time to skimp."

"Agent Iverson, you are not on vacation," Caine growled.

I sucked up my amusement. "Our well-appointed historic accommodation slash prison begs to differ."

"Stay well."

"Okay. Keep in touch." Before he rang off, I managed another plug. "We'd appreciate the tequila."

Smiling I put my phone down. Dane had found the remote for the television. He pointed it at the TV hanging on the wall of the living room and channel surfed.

That patch of cold came back, like an ice-cream headache. Maybe walking it off was smart. We had a stack of room. As far as emergency accommodation went it wasn't too shabby at all. I wandered around the downstairs rooms, taking note of where everything was.

The key was on a cherrywood coffee table in the living room with a note from Grant. He'd left medical supplies in the first office and written down the WiFi password. I smiled and entered it into my phone.

All we had to do was to maintain a positive attitude and lie low until we were no longer a threat to anyone. Seventy-two hours. We got this. I watched Dane for a moment, then a wall of frosted silence descended, where amicable brotherly hi-jinx used to reside.

Stu. Shit. "Dane?"

The color drained from his face. "I felt it too."

I snatched my phone from the table and called Kurt. "Stu?"

"I was about to call you. He crashed ... they could not revive him."

"But. He." Thoughts rammed into each other. "He was okay. He was texting us earlier. He was okay."

Kurt's voice changed, soft, concerned. "Ellie, it was a

blood clot. It's shitty but it happens."

"He was in a hospital ..."

I felt myself losing it. Dane reached over and took the phone. His voice crumbled as he tried to talk to Kurt. If anyone was going to lose the fight, it supposed to be me, not Stu, not Kennedy.

Dane spun around and stared at me. He shook his head and hung up the phone. "We all have our time, Ellie. It was Stu's. As far as we know, Kennedy is hanging on."

"How can you be so fucking philosophical? He's your brother!"

"He'll always be my brother. Death doesn't change that. He's okay. Everything is as it should be."

A tear slid over his thick dark lashes and down his face. I felt the burn in my throat of unshed tears. It was too much. My death I could face, but losing Cait, Misha, Iain, and Stu. All my vital organs shuddered as I fought to control the rising sobs. Chance's voice forced through the building sadness, "I got this. Let me help."

A disembodied hand-sketched black pencil outlines around the room, dodging Dane. By the time the lines were drawn it was Chance and me. He pushed me into a chair, dragged another chair in front of me and sat. His knees touched mine.

"You didn't do this, El."

"Yeah, I did." I lifted my head and felt his pale blue eyes draw me in. "I let the world think Cait was alive. Stu is on me. If Kennedy doesn't make it, his life is on me too." I wiped tears off my face; they sparkled on my hand.

"You made a call. If you hadn't …"

I blinked, more glittery tears dripped, this time onto my lap. "If I hadn't, Dane wouldn't have lost his brother. We wouldn't have lost another member of Delta A."

"You don't know that." Chance's fingers brushed my hair from my eyes. "When it's time, it's time."

"You don't know that," I countered, with a jerky breath and wiped away more tears. "I found out the truth but the cost was too high. And I can't un-fuck this." Swallowing hard I forged on, too hard to stop now I'd started. "I screwed up, Chance. I can't erase this and I can't ameliorate it. I am responsible for Stu and Kennedy. Me. My call to stand and fight. My fucking call and where was I? I was fucking safe."

"Did you go after them?"

I shrugged. "It doesn't matter, I was too late. I didn't get that drone up fast enough. I didn't get into position fast enough."

He shook his head. "El. Stop. You retrieved the drone." He poked his index finger at me. "You went up the tree with a rifle. Because you were there, those helicopters made it in safely. How many men would've lost their lives if you hadn't been there?"

"None. If I hadn't been there. If I hadn't made the call to stand our ground, none of them would've been in danger."

"That's bullshit. You're not thinking with clarity." Chance's voice softened. "You had no choice but to fight."

I stared at the pencil lines that created my jeans.

"You're missing the point. If I hadn't released a statement implying Cait was alive, none of this would've happened."

"You don't know that. Those bikers might've come anyway."

"Stu is dead."

Crawling into a dark hole seemed like a good thing but the thought of solitude felt like a reward, and I did not deserve a reward.

"Listen to me." He lifted my chin until our eyes met. "There's always a risk. The risk is there before we even wake up in the morning. Humans are fragile. They break, they die. Sometimes they go to sleep and never wake up. Sometimes a car comes from nowhere and smashes them into a light pole. Sometimes they put themselves in harm's way because it's their job to protect others." The skin around his eyes crinkled as a smile tweaked. "Stick with me kid, I'll never leave you."

"You're a pencil drawing, Chance. All it takes is an eraser." I wiped away more tears.

"And she's back."

"Someone needs to make sure Dane is okay. This isn't about me. Time to suck it up."

"Look at him." Chance leaned to his left and twisted to see. Dane sat on the sofa with Argo, his arm around the dog. Argo was doing what he did best. Being present. "It was your call to bring him on board, yeah?"

"Dane or the dog?"

Chance grinned and turned to face me properly. "Yes?"

I nodded. Sniffed. And attempted a smile. "They were

both my idea. And I went all out to convince my team that The Brothers Grimm and the dog were precisely what we needed."

Chance laughed. "The Brothers Grimm is probably the best description I've heard for Dane and Stu."

A couple of deep breaths later, I wiped the last runaway tears from my face.

"Thank you. You help more than you know."

"Happy to help, El. Always."

His edges fizzed. The lines blurred. Life pushed the blurred pencil sketches into a corner of the room. A dustpan and brush appeared and swept up the remnants. I wasn't sitting. I was standing near a picture window. Snow fell thick and fast. A shiver ran through me. Leaving the snowy vista behind, I joined Dane.

"I'm sorry, Dane."

He wiped his face and nodded. "Me too." He took a deep breath.

I knew I shouldn't ask but pragmatism got the better of me. "What do you want to do now?"

"Think we're stuck for the next few days," he said, rubbing Argo's neck.

"I didn't mean right now. I mean, do you know yet what your next jump will be?"

He shrugged. "Go to California and smoke pot."

"You've probably had worse ideas."

A mixture of amused and startled chased the sadness from his eyes as his eyebrows rose. "Are you kidding me right now?"

"No … not really. I've seen a lot of dreadful things over the years. A lot of drug-fueled fucktards, a lot of alcoholic rages. Personally, I cannot attribute any of the horrendous crimes I've investigated to recreational marijuana users." I sat in a chair close by. I wanted to be near him. "Other agents may have different opinions."

"Do you smoke?"

"Nope. It's illegal. I couldn't do my job stoned. Can you imagine what pot would do to my already rich imagination?"

Dane laughed, a proper deep laugh that vibrated his rib cage as it traveled from his belly.

"If you don't mind, I'd like to stay with Delta A."

"I don't mind at all. Your permanent partner will be Lee." My smile was real. I liked him. He was a valuable member of Delta A. So was his brother. "One thing though, you will have grief counseling once this is over."

"Thanks, boss."

I picked up my phone. "I need to make a call."

Three rings and Mitch's voice. "Babe, you all right?"

"Here's hoping." I knew what I needed to say but letting the words fall off my tongue, not so easy. "Mitch. If I'm not okay. If …" The lump in my throat tried to choke me. Breathe. "I need you to promise me that you and the girls will be all right. Promise that you can love them enough for both of us. Tell them stories, tell them who I am and that I love them."

"El, this is not how it ends. This is the beginning of our lives as parents." His voice hardened. "This. Is. Not. How.

It. Ends."

Always thought I'd end bloody but maybe I'm wrong.

"Tell them how much I love their daddy."

"Love you. We'll see you in a couple of days."

I ended the call, placed my phone face down, and wiped tears from my face. Tears change nothing. Innocence wrapped in bright blue eyes, a gummy smile ignited before hands grabbed handfuls of my hair. My heart hurt.

Dane reached out to the coffee table near him and held up the tequila. I nodded.

He stood, Argo followed him into the kitchen and followed him when he returned with a couple of glasses, then poured us a drink each. A meme I saw once came back to me. A quote on a sunset background and it was perfect for now.

I moved seats and settled into a soft leather-covered sofa. "So long as the memory of certain beloved friends lives in my heart, I shall say that life is good. Helen Keller." I held my glass out to Dane. "For Stu," I said, clinking my glass on his. "A damn fine agent."

"Brothers forever," Dane replied and sipped the warming tequila. Argo woofed then lay on Dane's feet.

"This is a delightful tequila," I said, letting the liquid trickle down my throat.

"It sure is."

I held up my glass, he clinked his to mine.

"Here's to not dying of the Qu Pathogen."

Time

Time runs like molten silver
dripping over the edge of life
joining the waterfall of memories
cascading from the cliff
Years splashed against rocks
months swirled
weeks drifted
days drowned
moments lost
Memories glisten on the surface
before sinking to the depths.

Keep reading for a sneak peak at the 11th Byte novel:

Cryptobyte

Chapter 2
Lookin' Out for #1

I opened some software on my laptop and added the phone number I'd written on my desk pad. It was not a surprise to find the number belonged to an unregistered mobile phone. Great.

An email notification popped up on the corner of my screen. The subject both intrigued and worried me. Second family vanished. I clicked on the notification.

The email was from a police officer I knew out in Missouri. He'd included an email from a colleague of his about another missing family. I read it twice. Then hopped into Law Enforcement Online and looked up the cases. We hadn't received an official invitation to meddle but Gary wanted to know what I saw and thought. A straight up second opinion. That I could do.

The first missing family disappeared eighteen months ago from Wichita, Kansas. The second, on November fifteenth twenty-nineteen from Jefferson City, Missouri. I read through everything the investigating officers added the files. Entire families don't usually disappear. Unless

... I stopped and checked the names of the parents against criminal cases from around the time of the disappearances. Nothing. Probably not WITSEC then.

The first missing family, the Johnson family. An elementary school teacher noted the absence of seven year old Janine Johnson. No one could make contact with the family. A week after the seven year old child was first noted as absent from school police were notified. A similar pattern occurred with the next family, the Abbot family. Once police were notified, it was discovered fairly quickly that neither parent had turned up for work, and two of their three children were missing from another elementary school. The third child was absent from daycare.

Whole families. Mum, Dad, two kids. Mum, Dad, three kids. Whatever happened to the families happened over a weekend. The kids were all last seen at school on a Friday. As far police could determine there was nothing unusual about the families. None of the adults had ever come to police attention before. None of the kids had either. They were regular families. Both parents worked. Kids attended school and did the normal amount of after school activities. They were both church on Sunday type families. Zero history of mental illness.

I sat back and thought about it for a moment. Even one family disappearing would've made the news. People don't just disappear like that. One person might. Two might run away together. But a whole family? Unless people assumed the families had moved away it was suspicious. And why would anyone assume a family would up and move like that?

I was still trying to find information when Kurt walked into my office.

"Got a minute?" He moved the chair Mike had vacated a bit closer to the desk before sitting.

"Be right with you." I fired a quick email to Gary and told him I wanted to look into the missing families cases and asked if he minded and who I needed to contact in Wichita. As soon as I hit send I looked at Kurt. "What's up?"

"A couple of text messages from an unregistered mobile phone."

"Oh snap," I said, raising an eyebrow. "What'd yours say?"

"Cryptozoology then cryptomnesia."

"Same as mine."

Dane appeared in the doorway with Lee right behind him.

"Boss," Dane said. "Something weird is going on."

"Lemme guess ... text messages saying cryptozoology and then cryptomnesia?"

Dane's forehead wrinkled into a slight frown. They joined us.

"Delta A is getting weird messages. Any ideas?" I said, rocking in my chair. I looked at Lee. "Word of the day stuff is right up your alley. What do you make of it?"

Lee cleared his throat. "It's pretty obvious that someone investigating Big Foot has come across research they think is new but it is in fact a forgotten memory." His straight-faced delivery was awesome. "They've plagiarized themselves and are now ready to report it."

Dane laughed so hard he snorted. Kurt lost it and spluttered coffee. Dribbling like a two-year-old, he wiped his hand across his mouth and chin.

"Hang on, there's a flaw in your logic," I said matching Lee's no nonsense tone. "In Twenty-Eighteen researchers proved that Big Foot did not exist, once and for all. So, I'm going to say the sender of the text is talking about Leviathan."

"Biblical Leviathan or Supernatural?" Dane said, controlling his mirth.

"Sea monsters versus something so awful that they were locked in purgatory because God couldn't control them?" I said, dropping my feet to the ground and bringing my chair upright. "Looks like we've got quite the battle in front of us. Anyone got any ideas on how to subdue or kill Leviathan?"

Kurt coughed. Reached for tissues from my desk and wiped up the coffee in his lap.

"Meanwhile back on dry land and in the real world," Dane said. "We all got the same text messages, it's got to mean something."

I'd like to think someone made a mistake. I'd really like to think that.

An email notification hung in the corner of my screen. It was from Officer Gary Singe. The official invitation to help investigate the missing family in Missouri and a contact for Wichita. The weird text messages would have to wait.

"We have a potential new case," I said, opening the email. "For now it's research based."

Everyone's heads lifted. Kurt balled up soggy tissues and tossed them at the waste paper basket.

"Who, what, where, why?" Lee said, moving his chair closer. Dane followed suit.

"Two missing families," I said, scanning the email for information to share. "They went missing fifteen months apart from different cities and States." I felt the rooms energy directed at me. "The first disappearance was in Wichita, Kansas. The second in Jefferson City, Missouri."

"Why aren't FBI in those cities looking into the disappearances?" Kurt said.

" Mostly because there is no evidence of foul play, as strange as that seems."

"Hard to imagine that families go missing without foul play."

My right eyebrow arched in his direction. Exactly what I thought. "A couple more reasons for our invitation, we're the experts in serial crime and also because a cop I know asked me to have a look at the files."

"Two isn't serial," Kurt replied quietly.

"No, it isn't. But something about this case tells me there is more going on here. Hence, research."

"Do we know if they're witnesses or criminals and now within the Witness Protection Program?" Dane said.

"I did a quick look at cases around the time of their

disappearances. Nothing that jumped out and made me think WITSEC were involved."

"But they just disappeared," Dane said. "That's a WITSEC trademark."

Sure is.

I filed the thought away with the intention of talking to Debbie Barnes down in her office. She was our resident expert on new identities.

"Let's let that simmer and in the meantime, I want to know if any other families have disappeared. If so when and where from. Nationwide."

Dane was making notes.

"Why do you think there are more?" Kurt said, he glanced around the room then back at me. "Chance? A song?"

"Not this time. Just my gut twinging."

Lee looked up from his phone. "Media has reports of a missing family in Carson City, Nevada.Twenty-one months ago."

"Any details?"

"The Gatewood Family. Scott and Kirsty Gatewood and their twelve year old twin daughters Josephine and Julie was last seen, separately at school and work on Friday April thirteenth." He looked at me for a beat. "Good chance they went missing over the weekend even though they weren't reported missing until two weeks later."

"Why did it take so long to report the missing family?" Dane asked.

"The parents signed the girls out of school for a week

from the Friday, they were going on a family camping trip before Scott Gatewood continued his cancer treatment."

Not good.

"Did they go?" I said thinking that maybe they were they eaten by bears.

"No one knows," Lee said.

I scrolled through the information I had about the other two families. It looked like they also disappeared over weekends.

"Weekends," I said, knowing the team would catch up.

"Looking into it," Kurt said, making notes in his notebook. "What events do families attend in weekends."

He looked at me but wasn't seeing me. I waited to see what he came up with.

To my surprise all heads came up and eyes focused on me. When did I become the expert on all things family?

Nope. Not even close to being ready for that role.

"I'm new to this family thing and my girls are a bit young to take to weekend events." My brain scrambled about in the dust and cobbled an answer together. "But, I imagine, when they're older we'll go to movies, parks, fairs, circuses, art galleries, museums, parties, theaters, concerts, and they'll probably play some kind of sport."

Heads went down. Pens and fingers added information to either notebooks or tablets. Locating all the events and places families could go in each city and within a reasonable day trip distance from each city or town with a missing family was going to take time. I envisaged spreadsheets and other annoyances.

Truthfully I imagined me getting a coffee and asking for a briefing once the boring stuff was done. Proving once again there was nothing wrong with my imagination.

The Gatewood family from Carson City, Nevada felt like an anomaly. The other two families went missing from their own towns, the Gatewoods may have gone missing camping or never got to their destination or taken part in some activity before the trip.

Maybe the families did the exact same thing but in different States.

I heard the word in my head before it tumbled off my lips. "Circus."

Lee's eyes met mine. "Carnie folk."

A shudder ran down my spine.

Acknowledgements

Qubyte was not the book I intended to write as the tenth byte novel, it started out as a very different story which is why you hadn't seen the first chapter prior to the launch.

I would like to acknowledge the characters who have helped me tell these stories and in particular the absence of SSA Sam Jackson during the writing of *Qubyte*. Your death made it hard, Sam.

Thank you to my youngest daughters, Caoilfhionn and Breezy, for listening to my ramblings as this story came together. You are a wonderfully supportive albeit captive audience.

Thanks to Charlie and my eldest daughter Bex for your willingness to read early on and provide notes.

I'd like to acknowledge the years I spent with Rebel ePublishers, in both its incarnations on two different continents. Thank you for making this journey possible and for believing in me.

To my glorious editor Jayne Southern – you've not seen the last of me or Ellie.

About the author:

Cat Connor is a prolific crime thriller author hailing from New Zealand. Her expertise in the genre is reflected in her engaging and suspenseful narratives, which have garnered a loyal following. Her work is known for its intricate plots, dynamic characters, and relentless pace, keeping readers on the edge of their seats until the very end. She has authored multiple books, including the popular "Byte" series, which follows the exploits of an FBI unit that investigates serial crime.

Cat's passion for crime and espionage is evident in her writing, as she strives to create a world that is both authentic and thrilling. Her meticulous attention to detail and extensive research have won her critical acclaim and accolades from readers and peers alike. In addition to writing, Cat enjoys speaking on topics related to writing and publishing. Her talks are known for their candidness, humour, and practical advice. With her unique blend of talent, expertise, and passion, Cat Connor has established herself as one of the most exciting and accomplished authors in the crime thriller genre.

Her other passions include music, reading, tequila, red wine, coffee, and chocolate. When she's not writing she can be found binge watching TV shows and spending time with her much adored animals; Diesel the mastador, Patrick the tuxedo cat, & Dallas the tortie Birman.

You can follow and contact Cat at the following places:

Website: www.catconnor.com
Twitter: @catconnor
Facebook: @cat.connor
Instagram: @catconnorauthor
Bluesky: @catconnor.bsky.social
Threads: @catconnorauthor

Also by Cat Connor:

www.ingramcontent.com/pod-product-compliance
Lightning Source LLC
Chambersburg PA
CBHW031950060726
47497CB00016B/1041

VISITE
AU MUSÉUM
D'HISTOIRE NATURELLE

PAR

GEORGES POUCHET.

PRIX : 1 FRANC

ROUEN,

A. AILLAUD, ÉDITEUR,

RUE SAINT-NICOLAS, 31.

1859